It Couldn't Be You

REBECCA JO JACKSON

It Couldn't Be You

SWEET RIVER SERIES

BOOK ONE

REBECCA JO JACKSON

It Couldn't Be You © 2023, 2025 by Rebecca Jo Jackson

All rights reserved.

Cover design by Melody Jeffries.

Editing by Jen Boles.

No part of this book may be reproduced in any form or by any electronic or mechanical means, including information storage and retrieval systems, without written permission from the author, except for the use of brief quotations in a book review.

This novel is entirely a work of fiction. The names, characters and incidents portrayed in it are the work of the author's imagination. Any resemblance to actual persons, living or dead, events or localities is entirely coincidental.

 Created with Vellum

For the overthinkers trying to muster the courage to reach for what they want.
You never know what is already reaching right back.

And for Joseph.

Playlist

I'm a music while writing kind of writer. So I thought I'd share the songs I wrote this story to, in case you're a music while reading kind of reader.

1. drivers license | Olivia Rodrigo
2. Out of That Truck | Carrie Underwood
3. Long Time Coming| Tomi
4. Psycho (feat. Mark Hoppus) | Amy Shark
5. Cruel Summer | Taylor Swift
6. We Don't Talk Anymore (feat. Selena Gomez) | Charlie Puth
7. Side Effects | Carlie Hanson
8. Notice You | LeyeT
9. The Slow Song | Amy Shark
10. Teenage Headache Dreams (with Ellie Rowsell) | Mura Masa, Wolf Alice
11. Stay | Gracie Abrams
12. Back in My Body | Maggie Rogers
13. Cold | Mating Ritual, Lizzy Land
14. Beautiful Wreck | MØ
15. Your Shirt | Chelsea Cutler

16. Mine Right Now (Acoustic) | Sigrid
17. Say It | Maggie Rogers
18. This Town | Niall Horan
19. Movie | Blake Rose
20. Clementine | Wet
21. skinny dipping | Sabrina Carpenter
22. Overkill | Holly Humberstone
23. Nocturnal | Aaron Smith
24. Smallest Things | Lily Meola
25. hurts like hell | Wrabel
26. Alone Together | Fall Out Boy
27. If the World Was Ending | JP Saxe, Julia Michaels
28. right where you left me | Taylor Swift
29. If I Can't Have You | Shawn Mendes
30. Ready to Love You | HEDEGAARD
31. Hold On | Colbie Caillat
32. COMPLETE MESS | 5 Seconds of Summer
33. Satellite | Harry Styles
34. Riptide | Vance Joy
35. Want Want | Maggie Rogers
36. So Hot You're Hurting My Feelings | Caroline Polachek
37. Silent Love | James Bay
38. 18 | One Direction
39. There's No Way (feat. Julia Michaels) | Lauv
40. When Emma Falls in Love (Taylor's Version) | Taylor Swift

Playlist on Spotify

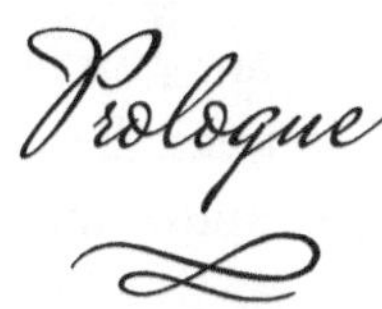

Prologue

I knew my boyfriend didn't want me to go to this party, but here I was at the Hernandezes' anyway.

Pulling up to the house and seeing Gabriel's—who was definitely not my boyfriend—janky old truck parked out front, felt like I had stepped into some kind of cruel time machine.

As I parked my car, I was suddenly sixteen again, my heart beating faster just at the knowledge of Gabriel's presence. My body felt electric, like someone had connected wires that had been left disconnected for too long.

No, I reminded myself as I unbuckled. I was a twenty-four-year-old woman. I was a college graduate with a career in a serious relationship (and not with the owner of the aforementioned janky trunk). I wasn't going to be affected again by this man.

But, as I went to open the car door, my mind raced with questions. Was he hoping to see me? Was he single? How long was he staying? *Was he even there?*

It'd been so long since I last saw him. The sight of that truck in the driveway still sent my pulse humming.

You will not be affected by this man, Emma, I repeated to myself.

What was it about Gabriel?

Well, okay, it was that I could always feel him. I remembered being sixteen and feeling my hair stand on end just knowing he was upstairs working on homework while I was downstairs talking in the kitchen with Gabriel's younger sister and my best friend, Katie. Existing in the same space as Gabriel made the air around me drum the chorus of a pop punk early 2000s love song. I was completely thrilled to know he was breathing and moving and living a flight of stairs above me. That maybe I'd get the chance to hear his thoughts, to hear his voice—to brush up against him.

Gabriel was thrilling, but I obviously didn't like him. He was off-limits with the whole brother to my best friend thing and kind of conceited. Plus, he always said whatever he thought without any kind of filter, which could sometimes piss me off.

He was just Gabriel. And no matter the jolt of electricity that went down my spine whenever he sat beside me—we couldn't be together.

Gabriel made me roll my eyes, but he also made breathing embarrassingly complicated when he let his eyes linger on me. Plus, there was his curly brown hair. He had this one curl that always fell across his forehead, and sometimes, like on my twenty-first birthday, I would wrap it around my finger—and he let me.

But that was the thing about Gabriel. Ever since I was, like, twelve years old, he made it hard for me to concentrate on anyone but him.

We would be at a Christmas party at his house or an English Club meeting at school, and I would have to literally make myself listen to whoever was talking to me and not tune in to whatever Gabriel was saying across the room to someone else. As if I cared what he had to say about the gas mileage on his truck or his chemistry exam grade.

And don't get me started on whenever he was flirting with some other girl. Okay, there was some part of me that felt some way about Gabriel. But it was the curly hair. And the sideways grin. I preferred that grin to be about me, and I felt lucky when it was. I would get nervous about losing his approval, his adoration —like when someone falls asleep on your shoulder, and you stay as still as you can so you don't wake them.

That was the thing about Gabe, I thought. There was some kind of heat between us. When we were in the same vicinity, you could follow the trail of sparks from me to him. Maybe it even stretched farther than being in the same vicinity. Maybe it ran from Texas to California, and we were just really good at ignoring it.

I thought to myself, *I'd hope all these years had blown every little spark out.*

The last time I remembered us really talking, just the two of us, face to face, was the night of my twenty-first birthday. I could still hear what Gabriel said that night. I felt my cheeks go hot as I remembered.

How could Gabriel's hand tugging on my elbow do more to me than my own boyfriend's lips on mine? How could Gabriel whispering my name in my ear with some dumb joke make me melt easier than a man I've been dating getting down on one knee?

I shook my head. *That wasn't true.*

I didn't want that to be true. Maybe it was true for teenage me, but it just couldn't be true anymore, not for twenty-four-year-old me. I needed a key to lock up these stupid thoughts.

I needed to get my mind in order. No one made me feel like my boyfriend, I almost said aloud. Except, how my boyfriend made me feel was a complicated issue lately. Like a song fading, and you didn't even realize you'd missed the last few lines.

But here I was outside Gabriel's house. I took a deep breath. He was just stupid, annoying, get-my-heart-beating Gabriel. It was just the way he was. It was about him, not me. Maybe he wasn't even here. I hoped he wasn't. I fidgeted with my keys.

I felt a thrill go through me at the idea he was standing in his kitchen all barefoot and grinning. One of his plain white tees on with a V-neck, the kind he usually wore under his other clothes.

The kind that smelled like him when he got close. His dark curls and amber eyes. He'd grin at me when I walked in. He'd greet me in the way he always did.

"Emma," he always said. Not "hi" or "hello," always my name first. Like when I was sixteen. The day after my birthday.

My mom dropped me off in front of their house like she always did. The anticipation fluttered in my chest when I spotted his truck that afternoon. That janky old truck. I bypassed the front door and headed around the house through the side yard toward the back porch, which ran along the pool. I was all timidity and reckless excitement for him to see me in my new yellow halter bikini—to get his eyes on me.

"Emma," he said, almost teasingly, when he saw me turn the corner toward the pool. The summer sun beat down on us, and I tossed a smile his way.

"Em," Katie, my best friend since kindergarten, called out. She was lying on her stomach, working on her tan. "You made it!"

"I did," I said. I was about to say something about being tired from my party last night, but then Katie's mom, watering their plants in the backyard, called out, "Did you drive yourself here?"

"Oh, no, my mom dropped me off," I said, thinking of my little cherry red car all un-driven and parked outside my house.

"Wait, do you not have your license yet?" Gabriel asked from his spot sitting in the shallow end. I felt his eyes on me like a spotlight, making me a little skittish, and a little pleased.

"Not yet," I said.

"Why? You always said you were going to get it right on the day you turned sixteen," he said.

"She's scared," Katie said, waving her hand in the air as if to brush away her older brother's question.

"Scared?" he questioned.

"Ah, you know, parallel parking," I said, looking down at my blue flip flops.

"That's all you're scared of?" he asked. I shrugged as I kicked off

my flip flops and sank into the deep end, a safe, agonizing distance from him.

"She can get it when she's ready, Gabe," Katie said, muffled from her face down on the outdoor lounge chair.

I dunked under the water, rising up to Gabriel, staring at me curiously. "What?" I asked, wiping the water from my eyes.

"Come on, let's get you un-scared. Fifteen-year-old you would be appalled at this news." He hopped out of the pool, splashing water all over the patio. "Let's go."

"Go where?" I laughed nervously.

"Leave her alone," a muffled Katie said, always my defender. I was waiting for her to click into her family's tendency to call each other out in Spanish, trading names and insults I could barely understand.

"If you can parallel the beast, you won't be scared to parallel any other car. Especially your little red thing," he assured me, referring to his beloved truck as "the beast," a new nickname he was trying out.

I rolled my eyes, wondering how I could drag out this special attention he was giving me.

"Okay, then." He marched back into the pool and then, to my own thrill and surprise, slipped his hands under me and scooped me out of the water. I was acting appalled but pressed myself against his chest and wrapped my arms tightly around his neck. I could feel his voice against me when he spoke, see his pulse racing in his neck.

His mom was laughing, finding the whole shtick entertaining, and Katie called out that she'd rescue me when the thirty minutes of tanning on her backside were complete.

He dropped me down in front of his truck. I landed on my feet with my face only inches—if that—from his face. Our noses could touch. My body was still tingling from where our skin had made contact.

"You sure are bossy," I choked out, attempting to play it with some semblance of cool. A big ask for my awkward sixteen-year-old self.

"You sure are stubborn." He stayed close to me, not moving at all, I noted, feeling the heat from his body.

"I'm standing here, aren't I?" Water was dripping from my dishwater blonde hair all over us, and his hand brushed up against my waist. Goosebumps on goosebumps under the Texas sun.

"Because I carried you," he countered. His hand touched my arm—gentle and intentional.

"I let you, didn't I?"

His eyes were wicked as he said, "Yes, you did." His voice suggested that me letting him carry me out maybe meant something. Maybe meant that I wanted him to.

My cheeks were red as a pepper because, yes, I definitely did let him carry me out. I was a willing accomplice in this whole flirty mess. I didn't know what to say. My eyes locked on his. My whole body buzzed. He was a kiss away. I could reach out for his loose curl if I wanted to.

I couldn't breathe a single breath. I could hear how uneven his breathing was, too. His hand was still on my arm. It felt like we were swept up in some buzzing current—swimsuits, warm skin, and us, just us two, alone.

Then his eyes dropped from my eyes to my lips. I felt my lips start to part because my body went on pure instinct when he was around. His other hand found my waist, pulling me in.

Suddenly, he backed away, shaking his head like he was trying to wake up from this dream. I went to speak, but he was already moving on, asking if I was ready for lessons. I was very much not ready for lessons. I was all breathless with wet hair, shaking hands, and very un-kissed lips.

"Keys are in the ignition," he said playfully as he casually walked over to the passenger side of the car.

That Gabriel, I thought, trying to shake off this consuming, confusing moment as he apparently could.

So ridiculous. So frustrating. How could he move on so smoothly from a moment like that? Like he'd light a match and then shake it out with one flick of his wrist, walking away grinning while I'm still choking on the smoke, wondering if I had imagined it all.

The guy thrilled me. But I completely and totally did not like Gabriel. I couldn't. He was my best friend's brother. I just really wished he would've freaking kissed me that day.

I thought this as I knocked on the door.

JORDAN BOYFRIEND <3

Hey babe, text me when you're leaving the
Hernandezes' house.

JORDAN BOYFRIEND <3

If you leave early enough, maybe you could
stop by my fam's?

ME

I might be here a while! It'll probably be too
late to stop by. There is wine flowing tonight,
and everyone's here.

JORDAN BOYFRIEND <3

Who is "everyone?"

There he was, standing in the doorway. His skin still caramel, but his dark curls longer, messier.

"Emma," he said almost teasingly, a grin tugging at half of his face.

Katie had invited me over to the Hernandez house for an impromptu Christmas party with her family. Because in this big family with six siblings, there were four brothers and two sisters. Katie was the middle child, and Tanya was the oldest. The youngest, Ricky, had a new girlfriend, and I was called in to help assess. Katie didn't trust the others to truly know how to evaluate the way she deemed necessary.

"Gabriel." I cocked my head curiously.

"You've come to be merry with us?" he asked, moving to the side and gesturing for me to come inside.

"Of course, I can't miss a Christmas party or Mama Linda's Christmas tamales." I stepped into the open concept entryway, which expanded to the left with a big living area with walls covered in family photos and plants in nearly every corner and a kitchen drawing me in with scents of cumin, garlic, and lime, or the right with the formal dining room in shades of red and green and the well-worn stairwell leading up to bedrooms and the loft.

I could see everyone, as usual, gathered in the living room and kitchen. We always turned left at this house.

"I hate to break it to you, but you might be a few days early for the tamales, Em," he said, closing the door behind me.

"I know there are some tamales somewhere in that kitchen," I said, "this close to Christmas."

The Hernandez house could be described in two words—loud but also delicious. Linda was always cooking something up in the kitchen. There was always some stain on her shirt since she constantly forgot to put on an apron until midway through a recipe.

"I didn't realize you were home," I said, avoiding direct eye contact with Gabe.

"I always make it home for Christmas," he said, stepping in closer to me. We were only a couple of days out from December 25. I don't know why I hadn't accounted for his eventual arrival.

"I guess I just haven't seen you in a while," I said awkwardly.

"So, you forgot about my existence?" His voice was low. This conversation was just for us.

"Of course not," I said.

"What then? Katie messed up your plan of continued avoidance by not mentioning I came in a few days before Christmas?" His voice was guarded, but there was a tremor of hurt I could hear. I knew this tone well.

"Maybe if you showed up for more than just holidays, we'd actually get to see each other, and you wouldn't be cooking up these little conspiracy theories," I said a little more bitingly than I intended.

Before he could respond, his eldest sister was waddling over to me. The two of us stepped apart.

"Emma," Tanya said, her pregnant stomach bumping into me before her arms could reach me. "Hey, you."

"Hey, Tanya, you're due..."

"January. Hence the size." She patted her belly.

Tanya was the closest thing I had to an older sister. She was in her thirties and pregnant with her third child. I'd been close enough through each pregnancy that I felt as if I knew all the pregnancy and childbirth secrets by now.

I could hear her other two children squealing and bouncing around in the living room off the kitchen. Linda always had a billion toys she pulled out when her grandkids' visited.

Luis is the second oldest—I think he was about thirty now—and had a couple of kids with his wife, Sarah, too. They were loudly playing in the living room. I knew each of them and their little voices. Luis asked someone if they wanted another beer.

Gabriel was the third oldest. He was twenty-six. Katie, my best friend since childhood, was twenty-five. And then there were the two rascally younger brothers, Victor, who was twenty-three, and Ricky, who was twenty-one. The two we were always worrying about. Not for any particular reason except we were the older ones with a hard-to-break habit of looking after the younger ones.

Wine splashing into glasses, bags of chips being poured into bowls, all while Christmas standards sang over the speakers.

As I walked into the house, it would be easy to be impressed by the light oaky hardwood floors that matched the farm-style home and rustic furnishings that looked straight out of a Pinterest board, but what I loved were the shoes all across the floor, the jackets thrown on couches, and the toys and toddlers underfoot. I felt instantly at home.

My shoulders relaxed as Katie spotted me and called me to her side. She stood in the corner of the kitchen beside the sink and the fridge, where the work was done, her raven hair loose around her shoulders, her skin the same caramel tone as Gabriel. I almost grabbed Gabriel's hand without thinking to pull him along with me.

"Okay, do you see the two of them over there?" she said, ignoring formalities, not-so-discreetly pointing to the wide kitchen island, where most of the food was laid out. Everyone stood around it or sat on one of the four barstools, talking and snacking.

Ricky was sitting on a barstool, and a tall, wispy girl was standing with her arms wrapped around his waist. I presumed said girl was the new girlfriend. I watched how she shyly buried her head into his arms like he was a little zone of comfort. I remembered doing the exact same thing when I first met Jordan's family. I felt instant empathy.

She was laughing a lot, nodding along to some story Luis and his wife were telling her. I noticed Ricky flailing his arms about in an attempt to defend himself, so it must've been a story about him.

"What's her name?" I asked Katie.

"Maggie," she said.

"I like her." I said, as Maggie's eyes met mine and she offered a kind smile.

"What? You haven't even met her yet," Katie said, laughing dismissively.

"First impression is that she's kind, likes him enough to be nervous, and is a quick laugh. I always like people who are quick to laugh."

"The laughter could definitely be fake to make us like her," Katie said. Now, I laughed.

Katie saw Gabriel still standing near the entryway where I left him. She waved him over.

"We'll see. I think Ricky works well with someone who laughs easy, someone a little humble," I mused.

I could feel Gabriel arrive beside me. I could've sworn I felt his breath on my neck, but he wasn't close enough for that.

"What are you two up to?" he asked.

"We're talking about Maggie. What do you think of her?" Katie whispered. But before I could hear his answer, Mama Linda spotted me.

"Emma, come get some wine," Linda called out.

I gave Katie a quick goodbye-for-now arm squeeze before weaving through the family festivities. Linda was digging through the antique wine cabinet that was caddy corner to the sliding glass doors facing out to the backyard.

I rested my head on her shoulder for a second, feeling instant comfort. "Hey there," I greeted her, remembering being thirteen years old as she supplied me tampons, Midol, and Reese's peanut butter cups when I started my period at her house. Like I said, instant comfort.

"How're you doing, sweetie?" She slid her arm around me and pulled me close.

"Good," I said. "What do we have here?" I eyed the wine collection.

"Well, let's see. We have a rosé, a moscato Tanya brought, of course, a cheap red blend, a cab, merlot, a pinot, a riesling, and of course, the boys brought some beer." She waved over toward the kitchen, where I was assuming the beer could be found.

"I'm going to have my usual," I said.

"No, no, no," Katie's dad, David, appeared next to us suddenly. "It is winter. It is Christmas. Plus, this is my house, and I do not stand for the crime you—"

But I grabbed a glass hanging from the cabinet, walked over to the ice machine, and pulled out a few cubes, keeping my eyes locked on his. I dropped them into the glass. He shook his head in disgust.

"Emma Brown, do not..." he said sternly.

I quickly brushed past him and proceeded to grab the bottle of rosé that most definitely was always on hand for Katie and me. I poured the sweet pink drink over the ice. He mumbled under his breath disgustedly but gave me a small smile before he walked away, anyway.

"He's a drama queen," Linda whispered under her breath.

I found my way back over to Katie, who was curled up on the nutty brown couch in the living room. We were surrounded by almost all the siblings. I squeezed in beside her. She tapped her glass of icy rosé to mine in solidarity, and we chuckled. I wasn't sure how much we loved this drink or loved annoying her dad together. We'd been making him roll his eyes since we were ten years old.

The living room was a cozy square made up of a lengthy maroon couch, its matching love seat, and a couple of mismatched armchairs piled with Christmas decorative throw pillows. It was set off the kitchen so you could easily carry-on conversation with people at the sink.

I settled into a conversation with Katie, Maggie, and Ricky, when Gabe came and plopped down on the back of the couch behind us. He was just messing around on his phone, but it distracted me. If I rested my head back on the couch, I'd make contact with his legs. I was acutely aware of this.

It'd been a while since I last saw him. Had it really been almost a year now? He wasn't home at all this last summer that I was aware of. I had only heard updates from the family sometimes. I barely knew anything about his current life. And I didn't ask because it felt like a confession when I asked his family about him specifically.

So, for all I knew, he was texting a girlfriend right now, behind my back, quite literally. I glanced in his direction, and his eyes caught mine. He grinned, and I turned back to my group.

Katie laughed at something Maggie said, and I joined in, but I'd missed what was said, which I knew was phony and rude. I decided to actively ignore Gabriel's presence.

"Em," Gabe whispered, sending a current of electricity down my spine. "I liked this." He held up his phone, which was opened to an article I wrote months ago. Then, he pulled up another article from a few weeks ago and showed it to me. "This one too."

I flushed in reply. He was reading my words, which was terrifying and gratifying at the same time.

He said, "I like your reporting."

"Well, thanks, Gabe. I'm glad you caught those." I was still reeling from the tension earlier, finding our rhythm again after all this time.

"I make sure to 'catch' them all," he admitted.

"Stalker?" I said, my eyebrows raised in question.

"The biggest stalker," he said. "I print them out and keep them all in a scrapbook. The comments, too."

"All two comments?" I laughed.

"I think the last one had at least four," he said, which was funny because the last one did have four comments.

"Well," I leaned closer to him, turning to him, "I like this." I stole his phone, pulling up the link to his recent work. It was a series on the wildfires across California.

Gabriel was a journalist, but he also focused a lot on photography—travel photography at that, to tell the story. His work made me feel a little small in comparison. While he had shown me an article of mine on our town's high school football team and another one on our "growing downtown," his recent work was serious, dangerous, and moving. Gabriel's projects would take great amounts of time and risk.

"Thank you," he said, his eyes cutting into mine. "Yours made me miss home."

"Yours made me pray," I said seriously.

"I read the one about the football team like five times over. It felt like I'd somehow flown out and made it to the game myself," he said. "So thanks for essentially making me be able to be in two places at once."

"Funny you say that, Gabe, because when I was reading your last piece—"

"What are you two talking about?" Katie asked, turning to us.

"Work," Gabe said simply, but it felt much bigger than that.

"The journalists," Katie said.

"Talking about journaling," Ricky said, patting the couch behind him.

"Well, we thought Emma could relate to Maggie's story about her friend," Katie said, drawing us back into the group conversation.

"What's the story?" I asked, turning from Gabe.

"Oh, I was telling them how I have a friend who has broken up with all her past boyfriends for the silliest reasons. Like she dumped her last boyfriend because he didn't like Taco Casa," Maggie said.

"Wow, I am definitely back in Texas," Gabe said, sitting up but still on the back of the couch.

"Wait, how could I relate to that?" I asked.

"You love Casa sauce. You would use like ten packets," Gabe said.

"No, no, Katie said Emma dumps guys like that," Ricky said, running his fingers over his buzzcut.

"Emma dumps guys over fast-food restaurants?" Gabe crinkled his nose quizzically.

"I do not do that." I rolled my eyes.

"Kind of..." Katie winced.

"How does she *kind of* do that?" Gabe asked.

"Oh, you know how Emma was with guys," Katie said.

"No, how was Emma with guys?" Gabriel asked with a raised eyebrow.

"Emma always has her disqualifiers," Katie said as if this were fact. "And sometimes they're just as ridiculous as the Taco Casa thing."

"I did not know this," Gabe said, liking this conversation too much.

"It is such an Emma thing. I could just wait a few weeks after Emma declared her love for someone for her to say, 'Well, he's really great, but he eats too much tuna.'"

"I have never stopped liking a guy over tuna," I defended myself.

"What's so wrong with tuna?" Ricky asked, defensive of tuna, apparently.

"Yes, yes, you did," Katie said, her voice rising. "That guy we met at the campus cafeteria. The two of you were always flirting and making eyes at each other, and then he finally came over and asked for your number at the end of the semester... And you told him flat-out no. When I asked you why, you said that he ate too much tuna."

"Okay, well, first of all, I never even knew him well enough to like him. He was just my cafeteria crush. Secondly, I had started dating someone else by the time he finally asked for my number," I said. "But he did, like *always* have a tuna sandwich every time I saw him, which is weird."

"*See*," Katie exclaimed, tipsy with wine and happy. This made Maggie burst into her own wine-fueled giggles.

"You'd already started dating someone. You heartbreaker. Poor cafeteria crush." Gabe shook his head sympathetically.

"You better act before it's too late," I said without thinking, looking him straight in the eyes. The wine was making me speak and move quickly—impulsive.

He didn't look away.

"But, like with tuna guy, there was always this one random thing that ruined every guy for Emma," Katie said. "Except Jordan. He can do no wrong in your eyes."

"Ah, so Jordan is flawless?" Gabe's cheeks were red from the merlot as he spoke.

"Jordan isn't flawless, trust me." I instantly regretted saying it. Why did I say that? Katie looked confused at me because I hadn't told Katie about any of Jordan's breakup-worthy flaws. I hadn't even dared to tell myself any.

"Dang," Ricky muttered.

"What are his flaws?" Gabe challenged me. "I bet you can't think of one."

"Normal relationship flaws." I brushed it off. "Nothing serious. He really is close to perfect." I felt protective of Jordan after I had accidentally, impulsively, slighted him.

"What would be my flaw?" Gabe kept leaning in closer the more we spoke. Ricky and Maggie had left the conversation. Katie was checking her phone.

"You're my best friend's brother." It spilled from my mouth easily, warmly, as his eyes burned into me. I shouldn't have said it, but I didn't care at the moment.

The room felt still, like everyone was suddenly far away. Where did the air go? Our faces were close. We kept leaning closer, closer. He opened his mouth to speak but didn't say a word. I saw his wheels turning, thinking through his words.

I put my glass of wine to my mouth when he finally said, "You—"

"Emma, you would not believe who just followed me on Insta," Katie interrupted us.

The air came back. The room was back in motion. People were around us again, and my skin cooled. We sipped our big glasses of wine, pretending we weren't staring at each other the entire time.

Two

ME

'Everyone' is all the sibs and their paramours.

JORDAN BOYFRIEND <3

Had to google paramour.

JORDAN BOYFRIEND <3

My mom made your favorite chili tonight. She
told me to tell you she'll set some aside
for you.

ME

Tell her thank you

JORDAN BOYFRIEND <3

It sure is getting late. Don't drive too late on
those country roads, babe.

Later, I was pouring myself a glass of the cheap red blend and thinking about what Katie said. I'd had a couple of boyfriends and a few almosts and maybes since knowing Gabriel and before Jordan.

But, as I sipped my fresh glass of wine, I realized, or admitted to myself, that Gabriel was always frustratingly hanging out in the back of my mind while different guys made it front and center. As is the case when you're attracted to someone entirely off-limits.

You just pretend you're not attracted at all, like it's not there. Like a really annoying itch you could never reach. You ignore it. You ignore your instincts because you couldn't scratch it anyway, no matter how badly you'd like to.

But what Katie said about my "disqualifying factor" was a little bit true.

There was a high school boyfriend my senior year, Matt, who I liked a lot but when he told me he wanted to apply to a faraway school, I immediately broke things off. Long distance never worked, right? His fatal flaw.

There was a guy my sophomore year in college who was such a know-it-all. He was handsome, kind, and thoughtful, and we shared so many of the same interests that we got along so well, but he was a total know-it-all. It was a small thing that our friends always laughed off as Jeremy was just being Jeremy. But somehow, each "actually" or "well, you know" response got more and more grating until I had to dump him.

I explained this to Katie at the time. She just cackled and said, "Found his disqualifier, huh?"

"Doesn't everyone have a disqualifier until you meet the right one?" I countered.

"No one will be perfect, you know. Not even the right one," she said, all wisdom and virtue.

But I kind of already knew this. Because I was assuming my right one would be a lot like Gabe. I had always had a soft spot for Gabe, and not one flaw had turned me off or disqualified him. And I was definitely well-acquainted with Gabe's flaws. He himself was a total know it all, probably worse than Jeremy.

After breaking things off with Jeremy, I was back home with Katie, and while we were hanging out at her house with Gabe, I started noticing how often he said "actually," and "well, I just read about this online," but it wasn't grating. It was kind of cute—Gabe just being Gabe. And I wanted to hear what Gabe thought, anyway. What *had* he read online?

I adored Gabriel Hernandez for the whole of him, not just the pieces that made him who he was. I liked his core, his center, his very essence, him as is. The proof of this was in all my years of knowing Gabriel. He had grown and changed since I first realized the effect he had on me, and no matter how much he had changed over the years—probably no matter how much he still would change and evolve—I never stopped viewing him the way I did.

No matter the silly flaws or the big flaws, none of them were disqualifiers because, after all this time, he had proven himself un-disqualifiable. Honestly, he probably had the biggest disqualifier of them all. He was my best friend's brother, entirely off limits, but my heart still sunk its anchor into him and said, "Let's stop here."

I guessed the right guy would feel like that, like Gabe. I splashed the wine in my glass absentmindedly. Wait, no, *like Jordan*, I mentally corrected myself. I was thinking this as I stood in the kitchen, the noise of the family laughing and celebrating around me. I took a sip of my wine and then corrected myself again—*the right guy would feel like Jordan*.

The right guy was Jordan, or *maybe* it was. It could be? I really adored him. He was kind, tender, patient, and the kind of handsome that belonged strutting down a football field or slamming the hood of a car closed. I knew he was the dream guy for tons of women. But it was almost as if I hadn't realized just how waning our chemistry was until I was standing in front of Gabriel again. That might not be a fair comparison, though. Gabe didn't count.

I took another sip, and my eyes locked with Gabriel's. He hopped off the couch and started walking over to me. Man, I hated how he would show up and mess with my head. My phone started vibrating in my back pocket. I slid it out and saw Jordan's name on the caller ID.

"Hey, you," I answered and slipped out the sliding glass doors onto the big back porch, twinkle lights hanging from the wooden beams overhead. I pulled my sweater over my hands at the chill of the upper thirty-degree winter night.

"Hey, Emmy," Jordan said. "Is the party still going?"

"Oh, yeah. You know how it goes. I haven't even checked the time." Their black German Shepherd, Midnight, came and licked my shoes. I rubbed behind his ears.

"Did it really end up just being the family? No one else?" he asked.

"Yeah. Only family, their significant others, and their...me." I glanced inside the windows. Tanya and Luis were ushering their respective little families out the door, sleepy kids in their arms.

"You're basically crashing another Hernandez family thing again?"

"Sort of."

"Why are they even calling it a party then?" He laughed.

His family was wildly different than the Hernandezes. Always with the extended relatives, family friends, and friends of family friends. The bigger, the better. Jordan couldn't understand the way the Hernandezes were sometimes really content with their own company—not in a cruel way. Jordan would never be cruel. He just couldn't quite get it. Or why his girlfriend was weirdly always invited.

"You know them. It's always a party." I laughed. "They'll all be together again for Christmas in a few days, cracking out the food and wine."

I could almost see him nod. I knew the very one. My heart staggered; that was my Jordan. I felt my face flush at the memory of saying, *"Jordan isn't flawless, trust me,"* to Gabe. It was an unfaithful move. I'd burn inside if he said the same about me. Or would I? I bit my lip.

"So, is everyone back?" he asked.

"Yeah," I said. "And Ricky has a new girlfriend."

"Ah." I wondered if he remembered Ricky. "Well, I'm over at

my mom's. We kind of had our own Christmas party, I guess. Mom made this big pot of chili, and we were all watching Christmas movies. My sisters were making cookies. Wish you could've come."

"That sounds fun. I'll be there tomorrow for the big shindig, promise." I felt guilty. I knew that Jordan, and his family, whom I loved, wanted me to pick them the way I always picked the Hernandezes.

"You better be," he teased. "I miss you, you know."

"I miss you, too," I said softly. Jordan was always with the "miss you" and the "need you" and all those sentiments that I wondered if he could truly mean them. Did he miss me?

I glanced back inside and saw Gabriel. I felt guilty looking at him. I felt guilty that he made my heart race as if I had any control over it—over chemical reactions.

"Gabe is here," I randomly said.

"Oh, yeah?" Jordan's voice cut a little sharper.

"Yeah, we were catching up. Talking about writing."

"Ah, good, I'm glad. I know you like to talk writing sometimes."

I nodded into the phone. Could he almost see it? Did he know the exact nod like I knew his? Did he know me like I knew him? I knew Jordan like the back of my hand, knew the scars, knew the shape, knew the imprint it could make. I had been memorizing Jordan since our first date, as if studying for a test. Like if you knew someone well enough, you would love them by default.

Or maybe, I thought coldly, *I was searching for the opposite of Jordan's disqualifier*. Maybe I was searching for his qualifier. That thing that would make him thrill me.

"How is ole Gabe? He was like your best friend for a while, right? Right up there with Katie," he said, his voice booming into this quiet night.

"Yeah, but it's been a while since then. He's fine. He just finished a project, so I think he'll be home for a little while."

Why was I talking about Gabe to Jordan? I desperately wanted to stop.

"Well, I'm not up for sharing you that much more. I want you for the rest of the holidays." He was joking, but he wasn't.

"Possessive, huh?"

"I just want you to get used to some of my family traditions. It'll be special to have you there. Tomorrow is a tradition for my cousins, but also my dad's cousins and his granddad's cousins. It's really fun."

"I'm really excited, Jordan," I said. I was smitten with the idea that all of Jordan's family all stayed connected like that.

They had this huge party every Christmas where the kids went wild, and the adults all caught up. I'd been excited to see Jordan with people who'd known him as an awkward twelve-year-old and a hyper two-year-old.

He'd told me about it so many times, and I would always think how sweet it would be to be an insider at these family events he loved. I had trouble envisioning myself as anything but an outsider hearing about it. But I was becoming an insider, wasn't I?

"How was work today?" I asked.

"It was great. I'm making so many new contacts. It was such a win connecting with that guy, Jon. What we do is what his clients need, so having me as a referral is a win for both of us, really. I swear I had so many calls today with so much potential."

"Wow, I'm so proud of you, Jordan," I said. Jordan had been planning, strategizing, and building his own construction company since we first started dating.

"*Making my own name in the town I grew up in,*" he'd said over that first dinner together. He already had his own name, his own reputation—and a deeply respected one, at that—his own life, and I knew that. Even on that first date, I knew that.

This company was his dream. But as much as it was his dream, it was also the next step in his plan. He had his plan, and he was taking it step by step. His steps were his dreams, or his dreams were the steps. It was funny to someone tripping through life like me.

The next step... I could barely swallow when I thought about his next steps—house, marriage, kids.

I thought about my tiny apartment with the windows looking out onto our little cityscape and my balcony full of potted plants. I thought about my little unattached life where I could stay at my best friend's family's house late into the night, drinking wine at the drop of a hat. I thought of having kids and almost blacked out.

"I'm excited, Emmy. Everything's really starting. It's all starting for me," he said earnestly.

"It is," I said.

I remembered that first date. It was funny how he'd only graduated college a couple of years before me, but his life was all mapped out before him. My life was the opposite. It had gotten all torn and tangled while unfolding before me. It all felt so easy that day as I sat across from him. I could just slip my hand into his and hop from step to step with him. I wouldn't even have to think about it.

But here I was on a December night, standing out in the cold, looking at another man through the window, thinking about it.

"It's starting for you, too, Emmy," he said sweetly.

"I sure hope so," I said.

"I know it is. It's happening for *us*." It was that sweetness that made me want to hop from step to step with him. That sweetness that I liked kissing me goodnight and sending me text messages every morning.

"For us," I repeated.

The sliding glass doors opened, making me jump. Out slipped Linda and David. They were all bundled up and shuffling out with their egg nogs.

"Hey, sweetie," Linda said.

"Hey." I gave a little wave. "Jordan, I got to go. I'll call you in the morning."

"Okay." He sounded disappointed. "We'll talk tomorrow."

"We'll talk tomorrow," I confirmed. "Bye."

"Hey, I love you," he said quickly.

"Love you, too," I said, then hung up. I turned back to Linda and David. "The party ending?"

"Well, now it's just the young crew inside, and they're trying to decide on a game to play. We're too old for that, so we're sneaking out while we still can," Linda said as if they were getting away with something.

"A little eggnog under the stars with my wife—that's the best way to end a Christmas party if you ask me," David said.

"I'll go check in with the young crew." I winked.

"Keep 'em in line, Em."

"Oh, you know it," I said as I slid the doors closed behind me.

Three

"What were you doing outside in the cold in just a sweater?" Katie said, appalled, as I stepped back inside.

"You're just now noticing I was gone?" I said.

"I noticed. I thought Jordan probably called. I just assumed you had a coat," Katie said.

"Well, I survived the cold. Somehow," I said like a survivor.

"So, how is Jordan then?" Gabe asked. I wondered if he was just confirming it was him I was talking to.

"He's good. He's good," I said. "So, what game are we playing?" The group sitting around in the living room was down to Gabriel, Katie, Ricky, Victor, and Maggie. I sat down beside Katie on the loveseat.

"We're thinking we might play charades or something," Victor said noncommittally.

"You know what?" Gabriel spoke up from his spot on the ground by the couch Ricky, Victor and Maggie were curled up on. "Let's play Truth or Dare."

"No," Katie said while Ricky shouted, "Yes!"

"No, no." I sided with Katie. "No."

"Why not?" Ricky protested. "I think it sounds fun."

"Because we're not sixteen," Katie explained.

"How about we play for our sixteen-year-old selves? In honor of them and all the dumb dares we used to play," Ricky pleaded his case.

"In honor of the nasty peanut butter and pickle sandwich, you guys made me eat when we were sixteen? No, thank you," Katie said. Maggie's mouth formed a horrified O.

"Come on, Em. What do you say? Why not pretend we're sixteen again?" Gabe said with a playful wink.

I could barely breathe, exactly like when I was sixteen, but I choked out, "Fine."

He punched the air excitedly, and it thrilled me. I rolled my eyes for show.

"Okay, but sixteen-year-old us didn't have red wine." Victor pointed to his glass.

"Put it away then," Gabe said, deadpan. "Okay, let's start with the guest of honor."

"Who's the guest of honor?" Ricky asked.

"Maggie, of course," Gabe said. "Truth or dare?"

I felt for her shy self, so I stepped in. "Okay, okay, let's take it easy on the newbie."

He was enjoying messing with us—with me. "For sure. You know me." Gabe defended himself as if shocked at the accusation.

Maggie laughed nervously. "I guess...truth?"

"Who is even asking?" Katie asked.

"Me," Gabe said.

"What? Are you the keeper of the game?" I asked.

"I'll ask for starters then she does the next one. The last answerer becomes the questioner. You guys, we're not so old that we don't remember how Truth or Dare goes," Gabe said.

Though, once the game got going, we didn't really stick to these rules. We were all joining in shouting out questions and dares until we settled on one as a group.

When it landed on me, it was technically Victor who asked me truth or dare, but when I chose Truth, it was Gabe who talked the group into asking if I was in love with Jordan.

"Yes," I said confidently. I'd been sure I would love him since we were walking hand-in-hand on our first date. "Of course."

"Told you it was a boring question," Katie said. "I could've answered that one."

Gabe narrowed his eyes at me. "Okay, I have another then."

"Not how the game works," I countered.

"I vote we get another question since the last one was so boring and easy," Gabe said to the group.

"I mean, we could all just go to her Instagram and see she's throwing around the word love," Victor said. "So, yes, another question."

"Sure, another question—but a juicy one," Katie said.

"Wait, I'm not throwing around the word," I defended myself. "I *do* love him."

"We get it," Gabe said sourly.

"Em, we know. You guys have been together forever. Love is a given. Gabe is just behind the times," Katie consoled me.

"Fine, another question," I complied.

"If he asked you to marry him tomorrow, would you say yes?" Gabe asked.

Katie's jaw dropped. My heart started beating so fast I felt it in my fingertips. It wasn't that shocking of a question, right? I wanted to casually and coolly answer, but then, when I went to answer, I realized...I didn't know how to answer. Yes didn't feel right in my mouth. Maybe didn't either.

If he asked me tomorrow... Tomorrow? We'd been together for a couple of years now. It wasn't that crazy of an idea. But I couldn't say yes. I wouldn't want to marry him right now. But it felt cruel, or wrong, to say no. I'd be lucky if he asked me.

"That's kind of..." Kind of what? I didn't finish.

"Wouldn't you say yes?" Katie asked me, her eyes wide.

"It's..." I don't know why I was taking a game of Truth or Dare so seriously.

I couldn't look at Gabe. I glanced at Katie, who looked concerned.

"It's just a game," I said to her.

"So then, why not answer?" she asked.

"I think..." I felt like I needed to talk it out, but this wasn't the right time. "I think I'd say no if he asked tomorrow."

"Why?" Katie was hijacking the game.

"It doesn't feel right to say yes right now. I was just thinking tonight on the phone..." But then I wasn't sure how much I wanted to share during this silly game with all her brothers and the man who made me feel guilty just for looking at him. "I'm not sure if our future..."

"She's just not there yet, Katie. That's fine. It's not like he's actually asking her to marry him. It's just a game." Gabe thankfully jumped in. "I think it makes perfect sense. He might not be the one."

Victor slugged him in the arm. "Shut up, Gabe."

"Hey, okay, do you think if he asked you to marry him in *a year*, you'd say yes?" Maggie asked.

"Okay, that's too many questions, now." I laughed awkwardly. "I get to ask now."

"Fine, fine." Maggie smiled at me.

But Katie looked at me with an expression I couldn't read. She seemed concerned or something, but I didn't have time to wonder what was going on.

"Okay." I turned to Gabe. "Truth or dare?"

"Truth," he said quickly. I felt lucky. I had a billion questions I could ask him.

"Is there anyone special in your life?" I asked.

"What does 'special' mean?" Gabriel scooted away from the couch, closer to the loveseat where I sat.

"It means...is there a girl you are dating or *want* to be dating?" I explained.

"I'm not dating anyone," he said matter of fact.

"Anyone you want to be dating?" Katie asked.

"I feel like this question is a sly way to ask two," he argued.

"Says the man who asked me like thirty questions," I said dryly.

He snickered. "Fine—"

"This has gotten boring," Ricky whined. Maggie gave him a shove. I wanted to shove him too.

"No, there's no one I would date right now," Gabe said curtly. "Now my turn. Emma, truth or—"

"What is with you two?" Victor asked, annoyed with Gabe and me.

"They get obsessed; you know that," Katie yawned in reply.

"Truth or dare?" Gabe continued, ignoring them.

"Dare," I was on the edge of the loveseat now, leaning toward him.

"I dare you to jump into my parent's pool."

"Nope! Gabe, it's like thirty degrees out." Katie tried to protect me.

I got up and walked out the door. His parents were already

tucked into bed, so no one was out there when I stepped in front of their inground wavy-shaped pool.

"Emma! I know you two always get competitive, but it's too cold to try and beat Gabe!" Katie said. "Beating him is absolutely not worth pneumonia."

I slipped off my nice cashmere sweater—no way I was getting that wet. I had on a little lacy white camisole underneath. I slipped off my jeans, too, to save my favorite pair. I had on boy shorts underwear, which were more modest than my usual bikini bottoms anyway.

I glanced back at the group. Katie was laughing at me, appreciating the drama. Maggie was chuckling, shaking her head at the silliness of her new boyfriend's family. My eyes found Gabe. His eyes were taking me in, making me warmer on this cold night. When he drew his eyes up to mine, they wavered between praise and challenge—same as always. I boldly winked at him. He laughed appreciatively.

Then I dove into the pool. It was so incredibly, awfully cold. I felt blue. I scrambled quickly out of the pool as everyone cheered. Katie helped me up while calling me crazy, and Gabe stripped off his sweatshirt and wrapped me up in it.

"Get her a towel," he exclaimed. Someone ran inside.

He pulled my forehead against his as I shivered proudly. "Can I tell you something?" he whispered.

My heart was thumping. My soaking body was fully against him. His hands were gripped around my triceps, keeping me close. He pulled his lips against my ear. His warm breath sent shivers down my cold, dripping skin.

"I don't think my parents have cleaned that pool in months."

I gave him a little shove, and with my trembling jaw, I said, "What? You think I'm scared to get a little dirty?"

He laughed loudly, wrapping me up in a warm hug and rubbing my arms to keep me warm. "Man, I've missed you, Em."

I was in his arms, teeth chattering, hair dripping, giddy at the closeness, and it felt like the distance and tension of the past couple of years had finally been washed away.

"You two," Katie said, pulling us both toward the house. Maggie and Ricky had a towel for me. The warmth of the indoors felt like a hug.

After everyone had left, I was side-by-side with Katie in her queen size bed. I had decided to sleep over since my underwear was soaked and I'd finished off a couple glasses of wine.

"Hey, is it true?" she whispered. "What you said about not being ready to marry Jordan?"

It was dark, but I could still see the pink of her walls, a color chosen at nine years old.

I sighed. "That bugged you for some reason."

"I just want to know. I love you both." Her eyes peered up over the fluffy white quilt.

"To be honest, Katie. I feel like I have so many doubts and questions about our relationship. About what we both want out of our futures. I'd have to say no. I love him a lot, but that doesn't mean we should get married..."

She sat up, looking at me with eyes full of concern.

"Katie, this shouldn't be that big of a deal. It's not like he actually proposed to me or anything. It was just a game. Who knows, if he actually asked me maybe I'd say something different. It's late, and we were playing a dumb game. For heaven's sake, I dove into the pool in my underwear. Let's sleep on it."

"You really think if he asked you, maybe you'd say something different?"

"Maybe," I said, but I didn't.

I think this conversation was making me feel less and less sure of Jordan. But she seemed so sad for some reason. I was too tired to ask her why. A few beats of silence passed, and I started to drift to sleep.

"You know," she said. "Sometimes, I feel like you and Gabe

have a secret language I can't speak. A secret thing I can't keep up with."

"But you're my best friend, Katie," I said. "There's no contest."

"I don't feel like it's a contest. It's not like a 'I'm left out' thing," Katie explained. "I was just thinking tonight how you two... You have... You guys are the same sort of..."

"Same sort of frustrating?" I joked.

"Exactly." She yawned, resting her head back on her pillow.

Gabriel and I were the same sort of something? I thought it was true as I fell asleep. I decidedly didn't let myself think about Maggie's truth-or-dare question.

Four

ME

It's so late and I drank a couple of glasses of wine, so I'm staying the night with Katie. I'll drive to the party from there tomorrow!

JORDAN BOYFRIEND <3

Good morning, beautiful. I'm so excited for today!

The next morning, I woke up disoriented and with a desperate need to pee. I trudged over to Katie's en suite bathroom, but the door was locked.

"Are you going to be a while?" I whined.

She, ever the morning person, cheerily called out from behind the bathroom door, "Yeah, sorry!"

I crawled back onto the bed and found my phone under the pillow. It was 7 a.m. I knew most of the house was probably still asleep.

I was in a white tank top and a pair of Katie's baggy sweatpants. My hair was a tangled mess, but I felt safe that no one would see me. I crept down the hall toward the bathroom off the living room.

"Good morning, sunshine." Gabriel was standing by the coffee maker with that smug grin of his.

"It's too early for you morning people." I covered my face as I passed by him.

He started chuckling.

"It's too early for you to *laugh at me*," I added.

He just laughed more.

"I haven't seen sleepy Em in a long time," he called after me. "I missed her!"

I ignored him, closing the bathroom door on the sound of his chuckling.

After I reappeared, he asked, "Would you like coffee?"

I thought about my earlier intention to sleepily fall back into Katie's bed, but instead, I snatched the throw blanket from the couch and wrapped it around my shoulders.

"I'd love some," I said.

"Do you still do equal amounts coffee and half and half?" he teased me, his curls freshly showered. He had on a gray hoodie, the hood all the way up, the way he always did when he first woke up or was feeling particularly moody.

"I've grown since then. Now, I do what Starbucks would refer to as 'a splash,'" I said proudly.

He raised an eyebrow as he splashed a little creamer into a teal ceramic mug of coffee.

"Okay, maybe a few splashes," I admitted, rubbing my tired eyes.

He put in a little more. I reached over and grabbed the spoon and creamer and made it to my liking as Gabriel judged me from behind his inky dark cup of coffee.

"So, tell me, how's life? How's things as a newspaper reporter?" he asked, leaning against the kitchen counter.

"Small staff, small pay," I said honestly. "But I do love telling the stories."

"Living the dream?"

"Not so sure it's 'the dream.'" *Or even my dream*, I thought.

"Your dream?" he asked like he could read my mind.

"I don't know," I said, hating how much I had said this phrase the last twelve hours.

"Well, I know 'the dream' we always talked about was you being a writer."

"Yeah, that's true. I guess this job is *part* of the dream. I just don't know if it's *the dream*. It kind of worries me because I don't know where I even go from here," I said, surprising myself with my honesty. It was like words just tumbled out around this man.

"I will say, you used to talk about magazine writing far more than newspaper writing."

"But I don't know how to do that from Sweet River." I blew on my coffee.

"You can write from anywhere."

"I can't afford freelance; I need the reliable pay."

"Well, have you thought much into the future? Beyond what doesn't work?" He set his mug down, putting his full attention on this conversation.

"Not really," I admitted. "Jordan has his life mapped out in all these steps. I feel like I let myself get swept up in his steps some-times," I said, verbalizing my thoughts from last night.

"How's that?" He cocked his head.

"He's always encouraging me to try and like become the editor at our paper. So, I've just made that my next step, my next goal. It sounds right." I took another sip.

"But your favorite part is the stories," he said like it was a fact.

"Yeah, I know. But it seems like that's the only forward momentum for me."

"That's not true. That's the only momentum at this partic-ular job, but when we were taking our writing classes, you never said you wanted to write for the local paper. You said you wanted to write for *Vogue Travel* or *Land & Sea*, and you wanted to write from hotel rooms in NYC."

"We both know dreams and goals change from when you're a freshman in college," I said as Gabe walked over closer to me.

"Dreams change, for sure. I mean, look at Katie, look at me. We're evidence of that. I went from wanting to write novels to pitching stories about living out of a backpack—but that's 'cause what I wanted changed. Did your dreams actually change? Is becoming an editor what you want now?"

"I tried that original dream, and I got rejection after rejection. The local paper is the door that opened. Sometimes dreams don't want you back. Sometimes, it's not that dreams change...it's that they flat-out reject you, Gabe. *My dream ghosted me.*"

"You got like two rejections." His words were hard, but his voice was soft. "Then you moved back home."

I swallowed. I hadn't consumed enough coffee for this conversation. I wrapped the blanket tight around me. "You don't understand."

"Make me understand." He was now standing beside me, his face so close I could smell his shampoo, fresh pine and something warm and musky.

"I felt really grateful for this job. It felt like I had passed a test or something. I was also grateful to be in the same town as Katie."

He was quiet. Waiting.

"I just... I feel like I took the job and did the opposite of my boyfriend. Instead of making steps and planning my future, I just stayed put. I accepted the job, rented the apartment, and then was done. I just stopped planning, stopped taking steps." I held my hands up as if to gesture the big halt my life had come to.

"You're only twenty-four. You have time to come up with the steps now."

"But how? I think I didn't come up with them because there aren't any to take."

"Excuses." He leaned across the counter to grab the cup of coffee he'd left behind. "There are a ton of opportunities *if you want them.* You have to start looking, start writing, and start asking around."

"Says the famous Gabriel Hernandez fresh off his latest project." I wiggled my eyebrows.

"Hey, you're still my favorite writer." He took another sip of coffee while I blushed. *She didn't look back, but she did look up, and there were those stars she always saw in his eyes.*

"Really, you remember the poem I wrote at fourteen?" A poem about him, I thought silently, embarrassedly to myself.

"I remember you and me swapping poems and stories," he said tenderly, like he was talking about something precious. "That's when you became my favorite writer."

"You're still my favorite writer, too," I said softly, hiding behind my mug.

"Don't stop here if this isn't it for you," he urged me, leaning in close again, making me feel off-balance. "Don't do something because it's what sounds right, or you don't know what else to do. Your imagination is too big for that excuse."

But it all felt more difficult than I could explain to him. I felt tied to Jordan's next steps. I felt tied to my fears. I felt tied to my choices. I felt tied in a thousand different directions, in a thousand different ways. I wanted to ask how I could cut myself free from all these knots. I opened my mouth, but then Katie walked in and asked me what time I had to leave for Jordan's big Christmas party. I told her soon. Gabriel scooted away from his spot beside me, walking back to the coffee machine.

"I have something for you in my room, actually," she said with a twinkle in her eye.

I left my coffee to turn cold on the kitchen island with those weighty conversations I didn't want to carry with me to my boyfriend's party.

"So," she said her voice rising with mischief as I followed her to her bedroom. "Jordan stopped by a bit ago while you were getting coffee to sneak over a little surprise for you."

She walked over to her closet and slid open the doors. She had a small closet with a rod of clothes hanging, but she pushed her clothes aside to showcase the red, sparkling dress hanging in the middle. It had a note paperclipped to it.

For Emma, this is just the beginning of Christmas memories with you. Love you, Jordan.

The dress was velvety soft with long sleeves. I smiled to myself at the idea of Jordan leafing through dresses at some department store. But then I realized one of his sisters or his mother, probably took the time to shop with him, considering my taste and discussing it with him. They probably thought how important I was to him, for him to plan this for me.

I imagined him setting his alarm on a Saturday morning to drop this dress off so I could have it on for the big Christmas party later this morning. This was so important to him. I was so important to him. *He's important to me, too,* I thought. I just couldn't explain the pit in my stomach.

"This is so thoughtful," I said absentmindedly.

"He had a cute little plan. He was texting me about sneaking it over last night," Katie said with a grin. "Got to love Jordan and his romantic gestures."

He was one for the romantic gestures—the bouquet of roses on our first date, the diamond necklace in a little bag on my doorstep the morning of our first anniversary, surprise tickets to see my favorite band perform live, a blindfold leading me to a surprise picnic in the park on my birthday. Memories that played like a rom-com montage across my mind.

I nodded, still rubbing the dress between my fingertips.

"Do you like it?" Katie asked.

"Of course," I said. "I would like whatever dress was hanging here."

I felt like there was some button that was supposed to click on when your boyfriend made a gesture like this that made you swoon and blush, but mine was defective.

I suddenly felt choked up. "Can I borrow your shower?" I asked Katie, swallowing the rock in my throat.

Katie nodded, her eyes considering me the way they did last

night when I said "no" during Truth or Dare. I felt on the edge of tears the entire time I got ready. I showered, fixed my hair, put on my makeup, and slipped on the dress with my eyes stinging all the while. I looked in the mirror at my loose curls and my red lips to match my red dress. A dress straight out of a Christmas movie. I felt a couple of tears creep from my eyes like a premonition.

"I shouldn't feel this way," I whispered to myself, alone in Katie's room. I should be swooning over this dress, the sweetest little note, and him planning it all out with my best friend. *Swoon,* I ordered myself.

"I'm just confused. I'll see him, and all these doubts will vanish," I encouraged myself as I slid on the nude high heels I was borrowing from Katie.

This had to be because of my old lingering feelings for Gabriel. Last night was just a nostalgia bender, and I needed to shake it off and move on. In January, Gabriel would go home, and life could resume as normal. I clicked into the living room in my heels, and Gabriel was kicked back on the couch with a newspaper in his hand. He peeked over it and saw me in my dress.

"You sparkle," he said affectionately.

And I hated the way it made me blush, the way my heart spun in my chest, making me dizzy as I walked to the door.

The Christmas party was a big brunch. Everyone brought homemade casseroles with tater tots or a big pan of gooey cinnamon rolls, so I was driving there with only a few sips of coffee in my stomach. A thought crossed my mind as the car bumped along the country roads that led to his uncle's big farmhouse. When was the last time I blushed over Jordan?

When was the last time I wasn't trying to correct my feelings? Ordering myself to swoon. When was the last time I wasn't thinking somehow our hearts, our desires, were going to finally sync up? Or the last time I felt seen by Jordan the way I felt seen by Gabriel in the kitchen this morning?

"Do I ever feel seen by Jordan?" I said aloud as I pulled up to the house. I pulled a shawl around my shoulders, thinking this was a terrible time to finally be examining these feelings.

The sky was gray this late morning, with a low grumble of winter thunder in the distance. I opened my phone to a message from Jordan, saying I couldn't wait for him to see me in the dress. The words tugged on my heart. I did love Jordan. That's why I didn't want to be flippant or careless with his heart.

He was the kind of man who set his alarm to leave presents for the woman he loved, and he deserved a woman who didn't have to fake a feeling over his romance. *He deserves a woman who wasn't blushing over another man while in a dress he bought for her*, I thought, ashamed.

I remembered the butterflies I felt when Jordan first held my hand as we walked in our little downtown, the way I would reread his text messages. I remembered studying a cookbook as I made him dinner all by myself. And telling my mom when we were on a family trip at the lake, "I think this is serious, Mom." She had brushed a piece of my hair behind my ear and said, "I think so, too."

I felt lucky that day. I still felt lucky, but like I had somehow wound up with someone else's winnings.

Five

J ordan's Uncle was a cotton farmer who saw a considerable
amount of success and liked to pour his earnings into his big
farmhouse. There was an Olympic size swimming pool, a
tennis court, a patio styled for entertaining, his souped-up truck,
and thoroughbred dogs that ran all over his property. There was
even a massive, loopy slide that splashed straight into his swimming pool. Jordan had fractured his wrist going sideways down it
once.

Jordan said that his aunt and uncle liked any occasion to show
these things off, or rather, "They loved to host lots of parties."

It was his house where the family hosted every holiday party,
from Christmas to Easter. But Christmas was the biggest and
best. I had been excited and admittedly a little nervous because it
was the first one where I was officially a guest.

I walked inside and was greeted by "White Christmas"
crooning throughout the house's speaker system. There were

people chatting, holding shiny red or green paper plates stacked high with food. Kids were squealing and hiding underneath the enormous Christmas tree in the middle of the foyer. I made my way through the people and decadent Christmas decorations until I found Jordan.

He saw me and took in a deep breath. "Hey, Emma."

I smiled at him. "Hey, you." He was cozy in a lush green cable knit sweater and dark jeans and his blond hair was cut short.

"Merry early Christmas," he said, then gave me a kiss on the forehead.

"Merry early Christmas," I returned.

He pulled me in close to his side. His heart was racing, and his breathing was shallow, much like it was when we were watching a close football game or his dad was talking about the business.

He was nervous, I realized, as he anxiously smiled and asked me if I wanted hot chocolate. The hot chocolate bar at this party was enviable with a dozen tall silver carafes of steamy cocoa and various flavored marshmallows and whipped cream options.

"Are you okay?" I said, keeping my voice low for privacy.

"Sure, of course, yeah," he said, agreeable affirmations tumbling out.

He was definitely *not* okay. I wondered if he was nervous to have me around all of his relatives. If he had caught on to my odd behavior last night. Or something happened that he'd tell me about later. I tried to tune more into the party and less into why Jordan was so jumpy.

In the following hour, I was introduced to various relatives of varying degrees of closeness. I was given so many delicious plates of food. I made so much small talk that I was starting to feel like a Christmas party robot. It turned out Jordan's family had a tradition of everyone piling into one of the family rooms to sing holiday songs while one of the uncles, or aunts, pounded away on the piano. Jordan's dad volunteered as tribute this year, making some funny remark as he donned elf ears to play.

I was grinning, caught up in the celebration. I felt like I had somehow been written into a holiday movie. But instead of playing some holiday classic, he started playing the "Wedding March." People started laughing, confusedly looking around at each other for answers.

"What's this about?" someone asked loudly.

"Come on, Mark!" they jeered.

He wiggled his eyebrows at all of us and said, "There's more to celebrate in my family this year than just Christmas." After this remark, he started playing with more gusto.

I turned to look at Jordan to see if he knew what was going on, but he wasn't standing beside me. I had to drop my eyes to find him because he was kneeling close to the ground for some reason. He was down on one knee. As he cleared his throat nervously, I felt my body flood with panic.

"Emma Brown," he said. "I saw you years ago after some time apart, and my heart stopped when I saw your face. My heart still stops when I see your face."

Funny he should say that, I thought, because *my* heart had just stopped. It felt as if my heart had plummeted right through the floor. He was proposing to me, down on one knee, with a romantic speech. Was the world playing a joke on me because of last night's game?

I said I couldn't say yes to a proposal from him to a room full of people, so the world decided to test me.

"You have become my best friend, Emma, and the love of my life. And now I want you to become my wife. I want us to have kids and grow old together." He was bellowing, so everyone around us could hear.

His tone sounded like a command and not a question. I wondered if he'd even need a reply from me, or if he'd just finish his speech, slip the ring on my finger, and wish everyone a Merry Christmas.

Then it was all quiet, everyone collectively holding their breath in anticipation as he pulled a little black box out of his jacket pocket and popped it open in front of me. I swallowed hard at the sparkling silver ring peeking up at me. He probably picked this out, imagining me in it, like he did my red dress.

"Emma Grace Brown, will you marry me?" he asked loudly, looking around at his smiling relatives who started clapping and cheering like we were at a football game and he'd just scored a touchdown.

I stood there in my sparkly red dress, holding my breath— holding in all the doubts and questions from the drive here so tight I could burst.

How could I look him in the eyes and say yes? But it also felt as if I couldn't say anything *but* yes to this party of Jordan's smiling relatives. My would-be-in-laws expected to be eating my own hash brown casserole for Christmas parties to come. I looked back down at Jordan's hopeful face, a face I knew like the map of my hometown.

I touched the ring. It was beautiful. It looked like a ring Jordan would choose. Gleaming silver, a princess cut, like something straight out of a jewelry store catalog.

Seconds were ticking by, but I couldn't find any words that felt right or even a little sufficient. The anticipatory silence turned to awkward murmurs. I felt like I was in a holiday movie, but someone had stolen my lines. I had no answers for the man in front of me, only questions.

I knelt to Jordan's eye level and whispered, "I am feeling really overwhelmed. Can I have a minute, please?"

His eyes squinted at me in confusion. He cleared his throat before answering me. It was painfully obvious that saying anything but yes in this moment was hurting him.

"Oh, okay?" he muttered.

"Sorry," I whispered as I backed away. "I'm so sorry."

I bolted for the family bathroom. I heard a murmur of confusion ripple throughout the room as I shut the bathroom door behind me. I couldn't catch my breath. My hands were shaking uncontrollably. My chin was quivering. I collapsed to the bathroom floor on my hands and knees. A sob escaped me. I buried my face into a towel hanging on the wall beside me to muffle the sound.

I hadn't expected this. I should've expected this. I couldn't believe I let it get this far. I thought I had more time to deal with these quiet doubts that had been piling up in the back of my mind, but now they were going to break our hearts.

I felt like a sleepwalker who woke up in the middle of a car crash. One she'd caused.

There, crouched on the fuzzy white bathroom rug, I had to decide what to do next. Should I walk back out there and offer a polite yes in front of his family and then explain no later? But would that hurt worse? To offer forever and then explain it was all a lie to save his pride. Or would it selfishly be to save mine?

There was no escape plan, and I felt completely trapped. I felt my heart breaking within my chest. Jordan had asked me to marry him, and I had to give him an answer. *Jordan asked me to marry him.* That thought sent more sobs through my chest because I loved Jordan—his beefy shoulders, his bear hugs, his southern accent, his hand around a football. He made me feel wanted. We had a friendship that comforted me. I could have a happy future with Jordan. I loved Jordan. But maybe it wasn't about if I loved Jordan. Maybe it was just simply about *what I wanted.*

I wiped my dripping eyes with shaky hands while I reframed Jordan's question from "Will you marry me?" to "Do you *want* to marry me?" And it was an easy answer—no.

The idea of marrying Jordan apparently gave me a panic attack and sent me into sobs. I could never marry a man who thought proposing to me in front of his family, whom I barely knew at a Christmas party, was the way to ask me to spend the rest of my life with him. Casually in his car, while we were driving to dinner would've felt more right than this.

Now here I was, trapped in the middle of a stuffy pink bathroom with reindeer decorated hand towels and gingerbread scented hand soap while a room full of partygoers awaited my answer on the other side of the door. I stared at an ill-placed window across from the toilet and wished I was anywhere but here. I did the only thing that made sense right now and dialed Katie's number.

"Hi." Her voice was tentative and tight, and I immediately knew that she'd known his plans.

"You knew," I whispered angrily.

"Knew what?" she asked awkwardly.

"That he was going to propose at his family's giant Christmas reunion party thing!" I burst into tears.

"Yes, I knew. Oh no, you're crying. What happened?"

I just kept crying, collapsing like a broken dam.

"Did he propose?" she asked quietly with a door closing behind her. "What's going on, Em?"

I took a deep, steadying breath. "He proposed during the Christmas sing-along."

"During the Christmas sing-along? Oh, Jordan," she moaned. "Okay, what did you say?"

"I asked to be excused to the bathroom."

It was silent.

"And you're there now, I presume?" she asked gently.

I pathetically nodded my head into the phone. "Yes."

She took in a deep breath. "Oh boy."

"I couldn't say yes, Katie. I don't think I could say yes today, or tomorrow, or next year, or decades down the road. I love Jordan...but I don't *love* Jordan. I love Jordan like you love someone you hug at the end of a really great night with friends, but not the way you love someone who you're going home with afterward. He's just not it. I think I was realizing it the past few—"

"I want to hear your epiphany, Em, I really do, but this isn't the time. Right now is proposal time, and it all kind of depends on you. You have to get back out there, champ."

I started sobbing again like a little kid being told it was time leave to Grandma's. But I was being told I had to leave the guest bathroom and the fuzzy rug I'd covered in snot and tears.

"Emma, you just have to go out there, pull him aside, and then explain to him you're sorry but it's going to be *no*. Then just run out to your car and drive home ASAP."

I was quiet.

"Are you there?"

"I'm here," I whispered. "I just wish I wasn't here."

"But, hon, you are. The longer you hide out, the worse it's going to be."

"It's awful no matter what... I can't tell him yes, then take it back. I'd be lying, and he'd have to tell everyone about it after I took it back. But I also can't march out there and tell him thanks but no thanks in front of his whole family..."

"Just pull him aside."

"They'll know what's going on..." I imagined them staring at me as I asked to speak to him alone—their eyes on me. His perfectly sweet mom watching me with sadness in her eyes. His dad cringing at the piano. I rubbed my forehead.

"Probably, they're already expecting a big ole rejection since you locked yourself in the bathroom."

I lay flat on my back, sprawled out on the floor. "Katie, I know Jordan. He is going to try and argue with me on this. He'll try to get me to change my mind. He'll want to talk this out for hours. He'll want my reasons; he'll want to talk me out of my reasons. He'll ask me to take some time and think on it. I'm going to have an hours-long breakup with him at his Uncle's."

"Could you ask him to go on a drive or something?"

"Driving around while I dump him is not the safest choice."

"True," she conceded. "You have the options you have, Emma. I think you're just looking for a way out that doesn't exist."

I glanced over to the ill-placed window across from the toilet.

"There is another option," I said, my heart racing.

"I'm listening."

"I break out of here." The window opened to the front of the house.

"How?" She asked as I estimated just how high I would need to hoist myself up to crawl out.

"There's a window."

"Do you even have your car keys with you?" I could hear the panic in her voice.

"I have my over-the-shoulder bag on. I was kind of just awkwardly wearing it around the whole time since I didn't know where anyone was placing their purses."

"Emma's awkwardness coming in clutch."

I walked over and slid the window open easily, like a ring that fit just perfectly.

"Hold on while I climb out."

I heard a muffled Katie yell at me from the other end of the phone, but it was already in my purse. I hoisted my body over the windowsill and dropped to the other side. Then I ran down the rocky gravel road to my car like a prisoner set free. I got behind the wheel, breathless. I didn't waste a moment, starting my car and hitting the gas almost simultaneously. Dust crackled under my tires. Relief flooded down my cheeks in hot steamy tears as I sped off.

"Emma?" Katie called from my phone. I scrambled into my purse with my right hand and shakily attached my phone to my car's USB.

"Em?" She boomed through my car speakers.

"I'm driving home," I announced.

"You didn't, Em!"

"I did. I escaped through the window like I'm a character on *Friends* or something."

Katie burst into laughter. And, with tears on my face, I did, too. We laughed so hard that I had to pull over in an old Baptist Church parking lot. We laughed until we were quiet, silent, and I could just breathe.

Finally, I said, "I did the selfish, immature, rude thing. I literally did the wrong thing, the thing you shouldn't do. I knew it was wrong, and I did it anyway."

"You're human, Emma. Sometimes humans do the selfish, immature, rude thing every once in a while. And I know you better than most, and can say, you rarely do that, so I think you're allowed this one."

I groaned.

"Man, you sure did save up for a big one, though. Didn't you, my dear?"

"That I did. But, while I did do it for myself—I also kind of did it for Jordan, too. Mostly for me. But a little bit for him, too."

"I know, hon. I really do."

With that, I put my car in drive and headed home. Not the tiny apartment with the windows overlooking my town, but my childhood home where my parents would probably have a fire burning in the fireplace and my dad would have his nose in a book. I parked outside their house, expecting to feel like a kid again, all reckless relief, but instead, I felt very adult.

Here I was, a grown-up, carrying in my grown-up burdens and problems to discuss with my parents. But there was no way they could somehow fix this for me like they used to help fix my cuts and scrapes, my torn stuffed animals, my lost homework assignments, and even some of my heart's very first bruises. I was home, I was theirs, gratefully, but I was also under my own care and supervision now.

Six

JORDAN BOYFRIEND <3

Hey, are you ok in there?

JORDAN BOYFRIEND <3

Emmy, you coming out anytime soon?

JORDAN BOYFRIEND <3

????

JORDAN BOYFRIEND <3

You left???

I was an only kid. My parents had always told me that they had "knocked it out of the park on the first try" and felt no need to try anymore after me. This kind of flattery was kind, but it also never really cut it for me.

My parents were kind of obsessed with each other, and I secretly always wondered if they just didn't want to deal with anyone else getting in the way of their little bubble. They allowed me, their lucky accident in, and no one else. I wouldn't have minded one other kid in our bubble—or at least a dog or something. But it remained just us three, for better or worse.

I hated it sometimes. Especially on the days I felt acutely aware of both of their eyes only on me, their hopes and goals for their offspring hanging solely on me. But, on the days I needed all the love, all the focus, all four arms around me, I loved that my parents were all mine. This December afternoon was a day I appreciated my position as the only child.

As the dark sky crackled and cried, I laid my head in my mom's lap and let silent tears fall as she rubbed my back.

"I remember doing this when you were two years old watching Barney," she said softly. I imagined my little two-year-old hands reaching for my mom's and placing them on my back. I glanced at my hands now, bigger but still no diamond rings.

"No, we didn't know," my mom and dad told me when I asked if they knew Jordan was going to propose.

"I'm not necessarily surprised, though," my mom added.

"If you feel anything less than a hundred percent 'yes,' then it should be 'no,'" my dad said firmly. "Marriage isn't something you should talk yourself into. Marriage requires a hundred percent."

It was reassuring, confirming even, but my anxious heart was still hammering away in my chest. As good as it was to talk to my parents, the person I needed to talk to was Jordan. But I really didn't want to talk to him even if my heart wouldn't rest until I did.

One of the big problems with making the rude, immature, and selfish decision was that it made it easier to continue making bad decisions. As if I had turned myself on the rude, immature and selfish setting, Jordan had tried to call me a few times, and I kept clicking "decline."

Each time I pressed "decline," I could see the hurt on his face when I walked away from him sitting on bended knee with a ring in his hand. I felt emotionally paralyzed. I couldn't think up any words to say to the man hurting on the other line. I was barely even saying words to my parents. I was barely even thinking words to myself.

Jordan was one of the closest people in my life over the past couple of years. He felt like my hometown in human form. He had been my shoulder to lean on, my self-prescribed balm for the wounds of growing up. We had lived in this same town since we were babies. We were in the same nursery at church. Our moms were friendly in hallways and at football games. We went to the same summer camps, studied for the same tests, and bruised the same knees as we learned to ride our bikes.

This wasn't a rarity with the people in my town, but it deepened our relationship like a gas on the pedal when we were first moving our relationship forward. Over the past two years, I had grown to know him even more. I knew his instincts, his reflexes, the black-and-white way in which he understood the world, how he thought literally and logically.

So, I knew his response would be, "Do you not love me anymore?" when I denied his proposal. But I did love him. Loving him felt like a natural reflex, like an "of course" to a silly question.

I had watched him from afar when I was a freshman in high school while he walked hand-in-hand with his high school sweetheart. All through high school, I had hoped, if he ever found himself looking for love again, he would ask me to the dance. I prayed he would see me in my new shirt and think I was beautiful. I wished for him to offer to drive me home. But he never did.

Not until we were in our twenties, at least. We found ourselves both recent college graduates moving back to our tiny Texas town, Sweet River. I remembered the day I saw him finally see me.

I was late to church on Sunday morning, rushing through the parking lot, and there he stood in the lobby as I rushed inside. Our eyes locked. I saw him notice me, like really notice me. I literally thought, *finally*. I forgot I was rushing as he walked over to me while I stood swaying in my royal blue wrap dress.

"Emma Brown, are you back home?" he asked me as if we'd

been keeping track of each other's whereabouts all this time aside from what we scrolled past on social media.

We both said that we couldn't believe we had lost touch the past several years, both wrapped up in lives at different colleges—mine a school only a few hours away, Tarleton State University, in a similarly small town to this one, and his school was a big state school in San Antonio. He had moved home only a couple of years before me.

We decided right then that we needed to catch up like we were old friends. I don't think we'd ever had a solo conversation in our whole lives. We made dinner plans. I found out over dinner at my longtime favorite Italian spot that he had come home to start his own construction company.

I told him how I had come home to take a job as a reporter at our local newspaper. I told him how the man who hired me had taught my high school journalism course. It all felt so nostalgic and welcoming after four years of growing pains.

As we walked back to his truck on that fall night, I just couldn't believe my luck. He reached for my hand, and I remembered giggly conversations about what it would be like to hold Jordan's hand at ninth-grade sleepovers.

I felt my life falling into place like dominoes. Jordan made coming home feel romantic and destined when mere weeks before, the idea of coming home felt like accepting a failing grade at adulthood.

Jordan and Emma. Didn't it make sense? Wasn't this the way the story was supposed to go? Didn't this mean it was always supposed to be him? Could I make Jordan my dream come true?

But nostalgia and romance aside, while the story might make sense written in black and white—Jordan and Emma, the two individuals in living color, didn't make much sense.

I guess I had started to realize slowly after I came down from the excitement of finally getting the school-age crush. It was hard to notice for a while because I never stopped liking him, not once throughout the whole two years.

There was a certain grief I felt when I lost the internship. I had applied for at my dream job in New York City, and then quickly afterward was rejected from another dream job I applied for in Los Angeles—at the same place that had hired Gabriel, actually.

I was grieving a certain belief I had in myself. A hope and dream I had to give up. A vision I had for my life that I lost by my own shortcomings.

Jordan was a salve, a comfort, and a distraction. I could lose myself in the butterflies, in at least one thing going right. There was this person who found me special and interesting when I felt like a giant disappointment. I let myself be distracted for two years, I guess. Distractions can last a while, especially when they kiss you good and tell you you're beautiful.

It was easy to lose myself in the relationship, to ignore the future because Jordan and I felt *good* together. We just didn't feel *right* like reaching for a strawberry but getting a bite of grape. It was good; it just wasn't what you were looking for.

Jordan was always planning for his future in a way that made me anxious. He would talk about neighborhoods in town where he wanted to potentially buy a house, and I would nervously start tugging at my hair. He would wonder about the local schools his children would attend, and I would pick at my nails. He would buy season passes for the high school football team, and I would feel suffocated at the idea of knowing exactly where we would be for the foreseeable Friday nights.

He was building his own construction company here in town. None of this rootedness surprised me. It was my own reaction to all of it that was getting harder to quiet. I could only hit the mute button on my own feelings so often until the button broke.

It was just last week that I sat in the passenger side as he drove us to dinner when a thought I desperately wanted to mute snuck through. *Jordan is barreling us toward a future that I hadn't realized I buckled up for when I sat beside him.*

It wasn't necessarily because I didn't want a future with him —though I suppose that was part of it—but it was how he mapped out his life in a way that made me realize that his map didn't match mine much at all.

What did my map look like? I wasn't sure. I just knew as I looked at his that it didn't look like *that*. But if Jordan was keeping me from what I wanted, I, too, was keeping him from moving forward with what he wanted. Being together wasn't fair to either of us.

I could say I didn't like breaking his heart, but really, I would be breaking him free to get what he wanted—because I wasn't it.

As I thought this through, phone clenched in my hand, I thought of all I would be breaking free from, including the sweet, distracting things that had me riding alongside him for so long.

I could feel his lips on mine. His big hand on the small of my back. The way his cologne smelled like my own personal "feel better" elixir. The adorable way he would get caught up in a high school football game, his sisters and I giggling beside him in the stands, and his mom saying, "He should've been a coach!" His passion for tradition and grand gestures. A man a romance writer would create. A life with him would be sweet, satisfying, and fun. It was sweet and fun, I admitted to myself. And why it was hard to let go.

To answer the phone.

To say it aloud to him.

To seal my fate.

To put the nail in the coffin of "us."

I couldn't do it anymore. I was done hiding away at my parents house.

The day was fading into late afternoon. My dad had fallen asleep in his armchair with a book on his chest, and my mom was on the phone to her sister, probably discussing my almost engagement. I slipped out the door quietly. I was still in my sparkly dress, just now, with my dad's sweatshirt over it. My hair was a messy knot on top of my head.

I drove to Jordan's apartment. I walked shakily up the stairwell to his third-floor apartment, careful with the rain turning to ice beneath my feet. I knocked on his door, but there was no response. I pulled out my phone and, taking in a deep breath, dialed his number. No answer. I sat down on the top of the staircase, waiting for him to arrive. The air stung against my raw, puffy eyes.

I remembered the dozens of nights he and I sat on this very step right outside his apartment door, stars overhead. My head would rest on his shoulder. He'd tell me some story about his job or his sisters, and I'd listen to him, finding a calm just being close to him. And now I was going to forfeit the calm that had been all mine for two years. I choked back another sob.

I saw his car pull into the parking lot beside mine. He cut the engine, and I saw him warily look over at my own car. He glanced up, his eyes finding me sitting on our step. He didn't move. I wasn't sure if I should sit and wait for him to come to me or if, after everything, it was my turn to make the move and go to him.

He just stared at his steering wheel. I knew he didn't owe me his time or attention after what I had done, but I also knew I owed him an explanation if he wanted one.

With that in mind, I walked down the staircase to meet him where he was at. I was standing by his car door when he glanced up at me and let out an angry, disgruntled sigh. The kind of sigh he released after his team had a big loss. I could hear it through the car windows.

He opened the door, so I stepped out of his way. He climbed out, slamming the door shut. Leaning against his car, he rubbed his hands aggravatedly over his forehead. It was silent and tense for a while. Water slowly coming to a boil.

"You just left," he said. "You just *left.*"

"I'm so sorry," I whispered.

"You just freaking left." He was all disbelief and hurt.

"I know."

"Why?" His hazel eyes cut into mine.

"I felt like there was no good option—either I lie and tell you what everyone wants to hear and then hurt you later, or I make this awful scene and have this awful conversation at your uncle's big, cheerful Christmas party...or I just—"

"*Run away*?" He spit out.

"Yeah, run away. Run away like a scared little girl. And I just... I chose that option."

"I freaking got down on one knee for you. And you couldn't just pull me aside and let me down easy."

"There would be nothing *easy* about letting you down, Jordan. There was a whole party watching us—a party of your family members. None of my family, not even a friend. Just people rooting for whatever you wanted. I-I freaked out—" I brushed a loose piece of hair behind my ear.

"I get that there was pressure. But you couldn't even tap my shoulder and take me outside and tell me no, or tell me maybe, or whatever it was you want to say?"

"I know. I chose what was easiest for me. I am so sorry for being so selfish."

He rolled his eyes.

"I am sorry. I am *so* sorry. I was wrong to run away. I was wrong to leave you there at that party with a ring and no answers. I'm mad at myself." I started to choke up. I could only imagine how long he waited for me to return from the bathroom. "I just didn't know what to say. I still..."

He reached his hands out, grabbed my sleeves, and then yanked me close to him. His waist against my waist. "Well," he said gruffly. "What would you say if we had a do-over? Just you and me."

I took in a jagged breath. "Jordan," I said. "The setting doesn't change the question. It doesn't change the answer."

"Come on," he said a little sad, a little desperate. "You still haven't really given me an answer. It makes me think you're not really sure."

"Do you still even want to ask me after what I did?" I whispered.

He looked at me funny. "What does that mean? What? Were

you hoping I would be so mad at you for running away that I would break us up so you wouldn't have to?"

I was stunned. "No," I said after a few seconds.

He cleared his throat. "Why did you run away then? I'm really confused. Everyone is. Why did you ignore my calls? Why are you here at my apartment? What do you want to happen?"

"I'm here because I want to tell you that I'm sorry, first of all." I rubbed my arms and bounced in the cold air. My dad's sweatshirt wasn't enough in this cold. "And I want to tell you why I can't marry you."

"Okay," he choked on the last statement. Then cleared his throat. "Why?"

"Jordan, I can't tie my future to yours when I don't even know what I want my future to look like. You're so sure of what you want, and all I'm sure of is that I don't want what you want. We don't want the same things out of life. I've been ignoring it for so long...because of how easy it all felt in the beginning."

"How can you know we don't want the same things if you don't even know what it is you want?" He exhaled, trying to find the right words. Hadn't I been sorting out what to say since I left his uncle's house?

"What if someday you realize that you do want what I want?" Jordan whispered. "I can wait. Maybe you just need some time."

"I spent the last couple of years focused on you and me. I didn't spend any time on myself or figuring out what I want. You know so clearly how you want your life to look, and I don't know much except...that I'm not going to ever want what you want."

"But how do you know that? You don't know the future. How can you possibly know that, Emma?" He flung his arms open wide in exasperation. It made my heart hurt.

"If I was ever going to suddenly want what you want—it would be right now. With how much it hurts to end this thing with you—hurting enough for me to run away from the pain—with how much I just love you and your big heart, it would be *right now*. This would be the time I realized I could want those things." My voice was shaking, and my eyes were watery. "If I can't find it in me to want what you want today with you looking at me like this, I'm never going to. I wish I could snap my fingers and feel what I need to feel to be with you. But I've never been good at telling myself what to feel."

"So, this means..." He jutted out his chin, holding back tears.

I closed my eyes and said, "It's a whole lot of words to say I can't marry you."

He took a deep, frustrated breath. "How can you say you love me and then reject me in the same breath? It makes absolutely no sense to me."

"I do love you. I do. Just not in the way we need to make a marriage."

"So what? Just *all of a sudden* it doesn't feel right when it's been right this whole time? You don't want what I want now? I'm just lost, Emma."

"It's not that sudden. I've been in this weird place for a while now. I just hadn't let myself really think about it or question it... then lately..."

He shook his head. "It feels sudden to me."

"I'm sorry for that," I said. "I really am. I'm sorry for how I acted today. I'm sorry that I hurt you." My chin trembled. "I'm just sorry for all of it, Jordan. I wish I'd figured this all out before you got down on one knee and put yourself out there for me." Tears streamed down my face, but I was already wet from the icy rain coming down on us.

He buried his face in his hands. "I can't wrap my head around this. I seriously thought we were about to start planning our wedding. I've been looking at damn houses for us to buy."

All tears and sniffles I said, "Jordan, I honestly didn't see this proposal coming. I didn't know."

"Well, I guess we didn't really know each other as well as we thought we did," he drew a deep breath. "I thought we were in love, Emma."

"We did love each other, Jordan. We did." I said, my voice small.

"Then can't we get back to that?"

My chest squeezed at his words. "We loved each other, Jordan, but even then, it wasn't right. I can't give you what you want."

"I just wish you would take some time. Maybe you'll feel differently in a few days," he said, wiping his tears. "Maybe we can just press pause for a while?"

I shook my head, tears dripping down my chin.

"What do you even want, then?" he demanded. "If you don't want *this*?" He gestured between the two of us.

I collapsed into a sob. "I'm sorry. I don't know. I just don't know."

And it was quiet between us, minutes passing, maybe more.

"What now? Do I just go upstairs to my apartment? How do I walk away? What about our Christmas plans? What about New Year's? What do I tell my family? What now?"

"I guess we figure it out as we go." I sniffled. I wiped my eyes as he searched my face for answers.

This little life we had built together came tumbling down all around us—along with all the doubts I had stored deep inside, Jordan's hopes and plans, and the cold, wet rain I'd thought would be snow.

Seven

I drove through the gray storm back to my own apartment.

My mom called me and offered for me to come stay the night at my parents. She was worried I would be too sad all alone, worried I might cry myself to sleep. And as valid and probable as her fears were, I just wanted my own bed. My own stuff.

My hands were icy and shaky as I unlocked the door, my face wet with rain and tears. My little home looked so simple and normal after such a strange, eventful past twenty-four hours. I dropped my purse on the floor. I immediately shed my borrowed sweatshirt and shimmied out of the scratchy red dress. I numbly poured myself a glass of water and crawled into my bed.

As I burrowed under the fluffy white duvet, I let my shoulders relax and started to sob.

My phone started ringing, "You've Got a Friend In Me," from my nightstand, where I had dropped it beside my glass of water. I crawled across my bed and hit ignore, but it started singing again. I smiled in spite of myself at my friend's persistence.

"Hi, Katie. I'm in my bed," I answered, sniffling quietly.

"Are you crying, babe?"

"Yes," I whispered, but she heard me.

"Oh, Em."

"I think I'd rather not be on the phone right now," I admitted. "Sorry."

"How about you come over?" she asked.

"I think I want to be alone."

"No, no, you shouldn't be alone. Come over, and we can watch sad movies or funny movies. And drink wine. We can talk it all out. This is the whole best friend gig."

I laughed a little, considering it. But then I could hear Gabriel laugh in the background of the call. I couldn't handle letting any other kind of feeling in my chest right now. No thoughts beyond the ones already in my head.

"How about we revisit that idea in a couple days? It's been a long twenty-four hours, and I need a little time to myself."

"Understood."

"Thank you for the offer, though."

"Anytime, Em," she said kindly.

I hung up my phone and burrowed deep under my blankets. I cried really hard until suddenly I wasn't crying anymore, and I was finally asleep.

A couple of days later, I drove home with my parents from my family's big Christmas Eve dinner. They were crooning along with old Christmas songs and gossiping about family members, and I watched Christmas lights twinkle outside the window.

My mind kept thinking, *what would I be doing right now if I hadn't left him?* I would've been showing off a beautiful ring, dreaming up wedding plans. I would've been nervously, happily planning to see my almost-in-laws for Christmas…like a real-life adult. He would've come along to my Grandma and Grandpa's. My Grandpa would've quizzed him on all his silly favorite conspiracy theories. Jordan probably would've challenged a couple of my cousins to play a game outside. I would've whispered about him and his proposal to those who stayed inside with me.

Instead, I sleepily spent the night at my parents after we got back to town. We drank spiked hot chocolate around their big brick fireplace in the center of our living room and watched *It's a Wonderful Life* on their sunken-in blue couch.

After my parents turned in, I slipped into my little twin-sized bed in my old bedroom. My mom had a little Christmas tree covered in twinkle lights set up in the corner of the room with all my "Baby's First Christmas" and homemade ornaments I'd made as a little girl. I tossed and turned, my mind still spiraling.

Back in my apartment, in my bedroom closet, I had hidden Jordan's Christmas gift. *Do I mail it to him? Do I keep it?* I curled up in shame, knowing he probably had a gift for me hiding in his closet, too. Unless he'd tossed it, burned it. Was he at home thinking about me? Was Christmas a nice distraction? Did his family hate me now?

I wished I could tell my mind to turn off for the night. It was late, and I needed rest. I wiped my eyes and wished the same for my tear ducts. I wasn't grappling with regrets or even doubts, but I was carrying around so much loss, so much shame, so much grief. But no one really knew what to say to me since I was the one who ended it. His name wasn't mentioned at my family's, as if they had all decided beforehand to act like Jordan had never existed.

I had rehearsed what I would say when people patted my shoulder and sympathetically asked me, "How are you doing, Emma?" But no one did because it was hard to feel bad for someone who climbed out a window and refused an engagement to such a sweet guy.

"I wonder why? Why wouldn't she say yes? Such a shame." I could imagine them whispering, wondering what was wrong with me. Wondering what I was holding out for. Jordan's family was probably cursing my name this Christmas, telling him, "You'll find someone so much better than her." I sickly wondered if his mom was saying, "We never really liked her much anyway." Or maybe they were all politely erasing me from his history, too. Like I never existed.

Emma, who?

What would I be doing right now if I hadn't left him? I knew I would still be awake on Christmas Eve, plagued with doubts and worries. Just twisting a silver ring around my finger instead of the empty space there.

I finally crawled out of bed, wrapped up in an old family quilt, and fell asleep on the couch watching *The Holiday*.

That Christmas morning, I woke up early like I used to when I was a little girl and crawled back into my bed. I watched the sunrise outside the window, all purple, pink, and white, like advent wax melting across the sky. I had originally planned to get all dressed up this morning and bring my parents over to Jordan's. I had felt a little sad to let my usual slow, pajama-clad Christmas morning go.

Every year since I could remember, my dad would always go out and pick us up coffee from our favorite coffee shop, leaving them an extra big tip. When he got home, we'd sip our coffee still in our PJs, exchange our presents, and then we made giant cinnamon rolls. We'd always have a heated debate over which Christmas movies to watch and in what order. *Why, when my dad always fell asleep, did he have such strong opinions? Who knows.*

Later in the afternoon, Mom and I would get into the kitchen and make the three of us a giant feast. Sometimes random family members would join us for dinner, but it was always the two of us in that kitchen. Mom and me making an absolutely delicious meal.

Such a delicious meal that one year, when Katie had been completely heartbroken, Mom and I made our traditional Christmas meal to cheer her up. I think our homemade garlic mashed potatoes had been a large part of her healing process, truly. Christmas wasn't hustle and bustle to me. It was the best rest of the year.

While I lay in bed this particularly heart-sore Christmas morning, I heard our front door close and lock. Then my dad's truck started outside my window. I could already taste the gingerbread latte.

The grief over losing what Jordan and I had was real. The *what if* anxiously was reeling in my mind. The sadness over what I'd broken was there in my chest. The shame over how I'd handled something precious to me had my stomach in knots for days and would for weeks to come. But I was still relieved that I didn't have to get dressed up that Christmas morning, that I didn't have to sacrifice being side-by-side in the kitchen with my mom, and that I still got to debate Christmas movie choices with my dad.

I let myself relish my gingerbread latte, letting any spiraling thought melt in the nutty steam.

Eight

I had a meeting on New Year's Eve with my editor to go over my story assignment, which was going to be a New Year's Day publication on our local New Year's Eve fireworks show. The assignment was to go to the firework show, take notes, then rush home and write it up so it would go up the next day.

I had pitched this assignment, happy to work on the holiday because Sweet River's firework show was one of my favorite traditions. Plus, originally, I got the idea to pitch it because I had plans to go with Jordan's family. His mom was a volunteer helping set up, so I could go early and interview all the different committees and volunteers who made the show possible.

That morning I got dressed, had a little bit of leftover cinnamon roll, and then rushed to my editor's office. It was an old building with dark wood furnishings and pharmacy lamps on every desk. My editor, Rich, with his salt and pepper hair and wiry glasses, had a tradition of greeting me with a dad joke. It was his thing.

But today, when I walked in, he just said, "Emma, hello. Please take a seat."

I should've realized then that he was firing me or kindly "letting me go." But I suppose I'm really bad at seeing things coming, be it proposals or firings. Rich felt guilty and sad, hence waiting until after Christmas. But the "higher-ups" had decided I needed to be fully let go by the end of the year...which was today. He'd waited until the very last minute.

"I wish things were different. I do," he said solemnly, avoiding eye contact.

I was in shock. I had been wondering if this job was right for me, but it never entered my mind that maybe the people who hired me were wondering if I was right for the job.

I heard Jordan, his voice raw the night we ended things, saying, "What now?" in my mind. "What now?" was becoming the title of this chapter of my life.

"We had to let a few people go; it's not just you. We're cutting our budget way down. Honestly, it's taking a lot of work to figure out how to keep our doors open," Rich said with a loaded sigh.

"I'm so sorry to hear that," I said.

I loved this newspaper. The Sweet River Gazette had printed so many of the highs and lows of my life growing up—big school wins, the aftermath of an awful summer tornado, or when the bank closed. My friend Lexi's dad had lost his job, and we all cried with her because she had to move. I could count on the stories happening around me being captured in black and white and laid out across our kitchen table every morning.

This job was my safety net when I came home from college. Wandering around our town, taking notes and finding my dad reading my stories at the kitchen table on a Saturday morning. Tears started to prickle behind my eyes, and I had to bite my inner lip to hold back the tears. I saw his face fall when he must have recognized what was happening.

"Emma," he said. "I really am sorry."

"No, no, no." I shook my head as tears dropped down my chin. "I understand the budget cuts. I know how hard things are right now for the paper. I'll miss my job, but also," my chin trembled. "it's just been a weird holiday season. My boyfriend actually proposed to me last week, and I broke up with him. It really sucked. I, like, climbed out his window, and am so embarrassed I did that. And my best friend's brother is back in town, and so I'm kind of avoiding her right now because I'm avoiding him because we have a really complicated relationship that I've made more complicated over the years." I couldn't catch my breath now, speaking through snotty sobs. "And...now, I'm just... I don't know what to do with my whole life. Like, everything is going to be different. Jordan and this job were my whole life."

He blinked at me.

"I dumped one half of my life, and the other half has dumped me," I laughed grimly. Or, pathetically, if we're being completely honest.

"I had no idea. I'm here if you need to talk." But he didn't sound like he wanted to talk. And neither did I.

"I apologize for this unprofessional display of emotion. I'm just going to go." I stood up, wiping my face with my palms as I walked toward the door.

"Emma." He held up his hand, stopping me before walking out the doorway. "You're a fantastic writer, and I always thought we wouldn't be able to keep you here very long, anyway. You're going to look back at this time in your life, years from now, and be happy everything changed. Sometimes, the best things happen when everything is different."

"Thank you," I said, quite professionally—if you ignored the running mascara.

I didn't go home. I went to Commas & Coffee, our little coffee shop and bookstore hybrid downtown. Katie had been a book-seller and barista there since we graduated from college.

It was a frigid morning with opaque skies overhead, so I held my scarf close as I hurried down the street. Inside the shop, it was warm with a soft glow from the hanging Christmas lights overhead. As I closed the door behind me, I took in the familiar scent of coffee beans, old books, and freshly baked sugar cookies. I felt my shoulders immediately relax.

The walls were lined with bookshelves, and there was a cozy brown sofa across from a big picture window that looked out into the downtown streets. And tucked away in the corner was a bar that served baked goods and coffee in case you got hungry whilst caught up in a good book. It was Katie if you could walk around her heart; welcoming, warm, literary, and sweet.

I walked across the wooden floors to Katie's corner. She was sitting behind the desk with a thick book open on the table in front of her, studying the pages with a furrowed brow. Her dark hair was falling out of the messy knot at the base of her neck.

"Hey, you," I said.

"Hi," she said, a sound of surprise in her tone. "You're running late for your meeting, huh?"

"No, I've already been." The shop was empty at the moment, aside from a couple of readers with their noses buried in books, so I felt safe propping my elbows on her bar. "Let me tell you about my morning."

"Wow, Em," Katie said after I told her everything. "What an ominous start to the year."

I started laughing. "Ominous is a good word for it."

"You know what they say, right? How you spend New Year's Eve sets the tone for the *entire* year."

"So, what does that mean for me?"

Katie gave me an apologetic shrug. "There's still hope. It's not midnight yet."

"Katie, I am starting the year as the woman who dumped the greatest guy in town and am now unemployed. Where is the hope?"

"I can help you job hunt after we get back from Ruidoso."

"Do you know anywhere looking for a reporter in this town?"

"Does it have to be reporting?"

"Well...I would at least like it to be writing. I might have to look outside of Sweet River."

Katie's eyes went wide with sadness.

"Or maybe something remote," I added gently.

"Emma! Happy New Year!" Katie's boss, Rose, said as she walked behind the bar.

"Happy New Year to you, too, Rose. Your hair looks beautiful," I said, admiring her afro. Rose was in her late fifties, but she had an energy that always made me forget she wasn't in her twenties like Katie and me.

"Well, thank you. I was wanting to let the curls be natural for the new year." She busied herself with the pastry display. "What are you two girls chatting about right now? It was sounding pretty intense when I walked up. "

"Oh, Rose, let me tell you this girl's story." Katie took in a deep breath. "Jordan proposed to her, with my blessing, I might add. She told him to hold on...and then *snuck out his window* while he was waiting around with the ring. A couple of hours later, she shows up at his apartment and dumps him. She's been crushed all Christmas. Then she goes into work this morning, and Rich *fires* her."

"Karma?" Rose whispers under her breath. Then she winks at me and says, "I kid, I kid."

"She is the dumper and the dumpee. Life is all about balance," Katie said.

"Okay, no one is trying to spare my feelings at all, I see," I said wryly.

"We could always bring you in for some part-time work. I'm looking to train Katie for some more managerial work anyway, so we'll need some upfront help," Rose said.

"That'd actually be amazing while I job hunt," I said, happy to grasp onto some hope.

"Let's figure it out the next couple days, then." Rose patted the table as if adjourning our brief meeting and then walked off.

"Are you getting a promotion?" I whispered excitedly to Katie.

"Sort of? Rose just really needs some help with some of the

money, buying, and management—behind-the-scenes stuff. She asked if I could 'be her' for some of the stuff," she leaned across the desk as she lowered her voice.

"That's great, Katie. If anyone could take over some of the stuff for Rose, it'd be you."

"Well, we shall see how it all goes," Katie said humbly.

"We'll also see how being coworkers goes. Since I'll soon be doling out coffee and books here."

"You are going to need so much training. You make the worst cups of coffee," Katie said seriously.

I was back at my apartment that evening, making myself some New Year's Eve dinner, when my mom called.

"Hey, mama," I greeted her.

"Honey, I just saw your message about everything that happened today. How are you doing?" I could hear water splashing in the background, I was on speakerphone. I could imagine her with her phone on the windowsill over the sink while washing dishes.

"I'm okay. I'm just trying to figure everything out."

"Oh, sweetie. You will figure it out. I know it. I think God is just nudging you in some new directions."

"You think so? What do you mean?" I walked from the kitchen counter to my four-person round glass-top kitchen table. I sat down, pulling my feet up onto the edge of my seat.

"Well, with your job–maybe it's time you step out and try something new. Something a little different. Something more like what you talked about doing in college."

"Where? There's literally only one writing job in Sweet River, and I had it. Rich has the other."

"I don't mean in Sweet River," she said this slowly, carefully.

"I was thinking about that today, too. Katie wasn't too fond of the idea."

"Well, Katie would be okay. I know we'd have you back home

all the time. And wasn't that what you said when you broke up with Jordan? That you didn't want what he wanted, and he wanted to stay here."

I was quiet. All thoughts led back to the breakup.

"How about you come home, hon? It's New Year's Eve. You skipped out on your beloved firework show. You're there all alone in your apartment. I think you should come home. We can watch a movie, or we could zip downtown and watch the fireworks, just us three. I don't think you should be alone."

"I kind of want to be alone, though," I said. "I was supposed to go to the firework show with Jordan, you know. He'll probably be there with his whole motley crew."

"Well, why don't you go with *your* whole motley crew? Isn't Katie going? She can make sure you don't rub shoulders with Jordan. Plus, I saw that Gabe is home. He'd probably tag along, too."

"I just..." I suddenly felt myself wishing I had a rewind button and I could push it back far enough before I broke up with Jordan.

My whole life felt too complicated now. I just wanted to have my old simple plans back. My old simple life when I spent New Year's Eve with my boyfriend.

"Things just feel kind of hard. I don't know what to do." I rubbed my forehead.

"Oh, Em," my mom said. "Should I come over?" But if I saw my mom with her mom hugs and her mom voice, I knew I would cry even more.

I needed to give my eyes, and my heart, a rest from crying.

"No, I need to go, Mom," I cried.

"Emma, I don't know. Maybe we should keep talking? I can't hang up with you in tears."

"If I keep talking, I won't be able to stop crying," I said through jagged breaths. I looked over at my bowl of pasta. "I need to eat dinner, too."

She was quiet, thoughtful for a moment. "Well, okay. Eat

some dinner. But come over if you need me. You could sleep over here, you know."

"Thanks, Mom," I sniffled. My mom was always offering for me to stay over lately like I was a wounded puppy who needed around-the-clock care.

We hung up, but I didn't eat my pasta. I curled up on my pale pink couch and sobbed into my throw pillows. Talking to my concerned mom just made me feel worse. So much for taking a break from crying.

Two halves of my world gone, I thought to myself.

Karma, I also thought.

I dump something good and then lose something good. I said I needed to let Jordan go because I didn't want to be tied here and lose one of the strings keeping me here. All of these changes were what I was wanting, right? But, as much as I had realized I wanted different things for myself, having these vital, consistent parts of my life ripped away in one big tear was brutal.

I lay there and thought, *Should I have broken up with Jordan?* No, I didn't want to marry him, but I did miss him. Why was it marriage or breakup?

I thought about all the time I spent shopping for his Christmas gift just weeks ago. How I almost gave it to him early because I was so excited to see his face when he opened it. I remembered planning out our New Year's Eve day with his mom. How easy it felt. How pleased she was to be included in my work. How Jordan was grinning at us while we talked it all out at their dinner table.

"My girls," he had said. I had given him a sideways grin.

How had things changed so quickly? Time felt like a sharp knife, slicing my life apart effortlessly, painfully.

Slice, one day, and he's gone. *Slice,* one meeting and so is my job. Shouldn't important losses like this happen gradually, over time? With warnings, preparation, and time to think. But then, time was sharp, clever. It knew with too much time, I would've clung tighter. I would've fought and made it messy when precision and clean breaks were the beauty of time's quick slice.

My phone buzzed. I looked down to see Jordan's name on the caller ID, along with the heart emoji I had yet to delete.

"Hi," I answered.

"Hi," he said hesitantly. "I wasn't sure if you were going to answer."

"I wasn't either," I pulled a velvety throw pillow close to my chest.

"Man, it sure is nice to hear your voice."

"It's nice to hear yours, too," I said. *Come over*, I almost added. *Let's just pretend none of it happened—for a little bit.*

"How've you been?" he asked.

I paused for a beat. "Not great. Honestly."

"Really?" His voice was a familiar, caring tone that felt like a hug over the phone.

"Yeah, there's a lot going on right now." A sob stuck in my throat.

"What's going on, Emmy?"

"Us. For starters. That was pretty brutal. Then today I was fired." *And I really wish you were here right now.*

"Oh man, Emmy."

"How've you been?"

"I've just been missing you." He cleared his throat. "Have you missed me at all?"

"Of course, I have..." I was on the edge of asking him if he wanted to come over and talk things out again.

"Are you alone?" he asked, hopeful.

"Yeah," I admitted.

"I still need a date to the firework show." If I were Jordan's friend, I'd tell him he was playing with fire.

I laughed a little. But then, I got choked up.

I sniffled. "I don't know, Jordan."

"I hear you sniffling over there. Are you okay?"

"Yeah." *Can you come over and talk?*

"I can listen to some of those thoughts rolling around in your head. I know you always have a lot of those."

"I honestly want a break from my thoughts." My heart ached at his kindness, at how I was letting it go, no longer in the safety net of being one of his girls.

"Do you want me to come over?" he asked.

My heartbeat thudded through my fingertips as it gripped the phone. *Yes.* I wanted my dear friend back for a little while. I could imagine the heat of his arms, his confident planning for how I'd rebound from this job change, how he'd bring over my favorite kind of coffee like he always did when I was sad, the sweet kind I didn't always order myself.

But it would be yet another selfish, immature decision. It'd be unfair to him. To me, too.

"I think I'm okay. I'll probably go straight to sleep after we hang up, actually."

There was a quiet disappointment on both ends of the phone call.

"I guess it's just nice to know you miss me, too," he said quietly.

"It's nice to know you're still my friend."

"Always." His voice broke, and so did my heart.

We were both just two heartbroken people, used to running to each other on our bad days, used to relying on one another's arms and ears for comfort. Now we were just awkward silence and aching hearts, tip-toeing around bad decisions. So, we hung up.

My stomach was grumbling. My mind was exhausted. I dropped my phone to the ground. Maybe I'd just fall asleep and wake up in the new year as a new me, I supposed. I closed my eyes but then heard a loud knocking at the door.

Mom? I wondered. Then, my heart started to anxiously hammer away. *Jordan?*

I rushed to the door, all puffy-eyes and messy hair, to find Katie and Gabriel with Santa hats on and a box of pizza under Gabe's arms.

Nine

"Hi," I said, teeming with gratitude.

"I told Gabe about your bad day," Katie said. "We both agreed you needed pizza and fireworks. Maybe some wine."

"Or hot chocolate," Gabe added.

"Come on in." I opened the door wider, and the two trailed inside.

"I see a bowl of plain noodles," Katie called out from the kitchen.

"I hadn't gotten around to making the pesto yet. I had a couple of phone calls." I turned to Gabe, who still had the pizza box in his hands. "But this pizza smells so much better than anything I was going to make."

"Let's dig in." Gabe dropped it on the blonde wood kitchen bar.

Katie pulled a few plates down from my cabinet, all of them

mix and match floral patterns I'd found over the years, much like the floral throw pillows on my couch. Pinks and greens sprinkled throughout my house.

"So, you told Gabe I was fired, I take it," I said, an awkward attempt at addressing my situation. We all gathered around my kitchen table.

"It did come up." Katie grimaced.

"Well, yeah," I said through a mouthful of pizza. "It was a bit of a bummer."

"You know it was because they couldn't keep you on payroll, not a reflection of your work," Katie said, all sympathy and comfort.

I nodded. "I know, or, you know, I hope that's true. It hurts the ego to be fired, but it also hurts the bank account. I'm bringing in the new year with no money and no prospects." I laughed as I said it, but no one laughed with me.

"No prospects, my behind." Gabe rolled his eyes. "Breakup with your boyfriend, breakup with your job, and you have a world of prospects waiting."

"Oh yes, I forgot I haven't seen you since I was let go from the girlfriend position, as well." I looked anywhere but in his syrupy brown eyes.

"I heard climbing out a window was involved?" Gabriel asked curiously.

"You heard right." I nodded.

"In that sparkly dress you left in?" He lifted an eyebrow.

"Sparkly dress and all," I said.

"I liked that dress," he said. A smile tugged at the corners of his lips.

"You liked the sparkly dress, but Emma wasn't a fan of the sparkly ring," Katie cracked up at her own joke.

I winced but laughed in spite of myself.

"We're only hours away from a new year—a fresh start." Katie leaned from her chair towards mine to wrap her arms around me. "Are you going to the firework show in this outfit?"

I set my pizza down and hugged her back. "Can we just eat pizza and watch movies? I'd happily fall asleep through the whole midnight thing."

"Sure," Gabe said while Katie said, "No way."

"Why is the word 'no' coming out of your mouth after I say pizza and movies?" I demanded.

"If it was any old day of the week, I'd be like, sure—" Katie started.

"No, it's the day I was *fired from my job*—" I interrupted her.

"But!" Katie said loudly, cutting me off. "It's New Year's Eve. Your favorite holiday. If I may add, it is also a metaphorical day. A day that means a fresh start. With how this year is ending for you, how you start the next year is important."

"I think starting it with a belly full of pizza and sweatpants on...is just the right way to start the year, metaphorically speaking, of course," I countered.

"Wait, wait," Gabe said, wiping his mouth with a napkin. "I actually agree with Katie."

"Wow, for once," Katie gasped dramatically.

"I think you've had some nice moping after the breakup—" he continued.

"*Moping*? Who said I was moping?" I asked.

"There were murmurs of moping. But, with that, I think you might need something new, especially since this is your favorite holiday. I don't want you to have a memory of that depressing New Year's Eve you spent passed out on the couch after a bad breakup on the day you were fired. I think you should have a lifetime of fun New Year's Eve memories. Where you look back years from now and say, 'Oh wait, I forgot I was fired that day. All I remember is having fun with Gabe. And Katie.'"

I felt myself soften to the idea. "Okay, maybe."

"Maybe?" Gabe said. "*Maybe*?"

"Okay, fine. Let's do it."

"Yes, let's do it!" Gabriel clapped.

Katie was already setting our plates in the sink.

"Let me go change first," I said.

I grabbed Katie's hand, and we went into my bedroom. I went straight to my jeans drawer, but Katie was in my closet. She held out a long sleeve black cocktail dress.

It was satin and shimmery with a cowl neckline. I hadn't worn that dress since college on my twenty-first birthday.

"A dress?" I asked warily.

"You wear that dress," she said. "And I'll wear this one." She had dug out a hot pink dress I'd bought for a wedding a couple of years ago. "Let's do this thing the right way."

I didn't even put up a fight. She was ready to march out in that hot pink dress, and who was I to stop her?

We donned the shiny dresses. I pulled my messy tangle of blonde hair into a big bun on the top of my head while Katie shook out her waves. Katie fixed my eye makeup. I threw on some heels even though it was freezing outside. I spritzed on some perfume. We walked outside to find Gabriel looking out the window.

He turned to us—to me—and said, "Wow."

I wondered if he remembered the last time I had worn this dress as I felt his eyes falling over me.

"We decided to do it up." Katie spun in her dress. "To end the year right."

"Do I look like I've been moping all week now?" I struck a pose.

"Not anymore," Katie said, proud of herself.

Gabe swallowed. "You look like you could get stuck in someone's mind all year in that dress."

"Dang, Gabe." Katie's eyes widened at the comment.

"Yeah, dang, Gabe," I said, trying to sound casual but I couldn't stop grinning the entire walk to the parking lot.

. . .

Downtown was bustling with people, cars, and music. A local band was playing for the event. Right away, we found a vendor handing out hot chocolate and grabbed a few cups. We weaved through the crowds donning festive hats and eyewear until we had a good view of the band.

They were playing covers by request. Katie and I started singing along, serenading one another like we did when we were teenagers at a concert when they started playing "Firework" by Katy Perry—because, of course, they were. Katie and I were giggling even though the music was so loud you couldn't hear us. We lifted our cups of cocoa in the air like lighters, everyone around us singing along.

Our downtown was all lit up. Shops were open late for the occasion. Some people were singing with us. Others were eating wintry treats on the sidewalk or walking around the shop corners, watching the performance artists and stopping by the vendors lining the streets.

The singer started crooning, "We Found Love," as we all cheered in approval of the choice. Katie grabbed my hand and gave it a squeeze; I squeezed back.

My eye caught with an old friend of mine, and I nudged Katie, who knew them, too. We both waved at them and then walked over, stepping away from the center of the music.

We chatted for a bit as I finished my drink. A few more people came over. They asked me where Jordan was tonight. This question felt like bumping against a bruise I forgot I had.

A reminder that I was usually part of a pair. I was supposed to be here with him right now. His ticket matched mine. I glanced around, wondering if he was dancing along with the crowd right now. If he had a front row for the show. Had he decided not to come? Would his sisters spot me and think, *The audacity of Emma. To dump Jordan and then go dance around at the party she was supposed to come to with him.*

I slipped back over to the concert area to avoid more small

talk. I took in a deep breath of frigid air to clear my mind. I found Gabe as the musician started playing "What Are You Doing New Year's Eve?" He spotted me and offered me his hand with a twinkle in his eye.

I grabbed hold without letting myself think much about it, and he twirled me around, my dress fluttering around me. He pulled me in, close, chest to chest. The whole world felt black and white around me as we swayed to the music. People were slow dancing all around us. The downtown lights were shimmering. Gabe's hand rested against my lower back as he held my waist against his. His warm breath against my forehead, humming along to the song.

"Maybe I'm crazy to suppose I'd ever be the one you chose?" the singer crooned.

I glanced up at him, and he smiled down at me. One of those rare moments where it was just us two. I rested my head against his chest as he tightened around me. *Ah, but in case I stand one little chance.* It was almost midnight, and I was dancing under the moon with Gabriel Hernandez.

As the song came to an end, we just kept dancing. *He doesn't want to stop either*, I thought to myself like I'd stumbled upon gold.

There was a drunken group behind us shouting for her to sing, "Don't Stop Believin'," but we just kept slow dancing, no matter the song, no matter what anyone else around us was doing.

Until Katie was suddenly standing with us. She yanked me out of Gabe's arms, saying we needed to find a better spot to see the firework show. That it was starting any minute now.

I felt dazed and dreamy from being buried in Gabriel's warmth, but I followed her. Gabe grabbed onto my other hand as we weaved through the people until we found a bench with a clear view. We all released hands as Katie started excitedly clapping and looking up at the sky. She was ready for the show. An announcer boomed from the speakers that we were thirty seconds away from midnight.

I looked ahead, and in the distance, I saw a group huddling close, laughing, and tapping cups together that looked so much like Jordan's family. *Was that guy Jordan?*

Then we all started counting along until it was "Three, two, one, midnight."

It was new day, a new year, for all of us.

There was screaming and clapping. Katie grabbed me and gave me a kiss on the cheek, and I kissed her cheek, too. On instinct, I turned to Gabriel, and he slipped his arm around my waist and drew my face to his like we might just start slow dancing again, and kissed me lightly on the cheek.

He stayed there for a moment as my breath caught in my throat, and he whispered against my jawline, "Happy new year, Em."

I forgot words, my voice catching in my throat. "Th-thank you," I finally stammered.

We stayed close for a moment longer.

"Happy New Year," I whispered, a few more words coming back to me. He smiled at me so warmly my whole body could've melted.

Katie bumped into me, saying, "Look up," and I broke away from Gabe, raising my eyes to the sky. Colors crashed and sparkled over us, booming and loud. Katie grabbed my hand and then leaned her shoulders against mine. How'd I get so lucky that no matter the change in my life, I still had her? The sparkly reds and greens lit up the sky, and I settled into the promise of starting over.

Another me, who made other choices, would be bundled up in the arms of my new fiancé and his family, thinking being fired gave her more time to plan her wedding and move into that house Jordan had his eye on. Maybe her soon-to-be-father-in-law could get her a job at his company. I'd have a different kind of fresh start waiting for me in the new year. I couldn't help this line of thinking. This painful game of comparison came from hitting the backspace button. The emptiness was now a question of what might have come next.

That me would be staring up at the sky, a ring on her finger, but the doubts would weigh her down. She'd be tired from trying so hard to make something feel right. And there's no way she would've gotten to dance with Gabriel.

I glanced over at Gabriel. He was gazing up at the sky, but then he looked right back at me with that same smile from moments before. And I felt the opposite of weighed down, the opposite of tired, not a doubt in my mind. I smiled back at him. Then we both kept looking up at the sky.

After the fireworks ended, the crowds began to disperse. People were either heading home or to after parties to continue celebrating. We made our way down the street and came upon the band again to find they were still playing.

The singer was softly singing "New Year's Day" by Taylor Swift.

"Oh, I love this one," Katie said.

A cute guy who had been walking beside us overheard her and boldly asked, "Would you like to dance?"

Katie grinned. "Why not?" She swayed with him.

Gabriel cleared his throat, so I looked over to him to see he was holding out his hand. Everyone else was leaving, but we started dancing.

One year came to end, along with my relationship, my job— the way I lived my life for years. Undeniably, things were ending, but, as Gabriel dipped me, I couldn't help but think they were also undeniably just beginning.

Gabriel spun me in, placed his hand against my chin, and lifted my head gently so we were looking into each other's eyes.

"It's going to be a good year, Emma," he said it like a promise.

The fireworks were over, but I was still all lit up inside.

Ten

The aftermath of Gabriel always felt a bit like a hangover. I felt a little dazed, a little confused. I had to reorient my feelings and my choices the way people usually took aspirin and tried to hydrate.

January 1, I woke up around 10 a.m. and lay in bed dreaming off and on about Gabriel pulling me in while we danced, about his eyes on me as I walked into the room in my little black dress, about the earnestness in his voice as the scent of fireworks filled the crisp night air. I was in and out of sleep until my dreams filled with memories of Gabriel's lips against mine, of his hand on the small of my back, of my hand in his hair. My memories from last night, giving way to a memory I'd locked up tight in the back of my mind.

My twenty-first birthday fell on a Friday night. It was a cold October. Gold and red leaves were scattered across the streets, and the sun was setting earlier each night. I was fresh into my senior year of college with a heavy workload for my last fall semester. I was thirsty for a break.

All day long Katie had been telling me she had a birthday surprise for me—along with the birthday plans we'd already made together, which was basically just to go with our friends to a bar in Fort Worth on Sundance Square.

Our friend Marjorie had a big three-row SUV, so she offered to drive all of us girls. We stopped for burgers and fries once we got to the square, all hyper and loud. Then we made our way down for cheesecake, where waiters sang happy birthday to our giggly crew, before finally heading for drinks at the assigned spot.

We were already a little drunk on running around the square underneath the city lights and spotting cute guys—or really just any guys—along the way. So, we made a bit of a silly scene as we settled into a booth at the bar, but we made a scene everywhere we went that night.

I was sitting on the outside edge of the booth and proudly showing my ID to the server while ordering a spicy margarita when someone tall, dark, and mischievously handsome bent down beside me and said, "Hey, birthday girl."

My heart burned like a birthday candle at that voice. And my stomach dropped in that specific Gabriel way it always does.

"Surprise!" Katie cheered. "I got your favorite person to fly down to celebrate you!"

"I didn't need much convincing," Gabe said, scooting in beside me—to my delight. "I couldn't miss your twenty-first birthday."

"I can't believe you made it out. I know you've been busy, just moving to California and all," I said, still stunned.

"Who's this?" one of our girlfriends asked, interrupting us. She batted her eyes over at my personal birthday surprise.

"My brother, Gabriel," Katie said, a little proudly, the way she always was with her siblings.

"You live in California?" another girl asked, all curious and coy.

Suddenly my birthday surprise, my favorite guy in the world, was the main attention of a table full of tipsy college girls. I had to sit there and sip my spicy margarita as they asked him questions and flirted. Finally, I sipped the last dregs of my drink and marched over to the bar to order another.

"Another spicy margarita?" I asked the bartender. I could tell he was mildly judging my order. I turned around to find Gabriel standing behind me.

"Another spicy margarita?" He was judging my order too.

"Well, honestly, I don't know what else to order. And they taste really good. And it's my birthday, dang it! I should be able to order what I want without judgment."

"I wasn't judging." He put up his hands in surrender. "I thought it was cute. Only you could make ordering drinks cute."

I blushed. We didn't usually call each other things like cute. Though I'd always hoped he found me as cute as I found him.

"Are you ordering too?" I asked, gesturing to the bar.

"Nah, I just wanted to check on you. You seemed a little upset."

"What do you mean?"

"Back at the booth, you were really quiet. You seemed a little distant. I was wanting to make sure you weren't upset I came and crashed girls' night. I just wanted to see you, and Katie thought—"

"No, no," I brushed off his worries. "I'm really happy you're here. I'm touched, really, I know you're getting things set up in California. I, honestly..." It must've been the tequila lowering my defenses. "I just got a little jealous of all the girls taking up your attention. I'm so excited to see you and then... Am I gonna even get to see you? You're kinda busy flirting it up."

"You think I'm flirting it up?" He laughed, noticing my lowered defenses.

"Yeah, a little bit. And it's my birthday. Shouldn't you be flirting with me?" I said before I could catch myself. "I mean, if you're flirting with anyone, it should be me." I was attempting to salvage my mistaken remark, though it didn't really fix anything.

He started laughing, moving in closer. "I should be flirting with you, huh?"

"No, no, you know what I mean!" The bartender placed my margarita down in front of me.

"Ahem. I do know what you mean, Em," he said, but he had a

pleased grin on his face as if he'd won one of our playful debates. As if I'd told him he was right about something he'd known all along.

I grabbed my drink and said with warm cheeks, "Let's just go back to the booth."

"Wait." He grabbed my free wrist, stopping me. "Why don't we just sit here at the bar for a while?"

"Oh." I liked his idea. "But what about my friends?"

"They'll be there all night. And I flew all this way to see you."

"Well, okay. Yeah." I sat my drink down and scooted in close to him at the bar. "This is cozy."

He laughed. "Now that I've got you alone, I can properly flirt with you and only you."

"Gabriel, good Lord, with the flirting comments." I took a big drink and then said, "Fine, flirt with me if you want to."

"Oh, trust me, I will." His eyes gleamed playfully. I felt it all the way to my toes.

We never went back to the booth. We sat in our own little corner of the bar and talked about his new apartment in California and the magazine where he worked and how I would apply to work there too.

We dreamed about living in the same town again, about our shared hopes and goals.

We talked about my classes, and songs that were stuck in our heads and movies we'd recently seen, my friends and his, our parents, and we laughed at the idea we were growing up.

We talked and talked and talked until the bar was closing up and my friends had come and kissed me on the cheek goodbye. Gabriel said he'd drive me home in the car he rented.

We talked until the bar locked its doors and began to sweep the floors around us.

We talked until Gabe sighed the deep sigh of someone resigning to do something they absolutely didn't want to do and broke the spell, saying, "I guess we should head out."

The air was crisp with the hint of winter to come as we walked down the street. What was once busy and crowded was now quiet and empty. It felt like the entire street was just ours as we walked to the car—like the whole night was just ours.

It felt easy and right when I slipped my hand in his, and he interlocked his fingers with mine. I looked up at him to see him smiling back at me. We walked hand in hand the entire time to his car, giddy like two little kids getting away with something. He walked me to the passenger side. I leaned against the door instead of opening it, fingers still intertwined, laughing for no reason. He grabbed my other hand.

And there we stood, holding hands, our eyes searching each others. All the feelings still unspoken but visible in these touches, in this heat. If feelings were palpable, they were on us like sweat, like breath. Then, he was leaning into me, our foreheads together, hands still holding.

"Emma," he said in a rough whisper. "Do you know what you do to me?"

Our eyelashes brushed when I blinked. "I think I have a pretty good idea," I said back.

"Do you?" he said, his voice low.

"Trust me, I do," I said, my breath heavy, my mind swimming.

And just like that, his lips were on mine. I can never remember who kissed who first. But there we were, two magnets, finally making contact. He slipped his hands around my waist, his hands on the small of my back, pulling me closer to him like he'd been waiting way too long to do this. My hands were in his hair.

Never had a kiss felt so completely natural, so completely right. So completely desperate. We kissed until we were out of breath, like we couldn't get enough—like we should've been doing this all along.

We looked at each other for a while afterward. Our bodies were still pressed together. We laughed a little. What now? Would we just go back to normal life? Was kissing now normal life?

"I'd been wanting to do that forever," Gabe breathed into my ear. Shivers ran everywhere.

"I guess we should go?" I asked, dizzy, drunk from more than the drinks.

He nodded, a little hesitant, like he had something else to say, but he didn't want it to end just yet. He opened my car door, and I slid inside. As we zoomed through downtown Fort Worth, we held hands again, and I fell asleep safely next to Gabriel. I didn't wake up until we were on campus, and I directed him to my dorms.

When we pulled up front, we sleepily said our goodbyes. He was flying back home the next day. Maybe we could get breakfast? I asked. Maybe he'd let me sleep, he said. It was such a nice time, and we would miss each other, we said. Then I looked at his lips, he looked at mine, but we didn't kiss.

I slipped out of the car and tiredly walked up to my dorm room. I waved goodbye one more time as he waited to leave until I was safely in my room.

I lay in bed all these years later, still with Gabriel on my mind—still with that kiss on my mind. But he was off to California last time, and he would be off to California again. And, as usual, I was tucked into a bed in Texas, states away.

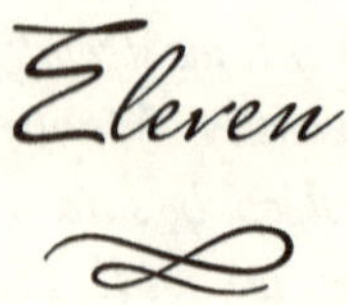

Eleven

KATIE

OK so send me all the updates while I'm away.

KATIE

I'm meaning work-wise.

KATIE

But of course personal too.

ME

I will send you all and any updates work and personal. Prepare to be inundated.

KATIE

Yay! You know how long this drive is. I need the entertainment.

ME

I actually do have an update. Jordan has been messaging me.

The Hernandezes were off on their annual ski trip. Well, all except Tanya, who was due to go into labor any day now. They would all caravan out to Ruidoso, New Mexico and play in the snow for a few days.

I had my first days on the job without Katie. The coffee shop felt different without Katie's warmth and energy. Her usual customers were asking when she'd return. I watched how even Rose felt her absence in her short trip away. I read the employee handbook she'd helped write.

My first days on the job, I could see that Katie didn't just work at Coffee & Commas, she was an axis on which it spun. It was funny how you could see someone do something for years, but it wasn't until you were in it with them, not just watching from afar anymore, that you really understood—like watching the sun through a window from an air-conditioned room then walking outside and truly feeling its impact on your skin. Sometimes, it took walking in it to get it.

There was someone else messaging me those first days on the job. But they had nothing to do with work and everything to do with complicated feelings I was attempting to navigate. I wasn't sure how to respond to Jordan. Was it rude not to reply, or was it unwise to reply?

The first message was a simple *Happy New Year* kind of message around midnight, so I didn't respond. Then the next day he sent:

> How are you feeling after last night?

This was when I wasn't sure how to reply. I screenshotted it and sent it to Katie, who didn't have a good signal in the mountains, so she didn't reply for a while.

In the meantime, Jordan sent over:

> For me, it felt really good to talk to you last night. I have to admit I've really been missing having you in my life.

I screenshotted that one, too, and sent it over to Katie. With no advice from Katie, I decided it was better to respond kindly but in a way that didn't open the door to further conversation. Later in the evening, after my shift, I sat in my car and typed up:

> I'm feeling a lot better. Thanks for being such a good friend to me last night. Have a good new year, Jordan.

Seconds later, he replied:

> I'm so glad you're feeling better. What's your plan for finding a new job? I have a few ideas. Want me to call?

I didn't want him to call, but also, a call from him felt very normal. It felt nearly routine like checking my phone before I went to sleep at night...or chewing my nails when I was anxious.

I wondered if communication here or there would be so bad. Also, knowing him, he had some grand get-a-job plan for me that was far better than anything I had planned, which was more of a plan to make a plan.

I told this to Katie when she finally got reception. She said there would never be "here or there" calls.

"Don't start something," she said bluntly. "Because I know you both, and this would start something. *He knows it*, even if you don't. He wants you guys to start something."

"But I can't just ignore his message. I don't want to reject him even more than I already have. I don't mind him messaging me, and I don't want him to thin—"

"Em." Her voice was loud in the phone. I could hear her family in the background noisily talking back and forth in their big, shared cabin. "You still really cared about and liked Jordan when you broke up—you didn't end things because *you didn't like him.* You ended things because you were thinking about the future. Now, every choice you make in regards to him needs to have that same kind of thinking. If you start chatting with him, how will that effect your future?"

I heard her and knew she was right. But I still responded to him because I knew I would run into him in this small town, and ignored messages would make the future awkward and cold. Plus, she was right. I still liked the guy, and I liked talking to him. And just like checking my phone at night or chewing on my nails, it might not be necessarily healthy, but it felt kind of good.

I told him I was still thinking through my future plans and I didn't think a call was a good idea right now, but thanks, and that I appreciated him. He told me to call anytime. Or message. The next day he sent me another message telling me he knew of some places hiring. The day after that, he sent me a message saying he was thinking of me and hoping my week was getting better. This was while I was at work.

I shoved my phone deep into my apron pocket and went back to practicing making lattes. I had told Jordan that I was thinking through my future, but really, I was just perfecting my latte skills.

"Looking good," Rose encouraged me.

On my break, I began typing up a message asking Jordan to send over his job leads, but then I deleted it. I told him I would let him know if I needed them and thanked him for thinking of me. Then I researched job openings in the area on my own because I needed to decide on my next steps. No more relying on Jordan to lay them out for me.

As I scrolled through the listings, I thought I could move into marketing, administration, or some other creative field since that's all I was finding. When I narrowed my search to neighboring newspapers—there were zero results. And even if they were...I wasn't sure I wanted to keep working as a reporter. I knew I could look outside Sweet River and the surrounding area.

But then, as my break was to coming to an end, I started

looking into freelance writing opportunities. I wasn't sure of the big steps in the future—the kind of stuff Gabe and I had talked about—or finding a position like Gabriel had in Los Angeles that had spun out into his career now.

But, for now, I could do something like this. It was small, but it was a step all on my own.

Twelve

"Gabriel was in a ski accident," Katie said, her voice raw with emotion on a middle-of-the-night call.

"Is he okay?" I gasped. It was late, and I was in bed. I threw off my blankets, standing up as if I was going to drive on over to Ruidoso myself.

"He's in the hospital. He's going to be okay, but he's really injured. *Really* injured." Her words were tumbling out, frantic. "He hit a rock while skiing. It was just a bad visibility day, and I knew they shouldn't have gone out there. When he hit the rock, he flew into the air and just crashed down really hard—he broke his femur."

"Oh, Katie," I said, breathless.

"It was terrifying. He had gotten far off from the group. When my brothers found him, they thought he might be okay. *He thought* he was going to be okay. But then, they said Gabe started screaming in agony when they tried to help him up. They had to airlift him out." Her voice sounded like she'd been talking back and forth with her family, with nurses, crying, and whispering for hours. Her voice was all raw, tired, and bruised.

Over the next few days, Gabriel stayed in the hospital.
"The doctors put metal screws in his leg to help hold him together," Katie said when I asked how they were helping him.

"Is that painful? How long is he going to be on the mend?" I had so many questions.

"The doctors said he'll be in recovery for the next twelve months, really. Twelve months before his leg is fully healed. But it will be in phases. The first few months in a cast. A slow gaining of mobility." Her voice faded.

I sat on my apartment balcony wrapped up in a quilt, watching downtown as the sun set overhead with my phone in my hand. An unsent text message to Gabriel sat open on my phone.

> I heard about the accident. How are you doing? I'm here if you need me.

I wasn't sure if I should send it. I didn't want to pile on or overwhelm. It wasn't like we were such close friends anymore. Then I thought of him in his Santa hat in my doorway only a week ago, and I hit send. Moments later, Gabriel replied.

> I feel like the pits. Ski accidents really hurt, in case you were curious. This will definitely go into my memoirs, you know. I just met with an orthopedic surgeon actually. He said I'll be beginning physical therapy when we get home. Thanks for reaching out, by the way.

When we get home, he said. *We.*
Did he mean his place in Los Angeles, or did that mean he was

going to be doing therapy here in Sweet River? I spent an embarrassing amount of time wording my next message to him.

> How are you going to make it back to Los Angeles from Ruidoso? Is someone going to fly with you?

> Not my place in LA, I meant my family's home. Sweet River. I'll be back for a while during recovery.

> My mom is ready to be my at-home nurse.

> Let me know if there's anything I can do

I sent that last message and agonizingly, full-heartedly meant it.

He asked if I could pick out some good books from Coffee & Commas for him to read while he was laid up.

So, of course, I started overthinking which books to bring over to Gabriel, whom I felt awful for, but also secretly, guiltily, felt elated he would be only miles from me for a little while. *Was it bad to see the silver lining?* I built a little book stack for him over the next few days.

And once Gabriel arrived safely at home, I left work with Gabe's get-well stack of books plus an assortment of cookies and cupcakes.

"You are a hero," he said as I set the box of sweets in his lap. "A true hero."

"Truly," Victor said, sneaking a cookie out of the box. Gabriel shoved him out of the way. Both of them in sweatpants and tee shirts laid-back on the couch.

"How are you doing?" I asked, sitting down beside Gabriel.

"I'm pretty medicated, so that helps with the pain some, which has been pretty bad," he said. "But I'm kind of in a state of shock. With the change of plans, change of *work* plans, being on crutches for a while, medical advice to not do things I do like travel, hike, climb, you know, things I often do for a living. I'm kind of reeling from all that."

"You should've seen how bad it was when we were out there, though," Victor said somberly. "The fact you're going to get better at all is pretty amazing."

"I know," Gabriel said, his voice smaller than I'd ever heard it before. "I know all that. I'm grateful."

"I'm sure you're grateful, Gabriel. Noticing the crappiness of the situation doesn't make you any less grateful." I said the last part tenderly.

Victor selected another cookie.

"Thanks, Em," Gabriel said sincerely, then to Victor, he said, "You know, she brought those for me."

"You can't eat all of these. There's like a dozen cookies," Victor said through a mouthful.

"But the medicine is helping with the pain?" I asked.

"Yeah, it is. I'm trying to not take anything too intense, though. My doctor worked it all out for me," he said. "But, man, it hurts. When it first happened, I think I was in shock at first, and it was when I was trying to shake it off and keep going that the pain just seared. It was the worst pain I've ever felt. I realized I couldn't shake it off. I couldn't even move. I can't imagine if I was out there alone."

"I'm glad you weren't out there alone. I know for your first book you were out there alone a lot." Since I got the call about his accident from Katie, I hadn't been able to stop thinking about how so often for writing he'd venture out alone.

His first book was literally about traveling alone, young and fresh out of college—part memoir, part handbook. It was completely different from what he'd been writing at work. It was meant to be an escape for him, but instead, it became a new career direction. After his book received some success, he wrote a lot of pieces for big magazines covering solo trips and adventures. Solo.

I knew Gabriel and how he was probably already itching to

get back out there. Now, whenever I knew he was on a solo trip, I'd be praying every other minute.

"I always knew this kind of thing was a risk. I'm just lucky I wasn't alone this time..." he trailed off. "I do think I still would've been found and helped if I was alone. Don't get all worried on me, Em."

"Mom and the girls have already been having all these long talks with him about his future trips." Victor rolled his eyes.

"Well, they're not wrong to worry." My throat was dry.

"Mom always worries," Victor said.

"What do you say to them?" I asked as a fellow worried woman.

"I told them that I'm not necessarily only writing about adventuring solo anymore. My latest project was about the wildfires. I did have to travel and go out there—but not solo. And it was a lot more research based." He sighed as he said, "I'm obviously putting any and all adventure on hold for a little while."

Victor wandered out of the room, leaving Gabriel and I alone on the couch.

"What does the next little while look like for you?" I asked.

He gestured to his bandaged-up leg laid out on the table in front of him.

"Seriously, Gabe." I urged him to continue beyond broad gestures.

"I'll be on the mend and laid up for a while. So, a couple of projects that did involve travel are on hold, one of which is being handed over to someone else. Two big projects, actually." He closed his eyes, shutting out reality for a second.

"You can write from the couch, you know."

"I write about things I see and do. All I'm seeing is my family. All I'm doing is..." He gestured to his sprawled-out leg again.

"You used to write about the thoughts in your head and your little musings before you wrote about all those wild things you see and do. Might I remind you of your angsty high school writing?" I said. "Or your angsty college writing, for that matter?"

He laughed. "I know, I know. Maybe I'll pitch some couch writing. I can't live off royalties forever."

"You could write a piece about the healing elixir in good soft baked cookies?" I offered, stealing one from the box.

He pulled the box of cookies close to his chest protectively. "Or how everyone steals from the sick."

"Poor injured, Gabe."

He cleared his throat. "Thanks for coming and seeing me. Katie's not even over here. I'm not just an add-on to a Katie visit. I have to say I feel honored."

"You dork." I gave him a little shove.

"You steal my cookies *and* hit me?"

Linda walked over to us in the living room with a cheesy grin. "I haven't seen you two like this in a couple of years. It's doing my heart good to hear your little chatter in here." Then, as awkwardly as only a mom can be, she added, "Gabe needs some cheering up, Emma, so come over more. I know you can work your Emma magic on him."

"I just have to break my femur to get Emma to come see me," Gabriel said, his mouth curving into a grin.

"A broken femur is the only thing that gets you to stay in the same town as me," I retorted.

Linda broke into a laugh at my last remark while she walked out of the room. Gabriel and I were both quiet for a minute, exchanging glances that I couldn't quite define.

"Well, I'm here for a few months at least. If I have another surgery, maybe even longer," he said. "So, am I gonna see you now that we're in the same town?"

"Sure," I said casually. "I just don't promise to always have cookies and books every time."

My heart raced in anticipation. Gabriel was staying put. He hadn't been in the same city as me for longer than a holiday since we were two awkward high schoolers.

Thirteen

A lot of my Coffee & Commas shifts began at 6 a.m. We had many early-rising customers, so we would get there and make sure we had warm coffee and fresh baked goods ready for them. This shop was my warm, glowing haven in the dark early mornings. Katie would be humming along to our ever-growing playlist as we ran the little shop.

Around late morning, things would begin to slow down, and I had time to mess around a little. I was stationed at the front desk, so sometimes I would pull out my laptop and fill out a few applications or browse job postings.

But during downtime, I often found myself writing pretend articles about places I'd been or takes on different things happening around the world as if I couldn't quite turn off the writer-on-assignment part of my mind. I'd even taken to crafting an outline for a book I'd been working on in the back of my mind for years. I had all this extra creative time, making my mind run wild with ideas.

"What'cha working on?" Katie asked, leaning on her elbows at the coffee bar where my laptop was open before me.

"I was taking a minute to put a few touches on a little piece I was writing," I said.

"A freelance piece?" she asked.

"No, just a silly piece I was writing for myself. Got to keep the juices flowing, you know."

"Why don't you reach out to some places for a little freelance work?"

"I don't have a lot of freelance experience," I said. "Since I graduated, I've only written for the Sweet River Gazette about things happening in Sweet River. I don't know if I even…"

I didn't even know what to say. I didn't really have an answer. I wanted to try freelance writing, but I also didn't want to. I wanted a new writing job, and also my heart beat frantically at the idea of any job that wasn't at my own local paper. Indecisive Emma strikes again.

"You're a writer, Em. What's the harm in trying? You don't have zero experience. Just put yourself out there and see what happens. You can't just hide out in our coffee shop for forever. Well, I guess you can, and I'd honestly kind of love it. But the most selfless side of me encourages you to just *try*."

I poured myself a coffee. My third cup of the day. Working here had done a number on my caffeine intake. "I guess I could try. It all feels daunting to try something so new. I feel like I should just go right back to what I had been doing, even though that isn't really an option."

Katie gave me a sympathetic nod.

"I'll ask Gabe for some advice. I know he knows how to pitch and how to connect with people. I won't be writing for the serious journals like he does, but maybe I can do some cute listicle or something."

"You *should* reach out to Gabe. But, speaking of Gabe, you two are such peas in a pod. He's all grumpy about his new writing prospects, too. Why is it so hard to get writers to write? You both want these perfect specific conditions and get so persnickety when you have to change things up a little."

"Says the woman who has never published her heart and soul for the world to read."

"Your heart and soul? You just said you might do a listicle."

I snickered into my coffee cup. "I'll stop being persnickety. I'll write—maybe even more than a listicle. I'll get Gabe writing, too."

"You better," she quipped. "Though, you'd write a fine listicle, Emma Brown."

We heard a bell ring as a bundled-up mom wheeled a stroller in, and our little break was over.

We were in the last days of a cold January. It was mid-afternoon, and my shift was nearing an end at the coffee shop. I had a question for Rose that I'd been meaning to ask her, but she hadn't been around the shop in a few days. I slipped off my apron and found Katie in the back going over some paperwork.

"Hey, Katie," I said. She glanced up at me. "When is Rose going to be in?"

She winced. "I'm not sure? I could call her for you."

"Does she have, like, an official schedule anymore?"

"She comes and goes as she pleases, really."

"She used to basically *live* here. Do you remember that?" I leaned against the desk.

"Yeah, the past several months, she's kind of checked out. I think that's why she trained me up a lot. She's had the shop for so long, I think she's gotten tired."

"You kind of run the shop now." I was only half-joking. "It's weird because you feel like my boss. *But you're Katie.*"

"I love running the shop."

"Well, you deserve a bigger paycheck with how much falls on your shoulders. I know Rose, and she would happily give you a raise."

"I got a little raise, actually. Rose has always given me a lot of responsibilities, but it's really been this past year that the load got so heavy. She upped my pay along with it. Rose noticed and took care of me," Katie said as she stacked a pile of papers.

"Do you know why she's offloaded so much to you? You said you think she's getting tired. Are you worried she'll close the shop?"

"Not really." She let her mind wander. "But if she did, I'd just buy the shop myself or something."

I sat down on the desk in front of her. "Do you want to own a place like this someday? You always talked about owning your own business when we were in school."

"I think I do. I love this place, and to be honest, there are a lot of things I wish I could change up around here. But Rose is a little checked out and just wants to maintain the status quo."

I hadn't known Katie was thinking like this about the shop, but maybe Katie hadn't known until recently, either. It felt as if our futures were starting to roll in like the tide. For so long, we could run out and get our toes wet and then skip up to the safety of the shore, but recently, the tide was rushing up to us, and the safe shore was getting smaller and smaller. Soon we would have to dive in, whether we were ready or not.

"Maybe you go start a business that's all your own? Or start working on it."

She sighed. "But I love this place. I love the customers. I love the location. I love the name. I love the history. I love our memories here. And I don't have the capital right now, anyway. I'd have to go have a meeting with the bank, and it'd be a whole thing. I'm happy here right now. Not ready to break up with Coffee & Commas just yet."

"You'll know when it's time to move on, or it'll be sprung on you at a Christmas party," I flippantly added.

"What were you wanting to ask Rose, anyway?" Katie asked, wrapping me up in a side hug.

"Oh." My mind was blank. "I don't even remember."

Katie batted her eyes. "Any excuse to see this face, huh?"

I gave her a hug goodbye and then made my way out of the shop. I took in the twinkling lights, the smell of coffee and old books while the sun was getting lower in the sky outside the windows.

Maybe I was a persnickety writer scared to write for new eyes, but there was also a safety to this in-between space, where the lights twinkled, and I only answered to my best friend. I felt like I could stay there a while, just chatting at the coffee bar. If it wasn't for that running wild mind of mine, itching to tell stories, opening up my Word Doc over and over.

It had been an unusually cold last week of January, and to our Texan surprise, we woke up to a blanket of snow on the ground. I looked out my window to see snow flurries still falling from the sky. It was a Friday morning, and I had the day off to run a bunch of errands. I went out in the snow a little hesitant and a little excited about being out in the weather.

I filled the back of my car up with groceries in the shivering cold then went to start my car so I could head home when my car wouldn't start. The key wouldn't even turn in the ignition, just a quiet hum when I tried to click it. I reached for my phone, opening Jordan's contact by pure habit. I stopped myself before pressing the "call" button.

Jordan was my usual "help" call when it came to my car. Fixing and rebuilding cars alongside his dad had been a hobby of his since middle school. His ability to fix my car troubles had been one of our early bonding experiences when we were first dating.

We had been dating for about six weeks when I blew a tire. I was speeding along a country road and spun out—luckily, I didn't hit anything—and my car came to a stop. But I was shaken. I scrambled for my phone and, with shaking hands, went to dial my parents, but they were off on a cruise. I scrolled through my contacts list, but then a message from Jordan came through.

I called him. He answered right away, then drove to my rescue. He held me close as I cried—and apologized for crying—and he replaced my tire for me.

"What's your favorite ice cream?" he had asked me as I climbed back into my car.

"Coffee with chocolate sprinkles and whip cream," I said.

"I'll follow you home in my car so we can drop off yours. Then let's go get you your coffee ice cream," he said, all soothing and strong.

"Why are you always so sweet?" I asked him as he kissed me on the forehead.

I used to tell people that I realized he was the perfect man when he fixed my car troubles and then bought me ice cream. *He knew how to meet all my needs,* I would joke. A couple of years later, I was alone, my hands icy, holding my phone, unsure who to call now that my old go-to was gone.

I pressed my dad's number, but no answer, to no surprise. He ran his own dentist office and was never near his phone. He probably was with a patient.

I called my mom, but no answer. I glanced at the clock. It was 11:39 a.m., and she was teaching an art class at the community center.

Katie was probably at work. Being coworkers now, I had

pretty much memorized her work schedule. Plus, Tanya finally had her baby a few days ago, and I knew Katie had been busy with the meal train and meeting her new nephew. Gabriel popped into my mind. But he had an injured leg. He was hobbling around on crutches.

I wondered if I should just go ahead and call up Jordan. Aren't we still friends? Didn't this fall into the friends helping each other out category? I called Katie on the off chance her work schedule had changed, and she wasn't with her new nephew.

"Hello," she said distractedly.

"My car won't start, and I'm stuck in the Target parking lot in the snow," I said quickly.

"I'm at work," she squeaked. "Maybe I can sneak out?"

"I just need your car so I can jump my battery. I'm pretty sure it's the battery, and I know how to jump my car. I just need your running vehicle. You can sit back and then drive off."

"I'm not sure. There's one other person here, but it's about to be the lunchtime rush..."

"I understand," I said. "Would it be weird if I called Jordan? He'd just drive up and then leave. It wou—"

"It would be weird," Katie said. "He might get the wrong message. You're trying to have some space to get over the relationship. Plus," she lowered her voice, "you *dumped* him. You can't reject a guy and then call for his help a few weeks later. It'd be weird in just far too many ways."

I groaned, "Fine. Are any of your younger brothers free? Or are they all at work?"

She was quiet for a minute. "Okay, you know what? I'll figure it out. Won't be longer than a half hour."

"You're amazing!" I said gratefully. We hung up.

I pulled a book out of my bag and cuddled under my coat to read as the snow fell outside the car window.

Fourteen

Then I heard it, the loud engine of Gabriel's truck. I sat up from my reading stupor confused. He pulled up across from my car. I slid out of my car and walked over to his truck window. He rolled it down.

"What are you doing here?" I asked, confused.

"Wow, what a greeting for someone coming to help you."

"Sorry, it's not that. I'm just surprised you are out here, what with the injury and all. I was expecting Katie," I said. "I didn't call you because I know you're all laid up on the couch."

"What a lovely depiction of how I'm spending my time. But Katie couldn't leave work and tapped me in," he said gruffly.

"I'm sorry. I can call someone else. You're hurt!" I pulled my phone out of my coat pocket.

"Emma, I'm not immobile. I have my crutches." He popped his hand out his car window and pushed my phone away from my face.

"Should you be driving on your pain meds?" I inquired.

"I've been weaning off onto the kids' stuff; I'm totally fine. I've been going on drives for my sanity lately. I've even been to see a movie. I'm reentering the world slowly."

I raised an eyebrow in suspicion. "Okay. I can jump it myself, anyway. I have the cables in the back. I just need your running engine."

In about ten minutes, my car started again, and the roar was a welcome sound. I closed the hood and went to the back to put the cables away and noticed Gabe had scooted out of his truck and was hobbling in the snow on his crutches.

"Gabe, you need to be careful," I said in a tone of maternal disapproval.

I was turning from the back of my car when I got hit on the head with a little snowball. I squealed, wiping the snow off, when I saw Gabe crunched over in the snow laughing.

"You literally risked *the health of your leg* to hit me with a snowball?"

"It's the perfect time. You won't take vengeance on me when I can barely walk."

"Yeah, I'd never stoop that low," I said in mock horror, then quickly gathered a handful of snow and threw it at him. It wasn't necessarily graceful, or even a formed snowball at all, but it was quick and landed right on his chest.

He threw another one at me from his crouched position, hitting me on the shoulder.

So, I made a big snowball and walked straight over to him. We were both shaking with laughter, barely able to breathe, as I smashed it on his head.

"You are a cheat," he said as he shook the snow out of his hair. I sat down in the snow beside him, breathless from the laughing, cheeks sore.

"You are the cheat, thinking you could use your crutches as an excuse." I gave him a shove. "You know I'm vengeful."

"You are vengeful." He said, dusting snow out of my hair.

I looked over at my running car. "I should get going. I'm nervous it'll die again."

"You should go by the shop and have them look at the battery. Make sure you don't need a replacement," he advised.

"I don't think I need a new one."

"Doesn't hurt to have a good mechanic take a look at it. You should go to Roger's Auto shop. Steve Rogers is a really good guy."

"I've never seen him. Where's he located?"

"Just a couple minutes down the street from here, actually. You can follow me," he said while I helped him up from his snowball sniper spot.

"Gabe, you sure you're feeling up to it?" I looked down at his casted up leg.

"Up to driving down the street to the auto shop and then just sitting there with you? I think I can manage." He laughed. He tucked his crutches under his arms and hopped over to his truck while I buckled into my car.

It didn't hit me until we had already checked in with the front desk and were waiting in the lobby as they inspected my car that I knew who Steve Rogers was. He was Jordan's ex-girlfriend's dad. The infamous Sophia's dad.

Only a few seconds prior, I had seen her with her dark brown hair swept into a glossy ponytail and her tan skin—even in the thick of winter—walk into the shop with two coffee cups in hand. *What is Sophia doing here?*

As if on cue, she said to the guy at the front desk, "I brought a coffee for my dad."

Steve Rogers was Sofia Roger's dad.

"Oh yeah," I whispered to myself. Gabriel glanced over, having noticed me murmur under my breath. I gave him a half smile.

Sophia looked around the lobby, and I saw her gaze fall on me. Her eyes went wide, and she awkwardly looked away.

She was Jordan's high school sweetheart. She and I had always been friendly with each other in school, sharing friends and attending the same events. She was a track star and spent most of her time with athletes, and I was a total bookworm and kept busy with the English Club and the Hernandezes. The difference in things keeping us busy was the only reason we didn't hang out more.

Jordan told me about his relationship with Sophia on our third date. We had just walked out of the movie theatre downtown. The streetlamps were glowing. It was a fall night with leaves underfoot, and I had mused, "Do you have any long-lost love I need to worry about?"

Like in the movie, I was implying. But his hesitancy before he answered reminded me of Sophia.

I had forgotten to worry about her in our little new-love bubble. But for years, I had known Jordan from "Jordan and Sophia." A pair. A duo.

"No, not really." He laughed uncomfortably.

"Not really? Not exactly reassuring," I teased as our holding hands swung.

"No. I meant a simple, no."

I sighed. "What was your last relationship?" I didn't want to ask, but I also knew it would get more awkward the longer I waited. We both knew I knew the answer.

"It was actually my high school relationship. Do you remember Sophie?"

"Yeah, I do. No one since her?"

"Nothing but a few dates here and there during college," he said, looking out at the street behind me.

Was I going to be another "just a few dates" on the road back to her?

"What happened, if you don't mind me asking?"

"Well, it's hard to say." He stopped walking.

We stood in front of an old building being remodeled. People walked by us, lost in their own conversations, as he found his words.

"I guess you could blame distance. We really tried to make it

work, going to two separate schools. Sophie had a scholarship she couldn't turn down. I needed to keep working with dad to pay off my schooling, so I had to stay close to here, you know. Maybe I should've budged, in hindsight, and followed her. But we really thought we could make it work. We were nuts for each other all through high school."

"I remember. Prom king and queen." Sophia and Jordan, two names always together.

"Yeah, yeah. We thought it'd be okay. We'd have school breaks. But she got caught up in her own world, and I did, too. Then, I got a little jealous of this guy she was doing everything with. They were the center of their little social group. We started fighting more than sharing. I was being selfish; I see that now."

It was quiet between us. He cleared his throat.

"We decided to take a break. But it wasn't a break. A week later, she ended things completely... During our week 'break,'" he did air quotes with his fingers, "Cole, the guy I was jealous of, confessed his feelings. She didn't want to regret not giving it a shot with him. That's what she told me. It was hard."

"I bet it was hard."

"You know, she told me she still loved me. She said she had feelings for us both. She was confused. That's something I don't want to happen again... I don't want some girl who's confused. I want someone who knows they want me just like I want them. That hurt." His eyes glistened like maybe he would cry. "We'd been in love for years—what's there to be confused about?"

I nodded. Though, deep down, I knew there was so much to be confused about, especially at eighteen-years-old miles away from the boy you loved.

"We were young. She actually married him last year. So, they were meant to be. They got a house. They'll probably have some kids. She always wanted all that, you know. We always talked about having that ourselves. She used to tell me she wanted to teach at the school where we fell in love."

I gave him a sympathetic arm rub.

"I'm over it. I guess that's what I was doing during college instead of dating much. I was getting over Sophie. I'm happy for her, really. It was high school. She's married."

She's married. If she wasn't married, then what?

He coughed, apologized for his long reply, and asked me if I had any long-lost loves. I laughed and said I'd never really been in love, so I'd never really lost a love. He apologized again. He swore he had moved on. He barely thought of her now, he said effusively.

And we never mentioned her again. His family sometimes mentioned her when she was tangled up in old family stories, and I would search his face like a map to doublecheck that his heart was still where he said it was—still with me.

Because he might not have understood how you could be confused about feelings or how you could have feelings for more than one person because love for one didn't always disqualify love for another. But I knew.

And I knew that maybe he wouldn't identify it that way, but I couldn't forget how he'd said, "She's married."

I always feared he loved us both. His love for me couldn't squash his love for her. Her only disqualifier? She was married.

But, about a year later, she wasn't married anymore. And now, here she was, in front of me.

Gabriel kept looking at me with questioning eyes. He could sense my discomfort.

I was wondering if Sophia knew Jordan and I were broken up. Or if she told someone after they asked her about Jordan, "He's with someone," as if that was their dead end. The locked door. The giant disqualifier.

Gabriel looked over at the front desk where, she stood sipping her coffee and looking at her phone, presumably waiting for her dad. Then I watched Gabe squint his eyes in recognition.

"I know you," he said loudly, ever a Hernandez. "The prom queen!"

She turned her head, putting on a polite smile before her eyes softened in recognition. "Gabriel Hernandez." Then she added, "The writer."

"You flatter me!" He stood up.

"Oh no, what happened?" she asked, noticing his cast as he hobbled over to her.

What. Is. Happening? The horrific idea of the two of them having some unspoken magic between them flitted across my imagination. I mean, she was single, and he was single. And, apparently, Gabriel found her memorable. And she cared enough to track his career like a stalker.

The idea felt like someone had heard about an old nightmare of mine and evilly laughed, "I can make that ten billion times worse."

I walked over and stood awkwardly beside him, prompting him to say, "Do you remember my fellow writer, Emma Brown?"

"Of course," she said. A little less warm, I noted. "Hi, Emma."

I gave a little wave. "Hello, Sophia. How've you been?"

"I'm good," she said. "I've moved back, actually. I'm teaching over at Sweet River Elementary, actually."

She was teaching at the school where she and Jordan met, where their love began like they had always planned.

"How are you?" she asked. Then in a rush added, as if she couldn't help herself, *"How's Jordan?"*

Gabriel let out a breath of air, always so dramatic. His gaze sideways on me.

"I'm not sure. I hear he's doing well," I said politely. "We're actually just friends now."

Her eyes lit up, but her voice didn't match her expression. She said softly, "Oh. I'm sorry. I didn't realize."

I shrugged. Then, thankfully, her dad walked in to update me on my car. As I walked toward him for the update, I grabbed Gabriel's arm to drag him along. I wasn't going to leave him alone with the memorable prom queen.

Fifteen

We were heading back to our cars, snow flurries falling around us like glitter in a globe, when Gabriel asked me if I was okay.

"Yeah, why?" I asked.

"In the lobby, you seemed to have something on your mind or like something threw you off for a minute. Maybe I was imagining it, though." He leaned against his truck, both crutches to the side for a minute.

"Oh." I laughed awkwardly. "Sophia, the girl we ran into in there—"

"Sophia! That was her name!"

"Yes, Sophia. She was Jordan's high school sweetheart. And even though they weren't on bad terms, and I didn't have any bad feelings toward her, things are always very awkward when we see each other."

"Ah, okay," he said, rubbing his cold hands together. "That explains the vibe."

"My ex's ex."

He cocked his head and looked at me. "Look at you with this sordid past."

"Sordid past? Please." I rolled my eyes. "Aren't you the one always dating someone new?"

He looked a little hurt. "Who says that?"

"I don't know," I said, instantly regretting what I'd said. "I just assume, I guess, from the tidbits I hear."

It was quiet for a beat. I sniffled, feeling my nose turn pink from the frigid air.

"Have you...you know...had anyone serious? We don't really talk about that," I finally mustered up the courage to ask.

"Do I have a Jordan?" he clarified.

"Just anyone serious or semi-serious? Like, anyone that went beyond a few dates?"

He sighed and looked as if he was thinking about what to disclose, carefully choosing his words. "Sort of. I guess I never had a Jordan. You and Jordan were really official and looking to the future and stuff. I haven't had that. But there were a couple of girls that it did go beyond just 'dating.'" He chewed his lip. "There was Heather. I think she happened the fall you moved back home. We were an unspoken item. We just kind of happened. Our friends were all the same, so we just fell together so easily. We matched. But it never went very deep."

"Heather," I said her name as if a mythological creature.

"That was the thing she said when we were breaking it off, that 'we never went deep enough.' She asked why we were 'unspoken,' why we weren't official. According to her, I had a wall up."

I wanted to know everything, even though the idea of a Heather bothered me. I was desperate to ask what she looked like. What was her job? Did she kiss him against his car? Did he say Heather's name almost teasingly?

"That was the case with Lila, too. She, uh, was an *official* girlfriend. We met about a year ago. We hit it off right away. We were dating and pretty quickly had the define the relationship chat. We really liked each other. We lasted about six months, and then she also asked me about this wall. She said there was a wall up when it came to the future. She said, and I quote, that I felt hesitant."

"Hesitant," I said.

"Hesitant. Like I was holding back."

"Was she right?"

He laughed, his eyes cutting into mine. "Yeah."

"Yeah?"

"Yeah. I could feel myself holding back. Like I was waiting it out. I don't know why, but I do that every time. I guess I always feel like..." But then he trailed off. He looked away.

"Me too," I said suddenly. "You know, me and the disqualifiers."

"Oh, yes, the disqualifiers," he said, but then he looked at the ground. "But not with Jordan."

"Well, I obviously found a few disqualifiers, didn't I?" I joked sardonically. "You know, you said the same thing at your family's Christmas party. As if Jordan is perfect or something." I paused, but he just blinked at me. "Why do you say things like that?"

"I don't know. I've never seen you be like that with a guy before. I just assumed he must be just the perfect guy. Or, at least, you think he's the perfect guy. Or something like that."

"I've never been looking for anyone perfect."

"Well, perfect or not, you guys seemed *perfectly* in love for years." He seemed a little agitated like he was wrestling with some thought.

"Yeah," I said, navigating the maze of this conversation. "But we broke up, so..."

"Are you still in love with him?"

My eyes widened in surprise at his directness. "I don't know. No? But with an asterisk? Because I will always love him."

"You'll always love him?"

"Why are you grilling me about my recent breakup?" I asked on the verge of frustration.

"Sorry, sorry, we just never talked about it. I've always had my questions. You two came out of nowhere and were serious in, like, seconds." He sounded exasperated.

"Why would we have talked about it?" I asked.

"Because you met him when you were twenty-one."

"Because I met him when I was twenty-one?" I repeated it back as a question.

"When you were twenty-one things were…" he said softly, almost a whisper.

"Things were?" I gestured for him to continue.

Then he said quickly, "Well, I feel like we've dug up enough relationship history for one day. I should probably head back home since your car is obviously good to go."

I nodded, even though I remained standing there, frozen as the snow on the ground. He hopped on his crutches back to the driver's side of his car, away from me.

I stayed standing there. *When I was twenty-one things were…*complicated.

Gabriel and I kissed when I was twenty-one.

We had high hopes. But I didn't get that job near him in Los Angeles.

I didn't even try afterward, even as he urged me to try other options.

I moved home when I was twenty-one.

I bowed out.

We talked less and less. I ignored so much.

I said no thank you to anything scary when I was twenty-one.

And Gabriel Hernandez had always scared me.

He started his car, waking me from my memories. He looked out his window at me still standing there in the parking lot where he left me.

He rolled down his window. "Em? Are you okay?" he asked, a little confused, half smiling.

"What were you going to say? When I was twenty-one things were, what?" I asked, even though my voice was a little shaky.

"Nothing, nothing. Don't worry about it," he said casually. A hint of what Heather and Lila might've encountered.

"Gabe," I said. "It's me. I know you meant something. "

He looked at me with eyes a little darker, his voice a little lower, "Can you guess what I meant?"

"I don't want to play a guessing game."

He started laughing a little sadly. "You're right. I shouldn't have said anything."

"I didn't mean that. I meant, if you want to say something, you should say it."

It was quiet for a minute. I looked up to see flurries falling harder than before. He noticed too. "Go get in your warm car and forget about it. I was being a jerk."

"You weren't being a jerk," I said, willing to wait it out. Should I just say it? Say what we never said? Talk about what we never talked about? Admit what I didn't want to admit? "I just want to know what you meant."

"Em, don't get all up in your head. I'm sorry. I shouldn't have said anything. Let's just go back to normal, yeah?"

I felt a door had been cracked open for a second, and now it was closing in my face.

Snow was on my eyelashes, my fingertips. I felt numb in my shoes. "Okay," I said unsurely.

"Okay." His voice was as unsure as mine.

"Okay," I said sadly, resignedly.

I got into my car and started the engine as he drove away. I went to put my car in drive but instead buried my face in my hands. Did I want to talk to him about the kiss?

About that fall, almost an entire year after the kiss? And what was going on in those in-between months?

About this never-ending childhood crush? Or the fear that it was more than a stupid crush?

About all of it? About any of it?

What even was it?

"What good would it do?" I asked myself. It felt off-limits. It felt useless to even talk about it. To think about it. It'd probably just make things messier, worse.

I didn't want to imagine the ramifications it would have on my closest friendship—on the family that felt like my own family.

And what if I brought it all up just to find out it was all in my head? I could lie in bed and think through every word he said and analyze why it meant something, but I could just as easily logic myself into thinking it meant absolutely nothing.

Plus, he doesn't even live near me. He'd move back to Los Angeles soon. He'd go back to his work trips, meeting Heathers and Lilas, and I'd be left here.

He'd drive off and leave me behind, like right now. He just left me there, crying in a parking lot. Snow still in my hair and on my lips, like the stain of an untold kiss.

Sixteen

ME

hey, I know things got a little deep earlier, but I forgot to say thanks for coming to my rescue today

GABRIEL

Happy to help!

GABRIEL

plus I like talking to you, even if you're grilling me on my exes and I'm grilling you on Mr. Perfect

ME

shall I start nicknaming Heather and Lila now?

GABRIEL:

wow you remember their names huh?

That night, I couldn't sleep. I tossed and turned in between dream and wake, unsure of where I was in time. As if I were still the twenty-one-year-old girl torn between risking it all on her dreams and a boy she'd just kissed by moving to Los Angeles or coming home to Sweet River to a sure thing and dating her high school crush.

As if it was as simple as one choice. As if life was just a series of forks in the road instead of a free fall of maybes and never landing where you'd planned.

I woke up the next morning restless and tired. I drove to my parent's house on an empty stomach and in sweatpants. I'd told my mom I would work with her on repainting the living room—for the sixth time.

My mom was an art teacher at our local community center. She'd taught art to children and adults my entire life, at the same time on the same days, for years. Her art spilled all over her life, her world—and my world, too. Her art even spilled all over my childhood home.

Our house was always being changed—the furniture rearranged, the walls painted different colors. She was always finding new treasures to replace décor, always painting murals in our backyard, over our sink, over the fireplace.

Mom was always chasing a vision, but the vision changed daily.

How my mother could always be changing and evolving herself and everything around her yet remain the most consistent and reliable woman in my life, with the same work schedule for over a decade, was the miracle of my mother.

Our home might look completely different, but it was still always *my* home. It was perpetually waiting for me to relax into it whenever I needed it, no matter where I was coming back from.

When I walked inside, there was no paint, no usual decorating project set up. "Hey, where's the paint?" I asked.

"Oh, I woke up this morning, honey, and I'd changed my mind. I think I like it how it is for now," my mom said plainly. She was in an old white tank top, I think used to be mine, and a pair of overalls. She was long and tall, like me. Her blonde hair turning silver. "Dad and I thought we would just make a big breakfast and catch up with you."

"That sounds perfect, actually." I sighed contentedly.

I could smell the bacon in the oven and hear the sizzle of eggs cooking in the frying pan. I walked into the kitchen and began to set the table for the three of us.

Dad walked into the room moments later, his reading glasses still resting low on his nose. "Good morning," he said.

"What were you reading, Dad?" I asked.

"Oh, I've been caught up in this little mystery series set in Edinburgh, I recently discovered. I think you'd like it. Remind me to lend you the first book in the series."

I wondered if you put together a creative artist, like my mother, and a nerdy bookworm like my father, you couldn't help but wind up with a daughter who wrote.

We were sitting around the dining room table eating our breakfast while mom told us some recent stories from her class-room, and my dad talked about slowing down at the office, poten-tially bringing in a new doctor to take on more of the heavy load of patients.

I curled my legs up under me as I finished my last bite of food. I chewed thoughtfully, realizing I had no new or interesting news to share except that I was getting fairly skilled at latte art now.

"How are things on the job front?" my father asked. I told him I was applying, searching and recently asked Gabriel for a few contacts that might be interested in some freelance work. I was trying; I was hopeful.

Then, I asked, "How did you know that you wanted to settle down here, in Sweet River? How did you know this was right?"

A lot of people in this small town had aunts, uncles, grandpar-ents, cousins, and kin. Deep roots that kept them in this city. But my family was just us three. My kin spread out across this whole country. I even had a cousin in London. What kept us here?

"Well, you know we went to school in Austin," my dad said. "We met there originally, as we've told you. But after I worked in

Dallas for a while building up my career, it felt like the right time to open my own practice, and we just..." He sighed thoughtfully. "Landed here."

"You never had a dream of seeing other places? Of moving around?" I wondered if this longing in me could've been passed down to me from my dad like my blue eyes.

"Well, honey, you know we found out we were pregnant with you. A sweet little surprise. It helped us realize we wanted to find our own spot to watch you grow," Mom chimed in, coming up behind me and rubbing my shoulder.

"If I remember correctly, I had an old colleague who told me someone was retiring out here. It felt like serendipitous timing. We felt a little anxious for a job to open up, and here was a perfect opportunity at just the right time," Dad said. "It felt meant to be."

"If you hadn't had me, where do you think you'd have gone?" I asked. Did my mom have a secret dream of Somewhere Else that never came true? Like me?

"Honey, it's been over two decades, I can barely remember the girl I was before you," Mom said with a gentle laugh. "I think life just happens, and you go along with what feels right. Sometimes, all you can do is follow the opportunities that arise and chase what you feel an ache to chase. For me, that was always art, that was teaching, and that was you. I never wanted to chase travel. I would dream up paintings. I would dream up classroom projects. I dreamed up raising you with a little backyard and a little city of our own, and that's just what I did."

Dad nodded. "I guess I was a little boring. I wanted to own my own practice since I was in school, so I charted out that path."

"Were you ever deterred from it, Dad? Were you ever scared? You've never seemed scared about any of it," I said. "But maybe that's just my perspective from being a kid."

Dad let out a big laugh. "Emma, of course, I was scared. I went to medical school! I remember failing out of a particular class over and over, and your mother telling me I just had to keep it up until I made it. This career has sometimes cost me more than I thought I could afford. I mean, heck, it was terrifying a lot of the time, and I don't think I ever felt smart enough... But I really liked it, so I kept at it." He reached over and grabbed my mom's hand. "Your mother really held my hand and led me through it, too."

"And moving to this random town with no family wasn't necessarily easy, but it was the right opportunity at the right time. It was our dream for the moment. It was scary, but we did it. We did it together," Mom said.

I sighed. I wanted so badly to be able to peer into my parent's history and find some sort of roadmap for my future. I think part of me had expected them to tell me of course they'd longed for something different all along, but for very good reasons they'd ignored those silly desires, so I could have a good reason to ignore my own silly desires.

I went to speak, but then closed my mouth.

Mom noticed, of course. "Honey, I fear you're having one of those early-onset mid-life crises."

"You mean a quarter-life crisis?" I groaned.

"Yes, that!" She pointed at me. "That's it."

"No, no. Where did you read about those? I'm not having a quarter life crisis. I'm just trying to figure out my next steps, I suppose. Which dreams do I chase? How do I know when to go and when to stay?"

"I think right now is the age for trying," my dad said. "Write for a magazine, Emma! Write your stories. You can write while you're at the coffee shop, can't you?"

"It's not that. I know I should write." I fiddled with my silverware. "I guess I'm trying to figure out what it means that I've always wanted to travel. Should I try to move somewhere? Should I apply across the country? Or should I just book a few fun future vacations when I'm not so strapped for cash? And, like, what should I do about writing? Don't get me started on that. Gabriel thinks I should go back to what I wanted to do fresh out of college. Katie thinks I should do freelance." I looked up at my parents. "Dad thinks I should write for a magazine, I guess."

"I think you should do what you want to do," Dad clarified. "Little you was always making me those pretend magazines, so that's what I think you should do. Little me was always offering fake dental exams, you know."

"You're cute, Dad."

"Honey, I say you should calm down," Mom offered. "Don't put so much pressure on yourself. You're twenty-five. You're not supposed to know where you'll be for the rest of your life at twenty-five. You want life to surprise you a little. Write, reach out, and see what happens. If you wind up with an opportunity to travel—take it! If nothing happens—well, I think something will happen."

"Something will happen," Dad's voice boomed in agreement.

"But, mostly, sweetie, calm down." Mom was rubbing my shoulder again. "No little life crisis for our Emma."

"No *quarter-life crisis*." I laughed. "Well, now, tell me how you knew each other was the one."

They both laughed at me. Mom started clearing our plates.

"Really, guys, come on. How did you know?" I said, even though they'd told me this story hundreds of times.

Mom stopped clearing the plates and looked at Dad. She grinned at him and said to me, "How could I not know?"

"What did you write in that note?" my dad asked.

"Magnets," Mom said delicately.

"We were magnets," Dad said.

"I mean, honey, when it's the one, you just think, *of course.* It's not a question of *are they the one*, but of *who else could ever be the one* now that I've met them?"

"Oh my," I leaned back in my chair. "You two sure are cheesy."

"Sure, Emma. I used to read those poems you and Gabriel wrote. Now those were cheesy." My mom wiggled her fingers at me.

"Let's let those die." I covered my face as visceral memories of Gabriel and I passing poems back and forth so dramatically, so seriously came back to me.

"Oh, speaking of the one. I have a boy I want to set you up with," my dad patted the table excitedly.

"Dad! I just broke up with Jordan."

"He's a great guy, and you don't want to miss your chance!" Dad urged.

"Who is this guy?" Mom asked from the kitchen sink, dishes clattering.

"He's the son of one of my patients. He's moving home. I think he's a great kid."

"Kid?" I asked.

"He's a little younger by a few years, but a great catch. He's a teacher," Dad bragged on this guy.

"Dad, I'm not interested in dating anyone new right now."

"Are you interested in dating someone old?" Mom asked over the sink water. I felt my face flush, instantly thinking of Gabriel.

"You guys," I said, half laughing, half serious. "I am taking a romance hiatus."

Mom turned off the water. "Isn't that a line in one of those romantic comedies? Saying that usually means you're about to fall in love."

"And Valentine's Day is around the corner, Emma," Dad wiggled his eyebrows.

"Valentine's Day hiatus," I said seriously.

"What about from dear old dad?" Dad said with puppy dog eyes. "What if I want to pick you up some flowers?"

"Dad, you're always an exception." I walked over to his seat and gave him a hug. He patted my arms.

"I'll let my patient down easy about the blind date we were planning," my dad said wistfully. I buried my head in his shoulder, muffling my laughter.

Seventeen

One morning in early February, I was on my lunch break while scrolling through pictures Katie had posted online of her new little nephew. They were at the high school football field for some reason. I was squinting at the caption to see if she explained the location. It got me thinking about the article I wrote on small-town Texas football.

That particular piece was a point of pride for me. It had generated a lot of positive feedback. The founder of one of my favorite online travel magazines had even reached out to me. It was back when his magazine was just starting out. He praised the article and said they were looking for freelance writers if I was interested.

I stopped scrolling and thought about that. Terrence Pell with *Here & There* Magazine had reached out to *me*. It felt too good to be true, even at the time.

I had been following *Here & There* since they published their very first pieces. They offered what were essentially intimate or thought-provoking takes on various places around the world. It wasn't merely a rundown of the best places to see and the fun things to do, but it often felt like you were traveling with a friend who really wanted to get to know the heart of a place.

I would read the articles and wish I had written them. Why hadn't I replied to him? Why hadn't I thrown myself into that opportunity? *I was scared.* Scared Emma of the past couple of years at the wheel again.

"Can you believe he reached out to me?" I remember telling Katie about this miraculous email over a year ago as we walked around downtown.

"Of course, I can believe it, Emma. I can easily believe it because it was a beautiful article, and you're a beautiful writer," she'd replied, stopping to look in a store window. "Have you replied to him yet?"

"No, no. I don't think I'm going to reply to him, at least not about the offer to freelance. I am not his kind of writer. And I'm busy anyway." I had shut it down, peering in the window beside her.

"Come on. You should at least think about it. It's right up your alley and could lead to something, you know." She turned to look at me.

People walked by us, having their own conversations, their own feelings, their own fears and hopes, just brushing by ours for a second.

"Katie, that's not my alley anymore," I remember saying defensively. I tried to start walking on.

She touched my arm gently, stopping me from going, and said, "Will you just think about it?"

I took in a deep breath and then breathed out two words, "I guess."

But I didn't. I didn't think about it. I took it as a fine compliment from an interesting man and then tucked it away in my mind, forgetting all about it until now. I opened up my laptop and clicked around until I was deep into my old work inbox. Until there it was, the email from Terrence Pell, open before me.

Hi Emma,

I'm Terrence Pell with Here & There *magazine. You wrote a piece for your local paper on the camaraderie and community surrounding Sweet River 's small-town football team recently. I really loved it. I actually bookmarked it and have returned to it a few times. I'm Canadian, but something about it made me relate with my own small-town community growing up. The piece was about high school football, but really it was about the heart of a small town. That's exactly the kind of writing we're doing at* Here & There. *I went and read a bit more of your work, and I'm a huge fan. If you're open to it, we're looking for more freelance writers. Most of our opportunities require some travel, but not all of them...*

A little miracle flickering into my life, and I had snuffed it right out. Scared Emma and the choices she made. I scrolled down and realized I had replied to him a few days later, but just to send a thank you for his kind words. I closed my laptop, all regret. It was too late now. An opportunity lost. Now it would be far too rude to reach out. Awkward and rude.

I weaved through the coffee shop, picking up used mugs, tossing trash away, checking on customers, and wiping tables. There were people typing on their own laptops, people cozied up to thick books, people chatting over lattes, and I thought to myself, *I don't know this guy. Who cares if he finds me awkward and rude?*

He'd probably just ignore me if he did. But if he didn't find me awkward and rude, he'd probably give me an opportunity to write. I didn't mind being the awkward, rude girl, but I was so over being the scared girl.

After I finished up my work, I whipped out my phone and typed up an email to Terrence, apologizing for reaching back out over a year later and asking if he was still interested in having me write for *Here & There.* I wrote boldly, and maybe a little desperately, *If there are any opportunities available at all, I'd be interested.* I reread it a few times, took a deep, steadying breath, and hit send.

A few hours later, as I was finishing up my shift, my phone pinged and to my surprise, he had replied.

Hi Emma, how nice to hear from you again! I still remember your work. Funny enough I'm visiting Austin this week, and your piece had actually come to mind—what with Texas high school football and all. Let's meet for coffee tomorrow morning. Send me a place in your town. I'll drive up and meet you. Write something about your town and send it to me tonight. But put a twist on it. You know we don't like the basic travel pieces. Give it some feeling. Some love. Let's see if your style and voice still work for Here & There. *I'll read it before we meet so we can discuss it tomorrow. You can send it to me here. I trust you know format, etc.*

I reread the email a few times. I felt like Scared Emma again. I was shocked at his bold offers to not only meet in person, but to also request I write something *by tonight.* I was at a loss for words, so I went and got Katie to see what words she had about all of this.

"Isn't this weird?" I demanded, leaning over her shoulder after she read his email.

"Yeah, but who cares if it's a little weird," she said, turning to me. "It might be weird, but it's the best offer you got right now."

"But I don't want to meet him in person..." I whined. "Doesn't writing freelance usually mean you can be distant with employers or something?"

"Em, I reiterate, it's the best offer you got." She then added, "And don't most jobs involve meeting with your employer first? It's really not that weird. He wouldn't do this if he wasn't a couple of hours away. It also weirdly makes sense for this travel guy to be spontaneous and adventurous. I think it's kind of cool. You get to meet someone new in the industry, someone who created a magazine you adore. Honestly, it's kind of awesome."

"But, beyond the issue of the meeting, which is maybe cool. Isn't it weird that I have one night to write this piece for him with the vaguest description ever? Write about your town with a twist... A twist on what? What is this, like an audition?"

"His magazine is known for its quality, sending a sample over seems normal. It's not like he's publishing it. He's just checking your style, like a peer review. And neither of us know if the time-line is weird because neither of us have ever done this."

I released a big sigh. "I'll go through with this, but if he's some creep or if he ghosts me, it's on you."

"Here, let's email him and tell him to meet you here at Coffee & Commas. I'll hang around. If he's a creep, I'll have your back. But what if he's great? And you get a new industry friend." Then with a voice all sugary, she said, "Or what if he's hot and you fall in love?"

I raised an eyebrow. "What if he's hot?"

"Hey, you're single, it's February, and a handsome traveling man wants to meet. And he loves your writing." She wiggled her eyebrows. "What if your life becomes a Hallmark movie?"

I shrugged, too anxious to joke. What if he was hot and that made this even more nerve-wracking? I could not handle putting my career *and* my heart in someone's hands at the same time.

"Goodness, calm down, Emma." She put her hands on my shoulders and looked me in the eyes. "He adored your writing and still remembered it. That's a good sign. He wouldn't drive a couple of hours out of his way to meet with you if he wasn't already assuming he was going to like what you write. These are all good signs. He's setting you up to knock it out of the park." She gave me a big sisterly grin. "What if he loves your writing, and you end up getting paid to travel and write about it? This could be wonderful. You do see that, right?"

My heart was racing. I could feel it pulsing beneath my shirt. "I'm just really nervous." I wondered if I'd ever grow out of finding things other people found exciting, fun and wonderful, absolutely terrifying and dreadful.

"Good," she said, wiping the counter randomly, as if remembering we were at work. I realized for a second that my shift had probably ended by now.

"Good?" I asked.

"Last time you spoke to him, you were pretty dismissive of a dream opportunity showing up in your inbox like magic. Now you have chased it back down. You finally care again. You are nervous and excited like you should be." She walked back over to me.

I said nothing, just resting my head on her shoulder

"And it is magic," she said. "You went from randomly having some magazine show up in your inbox to having him show up on your doorstep."

"Well, the coffee shop doorstep. Tomorrow. If he actually shows up."

She pulled my laptop from me, opened up a Word document, then pushed the laptop back in front of me. "Let's take it step by step. Don't think about the meeting tomorrow. This afternoon just think about writing something that gets him even more excited to drive hours to come and meet you face to face."

I nodded. I preferred thinking about writing more than thinking about meetings.

After I got home, I sat at my kitchen table and did as my best friend said and wrote the article. I wrote in a way that made me forget I was writing for anyone other than myself. I wrote for past Emma, who was so scared it hurt, and present Emma, who cared so much it hurt. I was still Scared Emma, after all. But I was Scared Emma, who cared. I was Scared Emma, who tried.

I took my hands off my eyes, no more shielding myself, and put them on my keyboard.

I thought about my feelings for my hometown and how these feelings felt so tangled up with my feelings about my future, my dreams, and my relationship with Jordan. I wrote about how I loved this town, even though I wanted to leave it, just like I loved Jordan, even though I wanted to leave him.

About the sometimes-complicated relationship one can have with their hometown—the love, the nostalgia, the comfort of home, but also the growing pains, the moving on, the letting go.

How it can be so similar to a breakup with someone who maybe you've outgrown, or who just doesn't fit.

I wrote and wrote until there was nothing else to write.

I titled it, "I Love You, But." Then I hit the "send" button, even though my hands shook.

Eighteen

W e had decided to meet for coffee at 8 a.m. I arrived at Coffee & Commas at 7:30 and sat with Katie as she chattered encouragingly. My heart was rocketing out of my chest until I looked out the window. There was a tall, handsome man walking up the sidewalk. My eyes followed him as he opened the door to the café. He was wearing dark jeans and a navy cashmere sweater that made him look like the lead in a romantic holiday movie. For a moment, I wondered if Katie's prediction would come to pass.

He walked in the door, and Katie turned excitedly in his direction, whispering to me, "Is that him?"

He walked a few steps into the shop, his eyes scanning the tables until he set his sights on me, quickly saying "Emma?" as he walked toward me.

I nodded and gestured for him to come sit down.

"Hi, Terrence." His smile was wide and kind. His coffee-colored eyes were as dark as his skin. "I'm Emma Brown. I'm so glad to meet you."

"Likewise," he said, shaking my hand.

"This is my friend, Katie," I said. I glanced at her and noticed her cheeks were flushed.

"Hi," she said, her smile twisting up in a way I rarely see.

"Hi, Katie," he said, taking his seat at our little table. "How are you guys this morning?"

"I'm great," we both answered in unison, then laughed.

"How are you this morning?" I asked.

"I'm happy to be out here," he said. "Ever since I read your piece, I've wanted to check out Sweet River for myself. I have a bad habit of wanting to see every place I read about."

"It seems you found the right line of work, then," I said cheerfully. He nodded to the coffee bar. "I'll go place an order, then we can begin our chat. Would you like anything?"

"I actually already grabbed a cappuccino but thank you." I held up my mug.

He stood up from the table, and Katie said, "Oh, here, I'll actually be taking your order. We can walk together."

"Lucky me," he said, and my ears perked a little. I shot a look Katie's way, but she was busy giggling at something he said as the two walked away. Katie helped him decide on what he'd like to drink, and he stuck around the coffee bar as she made the order.

It was a little while until he made his way back to our table. I briefly wondered if his latte was cold by the time he sat back down. Was this a bad sign? Him making me wait so long before our meeting? I was considering this, but I looked over to Katie. She was grinning as she cleaned the coffee bar. I decided it wasn't a bad sign, or a good sign, because it wasn't about me or our meeting at all. He was distracted by the gorgeous barista, simple as that.

He sat down in front of me, finally, and said, "So, your piece last night."

"Yes, my piece last night?"

"It was beautiful. It was cutting. I've never been in that situation, but it felt universal somehow." He sipped his drink. "It gave such a picture of Sweet River, of small-town Texas, or really of small-town community and sort of growing up in one place. I liked how it did that, but it was also such a universal dive into growing out of a relationship. I didn't intend to publish it. I meant it as more of a sample of sorts, but...I forwarded it to our editing team and got the go-ahead."

"Oh my gosh, really?" I was breathless.

"If you are good with it?" he asked. "Obviously, we'll get a payment transfer set up. We'll need to get all that set up anyway to bring you on the team. I think we should schedule it to publish two weekends from now. It would perfectly coincide with Valentine's Day."

I nodded eagerly. "I would be honored." It was a dramatic thing to say, but I was too happy to care.

"I must say, I loved your old work, but this one...I think you've gotten better. If you can continue to bring that unique style to your travel writing, being more than just a tourist. We want the writing to reflect the real way places we visit or live in can help people grow and change and think."

"That's what I want to write," I said honestly. "That's what was missing from my old job."

"You're not with the newspaper anymore, you said?" Terrence double-checked.

"That's right."

"You'll be a little freer to travel then," he said, putting a positive spin on my career collapse. "What got you into writing?"

"I've always been into writing since I was a little girl scribbling in notebooks. It's come natural to me like how runners run, how singers sing. I write. It's what I do everywhere I go. I write about my hometown, my school, the park. Every trip I take gets me inspired, gets me thinking about myself and the world around me. I studied journalism in school with this in mind." The door of the shop rang as a group of friends piled in, giggling and loud.

"I'm not much of a writer. I wanted to be because I've always loved reading and creating. I'm more of a business guy. I own this magazine with the hope of it becoming a print periodical—which is actually coming to fruition soon. But I own a few businesses, whether as the founder or a partner. I'm creative, just in a different way than you."

"You gotta have all kinds of creative in this world," I mused.

"Otherwise, who would print those words you write?" He agreed. And he was right, but I sipped my coffee and thought, *I'd be writing these words even if they were only ever scribbled in journals.*

"And I'd love to print your words. We're in the middle of some big transitions so all we have right now are some freelance opportunities. But you said in your email that freelance was what you were interested in?"

"That would be perfect," I said, though something in me, hidden back behind all the fears and doubts about my future, was disappointed that there weren't bigger opportunities with the magazine. Part of me, way in the back, was aching for something more.

"I'll get someone to connect with you about this." He opened his phone and typed away. "Right now," he laughed. "I've sent your info over to Marianne. She'll get you set up."

"Thank you," I said. It felt like this meeting was coming to an end, but then he asked, "What happened with your reporting job anyway?"

"Oh," I said. "Well, they had to downsize. In the wake of that happening, I kind of realized I hadn't exactly been writing what I wanted to write..."

"No, no, I was meaning... You'd mentioned in your email that you wanted to travel write, and you were just saying that you went to school with travel writing in mind, so when you graduated, you wound up at the paper instead. I'm wondering why?"

"Well," I cleared my throat. "I tried to find a position that looked more like 'the dream' after I graduated, but I got a couple of...rejections. Right when I was looking for something outside of those dreams, the position with the newspaper opened up. The editor was someone I'd known growing up, an old teacher, actually. He reached out to me and asked me to come interview. It felt like a gift. Plus, the job was journalism. It aligned with my major, and it felt comfortable. It made me happy for a time. You know, in a way, I did love it."

He nodded. "You loved the job, although it wasn't the perfect fit." I grinned at the reference to the article I had just written for him. "You maybe just *outgrew* it, and it was time to move on."

"I guess I wasn't the only one wanting out of the relationship in the end," I joked along.

"Well, I hope writing for us is the first step toward finding... what's *meant to be*." He winked.

"A girl can dream," I said.

"As a guy who has often stumbled along through missteps until I found what I actually wanted, because, let me tell you, while studying business management in school, I wasn't sitting around thinking about founding a very specific digital travel magazine, or juggling a bunch of startups. I never had a clear-cut direction like you had since you were a little girl. I was just energetic, creative, and wanted to make things, and I realized business was exciting enough for me. Figuring out life, and what you want to do, is a different story for everyone. Sometimes it's stumbling along until you go, 'Oh, this is right,' a lot like finding the one. Or, sometimes, it's knowing what you wanted all along and getting the guts to go after it—"

"Also, sometimes, like finding the one," I added with a laugh.

"Ah, that sounds—" But then suddenly Katie was standing by our table.

"Just wanted to check if either of you need anything?" she asked. Since when did we offer tableside service? I wanted to tease her about it but knew better.

"Do you recommend anything?" Terrence asked, turning his entire body toward her.

"You know, as a little welcome to Sweet River, we have some butter pecan scones fresh from the oven," she said, eyes sparkling. "The pecans come straight from our own trees."

"She made them herself, and they're perfect," I said. "Truly the perfect welcome to Sweet River for any out-of-towner."

"I'm sold. I'll take one of those then," he said. But before she could leave, he asked, "So you're the chef here?"

"Oh," she said, and there were those flushed cheeks again. "No, I'm the manager. But I do some of the baking, too."

"She does *a lot* of the baking, and she's fabulous," I said.

"Wow, a baker and a businesswoman," he said. "I'm already impressed."

"You should probably try the baking before you get too carried away," Katie said, my exuberant friend, suddenly a little quiet and batting her eyes.

"I don't need to try the baked goods to be impressed by you," he said.

I thought about how he knew he wanted me to write for him, and he immediately reached out by email, then drove to meet me —bold in his intent. Now, here he was, looking into the eyes of my beautiful best friend, and there was still no question about his intent.

"Are you born and raised in Sweet River, like Emma?" Terrence asked, keeping her at our table.

"I am." She nodded. "You're visiting Austin, right? Just stopping in our town for the morning?"

"I might be able to extend my stay into a day trip," he said, a little mischievous. "If I happen to get lunch plans."

"You should stay here a little longer. I highly recommend it. But I'm curious, where are you from originally?"

"I'm from Canada. Vancouver, to be more specific. I went to college in the States, though. I have a place back home but also another in Seattle. A man with two countries."

"I have *one* place here in Sweet River. A tiny room," Katie said playfully. "A woman with one tiny town."

"Have you always lived here?" he asked.

"I went to school a few hours away, but then I zoomed right back here after graduation."

"Do you travel much?" He tapped his fingers against the table.

"I love to travel," she said. "But I also love coming back home."

"Well, being the Sweet River expert," he said, completely ignoring asking me, the person who literally wrote about Sweet River, "you got to tell me where should I go next?"

"Oh, you have found the right woman," Katie said excitedly. She pulled out a chair and sat down with us at the table. My friend's voice might be a little quieter around this man, but she was just as bold.

From there, I lost them both.

I tip-toed over to the pastry display, grabbed two scones, and set them on the table between the pair. They both laughed and thanked me.

My meeting was obviously over, so I got to work and started handing out coffee and baked goods. They stayed in the same spot talking for *nearly an hour*.

Finally, I walked over to Katie and Terrence, "Katie," I said, interrupting them. They glanced up at me. "I can run this place if you're hungry and in need of a lunch break."

"Oh, Em, don't worry—" Katie was beginning to protest, the loyal worker bee she was.

But Terrence was wise enough to say, "Maybe we can grab lunch together at that sandwich shop you were telling me about?"

"Oh." Katie was clearly torn. "If you're sure you're okay without me, Em?"

"Definitely. Go. Eat food." I couldn't stop smiling, holding back a laugh, remembering her wondering if my meeting was going to turn into a love story—if Terrence was going to be hot.

"Well, yeah." She turned to Terrence. "That sounds great. Let me just grab my bag."

"Perfect. It's a date," he said happily. Katie nodded at him with a grin in agreement. *It was a date.*

The two headed out together, and I watched from behind the counter, bagging a few cookies for a customer. I felt a subtle pang in my chest. An ache for something out of reach.

Not for something I'd had before, not like when a memory

sent a jolt of missing Jordan through me, but an ache for something I'd yet to ever have myself. Like when your mouth waters at the scent of something baking in the oven. You haven't tasted it yet, but you're hungry for it just the same.

My heart was hungry for something. I thought about how my heart hammered like a fist on a door every time Gabriel walked by, every time I breathed him in. But with him, it was never as simple as declaring, "It's a date." Never as simple as two eyes agreeing, *This is going to be something*. Oh, but there was that pang in my chest, all the same. I put my hand on my chest and rubbed it lightly, sending myself a little love.

If only it could ever be that easy for the two of us. In another story, Gabriel and I could meet at a café and get lost in conversation. We would talk and talk, like we do now, easy and passionate, words flowing like a strong current, but then he would ask if I wanted to go grab lunch. I would tell him that I would love that. I would grab my bag. I'd follow him out the door, my heart hammering away in my chest like a fist on a door, telling me, *"Open up! Something's here."*

I shake my head. I take another order. I ignore the ache—the pang—just like I ignore the hammering heart.

While the two were out for lunch, Marianne connected with me through a phone call, and thirty minutes later, she sent me an email offering me my first assignment for an article on a small town in Oklahoma that kind of reminded me of Sweet River, as well as an attached travel itinerary for this weekend.

I squealed in joy. It wasn't fabulous pay. I had never written a travel article like this, and I'd have to run this by Rose, but it was still a tiny miracle. I stared at the travel itinerary on my phone and heard Katie's voice say, "Magic."

Sometimes seemingly mundane things like emails, itineraries, and meetings over coffee were nothing short of magic.

· · ·

By the time Terrence and Katie returned, hours had passed, and my shift had ended. I stuck around to hear all the details from Katie on their impromptu date. I was eating a cookie on one of the café's old, fluffy couches, and flipping through an old copy of *Little Women,* wondering if it would be simpler to kiss your sister's best friend rather than your best friend's brother, when in strolled Katie with Terrence following closely behind.

"Well, I'm really glad you found your way to Sweet River," Katie said as the door closed behind them. "Even if it was just for a day."

"You know," he said, leaning against the door. "I could stick around. Make tomorrow's meetings virtual. Maybe you and I could meet up again?"

"You can do that?" Katie asked, her voice hopeful. "Tomorrow is my day off, you know. I'm free all day."

"I can be free all day if you're free," he said, his voice soft. I was slipping down the couch, attempting to hide. My face was red, and I wasn't even on the date.

"Em?" Katie asked suddenly.

I leaned up on my elbows with my head peeking over the side of the couch. "Oh, hey," I said, trying to sound casual.

Katie had a knowing look. "Our lunch break ran a little long."

"It might as well have turned into dinner," Terrence added with a chuckle.

"I noticed." I raised my eyebrows.

Then Katie walked back outside with Terrence, I'm sure for a little extra privacy. I looked away but did catch their hands intertwined.

What is going on? I waited around for another hour nearly, as they were still standing outside talking. I finally decided to leave. *She'll call me,* I thought. *She better call me.*

. . .

She didn't call until after ten. She explained they decided to just go get dinner, too.

"What is happening?" She howled with laughter. "Who is this man?"

"Canada Man," I teased.

"Emma, he is a freaking dream. I feel like I could talk to him for hours."

"*Feel* like? Katie, you did talk to him for hours. Almost twelve hours straight."

"I've never had a connection like this with anyone. It was like magic. I mean, you saw, he's really cute. But also, it was a lot more than that. We had a connection right away."

"I could tell," I admitted. "I saw it there right away."

"Right?" she said excitedly. "I shouldn't get my hopes up. He *is* Canada Man. He lives in a different country."

"Well, don't end it before it's even started," I interjected.

"But isn't Canada one giant disqualifier?" I could hear her frowning through the phone.

"Maybe it's not," I said. "You can't know that until you two have talked about it. I mean, he seems like he's kinda in charge of a lot of his work. What'd he say? 'If you're free, I can be free.' Seems like maybe he could be anywhere whenever he wanted."

She moaned all angsty and dramatic, as if in romantic anguish. "I don't even know what to do."

"What feels right?" I asked simply.

"Seeing him tomorrow feels right," she said after a beat. "I'd be a fool to do anything but give it a chance."

"I think so too. I've never heard you talk about a guy like this."

"I can't believe it..." she trailed off. "I've known him twelve hours, but I can't imagine not talking to him now."

"Crazy how it just takes one person to show up and change everything."

"One person, one day, one cup of coffee," she said, sounding like the tagline of a rom-com.

"Well, tell me everything about Canada Man. What's he like?"

Twenty

JORDAN BOYFRIEND <3

Hey, I haven't heard back from you since I sent my last message. Just wanted to say hi and that I'm thinking of you. Hope you're doing well?

ME

Sorry I got busy that day and forgot to reply. I'm doing well! Things are looking up in the job world. Hope you're good too.

JORDAN BOYFRIEND <3

I'm doing pretty good. Work is good, business is good. I've been missing you. I drive by Coffee & Commas and think about popping in like every day. Maybe I will. I was remembering last Feb when you tried skiing- how you never gave up until you got it perfect.

JORDAN BOYFRIEND <3

Do you remember how my whole family was calling you Snow Bunny?

ME

I remember. Great memories!

JORDAN BOYFRIEND <3

So many great memories.

Jordan's text came in while I was in a blur of packing and planning for my weekend trip to Oklahoma. I tried to be lowkey about it, like a casual friend replying to another casual friend's third—or fourth—message. I quickly replied without letting myself overthink it. But he sent another message. Then another.

I remembered that trip last February. The moment I read it, images of snow falling on us as he spun me around in his thick arms, hot chocolate with his family around a crackling fire, how he called me Snow Bunny while I learned how to ski, and I called him Coach. It all came back.

What else came back? How could someone go from your everything to someone you were praying didn't pop by your place of work? How you can be talking about forever, kissing in the snow, and a year later be living with a giant empty space in your life that you're trying not to feel. An empty space in your dinner plans, your text threads, your lunch breaks, your very brain space, your considerations, and comforts.

But it was a space I was getting used to...even liking, to be honest. A space didn't have to be lacking just because it was empty. I was starting to view that space as potential. I was starting to view it with creativity and even hope on my better days. Until I was sitting by a half-packed suitcase rereading his messages. His last message came through, and I purposely didn't reply.

I tried to go back to packing. I tried to regain the excitement and glee I had been feeling until my phone pinged. I didn't, but I tried.

• • •

Somehow, I was able to get Katie to leave the coffee shop for a couple of days and go with me on my weekend trip to Oklahoma. She said she wanted something to take her mind off Terrence flying off to Canada at the end of this week, anyway. Luckily a flight to Tulsa, Oklahoma wasn't too pricey, and she didn't have to pay for a hotel since she was just going to stay with me in my room which was covered by the magazine.

During the flight, I read the list of article requirements that came with the sponsorship by the Littleton's Board of Tourism that had made the deal—photo requirements, places I needed to see, etc. This kind of writing felt so foreign to me. I found myself starting to anxiously begin writing the article in my mind, even though we hadn't even touched down in the city yet.

We landed in the Tulsa International Airport and rented a red Jeep Patriot and drove it all the way to this little town in Oklahoma. We were booked in a local boutique hotel. We gushed over the handwritten welcome note waiting on the desk and the goodie back sourced from Littleton's shops and local businesses. And the hotel clerk chatted with us right away and had her own list of recommendations to add to my own to-do list.

Once we had dropped our bags in the room and changed clothes, Katie looked to me and asked, "So what do we do now?"

This was my work trip, after all. I was supposed to know and to have a plan ready. I felt in over my head like the sea of choices I'd made to get myself here was slowly rising over my capabilities. I pulled out my phone and nervously went over my to-do list for the hundredth time. Where to begin?

I finally guessed, "I'm not sure. I guess we just do something on the list and then keep going from there?"

Katie calmly and collectedly said, "Sure, that sounds good to me." She grabbed her purse as I almost walked out the door without mine. Luckily, she grabbed it for me along with hers.

I drove us to our first stop, hands shaking as I put the rental car in park. I was racking my brain, trying to prepare for what I should focus on, what I should be looking for. What would the readers what from my piece? Should I put a spin on it?

We wandered around the little town government building with a friendly tour guide. I anxiously took random notes about facts he was sharing as if I were studying for a test. Katie kept rubbing my shoulder in a way she hadn't done since we were in line for a rollercoaster back in high school... A roller coaster I ran away from once we got to our turn in line.

After that, we went to another stop and another. All the while, I was studying, taking notes as if I'd taken all the grind from my reporting with me on this trip but left behind all the fun and inspiration.

I was mindlessly leaving my things places, a habit I hadn't had since finals week my senior year of college. So far, I had lost my purse, my sunglasses, my wallet, and potentially all my creativity.

"Em," Katie said as we walked out of the Human Bean. She helpfully guided me back to where I had parked. "Do you really think you need this coffee?"

I laughed along maniacally but kept sipping.

"Em," she said again, a stern tone in her voice. "Are you okay?"

"Yes." I was trying to open the car door while balancing my purse, phone, and coffee cup in my arms. She came over to my side of the car and opened it for me.

"I think you're a little freaked out."

"No, no," I said, obviously lying, as I climbed into the driver's seat. "I want to write this."

"I didn't ask if you want to write this. I know you do. I asked if you were okay. You can want to do this *and* also be totally freaked out," she said after sliding into the passenger seat.

I put my coffee in the cup holder. I looked to her and just sighed, a deep, surrendering sigh.

"Em, you just got this job like two days ago. Now we're in this random town and you're supposed to write about it. You've never written an article like this. It makes sense to be freaked out. I'm in the freaked-out boat with you."

"You are?" I asked since she didn't seem freaked out at all.

"I am definitely freaked out. Just about different things, of course." She winked. "I guess Canada Man has really done a number on both of us."

"I guess he really has," I said, my voice small. She put her hand on mine, and I took a breath in and out. In and out. "I think I'm lost. I have no idea what I'm doing. I'm trying to report on this city when I know that's not what they want. I just don't know how to come up with what they want."

"Don't ask yourself what they want. What do *you* want to write?"

"It doesn't feel that simple. I came into this thinking I'd know exactly what to do. I've been a reporter for years, after all. Now that I'm doing this...I feel out of my element. Like someone asked me for a latte and now I'm standing in front of an espresso machine, but I've only ever made drip coffee."

"Oh, your first barista analogy. Makes me miss Coffee & Commas."

I sipped my own latte while Katie watched me thoughtfully. She said, "I'm not the person who can help you with this." She then pulled out her phone. "I know who to call."

I started to panic. The last person I wanted to share these anxieties with was Terrence, my very new boss. I shook my head no at her as the phone rang.

"Hey," a familiar voice said over the speakerphone. My whole body sighed. Tears of relief started to stream down my face as Gabe's voice, even velvety through the phone, said, "Hello?"

"Hi," I said, taking the phone into my own hands.

"Em? I thought this was—"

"I'm on Katie's phone," I explained, wiping my eyes.

"Are you crying?" he asked, concern in his voice.

"Yeah, sorry," I sniffled. "I'm having a little freak out over the new job."

"Oh," he said gently. "What's freaking you out?"

"I'm just a little lost," I said. "I feel out of my element. I had a whole espresso machine versus drip coffee analogy I used earlier."

"Yeah, you know, it's a whole other format, isn't it? Plus, you just get dropped in this new city, and you have to figure out what you're looking for—what you want to say about it."

"Exactly! I'm not used to just dropping into random cities in the first place. And now I'm taking these notes, like an embarrassing number of notes, but they're just like a bunch of random facts."

"Our reporter Em with her handy notebook. As you go, you'll find your own style and voice, of course, but can I tell you what I do?"

"Please tell me what you do." I said. Katie slipped out of the car to call Rose from my phone.

"I take notes on things like the feelings the places give me, the tastes, the people around me, the weather, you know...what actually makes the trip. Later, you can see what keeps popping up. It'll tell you a lot about the city and your experience. That's where the themes and perspectives will also show up—I know *Here & There* is big on that."

"Okay, that's a good tip. I like that." I felt my shoulders relax. "I'm also feeling kind of stuck with this to-do list that goes with the sponsorship and also the itinerary I have... I'm trying..." But that was all I had. I was just trying.

"I always remind myself—don't fit the story to the activities but make the activities fit the story," he said. "You know what I'm saying?"

"I think I do," I said. "Thank you." I leaned my head back on my driver's seat, closing my eyes for a minute. "I think I've been making it all about the checklist and the expectations, forgetting I'm hunting for a story and can use all this extra to help to tell that story."

"There's my reporter." His voice was soft like melted chocolate.

"I wish you were here," I whispered, the words only meant to flitter through my mind escaping from my lips.

"I could be," he said quickly. His voice was a whisper, too, making my body buzz.

"Really? Would you actually hop on a flight because I'm having trouble with a story?"

"Yes. Definitely. I'd hop on a flight because you were bored and wanted company. I'd hop on a flight because you forgot toothpaste and I had a tube. I'd be where you needed me."

I laughed. "I don't know if I believe that."

"Do you want me there?" he asked, his voice a challenge. A match against a box.

I always want him there, I thought. Then the car door opened.

"You guys still talking?" Katie asked. Her voice was loud and cheerful, like someone turning on the lights on a sleepy gray morning in bed.

"Yeah," I hiccupped. "He gave me just the advice I needed."

"Hi, you!" Katie grabbed her phone, turning it onto speaker.

"Hey, Little Sis," he said coolly. "Well, Em, you've wanted to travel and write for forever, just enjoy it. Have some fun. You *like* doing this, remember?"

"I hope I like doing this," I said a little cynically.

"Come on, you know you're excited," he urged me on.

I nodded. "She's nodding," Katie told him.

"You know me, I just get in my head," I said.

"That's a good thing. You're a writer. That's where you're supposed to be," he said, again, just what I needed to hear.

After the phone call with Gabriel, I drove downtown. We just wandered around. If it happened to be on the itinerary, great, but if it didn't, that was fine too. That became the mindset for the entirety of the trip. I found the first hint of the story, like an outline, as I lay in bed that first night. The rest of my trip, all we saw and did filled in the outline.

I met the people, I ate good food, and I wrote about all of it. I let the hotel clerk guide me more than the to-do list. I learned about the relentless wind that felt like a monument of the city itself, just as much as the downtown statue. I tasted the delectable barbecue sauce that literally everyone in the diner was ordering. I went over to the little church across the street from our hotel that was packed with people coming and going even though it wasn't even Sunday.

Once I found the story, the to-dos, the activities, and tourist traps fit in easily, helping the narrative as I went, like when you're falling in love with someone and everything you discover just keeps you falling. The weekend went by quickly, like any good trip. I stayed up writing as Katie slept, but I never felt tired. Maybe I was too happy and wired to notice it if I did.

On my last night, it was the wee hours, and Katie was fast asleep on her bed a few feet from mine. I was working, my mind getting fuzzy and tired as I reclined back on the fluffy hotel pillows. My phone lit up, and a message popped up on my laptop screen.

GABRIEL

When do you get back?

Seeing that message hit my body like a shot of espresso. I sat up straight and stared at the screen. I minimized my story and typed a reply.

ME

We fly home tomorrow.

ME

Why?

GABRIEL

Wasn't sure if I should book a flight out or not.
Would be embarrassing to land at the Tulsa
airport while you're flying away.

ME

You were not about to book a flight.

Then he sent a screenshot of flights from Texas to Oklahoma. My heart leapt into my throat. *He was looking?*

ME

Why not come yesterday?? Why'd you wait until now?

GABRIEL

well it's not like you ever did tell me that you really wanted me there.

GABRIEL:

I just couldn't take it anymore and decided maybe I'd just show up anyway, then I remembered Katie said she'd be gone 'just the weekend'

I typed out, *I always want you here,* but then I deleted it.

ME

I wish you'd sent me this message earlier.

GABRIEL

me too

GABRIEL

how's the story?

ME

it was a little tough at first, but then it came naturally. It's been fun to write. I'm writing right now.

GABRIEL

sorry to be interrupting!

ME

I like the distraction. I was pretty much done now anyway.

GABRIEL

I like to imagine you in your hotel bed, all propped up on pillows, typing away.

I took a selfie and sent it.
He hearted it.

GABRIEL

best pic ever

ME

how've you been?

GABRIEL

I've been working on my own story, too. I got an assignment that was more of a think piece about the travel industry. Not as fun as booking flights and eating new food.

GABRIEL

but it was fun to write, too. I had more opinion than I thought.

ME

hahaha

ME

I always assume you have a billion opinions.

ME

I could say 'cheese is good' and know you could write a think piece about it

GABRIEL

next piece I'm writing is on the cheese industry

ME

you're welcome for being your inspiration

On the drive back to the airport, I was excitedly giving Katie a rundown on my story.

"What do you think?" I asked her breathlessly.

"I think it's going to be a hit," she said, reassuring me.

"I'd love that, but I'm just hoping Terrence approves of it and then sends me another assignment."

"You know, he's going to be hiring some columnists, staff writers, and more editors. He's getting an office set up. The magazine is getting their print periodical, and they're starting a podcast, and they're going to start a book club... It's really growing. I wonder if you could become an official staff writer?"

"Let's just hope for another freelance project for now. It's all my heart can take," I said. But after a beat, I added, "Though that would be amazing."

"I could say something to him?"

"No, your relationship is just about you two." I shook my head.

"Though, you are the reason we met, kind of, sort of. You brought him to Sweet River, which brought us together."

"I'm a matchmaker, huh?" I said dreamily.

"Our matchmaker. Katie and Canada Man. Hey, you could write your next article about us!" Katie said all sappy and sweet.

We stopped at a red light when Katie said, "Oh, you know who we need to update?" She dialed up Gabriel before I could say anything.

"Gabe!" Katie cheered as his face appeared in the FaceTime window.

"Katie!" he cheered, then squinted and saw me. "Emma!"

"Hey, Gabe," I said, casual and cool.

"Are you two home now?" he asked.

"We're on the way to the airport," Katie said. "We wanted to tell you how great the trip went after your call."

"Yeah?" he said as if we hadn't been messaging about this just hours ago.

"Yeah, your advice was just what I needed to hear," I said, looking at the road but listening to him.

"Ah, Em, I didn't say much. You're a fine writer, though I'm always there if you need me. I can be *right there* anytime." We both chuckled, and Katie gave a half shrug.

"You're always my voice of reason," I said.

"Hey, you know, I got to keep my favorite writer writing. It's a little selfish, really," he joked.

"The feeling is—" but then another call was breaking in. "Sorry, we're getting another call." I glanced at the phone screen.

"Oh, it's Jordan!" Katie gasped. I realized Katie had called Gabe from my phone, as the incoming call was from Jordan—with the heart emoji still there. "You two were just texting, weren't you? All those mushy memories from that little mountain trip. What if he's calling to—"

"Here, I'll let y'all go. I was working on something anyway," Gabriel said abruptly hanging up. My heart sank.

Jordan's call was still incoming.

"Want me to answer it?" Katie asked.

"I guess?" I said, unsure. She answered the call, putting it on speaker again.

I said, "Jordan?"

"Em," he said, his voice shaky.

"What's up?" I asked.

"I was calling because," his voice broke. "Nana died."

Katie gasped. I went still.

Nana was his mom's mom. She was a huge part of his life... and our life together. She made us dozens of dinners. She was there at birthday and graduation parties. She read every article I wrote and always sent me little compliments, always including favorite quotes. She meant a lot to Jordan but also to me.

"Oh no." My hands trembled on the steering wheel. "I'm so sorry."

"Thanks," he said reflexively.

"What happened?" Katie and I exchanged a distressed glance.

"She had a heart attack. She was in bed asleep. My mom went over when she wasn't answering her calls the next day. I think she kind of had a feeling."

"That's awful." I could see her tight gray curls, her loose chiffon tops, and her little hand always grabbing mine and giving it a squeeze when she saw me.

"Yeah. I just thought you should know. You know she loved you," he said the last part quietly.

"I loved her, too," I said.

"I know. You loved all of us, huh?" he said roughly. "Well, day after tomorrow is the funeral. If you want to come."

It was quiet. "Do you want me there?" I didn't want to make it a harder day for him. I didn't want my presence to take any attention.

He didn't say anything for a minute.

Finally he said, "You know, I do want you there. It'd mean a lot to the whole family."

"I'll be there then," I said.

I hung up the phone and took in a jagged breath. Katie's hand was on my shoulder again, like she had done only a couple of days ago, a message of support.

I tried to get my thoughts in order after we parked the car. Katie was quietly on her phone, so I had a moment of quiet that felt like it was mine alone.

I had a billion thoughts in my head, like a server carrying too many plates, trying to balance, trying not to let one drop and crash. The grief over Nana, the excitement over my career, as well as the task ahead of boarding my flight and getting home, finishing, and submitting my story. Then there was Gabriel, our messages last night, and what he may or may not have heard Katie say during our call and…. All of this, I was carrying as I sat at the airport's car rental area.

Katie interrupted my moment of quiet. "Ready to go?"

"Yeah," I said, pulling the keys from the ignition.

My thoughts had no chance of getting in order, anyway.

Twenty-One

The funeral will be Wednesday morning at 10.
At Oak Grove Chapel.

I spent the airplane ride finishing my article. I bought Wi-Fi to send it in before we landed, and I had to put my laptop away.

As the plane landed, the escape of being in the air and being inside my laptop was gone. Airplane rides had always felt like a little bubble up above the rest of the world to me, where I could leave any worries or fears or sadness down below and pick back up once we landed.

We were back on land now, where someone I loved was gone —where a family I loved was hurting. Where a man I cared for was grieving and needing comfort. But I was not the one to comfort him any longer, right? Or was I? What were the rules? What was okay? Should I be reaching out? Was it heartless and cruel to not call or show up? After all we had between us. Or was it heartless and cruel to reinsert myself?

The thoughts came rushing over me as I waited at baggage claim. Katie was standing a few feet from me. She was quiet, too.

I kept opening Jordan's text thread, trying to muster up the right words of comfort that were genuine, but also, I don't know...*appropriate*, I guess. Was there a handbook on how to be there for your grieving ex? I kept wiping away tiny, warm tears.

Nana's homemade chocolate chip cookies that she always had on hand. Her laidback, loving attitude. She always said she'd seen enough in the world to know we shouldn't sweat the small stuff. She was running around in her sneakers, pulling out the paper plates, and laughing loudest at the party.

The baggage carousel suddenly roared to life and stunned me back to the present. I dropped my phone in my back pocket and watched for my bag and Katie's. I grabbed both and then walked over to her. She thanked me, and we rolled our bags through the parking lot in silence.

"Hey, are you okay?" she asked once we were on the road driving home. "You've seemed shaken since we stepped off the plane. I know you were close to Nana."

"Oh," I said distractedly. "Yeah, I'm pretty sad to have lost her. I'm sad for the whole family, you know. And I'm worried for Jordan."

She nodded.

"Should I call him or send him a message?"

"Yeah." She nodded. "I think so. I mean, you probably shouldn't show up at his house or start hanging out...but one of your sweet messages will probably go a long way."

We didn't say anything for a while longer.

Then, after some time, I said, "What do I say?"

She opened her mouth confidently, then paused. She didn't say anything. Finally she said, "I don't know. I don't think there are perfect words in this moment."

And before we could brainstorm a response, we were at her house. While she collected her things, she asked if I wanted to come in for a while. I saw that janky old truck parked out front and told her that I was too tired, but thanks anyway.

I got to my apartment and took a long hot shower and wrote messages to Jordan in my mind. I wrapped myself up in my favorite blue towel and then lay on my bed.

I wasn't sure how to be Jordan's ex or how to have him as my ex. For two full years, he was my boyfriend and one of the closest people in my life. He was top of the line for two years. My first call. He was someone I kissed on the mouth, someone I said "I miss you" to when we were apart, and someone who brought me soup when I was sick. Someone whose family called me their own. Nana had called me her favorite little writer. How to operate as anything other than that Emma felt fake.

If we rewound a couple of months, I wouldn't even be in my apartment right now. I would be at his house. I wouldn't be sending pathetic messages. I would be on the phone with him. I would be at his side. I would be mourning Nana with him. I would be hugging his mom close, sharing stories. I would be telling them, "She always put my stories on her fridge under a magnet."

I started crying. Tears falling from my eyes. I didn't message him. I called. He didn't answer, so I left a rambling, but honest, voicemail, telling him all the things I should've said when he first called.

I didn't listen to any music as I drove to the church the day of the funeral. I wore a black chiffon dress with lacy sleeves. My hair was tied into a knot at my neck. I parked my car and looked up at the sky through the window. The sky, which had been gray for weeks, was suddenly electric blue. The sun was so bright it was making me hot underneath my dress. I unbuckled slowly, searching the parking lot for Katie's car or my parent's. I spotted my mom and dad and let out a big breath.

During the service, a pastor spoke to us about life and legacy.

Later, one of Jordan's uncles gave a eulogy that made people laugh and also made them cry in that bittersweet way funerals of the elderly, of people who had a good and fair amount of days, can be.

I kept thinking about the time I was seventeen years old, and my mom and dad were going to the funeral of an old friend of theirs. I was eating a sandwich at the kitchen table. Mom and Dad were by the door, buttoning up their coats, when Mom sighed and said, "So it begins, the older you get, the more funerals you attend."

"Well, that's a little morbid, hon," my dad said, but he still laughed.

The service ended, so we all rose to give our condolences and leave the building and resume, what, normal life? Knowing full well that his family wouldn't be resuming normal life. They would be grasping at how to enter this new life, this different life.

I really wanted to see Jordan and his family. I wanted to give them hugs, to somehow send a message through my face and my touch that I loved them, that I cared, that I saw—that I was sorry.

I saw them huddled by the door, people giving kind words and touches as they exited the building. My parents and I got into line as a little three-person unit. We whispered about the eulogy, about things we were surprised to learn about Nana. As we got closer to the family, the line moving along, I noticed an extra person was standing with the family the entire time as if claiming themselves as a member.

Sophia. There she stood—in a black A-line dress and another glossy ponytail—*with Jordan's family*. She was being hugged along with all of them like she was one of them. I was completely confused. How long had it been since I was at her father's repair shop? A few weeks? The line moved closer and closer.

I turned to my mom, locked eyes, and nodded my head toward Sophia. Mom glanced in that direction but shot me a puzzled look. She didn't recognize Sophia as Jordan's ex, as

Jordan's biggest heartbreak and longtime girlfriend before his two-year blip with me. Was I now a blip?

I imagined him whispering, "I wished Emma was you the entire time," in her ear. I shook my head. I had no idea what was going on and no right to that information. My dad pointed out how cold it was in the chapel. I nodded in agreement. Mom said it was probably how close we were to the door.

It was almost my turn in the hug line. I looked at the family, and Sophia was standing by Jordan's side solemnly, consistently wrapping her arms around him, giving his mother a comforting arm rub, whispering things into Jordan's ear and his sister's. I had a little bit of an idea of what was going on.

It made sense, I admitted to myself. And he needed comfort, and she seemed to be doing a really good job at providing it. Plus, I thought of my two years, knowing Nana and being loved by her in comparison to the entirety of middle school and high school that Sophia had. Sophia *grew up* with Nana.

I was suddenly next in line. My body felt numb. My feet were shuffling me toward these people who had once felt so familiar to me. Now we were sharing formalities. I could see their pink cheeks, hear their sniffles, and I knew how big this loss was. Yet the familiarity was gone. I was another in the hug line. I wasn't on the sidelines any longer.

I had spent my Saturday afternoons cheering on their cousins at baseball games. I knew their holiday cookie recipe. I knew their food allergies. I knew the family stories, but I wasn't invited to their house after the service. I was fading out of their lives, bleeding into the borders then gone.

I said, "I am just so sorry," to his mother, and she squeezed my hand. I saw Jordan, and tears fell from my cheeks as we embraced.

"Emma." His voice was rocky and broken.

I whispered, "I loved her."

He said, "I know."

We went in for a second hug, and I said, "I love you," and he said it back.

Then, I was shuffled forward in line. As I passed Sophia, she gave me a polite kind nod.

I stumbled outside into the maddening sun. The air was wintry and cool, but the sun wasn't deterred. I waited for my parents on the steps of the church. I held my coat tight as a strong breeze blew harshly against me.

My dad cleared his throat, arriving behind me. I smiled at him.

He asked, "Who was that tall brunette standing with them? A cousin I hadn't met?"

I shook my head. "She..." was his ex? The love of his life? An old family friend? "She was Jordan's high school sweetheart."

I had been trying to deal with the blank space Jordan left in my life, but now I was faced with the blank space I left in his. Was I, to this family, just a blip? A bad memory that ruined Christmas one time. Someone who would show up at funerals and shake their hands. The treading of water after and before Sophia?

"Oh, I remember her," my mom said, standing beside the two of us on the stairs of the chapel. She grabbed my hand and held it all the way to my car.

Twenty-Two

ME

> Hey Gabe! I haven't heard an update on your leg in a while. How're you doing?

GABE

> same ole, same ole. I'm progressing little by little. Still on crutches. Lots of physical therapy.

ME

> I'm here if you need anything.

A day or so later, the sky was still a clear blue, and the sun was brilliant as ever. Katie threw a frisbee outside for Midnight. We were sitting on the grass. Our feet were bare even though the weather was only in the fifties. I had seen Gabe's truck parked in the driveway when I arrived and casually asked Katie if he was there. He was.

I hadn't heard a peep from him, but I'd felt his presence like a magnet pull. I lay on my back with my eyes closed, and I could hear Katie giggle to herself.

"What's got you giggling?" I asked. My eyes were still closed, guessing her answer before she said it.

"Something Canada Man said." Her voice was a little mushy.

As was slowly becoming the norm, she was with me, but also a little bit with Terrence. We would be talking then she would abruptly go silent for a few minutes to reply to a message. I found it adorable to see Katie so consumed with another person after years of being so elusive with guys before this—even the ones she liked.

We started discussing how old we thought Midnight was—potentially nine years old, or was he ten? Or even eleven? When her phone rang. I glanced down as she did to see the name Canada Man lighting up her phone screen as he attempted to FaceTime.

I wiggled my eyebrows, and she asked, "Is it okay if I answer?"

"I don't mind at all," I said, sitting up onto my elbows.

"Hi, you," she said in a tone I'd never heard her use before.

"Hey, beautiful," he said, smooth and soft.

I awkwardly looked toward Midnight, who had plopped down in the middle of the grassy grounds, frisbee abandoned just a few feet away. I tried to ignore the two of them as they shared updates. Vancouver was snowy. She had finished the book she was reading. He was going to get dinner with a friend tonight. She wished he was getting dinner with her.

"Who's that with you?" I heard him say later. I awkwardly sat back up and gave a little wave as Katie said, "Emma."

"How've you been?" he asked.

"I've been good," I said, squinting under the sun. "You?"

"I've been missing the woman holding this phone." He winked. I bumped into Katie's shoulder, playfully giving her a nudge. "How'd you feel about your last assignment?"

I bit my lip. "I had a lot of fun. I really liked where I took the story." I wanted to ask, what did he think? But I had promised myself I wouldn't bring our working relationship into Katie and Terrence's budding relationship.

Yet the question was there on my lips. I had seen and respected the taste and perspective Terrence brought to the magazine. His feedback or advice would be gold.

"That's good, that's good." He was in an office with a window overlooking downtown Vancouver. "Was it an adjustment?"

I briefly wondered if Katie had shared with him what an adjustment my first day had been for me writing-wise. "It was. I had to find out how to work with the new requirements and with the new way of traveling."

"You know, not every piece will be sponsored with the same requirements and specifications. But we do have to have a few," he explained.

I nodded. "I found my flow, anyway," I said chirpily. Some of the questions I had for him were waiting to come out, but I was just scared. Katie was smiling at me as we spoke, completely fine if I asked.

"Well, I'm glad to hear that. We'll send you a few more opportunities. I'll remind Marianne. You know, I was curious. Is this what you want to keep doing? Writing freelance? Or are you doing this while biding your time looking for another staff writing position or maybe reporting? What's the zoomed-out picture there?" He said all of this so fast, so easily, as if the question was at the top of my mind.

I swallowed hard. My heart said, *I want to be writing a column, writing whenever and however I can, and going out with my pen and notepad.*

But my mouth said, "I'm just trying to figure it out as I go. I have a few feelers out there." A vague job-interview answer.

I looked at Katie, who was frowning, but I wasn't sure if it were because of me, the sun shining hot on her face, or Midnight running toward us at that very moment.

He knocked her over with slobbery dog kisses, and she dropped the phone. I could hear her telling Midnight, "No, no, bad dog," and Terrence laughing from the screen.

I felt like I'd not only broken my promise not to interrupt Katie's love life with my work life, but I also felt I'd stumbled around while talking to someone I really respected and wanted advice from.

"Okay, so listen to this," Katie said, putting the phone back on herself.

I tiptoed off to the house as the two of them returned to their call.

Gabriel was upstairs doing something, maybe writing, or reading, or having a FaceTime call of his own. All afternoon I'd kept hoping he'd sit with us outside, that he'd ask me about my trip to Oklahoma, or that he'd tell me about trips of his own. I told myself I wasn't waiting, but when the clock kept ticking. Katie stayed chatting with Terrence, and even Midnight had enough of me and chose to stay behind. I knew I was biding time.

I should leave. I have things to do at home, I told myself as I padded barefoot, shoes in my hand, through the backyard toward the house. I should go pick up some groceries and clean my kitchen. I should work on one of my freelance projects. I should call my mom.

Instead, I slowly walked up the back porch, slid open the glass sliding doors, and meandered through the living room, stopping and looking at framed photos I'd seen a thousand times. I poured myself a glass of water and sipped it in the kitchen.

I "accidentally" or maybe subconsciously purposefully bumped loudly into a barstool and said, "Oops," loudly to the void of the kitchen. In case he hadn't known I was here and only needed to hear my voice. I blushed all the way to my chest afterward at how pathetic this was.

Gabriel stayed upstairs. After all these hours. After my loud "oops." He remained distant, a heavy pull, an undeniable presence, but distant.

I thought about the last time we spoke when I had to hang up because Jordan was calling. And there was the last time I saw his face as he drove away and left me in the parking lot. Neither of those times ended on a good note. I had hoped I could see him and smile at him and maybe make him laugh.

We'd become adept at brushing over things with small talk and pleasantries with "normal." The tension and pull between us, the intense conversations, the desperation for him to walk downstairs and talk to me—all of this was the unspoken "not normal" that we pretended wasn't there, or hadn't happened, by painting over it with "normal."

But instead, he was leaving everything sitting in "not normal" between us by staying upstairs. I emptied the glass and set it quietly in the sink. I walked to the front door, stood for a few moments, and glanced up the stairs. *What would happen if I went and knocked on his door? If I went to him right now?*

My core tingled, reacting to the thought as if my body was saying, "Yes, that's the idea, Emma," but my brain said, "Go home, woman."

Later that night, as I sat on my balcony wrapped in a blanket with a novel in my lap, replaying my earlier conversation with Terrence kept interrupting the story I was reading. He was this pivotal, important person for my writing career. Someone who I felt *got* my writing. He had asked me about my future, point blank, and instead of taking the opportunity to get advice or even plug myself into his magazine, I stumbled.

I looked out at the sunset, blazing pink over the edge of downtown like it was showing off for the last few moments it had left of daytime. I always stumbled around the truth like a boulder I didn't want to run into. Tripping over self-reflection like a trap I don't want to catch me. *What do you want out of the future, Emma?* And I'm scrambling for an exit route, a path around, a way out.

What am I so afraid of? I rubbed the spine of my book and asked myself aloud, "What box are you trying to fit into?" echoing a past conversation I had with Gabriel.

I could remember the late spring night like I was still eighteen, still sitting under the inky black sky beside Gabriel. I could practically hear the crickets even now. *The summer after my senior year, I had been accepted to two colleges, and I was torn between them. Typical indecisive Emma. Both schools had two big champions. The school Katie planned on attending a few hours away, and the school Gabriel was currently attending in New England.*

This particular night, Gabriel was sitting agonizingly close to me, our two lawn chairs pushed up close to each other, encouraging me to choose his school. He was home for spring break, and I'd felt the lack of him the past eight months. I had desperately missed his magnetic presence, his dinnertime conversation, the electrical rush of brushing past him at school, how he would drop book recommendations in my purse, his messy curly hair on lazy Saturdays in their backyard.

So, I was basking in his presence as he told me the wonders of his school's English Department. The firepit was crackling a few feet away from us, and everyone else was deep in other conversations. Only a few moments ago, he'd thrillingly pulled his chair up beside mine.

"Seriously, I think you would really like the professors and all the students in our department—I could see us taking a class together. It'd be so fun, Em," he said to me, earnest and excited.

"Oh," I yawned. "I probably won't major in English even if I do go to your school."

"Really?" he said, surprised. "What are you going to study? Journalism?"

"Business," I said matter of factly.

"Wait, what?" His voice went from surprised to appalled. "Why?"

"It just makes sense for my future. It'd fit most jobs, you know. I know Katie is majoring in business. My dad runs his own business,

so I feel like I kind of know it..." As I answered, I realized how lacking my reasoning was.

If I were honest and not stumbling around the truth, it was because Katie was studying business, I was afraid a real journalism professor would roll his eyes at me and tell me to change majors... and Katie was studying business.

Options first and last made me feel really comfortable knowing Katie and I could go to the same school, do our homework together, and I could just follow her to every class and all over campus. Like a high school do-over with higher stakes.

"Didn't you hate math? You know business degrees require a ton of math, right?" Gabe asked as if some college major expert after one semester in school.

"Katie could help me." I shrugged as if this conversation wasn't deeply serious to me.

"Em, she can't take the tests for you."

I looked at my hands. "I just want..."

"Well, what do you want to do after school? With this business degree?" Gabe's entire body was turned in his seat to face me now. He was leaning in toward me, which would usually thrill me. Instead, I was avoiding eye contact.

I had successfully put off thinking beyond college for months. I could write if I wanted with a business degree, like marketing or something. Or I could open a candy shop or something. I hadn't decided yet. I thought college could help me decide.

"I don't know. I thought college could help me decide." I spoke down toward the blanket on my lap.

"Sure, that works. But what do you like to do? What are you good at?" He was bending his head near to mine, trying to look into my eyes.

"I'm not that good at anything." I kept looking down.

"That's bull. You know you're good at writing. You run the school newspaper. You've won essay contests. You're best friends with your English teacher."

"I'm best friends with Katie," I said defensively.

"But that doesn't mean you're good at what she's good at!" He was getting frustrated with me, and it was making me frustrated with him, and myself.

"You don't get to decide things for me, you know," I said, finally looking up at him. "I'm eighteen years old. I can choose my own major."

"That's fine, Em. You're the only one who has to take the classes you enroll in for four years. The one who will take those tests and make those presentations. You're the one who will miss out on writing classes, English clubs, and meeting people who get all of that passion in you." He gestured toward my heart when he said that. Knowing better than most the passion and creativity I had living in my heart. "No one has to live with your choices but you."

"I'm just trying to do what's right!" I almost shouted, scooting to the edge of my seat like I might just get up. I saw Katie glance over to us. I dropped the blanket to the ground.

"What box are you trying to fit into, Emma?" he said, his voice deep.

"I don't think anyone wants me to fit into any box." My knees were knocking into his as we leaned out of our chairs toward each other.

"You're right," he said. He was thoughtful for a moment. And I've never forgotten what he said next, "No one has ever tried to make you fit into any box, except you."

"That's not it," I said weakly.

I felt exposed, like he'd walked in on me changing or caught me going through his phone or something. What made him think that? And even worse, how did he know? It wasn't necessarily me trying to fit into what I thought anyone wanted from me, but it was me trying to fit into whatever felt less scary, less demanding, or safest. What box could I hide away in? Or could squeeze Katie and my mom in there with me? Or came with instructions?

Even that English teacher, who was my "best friend," as Gabriel said, was the reason I felt safe running that newspaper. I hadn't *even submitted my essay for the contest. The teacher had. But that teacher was staying in Sweet River, and I wasn't.*

"Emma," Gabriel said kindly, waking me from my thoughts. He interlaced his fingers with mine loosely like a caring friend, I knew, but my heart raced anyway. "I just want you to do whatever makes you happy. What school would you be happiest at? Which school gets you the most excited to attend? What major has the coolest classes you can't wait to take? Which assignments get you buzzing—and make you happy. That's all." What he was saying was decision making 101, but I felt what he said like a dose of strong medicine.

"If business makes you happy, you'd probably be great at it. If that's what you really want, you should do it. Business majors are really cool. I mean, Katie is studying it, and I'm ecstatic for her. I have friends who are doing really cool stuff in their classes. I think I was just surprised. You know, I just thought you wanted to write. That's all. I shouldn't have assumed. I'm sorry if I came across pushy."

"You've never been pushy a day in your life, Gabe," I joked softly, not moving a muscle from our two bodies turned toward each other like a funny little heart, knees on knees, hands in hands.

"I care," he said. "I care a lot."

I shimmied my knees against his and said, "I know." I looked at his fingers. Wouldn't it be nice if he could transfer some of his bravery to me, right here, right now, through his touch?

I made the right choices that year. I chose the same school as Katie because it was the choice that made me happy, not just because it was an option that made me feel safe. The journalism classes and the internships made me buzz. I was happy and grateful to live with the choices I'd made.

Now here I was, years later, out of school and still having to make choices that determined my future. It wasn't a one-and-done situation. I didn't decide on journalism, and then a job and future unfolded perfectly before me. Life was a constant step by step up a never-ending staircase, and as much as I wanted a break, or for someone to please carry me up a few of these flights...These steps were mine to take. I might stumble, pause, and go backward or skip a few, but I'd keep going along.

For now, looking from my balcony, it was not a bad view.

Twenty-Three

It was early morning on February 14. I woke up to cloudy gray skies peeking through the curtains over my window, my thick white duvet heavy over me. Aside from a little Valentine's assignment helping Terrence out, I had a blank date on the calendar before me.

February 14 and not much to do. Katie and I had the day off work. Rose wanted to be in the shop, and she had some family helping her. They had decorated the shop festively and made special Valentine-themed treats.

Still in bed, I turned to my side and opened my phone to see my Google memories for the day. Photos from the past couple of Valentine's Days slid by on my photo album carousel.

Jordan and I were grinning over two big bowls of pasta, a tiny silver heart dangled from a chain, a gift from him that day. Another photo, this time it was Jordan and me at a concert, a gift from me to him. Another photo from the same day, one of him kissing my cheek.

I'm just somewhere so different than I've been the past couple of years, I thought to myself.

There was another photo with a big brunch with girlfriends in college. Photos flipped by of us drinking milkshakes outside the movie theater.

Then there was another photo from when I was nineteen. Gabriel, Katie, Logan, and me with big smiles over big burgers. Another one from that day where I'm on Gabriel's back, and Katie and Logan are holding up peace signs. I had forgotten that there had even been a Logan in Katie's life—not quite a boyfriend, but he had really tried.

That Valentine's Day, Katie and I had spur of the moment booked a flight to see Gabriel and cheer him up after he had a really rough week with one of his classes. His roommate, Logan, had an undying crush on Katie, and he had been texting and calling for a while. It was a little flame that flickered out after this trip.

I zoomed in on the photo, pausing the slideshow. I remembered how Gabriel nearly started crying when he spotted Katie and me running up to him on the campus lawn. He'd said, "My girls," when he hugged us.

We spent an exhausting, sweet, fast, fun twenty-four hours getting a little tour of his campus life.

I remembered realizing that Gabriel had a whole world that didn't include me. Friends, classes, a job, girls who said "Hi" and knew him from English Club. I wondered if I ever even popped into his mind, with us being so very far apart.

I had started building my very own separate life, too. It was my freshman year of college, and I had my own campus, my own friends. A life where I never heard the name Gabriel come up, but I still thought it all the time. He didn't need to be woven into my classes and campus. He was embedded into my brain like a favorite song.

I comforted myself by noticing how easily I fit walking by his side, meeting his friends and professors, and how conversation about our classes and new jobs felt effortless. We were growing up and seeming to fit even better. We were both college students mapping out our adult lives, the playing field more even. What we had in common was ever expanding.

"She's cute, Gabe," a friend of his, Chelsie, had said in a hushed tone when I had turned my back for a second in the cafeteria, assuming I was more than whatever I was.

He just "ahemed," not correcting her or denying anything between us. *Did "ahem" mean he agreed?* My cheeks had flushed as I pretended not to overhear anything.

This morning, years later, I threw my phone to the other side of the bed. Literal years had passed, and I was still pretending with Gabriel.

Terrence had emailed me a week ago and asked if I wasn't too busy on Valentine's Day—I laughed when I read that —if I could come up with a way to get Katie to a special surprise location. The location was a lake about an hour outside of Sweet River, where Terrence had rented a boat for the two of them and made reservations at a restaurant by the water. Katie didn't have any idea about Terrence's Valentine's plans. She had actually been mopey and sad that they were—to her knowledge— apart today. She thought she was stuck spending the day with me.

I had been doing my makeup and drinking my coffee when she called.

"Hi, friend," I said, putting the phone on speaker.

"Hey," she said, sounding a little down.

"How are you doing?" I said, putting the finishing touches on my eyeliner.

"I'm feeling like a bad girlfriend."

"Why is that?" I asked as it thundered outside my window.

"You're the absolute best girlfriend. Just ask your adoring boyfriend."

"I feel like I shouldn't be spending my Valentine's Day here in Sweet River. I'm actually thinking about buying a ticket to Vancouver. I could easily take tomorrow off work and fly out today and surprise him. He's so busy with work; it's impossible for him. But I could do it."

"Katie," I said, not wanting to ruin the surprise but at a loss for how to thwart her sweet idea. "You don't have the cash for a spontaneous flight to Canada, do you? Wasn't that one of the main reasons you didn't do that in the first place?"

"I could swing it," she said, warming to her own idea. "If ever a guy was worth a romantic gesture, it's Terrence."

"Are you sure Terrence is even free? If he couldn't take the time off to fly out, isn't he too busy for a visitor?" I was trying to put a crack in her growing resolve.

"That's the point—he could work, and I could be there for his free moments. I could make a romantic dinner or something. I could even make it for him in *his* kitchen. That would be really romantic, wouldn't it?"

"What if..." I was grasping. "What if he doesn't like surprises?"

"No, he'd love it. He's a big spontaneity guy." She took in a deep, excited breath. "I think I should do it. There's a flight around noon. I was scrolling this morning. I have a few hours to get to the airport. I could—"

"Wait, Katie," I said loudly, dropping my makeup brush.

"Why?" She sounded startled.

"I need you," I squeaked. "I was really looking forward to... our time together today. I just haven't been alone on Valentine's Day in so long... I just...I need...you."

"Em?" She sounded confused. "You haven't... I hadn't realized how important our plans were..." I hadn't shown any signs of being heartbroken lately. I had been doing fine. I had barely put effort or much thought into our faux plans either.

"I was just looking forward to getting brunch and then going and seeing that movie together. I already bought our tickets and everything," I said, trying to sound sentimental. I had only purchased one ticket to that movie.

"Well, okay, yeah, you know it's not like he's expecting me or anything," she said. "It was just an impulsive idea. I'd love to spend the fourteenth with you."

I breathed a silent sigh of relief as we sorted out what time I would be there to pick her up for our brunch plans that were out of town, which she thought was silly when we could just go to our favorite place downtown.

When I picked her up, she ran out her door in a red sweater dress similar to the cream one I was wearing. A light rain fell overhead as she held her purse over her topknot as protection. I could tell she was still doubting her choice to stay in town and not fly off to Vancouver, as she sadly mentioned that she hadn't had a boyfriend on Valentine's Day since junior high. She made a pathetic joke that she should've known she'd still be spending it with friends.

Then quickly added, "No offense." I was mildly offended. Though, I, too, would rather have spent my Valentine's Day with a handsome guy than with her.

She started to question me when I told her our out-of-town brunch place was an hour away. "Why are we going so far for pancakes?" We zoomed toward the lake.

By the time we were almost there, I could tell she had suspicions but was afraid to get her hopes up. She was questioning me but disguising it by pretending she was just making jokes.

"What, did Canada Man send some special gift out here or something? Haha, just kidding. Just kidding!"

At the parking lot where Terrence had set as our meeting place, he stood leaning against the car with a single red rose in his hand, resting against his chest. She was silent as we pulled up beside him. I parked the car and turned to look at her, and her eyes were brimming with tears.

"I've just never..." But she didn't need to say anything else because I knew.

I had been with her all these years, wondering why no one had ever noticed that Katie was, well, Katie. Every guy should have been buying her a single red rose and flying across the countries to kiss her on the lips. I realized now why they hadn't been. None of those boys we met along the way were Terrence. The one she was about to book a flight for, too.

I squeezed her hand and said, "And you almost flew off this morning."

She wiped her eyes, chuckling. "This is why you were being *so* weird."

He knocked on the car door. She pushed it open. "There she is," he said in a sing-song voice.

She threw herself into his arms, and he swung her around. It was sprinkling rain overhead while they kissed, but they didn't care at all.

Twenty-Four

I did treat myself to a brunch, all for me. My parents were off on a weekend getaway. Katie was off having rainy Valentine's kisses, and I was pouring strawberry syrup over a pile of pancakes and enjoying every single bite. I had two caramel lattes and cherished every sip.

I was walking from the café toward the movie theater under the thick gray sky when I spotted him. A tall curly-haired man standing outside the theater looking up at the movie posters while leaning on one crutch—though I was pretty sure he was still supposed to be using two.

As I glanced down at his casted-up leg, I remembered writing on his cast in seventh grade when he broke his arm. *Gabe drools, and Emma Rules* was my clever little remark.

"Gabriel Hernandez," I shouted, my mouth still sweet from breakfast. He was wearing a thick navy sweater with a beat up jacket overtop and dark blue jeans.

"Emma Brown." His lips curled into that mischievous smile, and my whole body felt warm.

"You have a hot Valentine's date?" I asked, arriving by his side. I felt the urge to touch him, to grab his sleeve or press my shoulder into his.

"Nah, just me." He shook his head. "Which movie are you seeing?"

"That rom-com, *Two for the Show*," I said. "Of course."

"Fancy that, me too," he said.

"Hey, want to sit together? I'll share my popcorn."

"Perfect, I'll share my candy," he said while we turned to walk into the theater. As the door closed behind us, he said, "Does that make me your hot Valentine's Date?"

Then he dropped his voice lower as the cold air of the theater hit me. "Or you mine?" He winked.

After the movie, we wandered out into the humid afternoon. The sun was hazily peeking out behind the rain clouds here and there.

"I don't know if the couple really liked each other," he mused as we walked out of the theater.

"Why do you say that?" I asked, checking my phone absent-mindedly.

"I think she was secretly into his best friend, honestly."

"No, no, Gabe you are not going to ruin this movie for me." I put my finger to his lips to hush him. They were soft and cool. He was quiet as I requested. I could feel his breath catching, like my own. I yanked my hand away, watching as he licked his lips. *I bet they taste like butter.*

I started walking. He tagged along.

"Are you hungry?" he asked, his pace meeting mine.

I had just eaten my weight in pancakes and then popcorn, but I said, "I could go for a drink."

We found a little Mexican restaurant and decided to see if they had a table, pondering Valentine's Margaritas.

"We are completely booked with reservations," the hostess apologized. We went to a couple more restaurants until we found a little Italian place. The spot was crammed with guests, but they had open seating at the bar.

The restaurant oozed romance with couples everywhere, red roses, hand holding, low voices, Champagne bubbling, and jazz coming from the speakers. I saw one man putting a ring in a Champagne flute. I started to sweat.

The two of us felt delicate and fragile. This little buzzing we had between us was sustained with jokes and making light of any tension between us. How would we handle this under dim lighting? Last time we sat at a bar, we made out that very night. I swallowed hard. I kept thinking of my finger on his lips and his breath catching.

As we slid onto barstools, he tried to rest his crutches beside us without taking up too much space at the bar. Once we were both settled, I could feel our shoulders touching.

"What can I get you and your girlfriend?" the bartender asked.

I started to laugh, but before I could say anything, Gabriel turned to me and said, "I have an idea."

We bought a bottle of Prosecco and took it to the park.

When we climbed out of his truck, I told him I was cold. He grabbed his sweatshirt from his car and tossed it to me like it was the most natural thing in the world.

Here I was spending the fourteenth with Gabriel while wearing his sweatshirt. What was this territory we're entering? Did it mean anything? But I reminded myself this was an accident. We just ran into each other.

I settled deep into his sweatshirt and thought how my fifteen-year-old self would've fainted at how good it smelled like piney aftershave, and mint gum, and him. Maybe my current self would faint.

The ground was muddy under our feet, and the picnic table was damp. But I was passing a bottle of wine back and forth with Gabriel, so I didn't care.

"Hey," he said as we sat on the table with our feet on the bench. "Can I tell you something kind of awkward?"

"Sure?" I said, then took a sip of the bottle.

"I saw Jordan with that girl from the mechanic shop. They were in one of those restaurants we stopped in." I was secretly pleased he didn't remember her name. "Just the two of them sitting at a candlelit table."

"Oh," I said. "That isn't too surprising. They seemed reunited at his Nana's funeral."

He nodded, gauging my reaction. "Sorry if I shouldn't have brought it up. I just thought I should tell you."

"No, I'm glad you told me. It kind of confirms my own suspicions. I'm glad to know."

"Are you okay?" he asked, a little hesitant, like walking on unsteady ground.

"Yeah, you know, it actually makes a lot of sense. The two of them. They were always so perfect together, all through high school. And the way he talked about her like, in his mind, it should've been the two of them, but she left so he was..." I sighed. "I guess he was settling for me until she returned."

"That's not exactly the story, Em. He wanted to *marry you*, and you broke up with him. Right now, *you could be engaged*." He took a big swig of Champagne.

I took a swig, too. "Yeah, he wanted to marry me if he couldn't marry her. I'm so glad I followed my instincts because there was so much we couldn't have survived, including the return of Sophia."

He shook his head. "Emma, you don't realize the force of a woman you are."

"I don't feel much like a force. This story with Jordan makes me feel like a little blip in Sophia and his story. I just look at what we had differently now. I had already questioned my feelings, and now I'm questioning his. Not angrily. Not bitterly. Just in hindsight. I'm not the main character, not the Sophia, just a little blip in the real love story."

"You are no blip, Emma. I don't care what guy it is or whoever shows up. You are impossible to be a blip in a story.

You're the girl a guy writes a story about. She's just him reeling from the loss of you, I'm sure." His eyes were soft on me.

I pushed my arms against his. He was absolutely wrong. Sophia was quite obviously now the story for Jordan, but Gabriel made my heart twist in my chest. I liked how he talked about me. I liked my name in his mouth. He handed me the Champagne.

"I think I'm happy for Jordan, actually," I said.

He had this little smile. He was trying to hold it back with the corners of his mouth resisting the pull as he said, "I'm glad you're taking it so well."

"You don't believe me?" I raised an eyebrow.

"I believe you."

"Why are you doing this weird little smile then?" I pointed at his mouth, almost touching his lips again.

"That's not what I'm smiling about," he said, trying not to laugh.

"What?" I asked. Our noses were almost touching. We were laughing with our breath mingling, and we both smelled like his cologne.

The sky cracked with loud thunder. My body was buzzing from the bubbly drink, from his closeness.

"It's probably about to rain," he said. His eyes were stuck on mine.

"I don't mind," I said. "I like to be in the rain."

"Me, too. It's one of the things I hate about California. It never rains."

"I remember. It's one of the things we have in common." I looked at the sky.

"One of the many." He was smiling again.

"I know. Katie sometimes calls us twins."

"I don't like that." He shivered dramatically. I laughed, but relished it because I always hated the nickname too.

"Do you still want to buy some big old house someday?"

"Yes," I said. "I want to break down walls and paint rooms strange bright colors." I

"Me, too," he said. "I like old houses." *And I like you,* I thought.

"Do you still want ten kids?" I asked.

"Not, ten. I never said ten. I want a big family, though."

"Me too. I want one of those loud families."

"Like mine?"

"Louder." I said emphatically.

"I want to pile them all into cars and take them road tripping with us." He gestured with the bottle still in his hand.

"I can see you with a baby carrier on," I teased.

"I bet I look good like that," he said.

Our arms were still stuck to each other like glue. We were so close we kept pushing into each other. We would turn to look at each other when we spoke, and our faces would touch. It felt like we were waiting for something, but I didn't know what.

"I want all that, too," I said.

"I remember how we even wanted the same jobs. The same school for a little while. The same awards," he said, almost wistfully.

"You're lucky we were in different grades," I said. "You'd have lost a lot more than you did if I were a grade ahead."

He sighed happily, so I did too. I rested my head on him.

"You know what's funny?" I said. "We even had the same Valentine's Day plans."

"Yeah," he said awkwardly. "About that."

"What?" I refused to move my head from its rightful place on his shoulder.

"I actually kind of engineered that. Katie had mentioned the movie you two were going to for your Valentine's Day plans. But see, Terrence had reached out to me as a backup in case you couldn't get Katie out there for his surprise and also so the family didn't worry about her and wonder where she was all day. So, when I heard about the movie, I assumed that you might still go. I decided to show up. I did plan on hanging around all afternoon because I hadn't thought to ask her which time you were going to, but luckily my first guess worked out."

"The first guess was also the first showing," I laughed. Feeling a little bolder, and without thinking, I tangled my fingers into his. He curved his hand around mine. We sat like that for a while, my head resting on his shoulder our hands laced together. We stopped talking, stopped joking.

"Are you really happy for Jordan?" Gabriel's voice was a whisper against my hair.

"I could feel you questioning that," I said. "Yes. I'm happy for him. I wasn't in love with him the way I should've been, and I didn't want to give him the things he wanted so badly. Sophia will give him all of that. She'll give him the love I didn't have for him."

"That all sounds nicely logical and wise, but..." He swallowed. "Are you missing him?"

"No." I shook my head. "I don't think I would call it 'missing' him. I've just had to adjust to his absence in my life."

He was looking down at our intertwined fingers, and I could feel how the idea of Jordan and me, and me missing him, or longing for him, had been bothering Gabriel, just like it had when we talked at the mechanics. It was blistering and bugging him all winter.

"He had been this presence in my life for years. I care about him. To just cut out his place in my life...I've felt that missing piece. It wasn't a piece that belongs. It's not a piece I'm up at night crying for, but I've felt it. I've had to get used to this new normal, and it is becoming normal," I said. "That's all. I'm not missing him. I'm not jealous of Sophia."

"Okay," he said. Nothing else.

"Can I ask you something?"

"Sure," he looked up at me.

"How're you doing being stuck home?"

He laughed loudly. "Why does everyone think I hate home just because I don't live here permanently?"

"I don't think you hate home!" Though I did a little bit. It was his reputation.

"No, no, I know how you and the whole family talk about me like I betrayed the family by moving off to California. I must hate Texas. I can write 'anywhere,' my mom says, so it must mean something if I'm not writing from Sweet River."

I had opened a can of worms. "Gabriel, I was meaning to ask how it felt being stuck with a broken femur and laid up in your house. I didn't mean being stuck in Sweet River. I mean literally stuck indoors and not traipsing around the country."

"Oh," he said sheepishly. "I guess I was on the defense. Mom and the family are always on me, trying to get me to move back, especially lately."

"It's their way of saying they miss you. Mostly everyone is proud of your work all the time, and we all understand that your work requires travel."

He nodded. "I appreciate that. To answer your actual question, it's been okay. I'm getting out of the house more lately. I feel a little more normal." He was quiet for a few beats, and I waited. "Okay, honestly, it's been tough. It's physically tough going through physical therapy. I felt like my career was really taking off, and now I'm kind of stuck and scrambling...so that's tough. I'm trying to view it as a pause...though it feels like a big fat stop and eject."

"Gabe, it's only been a couple of months. It *is* a pause—a short pause. You're not going to lose your momentum because it wasn't momentum that got you where you are. It was your talent. You can't stop and eject your talent. You're going to write that book. You're going to get even better projects. I'm not even saying this to be nice. I'm saying it because I believe it—I *know* it." And I did know it. I knew nothing could hold Gabriel Hernandez back.

He squeezed my hand. "I missed my Emma pep talks."

"I've missed my Gabriel writing crisis. It took me back to the Valentine's Day we came out to make you feel better because you got a *D* on your paper. You thought your writing career was over before it began. I'm pretty sure you had some insane graveyard metaphor you used. I much prefer this VHS metaphor."

He was grinning at me. "I need you around more," he said. "No one else appreciates me quite the way you do."

"I'd be around all the time if I could be," I said, my words spilling like the Champagne.

"Yeah?" he said.

"Yeah," I whispered.

Then it began to rain, heavy sheets of prickly hard rain. We were blinking it out of our eyes, immediately drenched.

"This isn't the good rain!" he shouted over the noise.

I said, "Your leg! Are you still bandaged up?" But he couldn't hear me.

We jogged in the downpour as best as we could as he hobbled on his crutch. I had my arm tucked under him, attempting to help. We stumbled as we got to the truck.

I turned to ask if he was okay, to check on his cast, and he crashed into me. We were suddenly leaning against each other with my back to the car door. I assumed he had fallen. I was worried he was hurt. But then I glanced up, his face to my face, and his eyes were on my lips.

Our breath was heavy and mingling. He slid his hands to my waist, his thumb curving into my side. I placed my hands on his forearms and then slowly slid them up to his neck. We stayed like that for a second, two magnets making contact. He held me close against him. I started to brush my lips against his, but thunder cracking loud across the sky like a slamming door stopped me.

We both paused.

He let out a low, frustrated grumble, kissed my forehead, and said, "Let's get into the truck."

I scrambled into the car, dripping rain, while he threw his crutches in the backseat. He got in the truck, started it, and I put my hands against the heater. He seemed very serious as he quietly drove me to my car. I didn't say anything, either. I kept looking at him, still reeling. My hands were shaking, maybe from the cold, maybe from the almost kiss.

He parked his truck beside my car. Still parked on the street by the café where I ate my Valentine's pancakes. I didn't want to get out of the truck. He didn't say anything. He tapped his steering wheel. I felt again like we were both waiting on something. An energy buzzed in the car. We were both breathing quickly.

I looked at him, and he looked at me. I wanted to crawl over to his side of the car, but I would settle for any little contact I could get. I turned to him, delicate like asking a question.

He twisted in his seat, his eyes looking torn, and said, "Em, last time, I was so confused for so long. You really messed with me. I don't want it to be like last time."

"I know." I pulled my hands away. A flush of regret. "I'm sorry. I never did tell you... I'm so sorry about that. I didn't know what I wanted back then."

He looked up at me like he had a question forming in his mouth. But, with the regret and embarrassment from his rejection, I reflexively opened the car door and got out into the thick rain. I didn't say anything. I closed his truck door and waved.

He waved, too, but also shrugged as if to say, *still confused, Em.*

I ran to my car in the downpour. I was shivering as I drove home, his sweatshirt stuck to me. I kept thinking about him saying how confused he was last time.

I told him *I didn't know what I wanted back then*...as if I knew now. The windshield wipers swished back and forth as my heart pounded. I didn't want to get out of his truck and drive home, shivering to the bone all alone. I knew that much.

I crashed through deep puddles, barreling on fast and wild, away from what I wanted. Whatever that was. I wasn't sure. But I knew what I didn't want. I didn't want to leave. *But did it even matter?* Because I did.

. . .

I took a steaming hot shower and crawled into bed early, but I tossed and turned until I wound up switching on my lamp. I wrapped up in my white quilt and trudged out to the living room, deciding to sit by the glass door that looked onto my balcony. I watched the rain splash hard on my outdoor metal chairs and cars splashing through the puddled streets. I watched lightning crash across the sky.

I kept hearing Gabe's voice in my mind like a skipping track.

I had my phone on the floor beside me, so I grabbed it and impulsively pressed his number. *I should ask him what everything means.* What had he meant? What had today meant?

I should explain what happened last time. I'd been a fool to think it would just be forgotten, swept up with the past two years like a silly miscommunication or mishap. Like it wouldn't matter. Like it didn't mean something.

"Hello?" he said groggily into the phone.

I hung up. Within seconds, he called me back.

"Are we in high school again?" he asked.

"Hi," I said like I'd been caught.

"Why did you call just to hang up?" His voice tenderly teasing.

"Oh, yeah, that..." I buried my face in the quilt.

"You know, it's not the 90s, right? We have caller ID. The call your crush and hang up thing doesn't work anymore."

"Don't flatter yourself, crush. I called but then immediately felt bad that it was so late. I was hoping your phone was on silent."

"What were you calling about, anyway?"

"I was wanting to..." *Ask what you've been meaning with all your little remarks. Ask why you orchestrated running into me on Valentine's Day. Talk about that time we kissed on my birthday, the time we danced on New Year's Eve, and this persistent, pulling thing between us.*

I went with, "Check on your cast. Is it okay after being stuck in the rain?"

"Yeah, I was able to salvage it all. I feel a lot more comfortable now. I rewrapped it."

"Okay, good."

It was quiet. Sometimes there simply becomes too much to talk about. You just remain silent because you become buried underneath all there is to say, unable to decide where to even begin.

"Em, you just left without saying goodbye," he started.

"I was a little bit embarrassed," I said. "It was like self-defense."

"You didn't need to be embarrassed, though. Of course, I want to hold your hand. Any touch from you is definitely wanted, trust me," he assured me. "I just was trying to think through everything. You didn't really give me much time to do that."

"What a bad decision it was to just bolt set in a little too late while I was driving home." I closed my eyes.

It was quiet again. The rain was letting up outside my window. I had a billion things I could say. He had a billion things I feared he would say.

Heck, I could ask him about "Any touch from you is definitely wanted."

I heard him clear his throat and, before he could speak, the part of me that ran away only hours ago quickly interrupted him saying, "You know, I always watch *When Harry Met Sally* on Valentine's Day and I didn't get to today."

"Oh," he said. "I didn't realize you had this Valentine's tradition."

"I do. It started with my mom and me. She'd always have her little date or whatever with Dad, but she'd always find time to curl up with me and watch Meg Ryan fall in love."

"Wow. Well, that's really cute. I never knew that."

"Do you want to watch with me?" I proposed.

"Like over the phone?" he asked.

"Yeah," I said. "Like they do in the movie."

He laughed. "I'd like that."

I put in my DVD, and Gabe found a way to rent it on his TV. We analyzed the characters, their relationship. We talked over them and rewound important scenes if we'd missed them while making jokes, and when they were on the phone while watching *Casablanca*, Gabe cheered, "They're just like us!"

I heard him popping corn at one point, so I told him what he missed for those three minutes. He shook hot sauce on it, the way he always does, and I judged him for it, the way I always did.

When the credits were rolling, I made a happy sigh from my couch, cuddled up in my fuzzy blue throw blanket.

"I always like the couple interviews best," he said. "I wish they were longer. It's always funny to hear how a couple's story unfolds. Was it right away, or did it take years?"

"I wouldn't want it to take years," I said, getting up from the couch and making the tiny trek to my bedroom.

"Me either," he agreed.

I yawned, climbing into my bed. "I should let you go to sleep, sleepyhead. You have work in a few hours," he said.

"I know. I'm opening the shop tomorrow, too."

"Maybe I'll come by for some morning joe."

"Ooh, I've figured out how to craft the perfect mocha with just the right amount of dark chocolate. I have to make you one."

"On the house?"

"Ha." I clicked off my lamp.

"Well, goodnight then. I'll see you in the morning for my mocha. Sleep tight, Hot Valentine's Date."

"Goodnight, Hot Valentine's Date." I turned off my phone and snuggled into my pillow. For a moment, all felt right with the world.

Twenty-Five

I'd never been able to pinpoint a specific age, time, or season when my feelings for Gabe became the messy, consuming thing it was now. But there were undeniable moments of significance. And one of those was when I was thirteen years old.

At thirteen, I started wearing mascara, I wrote through five journals, I went to the Grand Canyon for the summer...and Gabriel got his first girlfriend, Michelle.

Michelle Chung was older than Katie and me. She was one of our high school's track stars, with long glossy black hair and eyes the color of chestnuts. I would spot them outside sitting on the back porch, and she would laugh at the things Gabe said, her head tossed back, her long hair shimmering, and her laugh admittedly sweet like windchimes.

I would think, *What does he like about her?* Not in a spiteful or angry way, but genuinely curious in the way one might wonder where secret treasure was buried. *Where can I find this?*

I found out about Michelle and Gabriel's romance while I was eating dinner with the Hernandezes. We were in the living room with an opened box of pizza sitting on the little coffee table between all of us, a few slices left.

"How's Michelle?" Victor had asked Gabriel in a suggestive voice, drawing out her name all sing-song.

Gabriel didn't respond and all his siblings started jeering at him. Everyone was in on the joke, except me.

"Who's Michelle?" I asked the group, holding my gooey slice in front of me.

"Oh, didn't Gabe tell you? That's his *girlfriend*!" Luis said, jazzed to be the one sharing this juicy gossip. Gabe threw a pillow at him.

Tanya asked, "What, you don't want Emma to know?" Her voice was just as suggestive.

"I don't care if she knows. I just don't want everyone making fun of me!" Gabe said, grabbing another slice of pizza from the box.

"We love Michelle, Gabriel. She's a sweetheart," his mother said, joining in from the kitchen. "No one will make fun of you," she said the last line more as an order than a promise. Then she looked at me and winked. I looked away awkwardly.

"Girlfriends are gross," Ricky said from his spot, laying on the ground before the TV with a paper plate of a half-eaten slice resting on his stomach.

I was frozen as if I had just received crushing, earth-shattering news. We were watching the *Sandlot*, but I didn't laugh at any of the mishaps. I could only eat a few bites of pizza. I couldn't even look at Gabe. My face felt hot each time Michelle was brought up. I didn't understand why I was feeling this way.

I could remember that day so clearly still. Maybe it was the first time I had an inkling of what was to come, my first bout of jealousy, or it was the first time I felt like *I shouldn't be feeling this way* about Gabriel. Either way, I still remembered it well enough that the red-hot feeling in my face at the mention of Michelle's name still returned to me randomly when I was in the car listening to a sad song or trying to fall asleep at night.

I slept over with Katie that night, and as we lay side by side in her bed, I whispered, "Hey, Katie, are you still awake?"

She responded sleepily, "Yeah?"

"What is Michelle like?"

"Whose Michelle?" She yawned.

"Gabriel's...you know...*girlfriend.*"

"Oh, you know her. We've seen her at school. She runs track. She's super nice. She made our family cookies the other day." She was disinterested in this subject.

I couldn't decide how to respond. I wanted to ask if Michelle was pretty, if Gabriel had ever put his arm around her, if the family thought she was funny or smart, and were the cookies delicious. I'd never made cookies for anyone without my mom's helps. But instead, I just laid there silently until I fell asleep.

I soon became used to feeling this way whenever Gabriel had a girlfriend or a date. It was like how I could count on squinting when trying to hear someone better, how my knees were sore whenever I went for a run, and how I got a stomachache whenever I ate anything with too much lemon. It was just a part of being Emma, like a fact of my existence.

That Christmas, I brought over cookies for the Hernandezes that I'd made all by myself, and Mrs. Hernandez told me they were the best she'd ever had. As if this were some crucial, important part of my life, I remembered her telling me this clearly. Gabriel didn't say anything about them.

GABE

I'll be there this morning for that perfected mocha.

ME

I'll have it ready for you. As a second apology for running away last night. Still feeling sorry. Thank you for watching a movie with me anyway.

GABE

All is forgiven. It was more fun watching a movie on the phone with you than watching it in person with other people. It made up for the ditching.

GABE

Though I will happily accept this second apology.

ME

New movie watching tradition? Gabe & Em phone movies?

GABE

it was fun, but I'd prefer having you next to
me next time

.

ME

deal.

As February began to come to a close like the last button on a heavy coat, Gabriel started coming to the coffee shop for a mocha every single morning. Katie whispered to me once, as he was leaving, "I think Gabe really missed us. He's been here almost every single day."

"I think so, too," I said as the door closed behind him.

The other person who we kept seeing in February was our beloved Canada Man. He was flying down so frequently that Rose had asked Katie one afternoon at work, "How is that man paying for all these flights?"

"He's using his miles." Katie shrugged innocently.

"He's racking up miles, that's for sure." Rose winked, and I snickered in agreement.

I had noticed how Rose wasn't simply throwing a heavy workload onto Katie like a careless or busy boss might, but instead Rose was intentionally giving Katie more responsibilities, teaching her how to handle new roles for running the business. She was mentoring Katie, but could it be more? As Rose went over paperwork with Katie line by line and talked over the minute accounting details, it had to be more.

It wasn't just me who was noticing. During one of Terrence's recent visits, he was sitting with us in her family's kitchen as we poured tortilla chips into a big plastic turquoise bowl and Katie threw fresh tomatoes, cilantro, serrano's, onions, and garlic into a blender, the spicy aroma filling the room. She was telling us about one of the in-depth discussions she'd recently had with Rose about finances of the shop.

Terrence asked, "Did she talk with you about the future plans?"

"A little. We focused more on the necessities of keeping afloat currently. *I* have some future ideas, though," she said as she tasted the salsa and then added in a few more shakes of seasonings and then pressed blend again.

Terrence looked thoughtful. "I think you should talk about the future with her. Ask her the specifics. I know you want to share your ideas, but you should see what she's planning first."

"Yeah," I said. "I've noticed how she's kind of training you. I'm wondering if she's getting you ready to go out into the world. Like teaching you all she knows before she goes?"

Terrence was about to respond, but Katie blew past all of that and started talking about community engagement while she poured the salsa into a serving dish.

One morning in late February, Gabe was sitting at the coffee bar sipping one of his daily foamy, fresh mochas. I was talking with him while simultaneously trying to stretch my shoulder blades.

"Are you okay there, Em?" He cocked his head to the side as I laced my hands behind my back.

"I'm okay. It's just my back is really bugging me." I winced a little. I had reached out to other magazines and platforms and had a couple of new freelance writing gigs, which had me hunched over my laptop more often. But honestly, I felt a thrill with every sore muscle in my neck and gratitude with every shoulder blade crack.

"Here, turn around," he said after eyeing my little stretch session for a minute.

I turned around and backed up against the bar between us, and I felt him lean over, which probably broke some sort of barista rules, and place his big, warm hands on my sore shoulders.

The backrub was probably meant to help *relax* my muscles, but all of me clicked on down to every single hair on my arms standing to attention. He started to rub his thumbs in warm little circles behind my shoulder blades, and I closed my eyes.

He asked, "How's that?"

I choked out, "That's good."

"You are really tight," he said, moving his thumbs onto the sides of my neck, rubbing them down and across my shoulders.

It felt good—really good. Every touch with Gabriel just had to be perfect and delicious, even at an awkward angle across a bar. His fingers dipped under the top my shirt, and I could feel his rough fingertips directly on my upper back. My abdomen felt hot and syrupy.

He asked, "Is this okay?"

I opened my mouth to ask him to come back behind the bar when I heard a voice crash into our moment. "Oh, is Emma's back acting up again?"

Katie was by our sides. We jumped apart like we'd been caught making out on the bar, which, honestly, *I wish*.

Before either of us could reply, she was bouncing up and down, "Guess what! Guess what!"

"What?" I leaned on my elbows against the bar, curious. Shaking off the goosebumps and butterflies from mere moments ago.

"You are bouncing like a three-year-old," Gabe observed. "What's up?"

"Canada Man just told me he's getting a short-term rental here in Sweet River. He'll have a place of his own. He can move some of the things he needs for work into his new place, and he can stay for longer than a few days at a time. He can actually do life here."

"Wait, wait. Is he moving here?" Gabe asked. "Planning on moving here?"

"No, well, *semi*-moving here. Is that a thing?" Katie furrowed her brows in question.

"That is not a thing," Gabe said deadpan.

"You've semi-moved here, though, Gabe," I said.

"Yeah, okay. Yeah, but that's more *temporary* due to injury," he clarified.

"Nah, it's due to how badly you missed us," I teased.

"Terrence wants to work here and live here sometimes. It's simple as that," Katie said. Her defenses were up.

"Also, because he misses someone." I wiggled my eyebrows.

"I'm just curious about the long-term plan since this is a short-term rental," Gabe said.

"We're in the middle of figuring that out, Gabriel. This is the first step, the temporary fix. Though, I mean, with Terrence's work, he'll always be traveling around."

Gabe nodded wordlessly, skeptically.

I said, "I'm excited for you two. I think this is a good next step."

Katie breathed out a big sigh. "I'm just so happy he'll be here more. I want to do normal couple things so badly."

"Does any of this inspire you to move out of Mom and Dad's?" Gabe said, picking at a sore subject like only a sibling can. I heard Katie take a quick intake of breath.

I quickly busied myself with the espresso maker. Did it need cleaning again? I decided it definitely did.

"What does that mean?" Katie said, her tone all sharp edges.

"It meant simply what I said. I'm curious if any of these changes and the boyfriend getting a place here make you want a place of your own?" Gabe said slowly, carefully. Or patronizingly. I couldn't decide.

"Mom and Dad have all those empty rooms. It's not like I'm taking up tons of space," Katie said. Her voice was quiet, and she glanced around the coffee shop, aware of the customers. "Plus, it's temporary. I'm saving up to get a house downtown. I'm saving up for a future business, too. You know that."

"Katie, I didn't ask about why you're staying there or if you think you're taking up room. We all know Mom will miss you when you go. That's not the question. I just wondered if Terrence makes you want out of there?"

"I am fine there for now," Katie said shortly. "I've liked being there."

And for a moment, it felt like the conversation was ending. I turned from the espresso machine back to them.

"I feel like *you* want me to move out more than I ever have," Katie said like dropping something heavy she'd been hauling around. I turned back around.

"I don't care if you're living there." Gabe raised his shoulders. "I was just curious. We don't really talk about it."

"I feel like you're judging me. Like, you judge me for living at home because you don't, and you judge me for staying in Sweet River because you didn't."

"You're misunderstanding me," Gabe said, his voice softer. "That's not true."

"Yes, it is. The other day when Terrence was here, you said, 'Why make him get a place in Sweet River? You should be getting a place in Toronto or Seattle.' You're what? Judging me for wanting to live in this little town when I now have an opening to go somewhere *bigger and better*?"

Gabe opened his mouth to respond. But then Katie added, "And don't get me started on all the ways you whine about feeling like a child being at Mom and Dad's again when you know I've been there since I graduated undergrad."

Gabe was completely quiet now. I turned back to the espresso machine.

"We don't talk about it, huh? Well, here it is, Gabe. I missed home, here, this town, every day I was at college. That's just the truth. I have always loved it here. I have always loved family dinner nights and seeing my nieces and nephews grow up. I like knowing the city like the back of my hand and knowing my neighbors like family. I love being a part of the community. I like seeing trees grow in the neighborhoods. I like seeing the murals being added. I like my job, watching people grow and change as they come in and out of the shop. I've seen people fall in love. I've seen dads become grandpas. The girl I babysat is now in high school." She kept her voice quiet but strong.

"Katie." Gabe ran his fingers through his hair.

"Gabe, it's different from you. I get it. But you need to get it, too. I never question why you want to ping across the country all the time."

"Katie, I'm sorry that I've made you feel like you have to explain yourself to me." Gabe's voice was tender and shaky. "You know, I might like pinging across the country, as you say, but it's knowing you and the family are here having family dinner that makes me keep coming back. That makes this place home to me. I get that we're different. I more than get it... I like it, Katie."

Katie nodded.

"This town is lucky to have you. I'm lucky to have you. Mom and Dad are lucky to have you. I'm sorry I made you feel anything other than that." Gabe said.

I could see that Katie was wiping her eyes.

"And, really, I don't care if you're living at Mom's. I know you guys decided for you to save up to invest in your future for a few years. I respect that. I was being insensitive and not thinking about how my questions would make you feel. I was just talking to talk," he added.

"I might've overreacted. I think I had some pent-up feelings or something," Katie mumbled.

"Forget about it," Gabe said while Katie walked from behind the bar and over to his side.

"Hug it out?" she asked. It was the same phrase she'd said to him as we grew up. Every time they had a scuffle, it would end with one of them asking, all sheepish and sorry, "Hug it out?"

"Bring it in." Gabe opened his arms to her.

Katie had spent much of the past couple of years frustratingly telling me about how she felt Gabriel hadn't wanted her to move back home. She would wring her hands and say he acted like she was working at the coffee shop as a cop-out.

She would ask me, "How can you so easily understand what makes us different, but Gabriel can't get it?"

Once, I told her that it was because she told me how she wanted to move back home all through college—as if the tears in her dorm room weren't enough of a sign. She would dream up her own coffee shop plans while we ate lunch. She was confident when she told me she was staying in her childhood room for a while as she pocketed money to buy a fixer upper downtown someday and open her own business.

She would talk to me about the football games. She took me with her to the weekend farmer's market vendors. I watched how she knew the local shops and supported them. She would rally about changes that needed to be made and keep up with the town's governmental changes. She cared about what the town needed.

While I sat in our local church, I bounced my leg and wondered, *What else? What next?* She took a deep sigh and sunk into the pew.

Gabriel wasn't privy to this. She dodged and evaded the subject with him. Did she owe him an explanation? No. But if she wanted him to understand, I thought, this was a good start.

After they hugged it out, Katie went to help a customer, and Gabe took a sip of his mocha. He looked at me sheepishly.

"Sorry," he said, finally.

"Don't need to apologize to me. I've seen a billion Hernandez showdowns. This was teeny tiny in comparison to some."

"Indeed," he said. "Remember the time I forgot I was supposed to take her to Six Flags?"

"Oh, please, don't remind me." I winced.

"Do I..." He searched for the right words. "Do I come off judgmental?"

"In general? Not at all. You're genuinely one of the sweetest guys. Do you sometimes make comments to Katie about her life choices that rub her the wrong way? Yes, to that. I mean, I don't always pick up on them, but I think it's a sibling dynamic thing. I know she's always..." I lowered my voice. "She always cares what you think."

"I think I know that... I just forget." He sighed.

"You forget she cares what you think. You also tend to forget to think through your words a little more carefully when you're speaking to your little sister. It's not that hard. You might not care if someone teases you about your living situation, *supposedly*, but she does," I said, a little harsh but honest.

"Oh, I care," he said. "My family is always getting onto me. Why not move home if you can write from here? If you're not going into an office, why aren't you back home? Don't you miss us? Don't you want to see the babies? If you're going to be on so many trips, why rent a place in LA and not here by us? On and on. *All the time.*"

"Katie, too?" I set some fresh pastries in the display case.

"Not Katie so much. Though she has been in on it from time to time. I think since it's usually said as a joke, and with a lot of love and affection, they think it won't bug me. For the most part, it really doesn't." His voice was low, keeping this conversation just for our ears.

"Why don't you tell them it bothers you? Like Katie just told you. Help them get it."

"I don't want it to turn into a fight."

"If you say it right, it might not." I shrugged my shoulders as if to say, "Why not try?"

"I'm not exactly known for saying things right." He pushed the empty mug across the bar.

I rolled my eyes. "Says the writer."

"In pen, sure. In person?" He shook his head. "In person, not so much. "

"Gabe, for real, you're one of the least cruel people I know." I was looking at his mug, not in his eyes.

"Well, I feel bit like a jerk."

"I think that's a sibling thing. I wouldn't know, personally. But from my studies, I think they can sometimes make you feel very good and cozy, and then other times they make you feel like a big ole jerk."

"This is from your research, eh?" his eyes creased in a smile.

"Yes, my research." I nodded.

"Well, I'm gonna head out," he said. He patted the bar and then waved a few fingers goodbye.

He headed toward the door, but Katie crashed into him halfway there. She wrapped her arms around him and gave him a tight squeeze. He hugged her back, lifting her off the ground, and the two laughed like when they were ten years old. She told him to put her down, and he said "never," but eventually did.

The people in the shop were smiling because the customers knew the loud, loving Katie Hernandez. Honestly, most of them had known Katie *and* Gabriel both since they were kids and recognized that laughter almost as well as I did.

Twenty-Seven

I had been working on essays since January. I told myself I was writing them "just for myself." I saved them in a folder on my laptop I named "Reflections." I was getting back in touch with what it felt like to write as a teenager when my writing was often passionate, inspired, personal, and not written as an assignment or for a particular set of eyes.

There was a piece about Katie and her relationship with home. I was thinking about that piece after her argument with Gabriel. I found myself back at the keys that evening, curled up in a blanket on my balcony and writing as the sky went pink and purple over and around me. I reworked sentences, editing my wording.

While writing, I realized that I had figured something out after listening to her talk with Gabriel, and it made the whole essay click. Then, boldly, I emailed it to Katie with a message asking, *Can I send this piece out? It's about someone I love most in the world and the city she loves with her whole heart.*

A few hours later, while I was reading a book in bed, she replied to my email. *Yes. I love it, and I love you too.*

That was an early March night. Weeks went by as I carried this essay in the back of my mind. I frothed milk and poured it over espresso, wiped counters, finished the book I'd been reading that one night in bed, ate dinners with friends, and all with that very personal story sitting in the back of my mind, waiting in the little folder on my laptop.

To share with the world, or not? I didn't usually share the things I wrote just for myself. I could submit the stories that were very impersonal, about trips, morning routines, and news around the world. But nothing that sat in my little folder named "Reflections."

I would return to my place on the balcony. I would edit those essays. I even started another. I made lists of places I could, would, and should submit these essays. I found the requirements. I found the contacts. I was organized and prepared. But I couldn't bring myself to share them.

"Have you heard back about my essay?" Katie asked over cobb salads during our lunch break. It had been a few weeks since that night on the balcony. We were sitting at a diner a few doors down from Coffee & Commas at a table outside.

"*Your* essay?" I asked.

"The one you wrote about me," she said, as she poured dressing on her salad.

"*My* essay about you?"

"Yes, *my essay*," she said with a twinkle in her eyes.

"Well, I haven't actually submitted it anywhere," I said casually.

"What, why not? It was really good. I know I'm a wee bit biased, but it really was a great piece."

"I just..." I was trying to find the words. "I feel a little hesitant about submitting it. I'm actually sitting on a few personal essays that I really like that weren't writing assignments I picked up. These are pieces straight from my heart." I tapped my chest. "But every time I go to submit them...I just can't bring myself to do it. I just sit and stare at my laptop."

"Em." Katie stabbed a big piece of lettuce. "I'm just going to say it. These people aren't all going to be Terrence's who show up in your inbox singing your praises. You have to do it yourself now. You are a writer, and from what I've heard, it's a life of vulnerability. I've seen the Goodreads comments. It can be harsh out there."

I groaned into my salad.

"But it's worth it, right? Why don't you just send these essays out with zero expectations? Just put your goodness out there in the world, and if you get some good responses back, how amazing! How great. If you get nothing, or rejections, say, 'Hey, I kind of expected it might go that way' and move on. Kind of like that time I got on the dating apps. I put all the profiles out there. Do you remember that?"

"Yes, that was like not even a full year ago, Katie." I took a bite of tomato.

"I expected nothing, just did it to see, and hey, wasn't too hurt when I got nothing."

I took a drink of my iced sweet tea. "Will you send them out with me?"

"Of course. Let's do it after work," Katie said.

And so, that night after work, we sat together watching the sun go down and pitching people who didn't ask to see my work, asking if they'd consider me, my heart, and my thoughts.

I wondered if I could like my work enough for all of us. I told myself, *If they don't want me, that's okay.* I also told myself if it didn't feel okay at times, that was okay, too.

Twenty-Eight

March was coming to a subtle close. The only hint it had been there was the weather warming up often enough to fool me into thinking winter and cold were mostly done and that spring had already sprung. But Texas could be fickle and tricky.

I had been working the morning shift consistently. I had grown to enjoy the sunrise rhythm of tiredly tying on my apron alongside Katie, pulling baked goods from the freezer she'd made last night with Rose, and popping them in the oven. Our regulars, like Pastor Tim and Reverend James, came and went, being welcomed by the scent of hot espresso and baking scones and muffins. There were a few neighboring shop owners who came in nearly every morning for their coffee and scones. We had a few nurses who came by before or after their shifts, and police officers, firefighters, and teachers, who would bring in tumblers that I would fill with hot coffee every single morning. I knew their names and their tastes. I had started to know their orders, like memorizing an anthem.

It was later in the morning when students would come by with thick books and a desire for coffee as a treat more than a necessity. Moms with strollers who were onto their third cup by now and would try the sugary seasonal drink orders. Friends who would come in to talk and let their drinks get cold on the table between them.

It was after all this that finally Gabe would stroll in for his daily mocha.

This morning he was blowing on the steaming mug when he mused, "I'm going to adopt a dog today."

"Really?" I asked, my eyes wide in surprise.

"Yeah, his name is Jack."

"Wait, wait. When did this happen?"

"I've been in talks with the local adoption agency, you know Paws for Effect? I was emailing with one of the owners, and she told me this one dog—that they're calling Jack right now—had been there a while. He's a little scruffy, and they say he's a bit of a rascal, but he seems pretty sweet." His face was lit up with a hesitant excitement, like when we were teenagers and he was telling me about a book he'd just finished, one he wasn't sure I'd like but wanted to tell me all about anyway. "They don't know how old he is exactly, but their vet thinks he's probably just under a year old. They asked if I wanted to meet him. I've already filled out all the forms, so if we click today, I get to take him home."

"Gabe!" I clapped my hands. "Has she sent a picture or anything?"

"Yeah, here." He handed me his phone. There sat a pup the color of a Hershey's Kiss with floppy ears like a Labrador, a long snout like a German shepherd, and paws he hadn't grown into yet. In the photo, he had a bright green ball in his mouth.

"Does he like to fetch?" I asked, after noting the ball.

"I bet he does." He sounded a little nervous.

"Gabe, are you nervous?"

"Yeah, I'm way more anxious than I expected to be today." He let out a little laugh.

"Is there anything specific making you feel this way?"

"It just feels kind of big. Plus, what if he has temper issues or something? Or he has allergies—what do I do about a dog with allergies? Or what if he doesn't like me or feels nervous around me? I also hope it's a good idea that I'm going to take him home today just to move. He'll have to adjust to traveling around with me. The shelter said that's fine and tons of dogs like that and do that, but then I was wondering..." he trailed off.

"Gabriel, I know that you will be a fantastic dog dad," I said. He smiled at my words. "You laugh, but I'm serious. I think all this caring, as nervous as it is, will be good for this pup."

He sighed. "I hope he likes me."

"When are you going to pick him up?"

"I have an appointment for 2 p.m." He took a sip of his coffee. "When do you get off work?"

"My shift is until noon today."

"Want to come?" he asked, and my heart swelled in my chest at those three words. Gabriel Hernandez was inviting me into his life.

"For sure," I said.

Gabriel picked me up at my apartment about half an hour before two. Paws for Effect was a short five or ten minutes down the road from my apartment, but with all his excited energy, we left early.

I got in the car and noticed the backseat had a crate, a big dog pillow, chew toys, dog food, and lots of bags from Pet Smart.

"Someone is prepared," I mused aloud.

"I'm banking on the fact that we're going to get along."

"I don't doubt it," I said. "The pillow looks cozy."

He backed up his truck and started the drive toward the shelter.

"So, what made you decide you wanted a dog right now?" I asked, making conversation.

"To be honest, I've been a little down lately. I was Facetiming with my therapist, and somehow we landed on me talking to Paws for Effect."

"And one thing led to another?"

"Exactly." He kept his eyes on the road.

"So, you've been down. Would that have anything to do with the casted-up leg?" I wanted to reach out and touch his arm or his shoulder to offer some sort of comfort. I had noticed that Gabriel was taking this accident and all that shrapnel of his life that came with it hard.

"In part, yeah, the injury is part of it."

"I'd be down if I had sprained my ankle, let alone fractured a femur."

"Yeah, you know, it *is* the injury, sure, but it's also a lot more. It's like there is the cause and then there's the effect, and the effect is what has me...down." He hit the blinker. "Since that's the word we've been sticking with."

"Are you missing LA?" I was wondering what all could be labeled as "effect."

"No, it's not LA. I've liked being away from LA, to be honest. I didn't realize how much I would, but I do. What I've missed is my work. I'd just gotten a little momentum in my career, and now I've had to hit the brakes. I've missed some trips I had planned that were important for my book deal. You know it's my first collection of photography and writing, all based around hiking the PNW, and I've had to extend the deadline and move around dates...and I'm nervous." He sighed. "I guess I'm down, but I'm also the opposite of down—I'm all anxious about everything. I'm up, *and* I'm down." He laughed bitterly.

"Sorry to drudge it all up." But I wasn't, not really. I was always desperate to know what was going on in Gabriel's head.

"No, I should probably talk to someone about it. Not just mope around."

"Are you anxious about the extended deadline?" I turned toward him in my seat.

"I am. I'm also disappointed. I'd put a lot of work into the proposal and the plan. I'd mapped out the next year for working on it. Now every bit of it is under revision."

"I'm so sorry, Gabe." I felt frustrated for him.

"Did you know the doctor doesn't want me hiking for months and months? Hiking is a huge part of this book. I just don't..." He took a deep breath and turned into the parking lot. He put the car in park. "I don't know how to plan around all of this. I can guess about the future—but it's also just that, guessing."

"I thought you were healing really well."

"I am. Physical therapy is going great. But I'm still supposed to wait a while until I get back out there. Then I have to work to even get back to the level of activity I was used to." He turned to me in his seat. "This trip was planned around the seasons, as is the book. It's all delayed now. How does reworking the trip affect the plan for the book? Can we even bet on these new changes I've made? I'm nervous about these publishers scrapping it."

"All of those are just what ifs. *What if* they scrap it? *What if* I'm not ready by the new dates? *What if* I can't work with these changes and revisions? They're valid things to be anxious about. They're valid things to be down about. But they're not reality. Right now, in real life, you still have the deal, and they're letting you reschedule. In real life, they're working with you. That's the reality of this situation."

He rubbed his forehead. "I know."

"The reality is also that there is a rascally little pup in there waiting to meet you." I tapped on the window.

He grinned behind his hands. I could see it. "A nicer reality," he murmured.

"He will probably also need to be trained to the right level of activity to accompany you back to working on your book." I winked.

"My furry hiking companion." He was lit up again, that hesitant joy.

. . .

I've never been a big believer in love at first sight, but the day Gabriel met Jack made me question my stance. As they walked Jack outside of the adoption center and into the play area to meet Gabe, Gabe's eyes landed on the patchy brown dog. His shoulders dropped, and a calm smile rested on his face. His joy and excitement were not so hesitant anymore.

Jack was indeed a rascal. He was scrappy and energetic. When Gabriel went to play with him during their little introduction, Jack wanted to wrestle and jump pretty much the entire time, but Gabriel wasn't deterred by it. Gabriel was charmed.

"I would be jumping around too, boy, if I could." He laughed, rustling his furry head, leaning on his crutch.

Gabriel took him home that day.

On the drive home, I asked Gabe, "So, what are you thinking about his name?" I had a few names in mind, Fitz, Artie, or maybe even Comma.

"Oh, you know." He glanced to the backseat at Jack, who was intensely chewing on a squeaky toy in his crate. Between squeaks, Gabe said, "I think he's a Jack. He feels like a Jack to me."

"I think I can see some Jack energy." I looked back at him too.

"The world is full of great Jacks. Look at Jack-Jack from Incredibles. Jack who gave his life for Rose."

"I like how your mind goes straight to fictional Jacks." I laughed. "I thought you'd immediately jump to your undying love of Jack London."

"Oh my gosh, you're so right." His eyes widened. "How did I not think of that? I was obsessed with Jack London in high school."

"I remember vividly. You forced a few of those books on me growing up."

"Honestly, I still feel at home in a Jack London book," he said wistfully.

"So, our little Jack is in good company."

"Definitely," he said thoughtfully. We pulled into my parking lot, and as I unbuckled my seatbelt, I said, even though I was a little unsure if I was choosing the right words, "I hope you know I'm here for you. I know that this ski accident didn't just mess with your body, but it messed with your whole life. I'm here. I'm a drive away, or a phone call, or a text."

He gave a sideways grin. "Thanks, Em. I really appreciate that."

"I'll see you," I said to Gabe. "And goodbye to you, too, Jack." I turned in my seat and looked back at Jack.

He dropped his toy and looked at me, too, lifting his ears in attention.

Twenty-Nine

After slipping into a pair of baggy sweats, I started leafing through a cookbook to find a soup recipe I wanted to make. I had just put my big blue pot on the stove when my phone started to ring.

I walked over to my phone and saw Gabriel's face on my screen, trying to FaceTime. I slid open my phone and said, "Hey, Gabe."

"He's not just Jack anymore," he said, forgoing greetings. "*He is Jack London*. I don't know why we didn't think of it when we were talking about it earlier today."

"Well, I kind of did," I said. "I mean, I did bring up the reference."

"Well, to me, he was still just Jack. We were playing outside with Midnight when it donned on me. He's Jack *London*. He's not just a fellow Jack. He's his *namesake*." He said namesake like it was holy.

"What a burden for such a little dog to carry."

Gabriel's laugh lit up his whole face. "He carries it well!"

"How's Midnight like him?" I asked, resting my phone against the cookbook as I poured chicken broth into the pot.

"Midnight likes the company, I think. You know how Midnight is so old and chill, so if anything, he finds Jack London pretty entertaining."

"Ahh, Midnight has a little brother," I cooed.

"How far he's come."

"I wonder if he'll miss Jack when y'all move?"

"Or be relieved to get his yard back." He rustled with something out of the shot. "No, no, Jack London, that's Midnight's."

"So we're saying the full name every time, are we?"

"JACK LONDON!" he shouted. "Be right back!" He darted off the screen.

I folded my shredded chicken into the pot, then some sweet potatoes, carrots, and celery, all to the sound of Gabriel rescuing Jack from something that was "not a chew toy!" from the sounds of it.

"I'm back," he said, returning with the pup by his side. Jack London sniffed the screen.

"Hi, there," I said. I was grabbing a few seasonings from the cabinet.

"You cookin'?" Gabe asked.

"That I am. I'm making some soup for dinner tonight." I twisted the cap off the jar of garlic powder.

"Ah, I could go for a warm bowl of soup."

"They do say soup is good for the soul," I said. "Or something like that."

"You should bring some to Coffee & Commas tomorrow," he said as Jack gave his cheek a big lick. He pushed his snout away.

"You dork, if you want soup, why don't you just come get some tonight? I can't eat this whole pot anyway." That was a casual and friendly invite, right? Maybe how pathetically I wanted him to come over was not casual or friendly. But, I at least sounded the part.

"Could I bring young Jack London with me?"

"Is he housetrained?"

"That's what they told me. We could test it?" He gave a hopeful smile.

"Good Lord." I squinted at the screen. Gabe and Jack were both looking back at me. "Okay, but no accidents!"

"Yes, ma'am," Gabe said obligingly.

Gabe came by a few hours later, bringing Jack along on a leash. I poured us two mix-and-match ceramic bowls full of soup. We ate them sitting side by side at my kitchen bar while Jack rolled around on the kitchen tile with a chewy toy bone. We discussed Gabe's book and his original plan versus what it looked like now. He opened up documents and showed me outlines, rough drafts, and emails with his publishers. He laid it all out for me.

We wound up sitting on my couch, both with blankets, talking about the detours our lives had taken this year.

And, maybe it was shared ups and downs we were tussling with, or just the fact that he was Gabriel and I was Emma, but sharing it all with him, all the fears and hopes, Word docs on my laptop, emails with editors, and prayers in my journal felt as easy and restorative as exhaling after holding in a long breath.

"Maybe you can come along and be my assistant?" Gabe joked at one point in the evening. Jack London asleep by our feet.

"Hey, for some of the easier stuff, maybe I actually could tag along here and there," I nudged his leg with my toe.

"You really up for that?" he asked, but I wasn't sure if he meant the task of toughing it out in nature or something else, more akin to me running out of the car on Valentine's Day.

We ended up opening a bottle of wine, and our conversations moved from our careers to our families, then catching up on all we'd missed the past couple of years.

I could tell talking and brainstorming about his work had been therapeutic for him. His shoulders were relaxed, and he was laughing easily. We both felt like we could catch our breath. A little respite in the middle of it all.

It reminded me of when we were in high school. Gabriel and I had often helped each other with assignments, but there was one particular time when I was fifteen that had been far more dramatic and dire than the rest.

It was a crisp night in November, nearing finals, and Gabriel had been working on this long, taxing essay for one of his classes. I can't remember exactly which one. I had been around for the weeks of work he'd been putting into it. This essay had been a topic of discussion at his house a lot.

So, when I got this phone call on a school night saying, "Word crashed, and somehow, I lost all of it! I lost all of it, and it's due tomorrow, Emma!" I knew what a big, gigantic deal it was to him.

"I'll come help!" I said immediately. I got my mom to drive me over, it was 9 p.m., but she loved Gabe almost as much as I did.

She drank coffee with Mrs. Hernandez in the kitchen while I sat with Gabe on the living room floor. We put his essay back together again using his notes, his books, and our memories.

It was 2 a.m., and our moms were asleep on the couch when Gabe said to me, "I think it's better than it was before." We had just hit our final "save document."

"I'll give you author credit," he added seriously.

"Do not! They'll think you cheated!" I laughed, delirious with exhaustion and a little high on all these hours spent with Gabe.

"In my heart, you have author credit, Emma Brown." His voice was the sweetest and softest I'd ever heard it.

Then he looked straight into my eyes and said, "I know you're Katie's best friend, but you're also one of my best friends too. And I don't know anyone else who could've helped me like you."

I was deeply tired, but in that moment, I felt like I could fly. "I actually really liked helping you," was all I could come up with to say.

He smiled at me like he got what I meant.

"I guess we're done," I said. I almost wished we hadn't finished it yet, that we could've kept working together a few more hours.

"Our moms are pretty cool," he said, looking over at our sleeping mothers.

On the drive home that night, or rather, early that morning, my mom said to me, "You would do anything for that boy, huh?"

"Sort of. He's one of my best friends, you know. Just as much as Katie," I said, newly affirmed in this information.

"He's like a brother then." I realized now that she'd said gamely.

"No, that's not what I said," I snapped. "Gabe is not like my brother."

All these years later, and I would still sit around with him for hours and hours and try to piece things back together. Just happy to be there.

Thirty

The Hernandez kids were hosting a Taco Bar for Katie's birthday at their house one night in April, a couple of weeks before Easter. The nights had been cool but the days were sunny. I drove to their place wrapped up in an oversized gray cardigan, the heat in my car on low.

Katie squealed, all wrapped up in Terrence's arms, when she saw me walk into the kitchen. Her mom had grilled shrimp, pulled pork, and shredded chicken for our taco meat, and I could smell the spices as I joined the group.

"Happy birthday." I wrapped Katie up in a hug. She held me close, and we swayed like that for a minute.

"How's your day been?" I asked her, even though we'd spent the morning together at work. She told me about Terrence's sweet notes, about Gabriel making her blueberry pancakes, and about Tanya visiting her this afternoon and bringing her cherubic baby.

I leaned in close to catch every word. It was loud with almost all the Hernandez crew squeezed into the kitchen, the blender buzzing, and laughter spilling. I spotted Gabriel making the margaritas. He winked at me.

"Oh, you found our mixologist for the night?" Katie snickered, watching us watch each other. "His margaritas are really sour, I warn you. Gabe overdid the lime. You have to go try one."

I weaved through the kitchen to Gabe. His eyes were on me the entire time.

"You want a drink? I'm in charge of making these, and not to toot my own horn, they're a hit." He was using his crutch less and less, so it was leaning against the bar as he balanced on his own but still in a cast.

"Get me a cup full, bartender." I slapped the bar playfully.

"Order up." He proudly poured me a cup.

I instantly puckered my lips at the overwhelming sour. He had a big smile saying, "Good lime, huh?"

I nodded and gave him a half-hearted thumbs up. I searched the kitchen for tortilla chips to help soften the sting.

"Did I tell you it's my own recipe?" He beamed.

I drank it anyway. We all did.

We piled our plates with tacos, took pictures with the birthday girl and told Terrence all the funny stories we could think up. Later that night we put candles on a cheesecake and sang to Katie. It all felt right—Terrence fitting right into the group and Gabriel back with our little group. A perfect moment in time, all of us together.

As the night ended, we were gathering in the kitchen, some of us cleaning up, some of us picking at leftovers and talking.

"So, how's all the back and forth going, Terrence?" Victor asked as he poured some of the last remnants of the margarita from the pitcher into his plastic cup.

"Ah, it's a little exhausting to be honest. I was just in Seattle a week ago, and a few days prior I had flown out to Toronto for a day from here. It's been a lot of time changes in a short span of time," Terrence said, scraping food from plates into a garbage bag.

"You're basically living in three different places right now?" Victor said.

"Basically," Terrence sighed. "I've always traveled a lot, so I thought it'd be easy for me. But this being my daily life, my day-to-day, it's a little tough."

"How long do you think you'll be tri-city?" Ricky asked, standing beside me, picking at the cheesecake.

I watched Terrence shoot a glance at Katie. "It's unclear," he said.

"Oh, yeah?" Ricky laughed dryly.

"The stubborn girlfriend in Texas can make things pretty unclear, huh?" Victor teased. I shook my head to nobody in particular.

"Something like that." Terrence shrugged, maybe unsure of how to field the jokes from the little brothers.

Katie's shoulders tensed as she asked sharply, "It's your stubborn girlfriend making things unclear? How's that?"

Terrence dropped the plastic bag to the ground. "Babe, your brothers are just teasing me about my living situation."

"I didn't ask about them. I'm asking *you* since you agreed. How am I making things unclear?" Katie said.

"Come on, Katie, why do you have to get so heated?" Ricky whined. "The man is jetlagged."

"Yeah, Katie, I didn't mean anything," Terrence said, and in his defense, he did sound tired.

"It felt kind of like you did," she murmured.

"I just said 'something like that.' That's all I said," Terrence said.

"That's true," Ricky added. I elbowed him.

"That's not all you said, though. Before he even asked you if I was making it unclear, you were going on about how much you hate the situation, *our* situation. Plus, you didn't deny that it was the stubborn girlfriend's fault you're in this predicament," Katie said. Katie and I rarely fought, but this was the second time I was privy to a Katie clash. It wasn't lost on me that both fights were circling living situations.

"You realize that where you live, or how many places you live, is a *thousand percent* up to you, right?" Katie crossed her arms.

"Katie, it is *zero percent* that simple. My work, my love life," he gestured to her, "which does involve a stubborn girl from Texas, my family, all of these things determine where I live."

"You determine where you live," she said flatly. "Those things can all work around your location. You are not at the mercy of everything."

"Says the woman with a ten-minute commute," he said quietly, barely.

She took in a deep, angry breath. "I choose that commute. You choose your commute, too."

"It is not that simple, and you know it." If Katie was the fire set to high, Terrence was a consistent simmer, low and steady.

"Oh, don't I know it. We talk about how un-simple it is a lot lately. It's like all we talk about. You know what I want for my birthday, Terrence? For you to decide what you want to do with your life!" Katie said.

"You know, you're not helping any. Tell me what you want me to do, huh? You never just tell me!" Terrence walked over to her, his hands around him.

"I am not going to tell you where to live. I cannot do that." She started to walk away from him. Like maybe she was going to leave the kitchen entirely, her voice on the verge of tears.

"Katie," Terrence called after her.

She stopped walking, turned to him, and said, "I'm fed up with you acting like you don't know what I want because I don't tell you what to do. You've known from the start what I want. I want a life here in this town. I want the coffee shop. I want my regulars. I am not moving. That's never been on the table," she said, her voice shaky. "*You're* the one always zipping around. If you want to be around me, be *here*. It's that simple. Moving is always on the table for you."

Terrence looked awkwardly around the kitchen, remembering this boiling conversation had simmered over in the middle of his girlfriend's kitchen.

"Is it a place or is it me you're so afraid of choosing?" Katie demanded.

The air left the kitchen.

"I'm going to finish these later," Gabe said suddenly, turning off the water at the sink where he'd been quietly doing dishes. He started heading out of the kitchen, and like he was the captain of our motley crew, everyone filed out after him except Katie and Terrence.

Gabe turned at the bottom of the stairs and looked at me, his gaze pointed, pressing. We both wanted to talk, to debrief about what had just happened, and to pick up where we'd left off the other night in my apartment. Suddenly he was someone I wanted to talk through everything with. *When did our relationship get to this point? And why did I love it so much?*

Here we were tonight, and saying goodbye like this felt wrong. He felt it, too. I hung by the door, hearing Terrence and Katie's voices in the background. He opened his mouth to speak, but Victor and Ricky interrupted our silent conversation, breaking the tension.

They dragged Gabe upstairs. I took my leave and slipped out the door.

I had left that night in such a hurry that I hadn't been able to confirm that Katie still wanted to ride along with me for a day trip to Austin, as we had initially planned. *Here & There* had asked me to visit a chili cook off in Austin and write about it.

That night, when I got home, after crawling into bed I tried to call her, but it went to voicemail. I had wanted to check in on her after to see how things ended between her and Terrence and to make sure her birthday wasn't ruined. I sent her a message telling her to call me anytime. My ringer was on. But she didn't.

She sent me a text.

KATIE

> No worries, lovely. T & I are ending things on good note. Sorry things turned so dramatic. Talking it all out with him. I'll fill you in tomorrow. I'm still down for our Austin trip. See you bright and early.

I read her message, remembering how things used to feel unfinished until I talked them out with Katie, and presumably vice versa. But lately, things had shifted for Katie, and her late-night call, the one she talked things out with was transitioning to Canada Man. It was bittersweet. I'd spent years perfecting this role, earning this position, and so easily Terrence had slipped in and stolen my spot.

GABE

so tonight was weird

ME

who needs Taco Tuesdays when you can have Taco Turmoil?

GABE

Taco Tirade?

ME

Taco Tension

ME

you bolted right up the stairs

GABE

I almost followed you out the door, but then you slipped out before I had a chance

ME

you could've chased me out

ME

it would've fit the vibe

GABE

Taco Takeoff

Linda answered the door the next morning.

"Coffee?" she asked as I trailed in behind her.

"I'm all set, but thanks," I said, noting that somehow the kitchen had been cleaned last night, even after all the cleaning crew jumped ship.

"How are you this morning?" she asked, walking to the coffee maker.

"I'm good. I'm a little tired but good." I glanced around, looking for something, not sure what... Okay, I knew what I admitted to myself. I was wondering if Gabriel was up yet.

"Where's Jack London?" I asked, half expecting the pup to be bouncing at my heels like he'd been so much of last night as we snuck him bites of taco.

"He sleeps in a kennel in Gabe's room," she said. "Those two are probably still asleep. Especially after that margarita night. How late were y'all up?"

"We actually weren't up too late," I said.

"Surprising. When we turned in it felt like the party was still roaring." She turned her back to me as she poured herself a cup of coffee.

"You know, speaking of late nights... The other day, I remembered that night you and my mom stayed up until like three in the morning while Gabe and I rewrote his essay, the one he had spent weeks writing but then lost. Do you remember that night?"

"I forgot about that. I do remember. Your mom and I gave up around midnight and fell asleep on the couch if I remember correctly," she said, turning back to me.

"You two were troopers," I flung my hand to my heart. "Gabe and I were in awe of you both even then."

"You two were the troopers. I can't believe you were able to write in one night something he'd spent such a long time working on. Your mom and I were always in awe of what a little dynamic duo you two can be."

"We can be a good team when we want to be." I could see the morning sun glimmering through the kitchen windows.

"Man, I remember how stressed he was. Computers are fickle."

"Typing on computers went on to be both our jobs, even after such a traumatic night because of them!"

"Traumatic, sort of." She giggled into her steamy mug of coffee. "I remember you two laughing and snacking and having a bit of a ball. As dramatic as the stakes seemed, you two still had some fun. What was it Katie used to call you? The twins? Since you two are such peas in a pod."

"Gabriel and I both hate the nickname, twins, actually," I chuckled.

"Oh, you shouldn't. We don't mean it literally. It's always meant you're such a good team. We wouldn't dare mean you're anything like *siblings*." And the way she emphasized siblings made me want to blush.

I opened my mouth to protest, but she continued. "And it's been so good to see the twins, or dynamic duo, I guess might be safer to say, no relation implied, back at it again. The past couple of years, I could feel him missing your presence. Like a little light was switched off."

"Oh, I don't know." I was definitely crimson now.

"I'd venture to say the lack was felt both ways." She was all calm and collected.

"Of course," I crossed my arms. "I missed him, too. We just... you know, lost touch." I looked down at my feet. "He was there, and I was here."

"Here with *Jordan*," she said. And there was something about how she emphasized Jordan's name.

"Well, I mean, that's..." I wanted to minimize it, but it felt like a lie. "Our dynamic duo has always been... Boyfriends just don't get..."

She grinned at me like we were in on a joke together.

Katie walked into the kitchen singing, "Good morning!" the same way she did on work mornings, and we both broke away from our conversation.

"Good morning to you, too," I said. "How's our birthday girl this morning?"

She walked straight past me, proceeding to pull a powdery blue Yeti from the cupboard and fill it with coffee. "Does my birthday last into the weekend? I don't get just one day?"

"Didn't we used to claim birthday weeks?" I reminisced.

"Well, if they have cake at this cook off, I'll get some then," Katie said.

"This chili cooks off sounds fun," Linda said. "Do you two get to vote?"

"Sadly, no, we're not judges. But we do get to try all the different chili." I clapped my hands excitedly. "I'm so excited. I was researching a little the past few days, and it's a really big deal. It's all supposed to be such good food and music that people come from all over."

"Enjoy the chili for me," Linda said while Katie finished gathering her purse and coat.

Katie kissed her mom on the cheek and said, "We will, Mama."

It was a couple hour drive to Austin, so as we buckled up, I told myself to wait a bit before I brought up the fight from last night. I pulled away from her house, and as I got onto the road, I saw her check her phone. I glanced down at the screen for just a second.

Katie shook her head in disbelief. "Emma, are you trying to snoop on my messages?"

"Not at all. Well, not really. I saw you open your phone, and I was *a little* curious if you were texting Terrence," I said. "Last night was just intense, at least the bit I saw before I left. I've been curious. How you're doing?"

"It was just intense because Terrence and I have been going back and forth for weeks about our future—his future. It's like we've been simmering for weeks before we hit a boiling point last night," she said. "But we're okay. We talked it out last night."

"Is it okay if I ask what the back and forth has been? You haven't let on much." I tried not to sound hurt about my lack of inclusion.

"I've kind of told you. I've said how we're trying to figure out what our long-term living situation is going to be. He got his short-term rental here, but it's been killer on him to be bouncing between three places. We keep fighting because he wants me to tell him what I want him to do, but I want him to decide what's best for him and his work."

"Plus, maybe you want him to *want* to move to Sweet River?"

"Sure. I know he wants to be with me. But I can tell he's torn because we've been moving so quickly. We keep talking about our future with a marriage and kids, and we just met months ago. It doesn't *feel* quick, though. It feels natural—right." She sounded so achingly earnest.

"Okay, so you're having these long talks, but you're not asking him to move here?" I toyed with the air conditioner vent.

"Basically. Last night when he was griping about how awful things are, then didn't deny it was my fault...I just snapped. I know it was dramatic, but I did have some tequila in me... And like I said, we were at a boiling point."

"Now it all makes sense." I nodded. "Leave it to the two dorks to get you guys fighting."

"Of course. You can always count on Ricky and Victor. Little instigators," Katie tapped the steering wheel. "Though, honestly,

I'm kind of grateful. You guys ran off, then we laughed about you guys running off, and once the tension was abated...we started really talking. Defenses down. I started crying and said, I don't want to be anywhere but Texas, but I also don't want anyone but him. I asked him, what does he want?"

"What did he say?"

"He said he just wants me. He said it's scary and complicated, but he wants to be with me. He wants the kids. He wants the Texas sunsets. He wants to come get coffee at my coffee shop someday. He wants all of it."

"Of course, he does."

"You know what else he said, Emma? It's cheesy, but I know you'll appreciate it. He said, 'If you're in Texas, I can be in Texas.'"

I remembered him in the coffee shop when they first met, saying, *"If you're free, I can be free."*

"Wow, it's like you're living in the dang *Notebook*," I said in awe.

"I know. It's so cheesy, but it melted my heart. It really did," Katie sighed happily.

"So, what does this mean?" This sounded big. Like marriage proposal big.

"It means he's going to move here. He's going to make Sweet River the home base. When he travels, I'll go with him sometimes. We're going to do life together."

"It sounds like you're really doing this, Katie," I gave her an encouraging smile.

"We're committed," she said. We exchanged excited glances.

I pulled my purse into my lap and started digging around for my sunglasses.

"Are you upset I wasn't sharing much about the long-distance struggles between Terrence and me?" Katie asked out of the blue.

"No," I said, pausing my purse search. "Not upset. But I think it made me notice that our friendship is changing a little."

"Emma, I don't want you to think that!" Katie pouted.

"It's not changing in a bad way, though. We're making room

for someone new. We've never really made room for a guy before-hand. Terrence is the first one." I reached over and gave her arm a little squeeze.

She was quiet, mulling this over. "I guess you're right."

"I used to know what you were feeling about a guy before he did—even guys you were in a relationship with. Now I'm finding out post you guys already sorting it out."

"I wasn't hiding it from you. I think this relationship just feels so serious, and so...ours." She tried to find the right words. "I don't even know how to explain it."

"You don't have to explain it," I said tenderly. "I wasn't expecting you would be married and calling me when he didn't take out the trash or something. Or maybe I did. Either way, if I had to finally scoot over and share some of your time and attention, Terrence makes it easy."

The rest of the day, we talked even more about Terrence—about their future, about his family, about how good of a cook he is, about his ambitions, about silly things they had in common... And on the drive home from Austin, the sky going dark overhead, I had the urge to tell her all about Gabe and me. It felt like the right moment.

She was telling me a story about Terrence, and I had the perfect opening. I had the words. Like God had opened a door for me and said, "This way, Emma."

But I didn't say them. Katie kept talking. She made a joke. The song on the radio changed. Then the moment was gone.

Rose called to talk about work shifts. Katie asked me about what I was going to write about the chili cook off. My mom texted me, and Katie read it out to me. A deer ran out in front of us at one point, and we both screamed and belly laughed. We stopped for water bottles and gas. I forgot I had even wanted to tell her.

Thirty-Two

My dad was up to something. I realized this a couple of days before Easter when he gave me a call one afternoon. I was walking to my car after an early morning shift.

He said, "I'm thinking of planning a little Easter barbecue. You know, the weather's been so nice lately. It'll feel like a little kick-off to spring."

My parents rarely hosted events at their house and even more rarely made much of a fuss over Easter. It felt a little peculiar. I told him I would be there that Sunday after church. We agreed that he could handle the brisket, and I would handle the deviled eggs.

A couple of hours later, I was pushing a shopping cart through Target when I received a text from my dad. It was a group thread—in all caps.

DAD

ALL ARE INVITED TO AN EASTER BBQ AT MY HOUSE THIS SUNDAY AT 2 P.M. BRING YOURSELF AND AN OPEN HEART! SEE YOU THEN!

Bring yourself and *an open heart*? I scrolled through the contacts in the thread, but aside from a few unrecognizable numbers, I knew everyone. I made a mental note to discuss text message writing with my parents at a later date.

Easter Sunday, I wore a blue gingham sundress to church with a white cardigan, and a pair of white flats I'd had since I was seventeen years old. They were scuffed but fit like a dream. My hair was in a loose braid over my shoulder. I sat with my parents, we sang some of my favorite hymns, and then I drove behind my parents' back to their house.

My dad had woken up early that morning to start smoking a couple of briskets. Mom had made a few sides and enlisted friends to bring things potluck style. I had made deviled eggs early that morning, making me late for church.

We set things out and puzzled over why Mom and Dad's outdoor speaker wouldn't turn on. Mom had a special punch recipe she was making. My parent's had a big backyard so we set out a few outdoor tables and chairs for seating, as well as a long tables for the food. Then, people started showing up. Not long after the party had officially begun, I was standing with a plate of chips and French onion dip, chatting with Katie when my dad came over to us.

He looked at us earnestly. "You ladies need to socialize with the other guests."

"What? We have been, Dad." I laughed, a little perplexed. I glanced around the party. Everyone seemed content and happy.

"You're not socializing hovering over by the snack table," he continued.

I shot a puzzled look at Katie. *What was he up to?*

"Okay, okay, we'll get back to socializing. Who knew you were such the host?" Katie laughed good-naturedly.

"My dad is in a mood this spring," I said under my breath as we walked over toward a group of family friends sitting around a table. I had just settled down in a chair to chat with them when Dad popped back by.

He put his hands on my shoulders and whispered, "You should go make some of our *newer* friends feel welcome." He pointed over toward the kitchen where a client of his and her son were talking with my mom.

My mom saw me looking, and as we caught eyes, I watched her stifle a laugh. She shot a glance at the client's son. Things began to click.

Dad was trying to set me up.

"You want me to make your clients feel welcome?" I asked slowly.

"Yes! Come along." He grabbed my hand and led me inside.

"*Dad*," I said, feeling like a disgruntled teenager.

"Hi, Marjorie. This is my daughter, Emma." My dad beamed as we arrived in the kitchen. Marjorie, an older woman with salt and pepper hair and a warm smile, shook my hand eagerly, "Oh, your dad just raves about you, sweetie. I'm so glad we can finally meet."

I smiled politely. "I'm happy to meet you, too."

"Emma, this is Marjorie's son, *Nathan*," Dad said as if he were pointing out a really good deal, all pride and encouragement.

"You and Nathan are the same age. I think your dad and I did the math and realized you were born only a month apart!" Marjorie said.

"A month *exactly!*" Dad added.

I smiled at Nathan. He had a big grin that told me his mother had actually made him privy to this set up. I nervously crossed my arms.

"The twenty-first is a good date to be born," Nathan finally chimed in. He had a warm voice.

He was taller than me with broad shoulders like someone who swam a lot. He wore light denim jeans and a big belt buckle. I glanced down and took in his cowboy boots, scuffed and brown.

"I couldn't agree more." I smiled at him. "Do you live in town?"

The parents immediately hushed, pleased with themselves. We were about to embark on our own conversation; their work had been done. I half expected them to high five.

"I live about half an hour outside of Sweet River, over in Ambrose."

I nodded. "Where that big rodeo is every year?"

"One of our claims to fame," he said as my dad and his mom slowly backed away. "So, you're a writer?"

"I am a writer. And a barista."

"A full plate then."

"How's your plate?" I asked awkwardly. "I mean, is your plate...full?"

His smile was friendly, wide, and charming when he laughed. *He was cute*, I decided. "My plate probably isn't as full as yours with the two jobs. But I'm a teacher over at Ambrose Elementary, second grade."

"Well, your plate is probably very full as a teacher—and far cuter than mine," I said, not letting the analogy go. Because, *awkward.*

"Second grade is my favorite grade to teach. It can be loud and silly, but always really cute."

My dad stood over by Katie. He gave me a thumbs up while Katie mouthed silently, "Are you okay?" I stifled a laugh at the juxtaposition of the two of them, then nodded to Katie, letting her know I was fine.

Nathan began telling me about a field trip to the zoo gone awry when in walked Gabriel. He was in a white button down that I couldn't help but notice made his tan skin look bronze, I bit my lip. He immediately found me with his eyes, but his eyes quickly shifted to Nathan.

I tried to focus back on Nathan's story. "So, the kid thought basically all monkeys ate like Curious George..."

Gabriel joined my parents and Katie, who appeared to be filling him in on my blossoming love story, I realized, as they blatantly pointed over toward Nathan and me. My cheeks were fever hot as I politely laughed along with Nathan.

"You must have some cool stories, being a writer." He wrapped up his second-grade tale.

"When I get to travel, I get some neat stories. But nothing as hilarious as the one you just told me," I said. "So, how long have you been teaching?"

We kept talking. I quickly realized that Nathan didn't know anyone else at this party and didn't intend to. He was wholly committed to our setup. He asked me to sit with him while he ate his supper, he got me any and all drink refills, and he remained dedicated to learning about me all afternoon, with question after question. I, guiltily, felt a little frustrated to be so occupied while Gabriel was sitting around talking with everyone but me.

Nathan went to get us a couple of lemon bars, and I had a moment of quiet. A table away Gabriel was talking with my mother, and I could hear them clearly.

She was asking him, "How long do we have you until you jet off to LA again?"

"A while. I don't know if I want to go back to LA. I've got all my stuff in storage since I came back here. And you know, it was cool for a couple of years, but I don't think I want it to be my home base anymore."

"Will *here* become your home base?" Mom asked. I sat up straighter, straining to hear his answer.

"That's my family's constant question. My mom wants all her chicks in one nest, she always says. It's always an option, of course, and I'll always come here so it is a home base in sorts, but I've actually been thinking I'll—" but then Nathan set the lemon bar in front of me, waking me from my snooping.

"Do you like lemons?" he asked, grasping for conversation. And I couldn't make out what else Gabriel said after that.

But I could feel Gabriel's eyes on me the entire party. I wondered if he could feel mine. I wondered if he had eavesdropped on my table like I'd eavesdropped on his. Then, morosely, I watched him kiss his mom on the cheek and say he was heading out. As Gabriel walked out the door, I picked at lemon bar crumbs on my plate while Nathan told me about his horseback riding.

Gabriel stopped at the doorway, turning around, appearing to hesitate, and we locked eyes. I didn't know what else to do, so I gave a small smile. Nathan noticed my distraction and glanced over toward Gabriel, then back at me. Gabe gave a wink and then left.

The party was over for me. I sank into my chair and waited for Nathan to leave, too. Nathan asked for my number, but I only gave him my email address. He was handsome and friendly, and I spent this whole party getting to know him. Yet, for me, as always, the party began when Gabriel arrived and left with him when he closed the door behind him. The past couple of months had removed the mystery of it. I couldn't pretend or deny.

It hadn't somehow stopped when I moved back home instead of joining him in LA. It hadn't faded with age. I couldn't kiss it away with other guys. It appeared it was a chronic condition.

GABE

I have to admit I'm hurt

ME

?

GABE

I was completely ignored at the BBQ. I understand you were falling in love, or what have you, but still. Not even a 'hello.'

ME

you know how it can be with all-consuming love

GABE

so there was a 'love connection' as your dad kept referring to it?

ME

yes. Planning wedding now.

ME

Not at all. We didn't even exchange numbers. Truly I'm the one who is hurt that NO ONE came to save me or at least help divide up Nathan's attention.

GABE

tbh we all were busy laughing at you.

GABE

and also, admittedly, it was hard to tell if you were into it or not. Didn't want to be a distraction.

ME

YOU, not want to be a distraction?

ME

that's like your whole thing

Marianne called me a few days later, asking if I would fly to California and write about a little central coast town called Cambria.

"Write about it as a hidden gem, perfect for a getaway," she said. I would need to go in May before June Gloom hit. Could I go? She asked.

I said, yes, yes, *yes*. I could go.

"Oh," she added before we hung up. "We can pay for an extra guest if you want to bring a friend or significant other. Just email me the details by the end of the week."

I immediately dialed Katie's number, and she agreed to go on the trip with me. I compiled everything Marianne requested, and our flights and hotels were booked.

So, days later, Katie and I sat in her kitchen excitedly planning for our coming trip. This city, Cambria, was close enough for a day trip to a city called Paso Robles where we could do a wine tasting. And we were researching all of the little shops and cafes along this strip of coastline.

"There's even this Ranch Preserve where we could go on a long walk and get the prettiest pictures," I said, zooming in on the map on my laptop.

Katie peered over my shoulder. "I can't believe how many dreamy little cities exist that I don't even know about."

"It's why I'm writing about it," I said as if I had known it existed all along.

"There are actually tons of little coastal cities like this all along the central coast of California," Gabe said, walking into the kitchen with Jack London hopping between his ankles. "You hear a lot about the southern coast, like Malibu, Laguna, San Diego, and the northern coast, like San Francisco and Monterey. But there are other places to see along the ocean."

"Since you know about this stretch of coast, maybe you can help me plan?" I asked, slipping from my seat at the kitchen island.

"I'd be happy, too. I'm no expert, though, not trying to play it like that."

"Neither of us thinks you're an expert, don't worry," Katie said pointedly. I kneeled down, scratching Jack London behind the ears.

"Getting some good pets, London?" Gabriel said, pouring himself a glass of lemonade.

"London?" I asked, still crouched down beside the dog.

"We've slowly dropped the Jack," Katie said, clicking around on my laptop. "I think we need to try every place that has fresh fish. I am in desperate need of good fish tacos."

"How's the leg?" I asked Gabriel, noticing he was off his crutches today.

"Uh, a little wobbly still, but my physical therapist said I'm good to start putting weight on it. I should watch how long and manage the pain. But honestly, I feel a little *free* without the crutches."

"He's been giddy," Katie added.

"I have been giddy. It's true. Wobbly and giddy," Gabriel said, walking over to London and me. I glanced up from beside London and smiled at him.

Without thinking at all, I stood up as I said, "I'm so happy to see you back on two feet." I wrapped him up in a tight hug, all instinct. He hugged me back tightly, and we swayed for a moment, my cheek against his shoulder. It was unintentional but felt so natural. He let his fingers trail down my spine sparking goosebumps everywhere.

"Thanks, Em," he said against my hair. He somehow smelled like a fresh forest.

I pulled back, surprised at myself, and glanced awkwardly at Katie. She was still on the laptop, immersed in trip planning.

Gabe and I beamed at each other, feeling a little tipsy from the hug as we slowly let go of each other.

A few days before the trip, Katie and I were weaving through a favorite shop trying on sundresses and floppy hats for our trip. Katie had found a big, chunky gray sweater to wear with linen shorts.

We were sharing a dressing room and wound up sitting on the scratchy store carpet talking. Katie was beside me wearing her own jeans but had on a new top she was trying, price tags still dangling. We had just been laughing about my first attempts at latte art as a new barista, and Katie was telling me I'd "come so far."

Then she turned to me, suddenly serious, and said, "Can I tell you a secret?"

"Of course," I said.

"I've been working on all these plans and dreams for Coffee & Commas. I've literally been writing it all up."

"Yeah?"

"You know how Rose has been really, like, mentoring me? She's taken me through so much that I feel like I have such a good grasp of how we could grow the shop." Her eyes gleamed with excitement.

"Have you shown Rose?" I was so proud of Katie I could just burst.

"I haven't shown Rose yet." She started messing with the dangling tags, looking down. "I'm kind of nervous to show her. Rose and I have always worked together so well. I couldn't ask for a better boss and mentor. But lately, she's felt a little checked out. Or maybe, distracted is a better word for it? I know she still loves the shop and our customers. I just feel like..." her voice trailed off.

"Are you afraid she would be upset?"

"No, not upset..." She rested her head back against the dressing room wall. "Maybe I'm afraid she'll be annoyed by it or feel like I'm overstepping or being presumptuous."

"Why else would she be mentoring you if she didn't value your input and your position at the shop?" I tipped my head to the side, giving her a small smile. "I think you should share them with her."

"Maybe I will. If I get the right moment."

I put my hand on Katie's. "Maybe we just steal Coffee & Commas?"

"We kind of already have." Her eyes twinkled.

"I like what we've done with the place." I put my head on her shoulder. "Can you believe we'll be sitting on the beach like this in California soon?"

"At least we know the future week by week, huh?" Katie said. "We might not know where we're going to be a few months from now and definitely not a year from now. But I've got a good idea about next Tuesday."

"*Week by week*, maybe that's how you take life on? Forget five-year plans." I looked at us in the mirror, still playing dress up even now.

. . .

The next day at work, as I was sliding a plate with a big blueberry muffin toward Gabe, Katie rushed in the door. Immediately, her eyes looked sheepish.

"Hello, Katie," I said suspiciously as she slipped behind the counter beside me uncharacteristically quiet.

"I have bad news," she murmured to me, dropping her bag behind the counter.

"What's the bad news?" I asked, knowing our trip was tomorrow. Knowing how you sometimes do, that you couldn't even take things week by week. It was day by day, really.

"Rose had to leave this morning. Her brother-in-law is sick. So, she can't be here. She has to be at the hospital," she said it all quickly. "Which means I have to be here to run things the rest of the week."

I nodded, disappointed. But, I mean, none of that was anyone's fault. I was just really bummed my best friend couldn't enjoy the trip with me. "I'll miss you, but *you have to be here*. I get that."

"I'll miss you, too." She wrapped me up in a hug. "Have an extra fish taco for me."

"I don't even like fish tacos." I made a disgusted face. "How's her brother-in-law doing? Is he okay?"

"He's stable. He had a heart attack. The family just needs help. He and his wife are pretty old, from what Rose was saying," Katie relayed.

"I'll say a prayer," I said. Gabe murmured that he would too.

"Hey, maybe they can use my plane ticket to make your's first class or something?" Katie speculated.

"It's actually nonrefundable," I explained while spraying the counter. I wiped it.

"Yikes." Katie looked sheepish again. It was awkwardly quiet as Gabriel ate his muffin, I kept spraying and wiping, and Katie stood there chewing on her lip.

"Well," she said finally, "why don't you just take someone else? Take Gabe or something."

The two of us both looked at Gabe, who was dusting muffin crumbs off his hands.

He grinned, that mischievous gleam in his eyes. "You know I'm down for a trip."

Other people came to mind who could join me, friends who I had zero romantic feelings toward. Even my mom or dad could probably tag along. But there was that thing about Gabriel that put me in some kind of time machine like I was sixteen again and wanting to make the destructive but thrilling choices.

"Okay," I said, my stomach in happy knots. "Yeah, you should come with me. Can you be ready for a six a.m. drive to the airport tomorrow morning?"

"I'm ready for anything," he said, all cocky and cool, making me roll my eyes. But I couldn't stop smiling. Neither of us could.

He stuck around for a while longer. I filled him in on the trip details and forwarded him the flight information. We kept laughing for no reason—all destructive, all thrilled.

GABE

you sure you want me to come?

ME

yes.

ME

Are you sure you want to come?

GABE

yes.

When I told my mom the night before on the phone about how Katie couldn't come and how Gabriel would be coming with me to take her place, she chuckled a little and said, "Oh, you two are sneaking off together, huh?"

"What? Wait, wait. What do you mean by that?" I demanded, stunned. "Sneaking?"

"Oh, I'm just teasing, honey," she said. I could hear her shuffling around in the kitchen as we spoke.

"*Sneaking off?*" I reiterated, aghast. I had been in the middle of packing, but now I was just stood in front of my suitcase, holding a pair of sandals.

"I just mean, I feel like you two are always...*you know.*"

"I don't know. At all. How are we always *sneaking* off?"

"You two are just sneaky."

"How so?" I was tired of my mom and Gabe's mom's strange little remarks.

"I don't know, sweetie. Let's forget it." Mom was over it.

"Mom!" I shouted like a whiny toddler.

"Okay, fine. I mean that you two feel like you always have some little secret between you. It's like there's always a joke only you both are in on."

"How?" I attempted to fold a dress.

"Oh, come on, Emma. You know how. The eyes you make at each other, the whispers, the jealousy—he was boiling at that silly Easter setup. Your ears looked like they were burning to hear what he was saying. It's been a decade of it. *You know,*" she said. And I did know. I just didn't know that anyone else knew. Heck, I wasn't always convinced Gabe knew.

Mom sighed. "I mean, for being sneaky, you two aren't exactly good at the sneak part of it all."

"So, you think we..." I couldn't say the words aloud. I think all this time, I never had.

"Oh, I'll just say it, Emma. I know you two have always had a crush on each other. And why shouldn't you? How couldn't you? You're two peas in a pod. Always have been."

Tears came from my eyes, leaking over my phone. I felt seen, and there was relief in that. But I also felt exposed and embarrassed. I set the dress I'd been holding down.

"Am I not supposed to say anything? All this time, I've erred on the side of not saying anything. Especially with Jordan in the picture, but it's been years and you two are *still* all googly. I feel like someone ought to!" my mom said, and I could see her shaking her head at the two of us.

"Am I wrong?" she finally asked.

"I don't know what he feels," I whispered. I sat down on the ground beside my bed where my suitcase laid open.

"After all this time, you two have never talked about it?"

"I don't even know if there's anything to talk about, Mom." I pulled my knees against my chest.

"Babe, that's like a house on fire, and you're asking if it's really that warm."

"I think it's always been this way, at least on my end," I admitted. "It's been this way for him, too, at least for the last few years, I think."

"From where I'm sitting, it's been a two-way street since we first sat down beside them in church," she said, the sound of water splashing in the background. "His mama and I have always joked about it behind your backs. She stopped when you and Jordan were an item, but on Easter, we kept having to hold back our laughter."

My face was ablaze. His mom noticed.

"Does Katie..." I let my voice trail off.

"I don't know how she couldn't. But you never know with Katie. Has she never said anything to you?"

"Not a thing." I rested my forehead against my knees.

"How you guys have all resisted talking about the giant, noisy elephant in the room is beyond me." I could just imagine her rolling her eyes. A cupboard door slapped shut.

"What good would it do?"

"Oh, I don't know. *You two could start dating*?" Mom said bluntly. "Isn't pretending worse?"

"But us dating could ruin everything." How my mom couldn't see it was a lost cause was beyond me.

"Ruin what?" she asked incredulously.

"Ruin mine and Katie's whole friendship and our dynamic with the Hernandez family!"

"How would you two dating ruin any of those things?"

"If we broke up."

"That's a big if," she said. Another cupboard door slapped shut.

The next morning, my hands shook the entire time I finished packing my bag, put on my mascara, and slipped on my shoes. My hands shook as I toasted half a bagel. It was as if I had taken three shots of espresso and eaten a handful of sugar. I was completely wired to be spending a few days straight with Gabriel, just the two of us. It was like a toddler being told they could have unlimited access to ice cream.

Now, here I was, loading my bags in the back of his truck as he pointed it toward the airport.

"Good morning," I said through a yawn.

"Good morning to you, too." He glanced over at me.

"I can't believe you still drive this old truck," I said, yanking mindlessly on the seat belt.

"It feels like a piece of me now. Like an extension of me, like a limb."

"Feels like an extension of you to me, too." I patted the glove compartment lovingly making him break into a grin.

We went through a drive-thru for venti lattes and were waiting for our turn in line, when I asked him when he'd last been in California.

"Before Christmas," he said. "In a weird way, things kind of worked out. My lease came up right before I came home for Christmas. I was planning on coming back to LA in January and staying with a friend until I started my work trip. So, in a way, I had kind of already stopped living there. I didn't have a place there anymore."

"Are you planning on going back? I know your leg is getting better," I said, pretending I hadn't overheard him talking about this with my mom already.

"I don't really want to live there anymore. It was a place to get things started—what I needed at the time. But it's not what I need anymore. I'm trying to determine my next steps, especially with the book I'm writing." He hit the blinker before he switched lanes. "Do I get a new place until I take off for my trip? Do I stay put and write freelance until I take off?"

"Where would you go if you got a new place?"

"Wherever I find my next story," he said with a wink.

I just rolled my eyes.

"You know, I've been so focused on what I was supposed to be doing, but couldn't do now and trying to salvage my plans, that I haven't thought much about what I *want* to do in the interim. I've been in talks for a couple of stories, but none require jetting off somewhere cool. I can do most of the work from my bed," he said.

I imagined the two of us lounging in a bedroom working on our laptops, hot mugs of coffee on our end tables, the early morning sun peeking in through the blinds. I shook the image out of my head.

Gabriel was pulling into a spot in the airport parking lot. We yanked our bags from the car and chased after the airport shuttle. We bumped along in the shuttle, shoulder to shoulder. We were quiet, but Gabe kept looking over at me with a grin I could recognize anywhere.

The two of us jetting off on a trip together; the two of us navigating the airport. It felt like my favorite song had come on the radio, and I didn't want to miss a single second of it. I wanted to rewind and trace over these moments again and again while I was in the middle of living them. We trudged through check-in and security, then raced down to our gate to realize we, in our antsy excitement, had arrived early, *and* our flight was delayed. We had a good hour to kill.

I was standing by our gate, shoulders slumped. I shrugged. "I guess we could get some work done?"

"Nah, I know a place," he said, grabbing my hand and leading me to an airport gift shop full of snacks, mugs with Texas flags, books, and magazines.

"I kind of want one of these mugs," I said as we walked through the doors. I picked up a small white mug with a tiny Texas flag imprinted across it.

"One of these," he nodded to the mug in my hand, "or one of these?" He held up a giant mug with the slogan, "Don't Mess With TX!" on it in red, white, and blue font. He wiggled his eyebrows.

"Definitely that one." I put my mug down, laughing.

I walked over to a row of snacks. Gabriel stood by my side and then picked up two bags.

"This," he waved a bag of flaming hot Cheetos, "or this." He then waved a bag of Funyuns.

I snatched the Funyuns from his hand and said, "Funyuns forever."

I walked over to the tall shelves of books, then grabbed a small James Patterson paperback and a former *Bachelor* contestant's tell-all.

"Which one?" I said, holding them both up in front of him.

He tapped the tell-all, whispering salaciously, "You know I can't resist juicy gossip."

I nodded, "Plus, she was my favorite contestant that season."

After we purchased Funyuns and the tell-all for the plane, we found ourselves sitting by the gate waiting to board, still playing this or that.

"Coke or Pepsi?" he asked.

"Do you even have to ask?" I said, a woman with standards. "Okay, road trip or plane ride?"

"Road trip, every time," he said. I raised my eyebrows in surprise. Then he asked, "Coffee on the first date or dinner?"

"Depends on who I'm with," I said, twisting in my seat to face him. He turned to me, too.

"You're with me," he said, like it wasn't an option, it was a fact.

"Dinner," I said before I had anytime to overthink. "And coffee."

He liked my answer, I could tell by his smile as he looked down at his hands. He tapped his seat mindlessly.

"Dashboard Confessional or Fall Out Boy?" I asked.

He chuckled. "You know I can't decide between them!"

"Did I finally stump you?" I asked with pride.

Then, they began boarding. I felt like I was waking up from a dream as if the airport had been a little world where just the two of us existed for a bit, and I had forgotten we had plans and a place to be. We lined up together. Gabriel kept poking me with his boarding pass.

I anxiously kept checking and rechecking that I had my I.D. Gabriel saw me check for the third time and caught my eye and winked, and instead of feeling embarrassed, or like I needed to make fun of myself, I felt like somehow it was likeable, like it was seen, like it was okay.

"Remember how I almost bought a flight out for your last trip?" he leaned down a little, his voice low and breathy against my ear. "I knew I would end up on one of them."

We realized as we filed onto the plane that our seats weren't together. I felt my heart, which had been fluttering around my chest all morning, rebound a little.

"Oh," I said when I found my seat. I glanced behind me at Gabe who was looking at his seat number and realizing they were far apart. "I guess this way, we can get some work done."

"That doesn't sound like fun," he said low, just for me to hear. I gave a small, half laugh. I tucked into my seat as he walked away. It was a two-seat row, and I had the aisle seat.

I pulled out of my phone and was turning it to airplane mode when suddenly Gabriel was standing before me with a smiling elderly lady.

"Hi?" I said.

"Hi, I'm Doreen," she said, a small woman with a big voice.

"Doreen was my seatmate, but she offered to trade seats with you, so we can sit together," Gabriel explained.

"Wow." I stood up happily. "Thank you, Doreen! I'm Emma, by the way."

"I'm happy to help such a cute couple sit together," Doreen said.

"Oh, thank you," I said again, stumbling over my words. *Do I correct her?*

"How long have you two been together?" she asked.

"Since we were kids," Gabriel answered before I had a chance to think. "I had a crush on her when I was thirteen years old."

Doreen clutched her heart while I scooted into the aisle. "That is just a Hallmark movie, right there."

"I've always thought so." Gabriel sighed sweetly. I looped my arm into his. "Thanks again, Doreen. Have a nice flight."

My seatmate had his headphones on and was on his iPad. He hadn't looked our way once, and I don't think he'd even realized there'd been a switcheroo.

Off Gabe and I walked arm in arm to our own row for two. We settled in while people around us found their seats, and the flight attendants walked back and forth, getting everything in place before take-off.

"Hey, Gabe?" My tone was questioning.

"Yeah?"

"I know LA isn't where you want to be anymore, but do you ever miss it? I had forgotten I wanted to ask you that when we were driving earlier." I messed with my seat buckle.

"I do miss it, yeah. Not like I miss Sweet River when I'm away, but I miss some of my friends. A lot of people are kind of moving along in their lives, getting married or having kids, getting new jobs, going to grad schools across the country...life just kind of rolling along. I miss the people and how it was when we were all starting out together. I miss the beach, though I didn't get out to it as much as you'd think. I miss the weather, for sure. I miss the food. There was a ramen place I find myself hungry for almost every day. I miss that first job I had. It was a really cool season of my life."

"But it was over?"

"I could feel it was ending. It felt like reading the end of a book, the stack of pages getting thinner in your hands, and you know you're running out of story. It's wrapping up even if you aren't there yet." He leaned back against the seat.

"That sounds kind of sad," I said softly.

"Not if it was a really good book." His eyes flashed.

"Book or movie?" I asked suddenly.

"Book," he said. "You know that."

"I did." I pushed my shoulder into his. His hand was on the edge of his thigh, his knuckles against the side of my leg.

My dad always griped about how they "crammed people into planes like a bunch of sardines," but I was giddy to sit close like this to Gabriel for hours.

After about half an hour of chitchat, I slid my wireless headphones on, and Gabe did the same. I opened my phone and toggled between the Music app and the Netflix app when Gabe grabbed my phone right out of my hands.

"Hey," I said, reaching across him to try and get it back. He held his long arms up over our heads and tapped on the screen until my ears filled with the sounds of "Adore You" by Harry Styles.

"I remember you and Katie mooning over this song for months, blaring it every time I came home to visit. Truly annoying the whole house," Gabriel said, turning the volume down a little.

"Here I thought you were trying to say you adore me," I huffed playfully.

"Well, that, too, of course." He skipped back in the song a little. "It's true," he said, dramatically.

Then I stole his phone and put on "Alone Together" by Fall Out Boy. He broke into a wide grin. I remembered how we would play this song at full volume in his truck with the windows down.

He leaned in close, so I could hear him clearly, and I could feel his breath on my ear as he whispered, "You're telling me, you want to be alone together?"

I shook my head at him, ignoring his question and the goose-bumps all over my arms. I reached for my phone, but he, still scrolling through my music, said, "Wait, wait," while Harry Styles cooed into my headphones.

After a little more tapping, the song stopped playing, and he floated my phone before my eyes with a note open that asked, *Truth or Dare?*

"Gabe, we are not teenagers anymore. Plus, the last time we played, I wound up soaking wet in the dead of winter." I handed him his phone back.

"Emma, truth or dare?" There was a challenge in his voice.

"Fine, fine." I couldn't help but smile a little as he punched the air victoriously. "*Dare.*"

His eyes went wide. "Dare? Living on the edge, are you, Em?"

I took out my headphones and slide them into my bag as he tapped his chin, pondering a dare.

"Okay, I got it. I dare you to walk down the aisle of this plane singing 'Alone Together.'"

"*What?* Why would I just randomly walk down the aisle singing?" I immediately had my face hiding in my hands.

"Just act like you're singing to yourself, very loudly albeit, as you saunter to the bathroom."

"Saunter?"

"Yes, I've seen you. You saunter."

I took in a deep breath to steady myself.

"Come along now, Em," Gabe urged me.

I scowled at him. But, proceeded to slip out of our tiny row, walking down the aisle, and then shakily started singing the chorus, staring straight ahead, letting my voice get louder.

I ignored a few people who I heard whispering, "Does she realize we can all hear her?" and "Why are there are always weirdos on our flights?"

I got to the restrooms, then slipped inside. I hid out for a few minutes before racing back to my seat to find Gabriel shaking with laughter.

"Truth or dare?" I spat angrily.

"That was utterly beautiful. When's the album?" he asked, obviously pleased with himself.

"Someone literally said I was a weirdo." I sunk down into my seat.

"A beautiful weirdo," he said. "An angel."

"Truth or dare?" I asked again.

"Truth. I do not trust a dare made in vengeance."

"When was the last time you kissed someone?" I asked without thinking, almost wasting the question on impulse.

"Ah." He took a beat. "Last summer. I told you about her outside the mechanic shop. We were seeing each other. Then, we broke up, you know, with the holding back and all. But at least, I was one heck of a kisser."

"Last summer," I said, wondering...Heather or Lila?

"Your turn."

"Dare."

He raised an eyebrow. "Feeling bold today."

He brainstormed for a moment as I tried to not imagine what a girl Gabriel would kiss might look like.

"I dare you to go ask the guy down the aisle for his number," he said, his voice secretive and quiet. We both turned in our seats. "Him, in the blue cap." He pointed.

The people in the row behind us were staring at us. We noticed and jolted forward facing again. I nodded, bracing myself to go.

"You know, never mind," he said, placing his arm in front of me as I stood up to leave. "I don't like this dare."

"What? Why?"

"I just...I can think of something better."

"No takebacks," I said, suddenly set on completing my assignment.

"Wait, wait, don't ask for his number," he said, rushed. "Why don't you talk in a funny voice or like ask to take a selfie with him?"

"I'm going with the original, man." I elbowed my way out of the seat and sauntered down to the guy in the blue cap.

His nose was buried in a book. He was thankfully in the aisle seat, so I bent down a little and tapped him on the shoulder.

He looked up confused. "Hi?"

"Hi, there," I said, forcing confidence that wasn't there.

"Hi?" he repeated.

"I noticed you down here and thought I'd come over and introduce myself. I'm Emma. What's your name?"

"I'm Greg," he said awkwardly. "Can I help you with something?"

"I was wondering if I...um... If you don't mind, maybe I could have your number?"

Before he could speak, a beautiful dark-skinned woman poked her head out over his shoulder. She grinned. "*His wife* would say that's a big no, but thank you."

The couple broke into laughter. I tripped over my feet, backing up.

"I-I'm so sorry!" I stuttered to the woman.

She shook her head as if it wasn't a problem, as if she found the whole thing hilarious, and the man buried his face back into his book. And I couldn't get to my seat fast enough.

"Did you get the—" Gabriel asked as I fell into my seat beside him, mortified.

"He was *married*," I squeaked out the last word.

Gabe was visibly delighted by this piece of information.

"Truth or dare?" I moaned.

"Truth," he said, still beaming.

"Truth or dare?" I repeated.

"I already said truth."

"Truth or *dare*?"

He winced, realizing I wasn't giving up. "Dare?" he said.

"I dare you to make a very, very, *very* loud fart sound and then apologize to the whole plane."

He stared at me blankly.

"Go for it," I said, gesturing to the plane of people around us.

"That is absolutely childish. Totally immature." He shook his head as if he absolutely wouldn't do it.

"And me singing Fall Out Boy for the whole plane is a display of maturity?"

"Fall Out Boy is a display of good taste in music which can lend itself—"

"I gave you your dare." I cocked my head to the side.

"This dare wasn't made from a good place in your heart. I—"

"Do it now."

Gabriel's face was already red with embarrassment as he took in a big breath of air. He shook his head in judgment as he let out a long, loud flatulent sound. I started shaking with silent laughter as people around us started snickering and glancing around.

Gabriel then shot out of his seat and said loudly to the entire plane, "Oh, I am so sorry! Big burritos for lunch. You know how it is."

I could hear the plane reacting to his apology as he slid down in his seat beside me. "You are a child, Emma Brown. A total child."

"Everyone probably hates the two of us." I sighed wistfully.

"Truth or dare?" Gabe wasted no time.

"Truth. I don't think this plane wants to see another dare from us." I also had access to Gabriel's full attention for a couple of hours, I was going to use it.

"If you could live anywhere in the world, where would it be?" he asked quickly as if he'd been waiting for a chance to ask it.

"If I knew the answer to that…" I let my voice trail off. "I don't know. Maybe spend the summer in New York City."

"That's for the summer. That's a trip. Where would you *live*?"

"I don't think I'm looking to figure that out right now. I want to see some places first." I was slowly realizing it was okay to not know the answer to that question yet.

"Everyone keeps asking me where I'm going to set my *home*

base, so I feel that. I keep thinking in terms of phases of life when everyone's always asking about long term."

"I was just telling Katie that there is no five year plan right now. Life has been lived on a week-by-week basis."

"Truly, with my older siblings and even just recently from my own life, I've realized even with a five-year-plan, people still just take it week by week and see if that takes them where they're aiming to be in the next five years." Gabriel had a way of making me feel effortlessly understood.

"In the next five years, I'm aiming to be happy in my career." A flight attendant offered us drinks. I got a fizzy ginger ale and Gabriel got a water.

"Take it week by week. And this week, you're getting paid to visit a little beach town, so things are looking good," Gabriel said.

"Your turn." I took a sip.

"Truth."

"If *you* could live anywhere in the world, where would it be?"

"I like your summer in New York idea." I paused, waiting for him to continue. "I really would like to live in New York for a short time. Maybe Seattle. These are all places I could see myself being for a bit. But home base? Putting up a Christmas tree? Maybe Austin."

"Really?" My eyes widen in surprise. Gabriel putting down roots so close to Sweet River?

"I feel like I have a whole lot of questions to answer and things to do before I'm buying a house or anything like that." He waved his hands, as if to wave off any assumptions I might've been jumping to.

"Right now, we're off to New York for the summer," I said, feeling butterflies at the way my words made him smile.

"What would we be doing there in the summer?"

"Is that your truth question?" I peered up over the rim of my cup.

"No! Tricky, tricky. I have a question all queued up." He

wagged his finger at me. "When you first started dating Jordan, was there any other guy on your mind? What was going on?"

I closed my eyes, finding my words. "You know, some people are always on your mind. There in the background, like trees in the breeze or footsteps on the sidewalk. So perpetually present, you can force yourself to stop paying attention to it. To get used to it."

"Until it leaves and then comes back again."

"Yeah." I pulled at a loose thread in my shirt. "Exactly. I ran into Jordan, and in that moment of my life, with everything feeling so loud, so pressuring—I just let, even the idea of someone else, everything fade into the background. It didn't go away, but it just stopped being front and center."

"The answer is *yes* then?" His maple eyes were intent on me. Both of us knowing he was the other guy on my mind.

"Yes," I said, quiet as a soft breeze.

He didn't say anything for a minute. I dug in my bag for nothing really. I mindlessly leafed through my wallet.

"You going to ask me?" he said after a few moments passed.

"Oh, yeah," I said overly enthusiastically. I dropped my bag back under the seat. "Truth or dare?"

"Truth."

"Do you still write poetry?"

"Here and there." He pushed open the window.

"When was the last time?" I glanced out at pink clouds floating by us.

"That wasn't the question," he said, surprisingly dodgy.

"Why don't you want to tell me?"

"That also wasn't the question. Truth or dare?" he turned toward me.

"Truth."

"Have you and the guy from the barbecue been talking?" He tapped his fingers on his leg.

I burst into laughter, recalling my mom's words from our last phone call.

"What's so funny about this question?" he asked.

I kept laughing. "It's not funny. It's just... I messaged you about that guy, remember? I only gave him my email address. Nothing is going to happen with that guy."

"Hey, I had to check. Stuff can sizzle over email sometimes. I wasn't sure if things had changed since we texted about it."

"Had to check, huh?" I fight a grin.

"You guys were glued together the whole party."

"That does not mean anything. *My dad is his dentist*," I said the last part as if that was some nail in the coffin.

"Your dad is my dentist." His brows furrow.

"So?"

"Dare," he says through a yawn.

I grabbed his phone and said, "Let's see the last person to slide in your DMs."

He opened up his Instagram and pulled up a message from a couple of days ago. I squinted and realized I knew the girl.

"Is that the receptionist from Paws for Effect?" My jaw dropped.

"This is the second time she's slid in, too. Look." He scrolled for me to see.

I read her messages. "She could've at least pretended she was just wanting to check on London."

"She does ask how he's doing. But I can't blame her for shooting her shot."

"Are you going to reply?" I wiggled my eyebrows.

"Should I?"

"That is up to you. And London, honestly." I drop his phone back into his hands.

"Truth or dare?"

"Truth feels the safer option."

"You're wanting a safe question, eh?" He flexed his jaw.

I shrugged. "I'm not wanting to saunter down the aisles, is what I'm saying."

"I've always wondered," he leaned his head closer to mine, "have we ever kissed, or anything, in your dreams?"

My throat felt impossibly dry. "In my dreams?"

"Yeah, dream Emma. Is she kissing me?" His eyes gleam with mischief.

"Yeah." I swallowed. "Maybe a couple of times."

I was highly aware of our knees bumping into each other, our arms touching on the shared arm seat, and his mouth still only breaths apart from my own.

"Dare," he said, looking in my eyes before I ever asked.

"Dare," I repeated, mindlessly. All I could think about was kissing Gabe.

I'm sure the airplane was loud with the engine roar, with babies crying, with movies playing, with flight attendants attending, but I could still hear my pulse throbbing, hear him swallow.

I could dare him to kiss me. It felt like he was daring me to dare him to kiss me.

Finally, I said, without breaking eye contact, "I dare you to post a picture of me on your Instagram story, saying you have to finally admit that I am the superior writer, thinker, and person overall."

He leaned in close and whispered against my ear, "I didn't have it in me to pay for inflight Wi-Fi."

We both broke into laughter. Body shaking, tears forming, laughter. But we never lost touch, for even a second.

Thirty-Six

Sorry I couldn't make it for the trip. Thanks for understanding. Hope Gabe doesn't annoy you too much, ha ha

We booked a ride from the airport since it was almost an hour's drive to our hotel in Cambria. The driver was a chatty older man who talked with us about the times he'd visited Texas. Gabe and he got along well while I checked in with work.

The hotel was airy and laid back. They advertised excitedly that they had wine and beer on tap from the moment we walked in. The front doors were open, and I could feel the ocean breeze all crisp and cool on my skin, smelling like seaweed and hyacinths.

When we got our room cards, the woman at the front desk was trying to hide her apparent confusion that this couple traveling together was checking in separately and staying in different rooms. While walking down the hall, we realized our rooms were side by side.

"I guess I can just pound on the wall if I need you?" Gabe joked as he rolled his bag through his door. "Text me when you're ready to head out."

"I will." I gave a little wave and slipped into my own room.

The window on the back wall was open. I could hear the wind bristling through the trees outside. I had a little fireplace in the corner and a big canopy bed. I threw myself down on it, closing my eyes for a moment, letting the cool air wash over me.

It felt meditative. Fresh air on my skin, the sound of trees and waves outside my window. The quiet in my room. I listened to all of it, when, a little muffled, I heard "Alone Together" playing.

I sat up. I could definitely hear Fall Out Boy singing. I walked to the window to see if someone was playing it outside. I looked around my room for a second before I realized it was coming from my ridiculous neighbor on the other side of the wall. Pressing my ear against the wall, I could hear Gabriel singing along to the song.

I pulled out my phone and typed up,

ME

> I'm going to call the front desk and complain.

He replied telling me to invite him in—quoting the song and making a request at the same time. The music stopped playing, so I walked over to open my door, and there he stood.

He had two bottles of water. "I know they have wine on tap, but you need to hydrate after a flight."

"You're thoughtful. I guess I won't call and complain." I took one of the bottles from his hand.

"Of course not. I was just trying to creatively ask you to invite me over." He walked inside as I closed the door behind him.

"Oh, so you *were* speaking to me through the song, like when you told me you adored me?"

"Let's not pretend you weren't sending me a message with your song selection, too," he leaned on his shoulder against the wall.

"Yeah, how does the song go...something about ruin?" I said coyly.

"You wanted to get me alone." He winked. "And look, you got your way."

I gave him a shove. But he wasn't wrong. "Let's get out of here. There is an ocean just outside our window."

The walk from our hotel to downtown was short, so we picked up a pizza and then carried it down to the beach.

We sat on the pebbly shore, our shoes kicked off, eating slice after slice while watching the waves roll in and out. The sun was setting in different shades of pink. People were pulling out their phones all around us to capture it.

I was too happy with my circumstances to even think about breaking the spell between Gabriel and I by touching my phone. I wasn't even following my self-imposed itinerary at the moment.

Gabe had asked what we should do, I told him I just wanted pizza and the ocean, ignoring my little list. When the pizza box was empty, Gabe snapped photos, and I watched him from my spot with my head on his shoulder. He worked his phone like a professional camera.

He turned his camera to video mode to shoot the sunset, then turned it toward our faces, with my head still resting on his shoulder.

"A weary traveler," he narrated. I giggled and pushed the phone away. He put his phone back in his pocket then wrapped his arms around me, rubbing my shoulders to warm me up. I would've happily stayed like that for the rest of the night. For the rest of my life.

The sky went from pink to purple to indigo. The waves kept coming. People kept leaving. The tide got closer and closer until it finally chased us away. But we stayed as long as we could, finally alone together.

. . .

I t was bittersweet to close my hotel room door that night. It was chilly after the sun went down. I clicked on my fireplace but left the window open a crack, just enough to hear the ocean waves beyond the trees.

I had just crawled under my covers, content and sleepy when I heard the muffled sounds of a song behind mine and Gabriel's shared wall. Was he playing a song for me again?

I tiptoed from my bed, placed my ear against the wall, and could hear Jimmy Eat World singing about time in "For Me This Is Heaven."

Nostalgia crashed over me like a heavy wave. I could instantly see teenage Gabriel singing along to Jimmy Eat World in that old truck of his. The windows down, his messy curls making me melt.

The song begged questions from the other room.

I pressed my head against the wall and listened to the piano. My heart was stuck between the sweet nostalgia of memory and the painful hope of what could be.

I walked back across the room and snatched my phone off the nightstand. Impulsively, I sent a message to Gabe, asking my own question.

ME

Can you still feel my head on your shoulder?

I ran back over to the wall as the song came to an end and quickly queued up my own old favorite, remembering dancing around his kitchen in my pajamas, belting out the song "Teenage Dream" with Katie. As she sang about skintight jeans and forts made out of sheets, I heard Gabriel's raspy laugh from the other room.

Seconds later, my phone lit up with a message from him, with his own version of the song.

GABE

The way you're stuck in my head, I can't sleep

We flew to Cali and ate pizza on the beach.

I bit my lip, melting straight into the hotel's plush carpet when I read his next message.

Now every February you'll be my Hot Valentine Date

As the song came to an end, he started playing "Riptide" by Vance Joy. He used to play this song on the piano upstairs at his house. I would hear him while working on homework at the kitchen table or while sitting outside with Midnight. I closed my eyes and saw him sitting at the piano in his white tee shirt, hair falling in his eyes as he bent over the keys.

I miss your cover of this song.

so much I just gotta know

I held the phone to my chest, listening to the urgency, the fear, the hope in the song. I thought, maybe I couldn't relate to this song, but oh, how I could relate.

The song came to an end, and neither of us played another. It was quiet on both sides of the wall.

I sang the chorus to myself quietly. Just me and my feelings all alone on my side of the wall, so very aware of Gabriel on the other side. Was he sitting there, still? Like me? Basically together, but very much alone—a big, fat wall between us.

Was his hair wet from the shower? Was he in pajama bottoms, no shirt?

goodnight, little writer

I crawled back into my bed. The room felt too quiet now, even with the waves out the window. I pulled my laptop onto my lap to work on my piece for this weekend. Going over my notes from my first day of travel. I worked, trying my hardest not to be distracted by the ridiculously sweet guy next door.

Thirty-Seven

The next morning, I slid the balcony window wide open, letting the crisp, cool morning air fill the room. I wore the thick hotel robe as I got myself ready and pulled my hair back into a sleek ponytail. I picked out a flowy sundress and a beige and white cardigan with big pockets. I had just finished putting on a bit of mascara and tinted moisturizer when there was a little tap on my door.

In my doorway stood Gabriel with to-die-for sleepy eyes, holding two large coffees.

"You are a hero among men," I greeted him. "Come in, come in."

He walked in behind me, then sat down beside the warm fireplace. I plopped down next to him. "I got you a lavender oat milk latte with an extra shot."

"You know me." I happily started sipping. "How did you sleep last night?"

"Like a baby," he said. "I forgot how much I missed being on a trip."

"Sleeping to the sound of waves isn't half bad."

We discussed our plans to go to a winery on the edge of town, where I had booked a wine-tasting experience. We were going to get lunch while we were there. After we had finished talking about our plans, we quietly sipped our coffees and looked at each other as if there was something else to say, but we were just waiting on the other one to say it.

I let out an awkward laugh. "I guess we should go soon?"

"I feel kind of lucky. I have you all to myself. No sharing you with anyone. Not with my sister. Or people in the coffee shop. I can ask you whatever I want," Gabe said with a mischievous gleam in his eyes.

"What are you wanting to ask me?" I asked curiously, albeit cautiously.

"I have a list, you know." He scooted closer to me. My mind went wild with questions I could ask him, a list long enough to cross California to Texas.

I bit back a smile. "Hit me with one."

"Well, for starters," he paused to think for a moment, then proceeded with, "do you ever compare people to me, to us?"

"How do you mean?"

He went silent for a few beats. "I mean, I went out with a girl last November. We went on a couple dates, actually. She was cute, sweet. But, for some reason, I kept thinking about you and me. How *we* are when we're together. Comparing our conversations. Thinking how you might respond differently than she does. How we feel... Okay, like, she'd lean into me when I made a joke, similar to how you always do, but there's something about..." He went silent.

"Yeah, I do," I said, taking a steadying breath as I answered honestly. "I know exactly what you mean."

He turned and looked at me. His eyes were digging into me like he was searching for something buried, hidden.

"What do you think that means?" he asked, almost a whisper.

He was trying to get me to look at him. I looked at my coffee cup as if the cardboard sleeve was really something special. This conversation was a precipice we could carelessly fall into, the truth not that far, just a dive below, and he knew it.

"What do you think?" I asked, my voice weak, cautious. There was a line we couldn't cross, or it was game over, go home. I'd rather have the reckless possibility than any sort of honest closure.

Finally, he said, all jokes and false casualty, "It probably means you've always had a crush on me."

"You figured me out." I finally looked into his eyes. "I've been pining for you since I was thirteen years old," I said it in a sarcastic, rolling-my-eyes tone. As if it wasn't as real as my very hand reaching up to brush his curls back. He closed his eyes against my touch.

"Every poem you wrote was for me?" He played along.

"Except for the ones about my boyfriends."

The entire ride to the winery, the two of us were laughing in the backseat about old memories—things we'd never discussed before. Times we were jealous of each other's love interests or each other's attention. Silly, childish miscommunications. We asked about things we'd always wondered. It was as if something had cracked open between us, and instead of ushering in to glue it back shut, we were delicately peering inside. What was there? What had always been there?

We walked to our table, guided by a sommelier. The air was cool even though it was spring, so there were heaters on the patios.

The server set a big charcuterie board before us, and we dug in with gusto. Brie, prosciutto, peppery salami, olives, grapes, jams, nutty crackers, sourdough bread, goat cheese—all of it just for us two.

We ate. We sipped. We laughed. We became friends with Bridgette, our server. We became friends with a couple celebrating their thirty-sixth wedding anniversary at the table across from us, Michael and Laura. They bought a bottle of wine and shared it with us. My mouth turned purple, and Gabe's did, too.

Bridgette, Michael, and Laura all thought we were a couple. We didn't set anyone straight. We told our new friends about our mutual childhood crushes, about being in high school and writing poems for each other, all romantic and dramatic.

"I fell in love with her before I even knew what love was," Gabe said, tipsy and truthful. He squeezed my hand across the table. "She's how I learned what love was."

I swooned. *Does he mean it?* Deep down, as terrifying as it was to admit, I knew that he meant it.

"He makes me feel like I'm perpetually a lovesick teenager," I joked. But it wasn't a joke. It was the awful-break-my-heart truth.

We didn't tell our new friends about my twenty-first birthday. We didn't mention Jordan. In this perfect afternoon, we wrote the story the way it happened in my dreams. We stayed at the winery for the whole afternoon.

Our Lyft picked us up as it edged closer to evening and drove us home. I rested my tipsy, sunburnt head against Gabe's shoulder the entire ride back.

"Can this be my new spot," I whispered. My filter melted away under the West Coast sunshine

He laced his fingers in mine and said, "It's yours whenever you want it."

We held hands the entire drive home. My eyes were closed, I was almost asleep, but this moment felt kind of like a dream.

We got back to our hotel and started to rush, realizing the sun would soon be setting, and I still had a walking trail I wanted to visit.

We went to our separate rooms to change since the temperatures dropped later in the day. I put on a bulky, soft pink sweater and slipped on some comfortable sandals. I pulled my hair into a loose braid, down my shoulder.

I was drinking a lot of water and snacking after a day in the sun, drinking wine. Gabriel was waiting outside my door. His curls were loose, his eyes bright. All attempts to sober up felt pointless. I was sober, sure, but as we held hands down the hallway, looking at each other and laughing at a secret just between us. We were hopelessly drunk on the escalating feelings.

A car picked us up and cruised down the coastline until we hit the Fiscalini Ranch Preserve. We walked up the wooden steps and deck that led us to the walking path weaving along the coastline. Tall grass and succulents were afoot. Waves crashed out below. Gabe kept tossing my braid the way he did when we were in elementary school.

"Hey," he said as we walked along the path. "Let's cut through the grass. Do you see there's some worn paths from people walking out? Let's get closer to the edge. You could get some great photos of the sunset over the cliffs at golden hour."

"Good idea," I said. I had been so distracted by his presence that, for a moment, I had forgotten this was a work trip.

We walked further out until we could see the wild waves against the cliffside. Gabriel helped me take pictures with my new camera. I took notes on my phone as he gave me tips. Then he grabbed the camera from my hands.

"Look out at the view," he said, taking a few steps back. "I want to get a picture of the beautiful writer." He aimed the camera at me. My cheeks flushed at his words, my chest tightened.

I shook my head, "no," but he started clicking anyway.

I turned toward the coast line, my back to Gabriel, watching the golden thread over the sea as the sun disappeared. The rosy and peony pinks in the sky. I let myself forget anything but the endless sea before me, the smallness of this moment, the enormity of the sky. Gabriel came up beside me, dropped the camera back in my bag, and weaved his warm arm around my waist.

I realized at that moment that I had always thought my crush on Gabriel was so much bigger and more consuming when I was younger. That I could potentially grow out of these feelings like a pair of shoes that weren't the right size anymore. I had been lying to myself. Minimizing it so I could do things like fall for Jordan and endure living separate lives. But my feelings were stronger than ever. This realization took the breath right out of me.

To distract myself from these thoughts, these feelings, I dug the camera from my bag to see the photos he'd captured of me.

"The writer, always in her thoughts," he whispered over my shoulder as I scrolled through the photos. His fingers resting on my hip.

I turned my head and looked up at him, and he said, "Always beautiful." His eyes dropped to my lips.

I forgot about the lines I shouldn't cross, the need to just be closer to him pounded in my veins silencing everything else. Now his eyes were on me like a question, and I knew the answer. I slipped my camera back into my bag, then lifted my fingers to his curly hair, pulling his lips to mine. And just like that, we were kissing.

He wrapped his arms around me, pressing me against him. The two of us took turns pulling each other closer. Urgent, hungry kisses, after all this time. Finally, finally.

I heard footsteps and pulled away for a second to see a scruffy little puppy running toward us, his owner looking mortified as she chased after him.

"I'm so sorry to interrupt. Oh my goodness, so sorry! Come on, Mr. Flufferson," she said, her face all red and worried, as we told her not to worry about it. She grabbed her dog and then darted off.

I looked back up at Gabriel for a second from my spot in his arms. We were both grinning. I buried my head into his chest in giggles.

He whispered into my hair, "It feels so good to finally hold you close like this."

It feels so right, I thought to myself. Two magnets making contact.

I stayed in his arms, my face in his chest taking in his scent, feeling him breathe until I realized it was pitch dark around us. We stumbled along the trail back home, pointing up to the starry sky, stopping to kiss and pull each other closer—intoxicated by each other.

. . .

We stopped at a restaurant downtown that looked like a cozy cottage with a fireplace crackling inside.

"So good," I'd said about the food, although I barely even tasted the salmon salad I ordered. I was too jumpy and excited as Gabriel and I kept holding hands and kicking feet under the table.

"Why are you so cute?" he asked me randomly.

I stole a bite of his pork tenderloin and olallieberry marmalade just because I could. The waiter told me they were known for those berries in Cambria.

"I like to see you working," he mused. "I want to see all your notes and pictures later. I'm excited to see you typing away."

"I do that alone in bed," I said. "I can't write with someone over my shoulder."

"Even me?" He leaned closer.

"Especially you," I said, taking a big bite. My hand was shaking. My chest was shaking. The way you do when you're on the precipice of a big freaking deal.

Gabriel finished his food and asked me if I wanted to share dessert. I said, "yes," but I mostly just wanted to be alone with him again. But sure, we could stay surrounded by people in this restaurant. I gave the waiter my plate. We both ordered hot coffees and shared a crème brûlée.

We are sharing a dessert, I thought, as we both dug our spoons in. Was this crossing a line? He told me I was cute. Was that crossing a line? We just made out. That was *definitely* crossing a line. What should I do about the stupid line? Could I just deal with it later? Eat the dessert. Kiss the man.

"Man, this is really good," he said, a mouthful of brûlée.

I almost said, "I wouldn't know," because I couldn't taste the food. All my senses were focused on Gabriel Hernandez. I could feel every bump of his leg under the table. I was zeroed in on how his jaw moved as he ate, and I swear I could hear him lick his lips like it was right next to my ear.

"What's going on in that head of yours?" he asked, tipping his head in concern.

I want to climb over this table and kiss you again, I thought

"I think this coffee has me all wired," I lied.

"Oh man," he said. "It is strong."

I nodded, scraping the plate for a last bite.

"Should we head back?" he asked.

We got the check and left.

I could barely breathe in the backseat of the car. I could smell his cologne. I could feel his heat. My breath was quick and reckless. I said nothing while he chatted with our driver. He was all cool as a cucumber, as if we kissed every single day, nothing new. As if we caught fire every single day, nothing new.

We walked down the hotel hallway, holding hands again, slow and awkward. Should we take our time? Should we rush ahead? What was the pace when you were falling down a precipice, freefalling into the treacherous, messy unknown? Then, we were in front of our doors.

"I guess…" I said, breathless, shakey.

He grabbed my other hand and pushed me against my door, his body crashing into mine, and he kissed me. He was almost lifting me as he pulled me closer. We kissed like that, needy, breathless, reckless, burning. People might've passed by. The concierge maybe heard us. I didn't care. It was just us, for me. Our hips, our hands, our breath. Just Gabe pressing me between him and my door until I wondered if it'd collapse.

Finally, we stopped, and he leaned down to the spot between my ear and shoulder, saying, "I need to get a hold of myself." *I needed to get a hold of him.*

"I think you're perfectly fine," I whispered.

We were still leaning against the door, catching our breath.

He started to hesitantly step back. "I'll let you get back to work," he said.

Before I had time to remember how to form sentences, he'd disappeared back into his room. I just about fell into my hotel room. I felt disoriented, nearly wasted on emotion and desire. I walked straight to the window and let the cold air hit me. I knew we were running on pure feelings. It was like we'd let our minds run the show for too long so our feelings had grabbed hold of the steering wheel.

I just wanted to hold on for dear life and make sure our feelings didn't drive us over a cliff, drive us until we crashed and burned. But who was I kidding? We were already burning.

After a shower, I slipped into my cozy robe and curled up with my laptop to write. A message from Gabriel was on my screen, but I must've missed it.

GABE

Are you okay?

I was more than okay. I was jittery and happy and blissful and scared and confused. Was I stupid? That was another question. But I was happily stupid. I didn't want to lose whatever we had for however long we could have it.

ME

listen for the answer

I walked over to the wall and started playing "Kiss Me" by Sixpence None the Richer from my phone.

GABE

anytime.

Thirty-Eight

I woke up the next morning before the sun rose. I was still reeling from yesterday. I washed my face, brushed my teeth, threw on some clothes, and knocked on Gabriel's door. A few minutes later, a sleepy-eyed and shirtless Gabriel opened the door.

"Hi," he said, his voice thick with sleep.

"Hi." I waved.

"You're very cute, but it's also very early," he shook his wrist to look at his watch. "Yeah, it's six a.m."

"Let's go walk on the beach. We can watch the sunrise." I placed both hands on his chest, gripping his shirt in my hands and giving it a little pull.

"You can't watch the sunrise on west coast beaches." He said gently.

"The sun will still be rising, though. The sky and ocean will still be worth looking at."

"True," he yawned. "Okay, let's go."

We walked downtown. The early morning fog was still heavy over everything. The world was slowly lighting up. A café easy to walk to was open.

"Let's get giant coffees," I said as we walked inside, instantly hit with the dark, roasted smell of espresso.

"And scones," Gabe said, pointing to the counter full of fresh baked goods. "And donuts. And whatever that is." He pointed at a bear claw.

"Yes, please," I said beside him.

We got two big coffees and a bag full of treats. We found our way to the beach and ate them as the sky over the sea went all berry colored and sweet. I let the glazed donut melt in my mouth, still warm from my coffee.

"It feels like we're hidden away here," Gabe said, looking at the fog surrounding us.

"I can't believe we have the entire beach to ourselves." *How was this my life?*

"Well, most people are still asleep, Em."

I took a big drink of my coffee.

"I'm glad you got me up," he said with an earnestness that tugged on my heart. "I used to fantasize about moments like this with you."

There was a question forming in my mouth, but instead, I said, "Me too."

"I remember getting jealous of Katie, my brothers, and everyone who got all this time with you. It was like I was always trying to sneak it in. I'd wish something would happen that would make us wind up spending time together, let alone a whole day. Or a whole weekend, *like this*." He ran a hand over the sand. "Did you have any idea what you were doing to me?"

"I didn't know, but I hoped. It'd send me over the moon to find out you were going to be hanging around when I was over. I'd stick around your house for hours to see if you were going to show up or *finally* come downstairs," I admitted. Keeping to myself that only weeks ago, I was waiting around downstairs at the Hernandez home, hoping he'd come downstairs to me.

"I remember being a freshman in college and wondering why my mind was still hung up on the senior girl back home. I should be flirting and dating, and I tried, but... I was still just waiting to run into you. Waiting for our paths to cross. Waiting for you to walk in the door. Waiting for you to make fun of me," he said. The two of us laughed at his last line.

"Meanwhile, that senior girl at home was just so heartbroken sitting in your living room like holding my breath, just wishing for Christmas break to get here so I could exhale." The waves were a bruised blackish blue as they crashed at the shore over and over, relentless.

"I get that feeling. It permeates everything, even when I'm at work. Everything I write, I imagine what you'd say, what you'd think." Gabe took a long sip of his coffee. "I didn't realize how good I had it in high school, in junior high, sharing all our work. No one reads me like you do."

"Can we do that again?" I begged, turning to him. "It's never been the same. Why did we ever stop?"

"You used to make me read it back to you. Remember when you wrote short stories and wanted me to do voices?" He tucked a strand of my hair behind my ear.

I fell back on the sand in laughter. "Your voices were horrible. But I still appreciated the effort. You really tried."

"I did really try," he said. "For you."

We eventually had to leave the beach. I had an itinerary, you know? I had pictures to take and notes to write. I was trying to determine what the story was here.

In the deepest parts of my heart, the story was Gabe. Cambria was Gabe and me kissing in the hallway. Foggy mornings spent sharing donuts. Too much wine and pretending we were together. It was too much wine and winding up together. Sandy pizza and sunsets. Songs through the wall.

Cambria wasn't falling in love. It was finally letting ourselves feel the love that'd always been there pulsing under the surface. Gabe and me, *finally*. Cambria was the tide coming in. Asking me, what now? Over and over, rolling in like waves. What now? What now? What now? But I didn't want to answer.

Instead, we checked off our to-do list as the fog cleared, like rubbing your eyes in the morning. I tried to soak it in like a kid does on Christmas night, knowing this special time when we could be together was rapidly coming to an end.

Next thing I knew, we were sitting in my hotel room, it was way past dinner, and we were drinking wine as I typed away on my computer. Gabriel sat by the fireplace, watching me. I thought how beautiful life would be if this was what it consisted of daily. Us in our sweatpants at the end of the day.

"I missed watching you work," he said.

I grinned at him from my spot on my bed, perched before my laptop. He kissed me on the forehead and headed back to his room. It was getting late.

As the door closed behind him, I pushed my laptop away and started to cry. I didn't want everything to end, but tomorrow, we flew home. Was all of it just a fantasy? How would we revert to the way things were? The way we were? We had to do that, right? That was the plan, right? We had talked about our history, about our feelings, but neither of us had said one thing about the future. All the questions I wanted to bury were shaking loose, rising from the grave. Right around that time, there was a knock on my door.

"Hey, I know you're working, and I don't want to interrupt you. Just, all day long, we've been hopping around, but I've been dying to know what's going on in that head of yours." It was Gabriel at my door, immediately rambling. "What are we *doing*? What's *going on* here? What do you *want*?"

"Oh," I said, stunned like I'd been caught trying to leave this weekend without having to face up to any of these questions. "I don't know if I have any answers. I've been asking myself all the same things."

He leaned his head against the doorway. "What've you come up with?"

"I think, I guess," I stuttered. I looked down at my hands like maybe I'd find the answers there. "I mean…I was just writing, so you've caught me off guard. I feel a little surprised by this conversation."

"Why are you surprised?" Gabe cocked his head, furrowed his brows. "Emma, we've been kissing. We've been talking about how obsessed with each other since we've been since we were kids. Didn't a conversation like this seem inevitable? I feel like all of this was inevitable."

"See, you keep saying things like that *I'm cute*, and *this was inevitable*, and it confuses me. More than me being surprised, I'm confused by you," I said, like releasing a breath.

"What's confusing about those things?"

"Why are you saying them?" I was desperate to know.

"I'm saying it because it's true. Because I like you, and I've thought things like that for a long time. I want to start saying them aloud, or I'm going to lose my mind. Just like I kissed you last night because I wanted to, because I like you and want to kiss you on a regular basis. Just like I come to the dang coffee shop every single morning, not because I particularly care for mochas, but because I want to be around you preferably every day. Just like me flying out for your twenty-first birthday was because I like you and I want to be with you for things like birthdays." He sounded exhausted, depleted, like he'd reached his breaking point. "*I like you, Emma*. I've always liked you. And *like* is a small word. I've been falling in love with you since I was a kid. *That's why I do every freaking thing I do*."

I couldn't have dreamed up a more perfect speech coming from Gabriel's lips—and trust me, Gabriel had confessed his feelings for me in many of my dreams. I was ecstatic, shocked, giddy, terrified, all of it. And I could've said I'd been falling in love with him, too. I could've said *anything*. But it was as if everything I might've said disappeared into the hiding spot where I kept my feelings. We just stared at each other.

"Are you less confused?" he asked me finally. I nodded. "I was assuming all the kissing and the hand-holding meant you wanted the same things. But now, I'm feeling less certain. I'm getting confused myself."

"I do *want* those things, Gabe. I do," I said, but I said it in a hesitant way. A scared way.

"Emma, I don't want to force you into something. I also don't want to be the only one who tries when it comes to us. I want to do something about *this*." He waved his hand between us. "But I'm not going to force you."

"You know how I feel," I said. "But...I just..." I might've known what I felt, but I didn't know what to do with those feelings.

"You know what I want. I just said it. I want to do something about this. I want to try. I've said all this before. Now, it's your turn. *What do you want?*" Gabe said, all frustration and impatience.

"I don't know what I want, I guess. It's that simple. I don't know the right move here," I confessed. *How could he be so sure, so brave?* I wished he could feel enough for the both of us.

"Do you want to be with me?" His voice cracked.

"It's not that simple. You know that." I felt like I was pleading with him to not make us face this thing head-on, to go back to yesterday when it was easy and foggy.

He pushed himself off the doorway and turned his back to me. "What am I doing here? I remember regretting sending that stupid message, and now I'm going to regret knocking on your door."

I touched his shoulder, and he turned back to me. "I'm not saying I don't have feelings, Gabe. I've literally loved you since I was a little girl. That doesn't mean I know what I'm supposed to do right now. A few days ago, we hadn't—"

"A few days ago, we were still wanting each other. This has been going on for years," he cut me off.

"I mean, I wasn't expecting to be figuring it all out in a few days. Or ever, really, to be honest."

"Emma." He was exasperated with me. That fact alone pierced me. "What do you actually want? With anything? You never say! It obviously wasn't that life you had rolling ahead of you with Jordan, but it took a proposal for you to admit it, and even then, by the skin of your teeth. It obviously wasn't the reporting just like you had, but they had to fire you before you admitted it. *Why can't you just admit the things you want? Why can't you admit you want to be with me?*"

"Don't say that about me. I do know what I want. I want you. I want to be with you. I want to be with you so much it's broken my heart over and over and over again. I wanted you before you wanted me. Wanting you leads to me pining away as you run off to California. Wanting you just hurts me." Tears stung my eyes. The elevator doors pinged in the distance.

He grabbed my hands. "I'm not going to California. We can—"

"We can what? I live in Sweet River —"

"You don't have to live in Sweet River, though—"

"That's not the point," I cut him off sharply.

"Then what's the point?" His dark eyes searching mine.

I said nothing. I didn't have words, at least not the ones to save this. A sad silence stretched between us.

"So basically, no real response. No response—just like on your birthday." He dropped my hands.

"That's not fair!" My chest squeezed. "Last time, you sent me a text that was just so confusing during a time in my life I was already confused. I didn't know what to say or what to do."

"You could've said something. Anything. You never replied." He shook his head.

"I'm sorry. I'm *so* sorry. I've been sorry. I know it was hurtful. I even knew it at the time, but I kept thinking I would come up with a response until too much time had passed. It got away from me, Gabriel."

He looked down at his feet.

"I regret not replying to you. I thought about it every single day for a year. I was afraid what you thought it meant." Tears were dropping down my cheeks, my chin.

"What did it mean?" He kept looking down.

"It meant I didn't know what to say."

"Why are you so afraid to—"

"Stop saying I'm afraid to admit what I want. *I am trying.*" I ran my fingers through my hair. I crossed them over my chest. "I'm scared. Okay? It's terrifying to want you. I have been your sister's best friend, your family's second daughter, basically my whole life. If we get together, then break up, there's no more Christmas parties for me to attend, no more tagging along for family vacation, no more being Katie's maid of honor. You're not losing your second family if you lose me."

"If I lose you, I lose everything." Gabriel's eyes were serious. "And I would never let you lose my family. Your best friend. I would protect those with my life."

My hands were shaking. My heart was racing. I felt exposed for admitting so much—so much I don't think I had ever fully articulated to myself like a shield had dropped.

"Emma, please. I think we could figure this out. It doesn't have to be this scary or this hard just to give us a shot," Gabe said, his voice like an open wound.

"Oh yeah, because I'm just being scared Emma, making things hard. And you're super smart Gabriel, who knows everything," I said defensively, angry at myself, angry at him.

"That's not what I meant, Em."

"Yes, it is. You literally said I'm just too scared to admit what I want in my life over and over again."

"I shouldn't have harped so much on that. I'm sorry."

I could feel his disappointment in me, and it stung. I took in a jagged, indignant breath.

"Do you want to give us a shot?" he asked me point-blank, and I knew, for one last time.

I *wanted* to give us a shot. But I didn't want to flip my life upside down. Him or my safe, tidy little life. I couldn't choose.

Which, ultimately, and to my heartbreak, was a choice. I took in a deep breath. I said nothing. The Emma who doesn't claim what she wants, the Emma he had been talking about.

"Em," he urged me. He was squeezing the doorway behind me.

"We shouldn't have played with fire," I said, my voice raw from crying, angry that he called me out and that he was right.

I went into my room and closed the door on him. We didn't play songs that night. It was completely quiet.

Thirty-Nine

The night of my twenty-first birthday, after Gabriel drove away from my dorms, I fell asleep in a tipsy, happy little ball on my bed. My phone was left unplugged on my nightstand. I woke up the next morning with a headache and a dead phone. I plugged it in and washed my face, drank two big bottles of water.

I kept touching my lips thinking, Gabriel kissed these.

Oh my gosh. We. Kissed. Last. Night.

I crawled back into my bed, blanket over my head. I kept thinking about Gabe pushing my back against the car, lips on mine. I thought about us side by side at the bar, voices low, in our own little world and he looked at me. I still had the shivers down my spine.

Oh my gosh. We ditched everyone last night. It felt rarified. It felt cozy. It felt like last night Gabe just wanted to see me. I could've passed out at that very thought. Since I always felt that way about Gabe.

I remembered my phone on my nightstand, finally back to life. The lock screen showed there was a message from Gabriel. I dropped my phone like it was on fire.

Instead of reading it, I put on a show and tried to think of anything but any of the serious aftermath that came from a night from, oh my gosh, kissing Gabriel. I wanted to live in the bubble *where there was just the flirting, the streetlamps, and the teasing me about my order. What if he regretted it? What if it was a pity birthday kiss? What if I misunderstood it all?*

Other fears rushed in. What if he wanted us to date, but Katie got mad at me, Linda didn't like me anymore, or things got weird at the Hernandez home like they always did when one of them brought in a new significant other? All the tiptoeing, snickering, and waiting-to-see-what-happens.

Admittedly, my heart swelled at the idea of the two of us... If I got that job in California by him, and then we had good night texts, dinners just us two, more kissing, and long talks about our days— that's the stuff of dreams.

But then the reality hit me. What if I didn't get the job in California and we failed at long distance? Or he broke it off because his life was moving on, and I couldn't keep up. Or he because he was in California and I was in Texas, and he met someone else.

For so long, being with Gabriel had been a fantasy I could never attain. I had never thought beyond the want to the reality, to the dark underbelly of what if.

Finally, I opened the message from him.

GABRIEL

Emma, last night was one of the best nights. I feel like we need more nights like that. More nights just the two of us. I have to confess I've felt more than friendly for you for a while—I feel like there's something there between us. I think we owe it to ourselves to do something about it. Give it a shot. What do you think? What do you want to do? You can take some time to think it through. I know you have a lot coming up this semester. I'm here when you're ready to talk about it. I just really liked last night.

I reread that message hundreds of times. Over the next several days, I crafted a variety of replies in my head, telling him yes, I wanted to give us a shot. Telling him no. Telling him maybe. Asking what we would do if I didn't get the job and I had to work some-where else. Apologizing for the late response and requesting more time. I kept putting it off, telling myself he said to take my time, so it was okay. Weeks passed. Until I took too much time, and I realized it was too late.

Then, I was sick with anxiety over my lack of reply. I decided he probably hated me, and I'd lost him. I'd hurt him. Not only had I not replied to him, but we hadn't spoken since the night of my birthday at all. No calls, no messages, not even social media interaction.

But then holiday break came. We were both back home when I next saw him, and he didn't mention the message. It felt like old times.

It wasn't the response I was expecting. It was almost worse. Was he over me? Did he not care? Did I imagine it all bigger than it was? Maybe I had read the message in an intense tone, but he had actually sent it in a casual one. We were just old pals who had gotten too busy to talk, it seemed.

I had been expecting the next time we spoke, we'd discuss the kiss and the message. As nervous as I was to talk about it, I think I was waiting for it. When it didn't happen, it was like a balloon popping and deflating. All this pent-up emotion, expectation, curiosity, and hope falling flat.

We kind of started talking again here and there after the holi-days. He'd check in on my job hunt. I'd comment on something of his I read. Social media back and forth revived. So we weren't doing this. We'd avoided a big mess, mutually. I didn't text him back; he didn't bring it up. This was an "us" decision. Or indecision.

I didn't get the job in California, and another little balloon of hope popped. Even fate agreed with us that this shouldn't happen. I moved back home. Jordan invited me to dinner. From what I heard, Gabriel was dating people, too.

I assumed, irrationally and selfishly, that he probably hadn't even really meant what he said to me the day after my birthday. He meant it casually or something. Maybe I imagined it all to be more *than it was. Maybe he'd forgotten he ever sent that message. I decided to forget it, too.*

I settled on watching his life unfold from afar. I curled up in my bed in my little town, tucked into my covers, reading his writings, scrolling through photos of travels, and reading comments from his seemingly impossibly cool and beautiful friends. I caught everything his family said about him at every turn. I ached and wondered about his lack of trips back home.

Somehow, in my mind, he turned into the one who broke my heart. The one who left me behind. The one I couldn't keep up with, always off by one message.

Forty

It was all a blur the next morning. We took a car to the airport but didn't speak much, only communicating whatever was essential. We kept our eyes looking out the car window. I felt like a raw nerve, permanently holding back tears.

Our flight was actually running early—something I didn't even know happened—so we rushed through baggage claim and security. Racing down the airport, our bags flopped against us until we barely made it onto our plane before takeoff.

We were out of breath as we scanned the plane for our seats, realizing that this time around, our seats were side by side. Even with all the awkwardness between us, I couldn't help but feel a little surge of gratitude that we were together, at least for a little bit longer.

Once we were cruising in the sky for a bit, and Gabriel and I had yet to speak a word to each other, I dug my book out of my bag. I settled into my seat and flipped it open.

Not too much later, Gabriel set his phone on my book with his Notes app open. He'd typed out, *Want to talk about last night?*

Feeling suddenly on the spot and emotionally spent, I took his phone and typed underneath his line of text, *I think it's best we don't right now*

I glanced sideways at him and saw his face fall as he read my response. I instantly regretted it. Maybe taking our time writing out our responses while we had nothing else to do for a few hours actually was for the best. But I was too hesitant, too nervous to attempt reversing my choice. Instead, I stared at my book and pretended to read, blinking away tears, wishing he'd type out: *are you sure?*

He stared out the window the entire time, disappearing inside himself. We landed and were mutually task-focused. We got our bags, loaded his truck, and drove home in a suffocating silence.

Before long, he was dropping me off at my apartment, saying, "I'll see you later then."

I said, "You too," almost apologetically.

I could've said, "Wait, this is stupid. Let's talk." Or "I'm sorry I've been so confusing. I just have too much I'm terrified to lose, including you." Instead, I watched him drive away.

I stood in the parking lot with my bags. In my small town. In my time zone. I had never felt more in the wrong place at the wrong time.

Before we left for Cambria, Terrence had told me that he was planning a big surprise proposal for Katie at her family's house with a big party. The Hernandezes were going to be having a summer barbecue with everyone she loved there. Her mom was telling her this party was so that everyone could get to know Terrence better, and his loved ones.

Then he was going to walk her down to her favorite spot at the edge of their property, where there was a dip and you could watch the sunset over the hills. He would walk her there right as the sun got low in the sky and propose. After she—hopefully—agreed to marry him, Terrence was going to call over to the party guests, "She said yes!" and then we were going to cheer and have Champagne and make toasts.

When he told me the plan, pulled aside at her family's house for dinner, tears sprung to my eyes. "There couldn't be a more perfect proposal for Katie," I told him, honestly.

He'd sent me photos of the ring before he bought it, when it was just one of the ones in the running, and then again the day after he officially purchased it.

I would look at the picture and try to imagine it in Katie's eyes. She would first lay eyes on it in the glow of sunset, in her Canada Man's hands.

The proposal party, as we'd deemed it, was set for the day after we returned home from Cambria, so I spent the night I got home doing my laundry while trying to brainstorm an engagement toast. My mind felt foggy. My thoughts and feelings were disjointed.

I tried to keep Gabriel out of my mind, which was surprisingly easy since our time together felt almost unreal to me. Like our trip didn't really happen. Like it was some weird dream set in California. I was awake now, back in Texas. Except, my eyes would randomly fill with tears, little prickly reminders of him, reminders of what could've been.

The next evening, I sat in the Hernandezes' backyard with my parents at a table set up under pecan trees laced with twinkle nights. The warm spring night air dancing against my skin. I had been searching for Gabriel since I parked my car in the driveway. In their front yard, the side yard as we weaved toward the party in the back, and as we greeted Mr. and Mrs. Hernandez, almost asking them where he was.

I hadn't seen him yet. Was he inside the house? Should I fake needing to pee and go inside... To what, just lay eyes on him?

I just wanted to see how he was holding up. How was he doing since we got back? Did he feel like he was clumsily holding the pieces of his heart together right now, like me, ready to fall apart if someone bumped into him or if he forgot, even for just a second, to hold it together? Was he broken like me? But, I remembered, I'd left him confused and hurt before, like this was my habit. This thought made my chest constrict.

"Wow, I had no idea how many people Katie knew," my dad said, interrupting my thoughts, as we took in the big crowd awaiting Katie and Terrence's arrival.

"Some of these people are Terrence's friends and family who flew down for the proposal." I ran my fingers over the table cloth.

"Can you imagine the size of the wedding?" mom guffawed.

"Oh, you know Katie, she is going to do it big. She'll invite every customer at Coffee & Commass," I said.

"Every order will get an invitation tucked in with their napkin," my mom added through laughter.

"Oh, I can smell the pulled pork sandwiches." My dad sniffed the air. It was spicy, sweet, and meaty. They had a buffet with all the barbecue fixings, which included the famous Hernandez pulled pork. Plus, salsa, chips, queso and guacamole.

I sipped my large cup of icy sweet tea.

"Hey, we haven't heard about your trip with Gabe," my dad said suddenly. "How'd that go?"

I met my mom's questioning gaze for just a moment and then looked up at the sky. The sun would be setting soon. "It was quick, you know. We were hopping from place to place. I came back tired."

"It looked like fun, at least on the social medias." My dad always said the social medias, plural, even though he only used Facebook.

"It was really fun," I said. "Cambria was beautiful."

"How was it spending time with just Gabe? I know you're used to the two of you kind of revolving around Katie," my mom asked, her voice suggestive.

"It was..." I didn't want to start crying at the party. "It was complicated. I'll tell you all the details later."

Mom raised an eyebrow. "Was it good?"

"It was good…and then also bad," I whispered the last part.

Dad looked confused and worried. "Wait, what happened? Why was it bad? I'm lost."

"Bad, how?" My mom lowered her voice.

Out walked Katie and Terrence like a breeze of fresh air. Guests had been ordered by Mama Linda to be normal and to *hold all cheering and applause until after the proposal.* But tons of people started cheering.

Terrence started laughing, being a good sport about the lack of chill. Katie looked a little confused, eyeing the number of guests to her little family barbecue. I was sure she wasn't expecting this big of a "get to know each other" party.

She turned to Terrence, grinning expectantly, asking, "What's this all about?" He shrugged mischievously.

She then said loudly for all of us to hear, "This is an awfully big backyard barbecue, Mama!"

Linda cackled from somewhere I couldn't see.

"Why is everyone staring at us and clapping?" I heard her ask him.

"Let's go for a walk." Terrence pulled her away from all of us, ignoring her questions for now.

We all watched them walk toward the proposal spot, hand in hand. Katie kept glancing back at us, the wheels in her mind turning.

She stopped looking back once Terrence started talking. We could see he was making an impassioned speech, and then he dropped to one knee—lots of guests gasping and excitedly whispering when it happened. Katie put her hand to her mouth as some of us clapped and hollered. Then Terrence was holding up a ring box.

Katie jumped up and down, then stopped so he could slip the ring on her finger.

Then, as he spun her around, Terrence shouted, "She said yes!"

On cue, we all clapped and cheered as they ran toward us. Everyone immediately began crowding them, so I made my way out of my seat and got into the hug line to wrap my arms around the happy couple.

The air was cooling down. The sun was so low that the sky was shades of plum and amber. My best friend, the girl I knew when she was an eight-year-old learning how to ride her bike, a twelve-year-old when she got a period, who I went bra shopping with, cried to over boys, and had done life with all this time was now...engaged. To be married. To a grown man.

You know things like this might, or probably, would happen as you grow up. I knew logically that someday, my closest confidant might get married. But I don't think I ever knew in my heart that the girl I'd done everything with would someday promise to do everything with someone new. I wasn't upset about this; it was just surreal.

My mom and dad stood beside me, excitedly murmuring about the coming wedding. Everyone was laughing. I could see Katie's dad, Ozzy, had tears in his eyes. As Katie excitedly gestured to someone, I saw the new ring glittering on her finger. In a matter of days, I would hear this story from Katie's perspective in detail.

I finally got up close enough to give the couple hugs. I got to Terrence first, and he said, "The girl who brought us together," and wrapped me up in his warm arms.

"Happy to," I said as my eyes fell on Katie. She was hugging Gabriel as he whispered something in her ear. She smiled softly and said something I couldn't hear in response.

She pulled away, and Gabriel turned to leave. There he was. Gabriel's eyes landed on mine; my heart stopped for a second. But he quickly moved on. He walked away. His back to me.

And I was moving into Katie's arms because this moment was her moment, and she was squealing. I clicked back into the reason I was here. I was here to jump up and down and cheer on my best friend's upcoming marriage.

"Isn't this the perfect night?" she said, eyes big and watery.

"I knew it would be. Terrence knows you. I thought that when he told me the whole proposal party plan," I said, my eyes brimming with tears, too.

"Look at this ring. Can you believe it?" She held out her hand for me, wiggling her ring finger.

"I helped him choose, you know," I said, proudly.

She looked happily down at her ring. "This all feels like a dream. Like I'll wake up tomorrow to real life."

Forty-One

The party was winding down, the sky dark overhead and our bellies full. The laughter was loud. People were saying their congratulations and hugging goodbye.

I couldn't help but look at Gabriel, who was sitting with his brothers right in my eyeline. I'd been trying my best to avoid gawking at his table throughout the entire night. Now, hours into the party, I couldn't help but give in and look right at him.

But he didn't look back.

It was like that magnet thing between us had been turned off. Or cruelly, only my end was still on like a walkie talkie only picking up static.

I think it's best we don't, I'd typed on the plane. But I'd also written, *right now.*

I considered marching over to his table and saying, "I only meant we should wait to talk about it until *later.*"

I knew Gabriel. He would say, "Okay, is it later?" *Was it later?* What did I have to say? All I knew was I didn't want us to be over. And I wanted him to look at me, for heaven's sake.

But I couldn't move from my seat.

Katie was with Terrence's family most of the night. She was still there, talking with his grandmother. She wouldn't be free to talk for a while if she was at all tonight. My parents were at another table now, toasting wine glasses with Linda and Ozzy.

I was all alone. I kept watching Gabriel's table. His brothers seemed to notice. I didn't care. I felt restless, reckless, and after the proposal party, romantic.

Then Gabe stood up from his table and started to walk toward me. I put my eyes on his and finally he looked back with a resolute glint I sat up straight. As he got closer, I opened my mouth to speak when I felt someone's hands on my shoulders.

I saw Gabe's face fall then he gave me a shrug. I turned my head to see who had put their hands on me, to find Jordan standing over me with a big smile on his face.

"Hi, old friend," he said.

"Hi," I said distractedly. I looked ahead to see Gabriel had already walked away.

"I feel like we haven't talked in forever." Jordan pulled out a chair beside me and sat down.

"We haven't talked in forever," I said. "It's good to see you."

"I've seen how you've been writing a lot lately—the articles you've shared online and you've been traveling. I saw you posting in California. Emma the Jetsetter, who knew?"

"Yeah, I got hired to write a piece on a town in California." I sat back in my chair. "It was beautiful. I've been stretching my writing wings. What about you? How've you been?"

"I've been good," he said, hunching closer toward me. "I've been really good. Things are really falling into place. My business is taking off to a good start. I got that house I wanted. I've been renovating it. I'm doing well."

"I had no doubt things would fall into place for you, Jordan."

"I know," he said, his voice catching. "I thought I'd be broken for a while. But I see now what you meant about how I was just dragging you along to my own plans. I realized that my plans, my life, didn't change much after we broke up. I look back and see you didn't have much input, and part of that was you—"

"That's true. I didn't have much vision for the future to pitch." I shrugged softly.

"But I see a lot of that was me, too. I could've asked. I could've just...noticed. I think, in comparison to, uh, other relationships, when you're really *for* someone they don't have to tell you what they want, or what isn't right, all the time. When you know someone, sometimes that speaks for itself. With us, I never did *know* with you, did I?"

"You're right. But to be fair, I didn't always *know with myself* either."

He just nodded, waiting for me to continue.

"I'm sorry, again, for how I broke us up. I regret it. I've been learning how my fears don't only hurt me, and I am so sorry you, and your family, were along for one of my lessons."

"I forgive you, Em. That day sucked. It hurt, not going to lie. But in the end, we needed to break up." Then he added, "But thank you for some really good memories when we were together."

I smiled gently at him. "Thank you, too, Jordan."

Then he cleared his throat and shuffled his feet nervously. "I also wanted to tell you so you hear it here first. Um, I'm back with Sophie."

"I kind of figured that one out, Jordan," I admitted. Then, I bumped my shoulder into his with a little smirk. "I'm happy you're happy."

"I am happy," he said. A couple of little kids ran by our table squealing delightedly.

"I ran into Sophia at her dad's garage months ago. Did she tell you that?"

"Yeah, she did." his eyes twinkled.

"I felt like she was kind of happy to find out I was single. I picked up on a vibe."

Jordan let out the big-hearted laugh I knew so well. "It was meant to be," he said. Then, it was quiet for a bit. It was an opening for me, but I didn't take it so he added, "I know you'll find your meant to be someday, Emma. I'll be cheering you on."

"Thank you," I said, my voice small.

He gave my shoulder a little squeeze as he left. I was sitting alone at my table again. The party was significantly smaller. Terrence and Katie were slow dancing a few steps away from the rest of us under the blanket of stars. As a party, we had decided to give them their space.

I looked around for Gabriel. Everyone else in Katie's family was sitting together talking, but no Gabe in sight. I stood up from my seat. I craned my head to see, still unable to find him. But his presence lingered like smoke after a firework show. There I stood, alone, waiting for Gabriel to come back.

But he never came back.

Forty–Two

The next day, I had an early shift at the coffee shop. I frothed milk, plated scones, and watched the door hoping for my favorite customer. But he never showed. Every mocha I made that wasn't for Gabriel broke my heart.

I had wrapped my hand so tight around "the way things were," completely terrified of losing it, fracturing it, of it even looking a shade different. But as I looked around the coffee shop, feeling the lack of Gabriel, feeling the weight of secrets kept from Katie, I had to admit to myself...*things had already changed.*

I was fooling myself that I could keep it perfectly preserved, and I was especially foolish to imagine it had been preserved at all. As I sipped my own mug full of caramel, frothy oat milk, and espresso, I could see a new picture replacing the fractured image I wanted to keep.

A picture of what could be. A life that could be. Gabe and I walked hand in hand into this shop. Katie's hugged the both of us, saying, "How long are my brother and sister here for this time?" We set our laptops on the same table to write. Ah, a future where we have so many writing afternoons like in Cambria. My kids called Terrence and Katie's kids "cousin."

And what was so scary about that?

I left work late that day. I drove through my downtown, shops locking their doors and streetlights clicking on. This tiny town of mine that I loved so deeply, the axis my whole world spun around. My safe house in adulthood. But my sweet safehouse felt like reality was creeping in through cracks in the sidewalk.

I wasn't entangled in a messy relationship with Gabe, but I was still crying in my car. You could run home, ignore the emails, and close the hotel room door in his face, but chaotic, persistent, messy life found a way.

I was at a stop light, my foot on the break, and I knew in my bones that I would have to tell Katie everything eventually. Though, it was hard enough to track her down for a conversation right now. There was no hiding what happened in Cambria. Another crack.

I hit the gas, but my eyes skimmed right over my mom walking out of an antique store. I pulled my car into a nearby parking space. I scrambled out of my car and pounded down the sidewalk to keep up with her.

"Mom!" I called out.

She turned to me, surprise in her eyes. "Hey, honey."

As her eyes took me in concern furrowed her brows. She

reflexively opened her arms to me, the way she had since I was a one year old and toddling her way. I walked straight into them.

I weaved my body into hers, an eternal knit between us. A hug we'd mastered for twenty-some years now. She patted my back, and I started crying.

"Oh, baby," she whispered. Then said, "Work or boys?"

I sniffled. "Gabe."

A knowing, "ahem" from Mom. She led me to a Mexican spot for dinner a few doors down the street. We ordered two tall iced sweet teas and a big heaping pile of nachos to share.

"What happened?" she asked, finally, after our food was in front of us.

So, I told her. I told her about the songs through the wall, holding hands in the back of the car, and kisses in the doorway. My twenty-first birthday and the morning after message. The junior high jealousy of Michelle. How Gabriel complimenting my sparkly dress meant more to me than Jordan buying it for me. I told her everything, as she crunched on salty tortilla chips and nodded her head. After I had let every single word out, every single story, every single secret, Mom asked me a question.

"What is the hold-up, Emma?" She gestured her arms emphatically, a chip still in one of her hands.

I sipped my tea to bide time.

She dunked a chip in salsa as she said, "You have the feelings. You know what you want and how long you've wanted it. You know he feels the same. It's all there. Why are we crying in the car? *What is the hold-up?*"

"I'm afraid of losing everything." I let out an exasperated breath because I thought it should be obvious. "The dynamics with his family would be different with Katie. Gabe would probably want me to move, you know. It would change everything."

"Baby, everything's going to change anyway. You can't preserve everything like a picture. Katie's getting married and is going to have babies. Trust me. That'll change things. Dad and I are getting older. Life keeps going. You can only keep *yourself* in place—everyone else is going to keep going."

"I realize that things have already changed. I guess things were changing all along with Gabe and me. Since Christmas. Since college."

"Since junior high," Mom teased. "He's always challenged you."

"He's always seen through me." I winced.

"I think he just has always understood parts of you that you don't want to understand."

"It's like he sees versions of me that I'm scared to admit exist." The restaurant felt cold, I rubbed my arms to warm myself.

"Versions of you that you're meant to be, Em," Mom said tenderly.

She reached across the table and placed her hand on mine. "Nothing will ever change so much that you won't be able to come home to Mama. We'll order big cups of iced tea and talk about all of it. The same goes for Katie, you know. You two are strong enough to take on any big change. You'll just adjust and then keep plugging along."

"I know." I squeezed her hands. "I think I just get so stuck trying to determine the right move that I don't make a move. Until I'm scared of moving at all."

"You were that way even as a little girl. I can still see you standing in front of our little kiddie pool. Your friends were all splashing around, and you guys were like three years old. You were standing there in your ruffled swimsuit, trying to decide if you should get in and play. I called out to you, 'Get in and play, Emma,' and you said, in your high little voice, 'But I'll be wet!' So I go, 'Then we'll dry you off!' You looked at me with this quizzical little look. I was half expecting your toddler self to say, *'It's not that easy, Mom.'"*

"Gabriel would just throw me in," I slumped back in the booth.

"Or dare you until you wanted to splash in to prove something to him."

"He's always been okay in the unknown, even the unknown of us."

"He just wants you to enjoy the water with him," Mom giggled. "Mom's always here ready to dry you off with a towel if you change your mind and want to get out of the water, baby."

I nodded my head at her. "But you think I need to just dive in, huh? That's what you'd do."

She shrugged and popped a chip in her mouth.

I drove from the restaurant straight to the Hernandez house. When I pulled into the rocky driveway, I noticed Gabriel's truck wasn't there. I got out of my car anyway and jogged up the front porch steps to knock on the door, but no one answered. The house appeared empty. I called Katie as I walked back to my car.

"Hey, Katie," I said when she answered.

"Hey, Emma, what's up? I'm getting dinner with Terrence, so I can't talk long," Katie said, her voice low.

"Where is everyone? I came over to your house to talk to Gabe, but he's not here. No one is from the looks of it." I glanced around the empty driveway.

"I don't know where anyone is except Gabe. Gabe flew out this afternoon."

"Flew out? Where? Why?" I could hear the desperation in my voice. I hoped it didn't carry over the phone.

"He's going to be in Seattle for a while. He said he wanted to get away and clear his mind—his words, not mine. Plus, he's meeting with his agent about his book." Katie was speaking muffled into the phone, trying to keep her voice down in the restaurant. "But I honestly don't know where anyone else is. Maybe my parents went to dinner? Sorry. Did you need something?"

"Oh, it's okay," I said, my voice breaking. *Gabe was gone.* "It wasn't important. I was just wanting to talk to Gabe about something."

"I can't believe he didn't tell you he was leaving. Lately, I felt like you two talked almost more than you and me. If I were you, I'd give him a call."

"Sure. I'll do that. It's my bad for driving out here without checking in with anyone first. Go enjoy dinner with your fiancé," I said, tears falling onto my steering wheel.

"Oh, I shall," she said, and I could almost hear her wiggling her shoulders

I hung up with Katie and immediately clicked on Gabriel's contact in my phone. I could call him. I could text him. But Katie said he wanted to clear his head.

I was tired of being that little girl standing by the pool, worried that maybe she'll get wet. Maybe she'll get hurt. Maybe she'll break. Maybe she'll regret it. Maybe her tiny, safe little world will spin right off its axis, and she won't be able to get it back quite the way it was before. Maybe, maybe, maybe.

On impulse, I clicked the "call" button. It went to voicemail.

While tears burned my eyes, I typed up a message.

ME

hi, I know you're clearing your mind. I just wanted to talk. Let me know when you're ready.

Forty-Three

ME

Got big plans tonight?

KATIE

Nope. Closing the shop, might be a little late because Rose wants to talk. Then Canada Man is in Canada the next couple nights, so I'm going home to watch the Bachelor and stuff my face.

ME

I might stop by the shop to say hi

KATIE

Come on over!!

When I returned from Cambria, I felt like I was hiding some big secret from Katie. Which, well, I was. She kept asking about the trip, and I would get all nervous and twitchy, and she'd look at me funny.

Katie would say things about Gabriel leaving like, "I wonder why he needed to 'clear his head' so suddenly. What do you think, Emma?" I took it as a personal inquiry into my relationship with Gabriel.

"You know Gabe, his head's always all stuffy," I literally said that at one point. Katie just nodded, like Gabe's head *was* always stuffy, wasn't it?

Any mention of Gabriel and I felt guilty, like a puppy caught with food straight from the table. Katie wouldn't dig much deeper, thankfully. She was too preoccupied with wedding planning since she and Terrence kept saying they wanted to get married as soon as possible. When people would ask, "How soon is soon?" They'd answer like they'd rehearsed it—and I do think they rehearsed it—"Soon, like we wish we'd gotten married yesterday."

And she was juggling the mounting tasks at work. That was another weird unspoken thing between us. Work was stressing her out, and I couldn't get her to communicate what exactly about work was making her so anxious. We were in two different worlds spinning around one another but never quite syncing up. I understood, but I also wanted to sync back up.

When I knew she was closing the shop late, and I had a free night, too, I picked up some of our favorite snacks and headed over. I was ready to hear everything bugging her about work and talk out all the wedding details. I was also ready to spill everything about Gabe and me. Bracing myself for any and all reactions. Writing messages in my mind alerting Gabe that *Katie knows*.

The dusk air was humid and hot. I jogged from my car, the door ringing over my head as I walked inside. My hands were trembling, nervous about the confessions I was about to make.

Katie was behind the counter when she looked up at me. Her eyes were rubbed red from crying.

"Katie, are you okay?" I asked when I saw her.

She shook her head. "No."

I ran over to her. "What's wrong? What happened?"

"Rose is closing the shop!" she said, her voice raw. I gasped. "I know, I know," she said, breaking into a sob.

She walked quickly over to the shop door and locked it from the inside, then turned to me and explained everything.

"Rose says she's ready to retire. She wants to move to Florida or something, I don't know. But the shop is closing." She led me to one of the cozier sofas.

"I'm in shock right now," I said, locking my arms around a fluffy pillow.

"I was getting kind of worried this was going to happen. I just thought I had a little more time." She sniffled.

"How are you feeling?" I asked softly.

"Heartbroken, which maybe is silly. But you know how much I love this place. It's the dream." She took in a deep breath. "I mean, I even had ole Canada Man move here because I love this job, this town. Now what?"

Everything's going to change anyway, my mom's voice flitted across my memory.

"It's not silly at all," I reassured her.

"I don't want a new job. I want to open and close *this* place. I want to see my favorite customers. I don't want to forget their 'regulars.'" She buried her face in her hands.

"Well, why don't you just open your own coffee shop then? You are marrying a man who loves investing in new business ventures."

She nodded. "You know, I've been toying with that idea. I'm just torn about it."

"What are you torn about?"

"Can I do it *here*?" She gestured at the shop around us. "I love *this* place."

"I know," I said, sighing a sad sigh. It donning on me that I was now out of a job, too.

"I think I *should* do it here," Katie said suddenly, jumping up on the couch. "I should call up Rose and ask if I can buy Coffee & Commas from her. Keep it going."

Katie and I had a joke that we were taking over Coffee & Commas, but I guess I had never realized she meant it.

But then, as if clues were finally coming together, I thought of Rose's mentorship for Katie, Katie's relationship with the customers, and her heartfelt plans for the shop's future. Of course, Katie should own Coffee & Commas next.

She looked at me expectantly, and I said, "Honestly, I think Rose would go for it."

"Me too," she said conspiratorially.

Katie began spinning out a plan. It was obvious she'd been ruminating on this for a while, preparing in the back of her mind. We talked it out until the city was black around us. Downtown was dark, except our little coffee shop lights blinking. Our shadows faced each other planning for the future—business ventures and wedding days.

I thought how on the outside, Katie might look liked she played it safe, but as she talked about the future of this business she loved so much, I knew she went always went *all in*. She gave it *all* to her dreams, to her love story, to the things she wanted. When she felt the spark with Terrence, hadn't she spent the rest of the day with him? She gambled all those hours, gambled all those feelings, pushing them to the center of the table, trusting her gut that this was it.

How often would I hold my cards close to my chest, waiting for the next time—the perfect time—until everyone left the table.

Now Katie was going to take the risk to own her own business —but not just any business, a beloved one. She and I knew that the town would be watching. Rose and her coffee shop had a reputation.

We were finally walking out the door, as she slid her keys into the lock, she said to me, "I'm gonna give it a future."

She was also giving herself a future.

. . .

That night Katie FaceTimed to tell me everything that had conspired in the last twenty-four hours. She had talked late that night with Terrence about her plan, then she woke up early that morning and called Rose.

They met and talked for hours. And agreed Katie would be the next owner of Coffee & Commas. They would begin the process the next day.

As I told Katie that night on the phone, "I'm so proud of you for just going for it like this."

I kept flashing back to shutting the door in her brother's face. I wanted to tell her, "I wish I had bet on your brother when I had the chance."

I wanted to tell her that there had been no returned call from Gabe, no text messages. That it felt painfully, cruelly fair to be agonizing over his lack of reply after my own silence years ago. How I always put silence between us, and he always put states. I wanted to tell Katie that I never said what I wanted the way she did to Terrence, to Rose. Even when her brother was begging for me to tell him what I wanted. I lost without even playing.

Telling my oldest friend in the world about how I'd been walking around with a shattered heart in my chest felt natural, felt like it would be a salve. But she was so excited, chattering away about Coffee & Commas and the wedding, her joy radiating through the phone screen, so I kept my feelings to myself. I knew I would share everything, eventually when the time was right.

As our conversation slowed, the two of us growing tired, Katie said, "Let's say it's your turn now, Em. What call do you need to make tomorrow morning?"

I knew just the number to dial, a number that would answer when I called.

I called Terrence the next morning and said, "I want work. I want a project. A big one. Lay it on me."

He sent me to NYC for three weeks.

Forty-Four

I went to Manhattan for the first time in the heat of summer. Instead of twinkling shop windows or autumn leaves crunching under my feet, I brought a suitcase full of sundresses. The heat was tangible, like dew on my skin everywhere I went. That dewy skin was most apparent on the days I rode the Subway, which was thickly humid. I was dripping the first day I arrived.

I was taking a complicated journey from JFK airport to my

temporary place in Manhattan. Taking the Air Train to the Subway and then, hot and tired, I gave in and took a Taxi, dragging my bags along with me. I got to my new place and immediately showered. I was exhausted and stressed but proud of myself.

I stayed in a little studio short-term rental on the upper east side. It was tiny, cramped, and old with a cranky air conditioner that sometimes worked and sometimes didn't. The fridge was small and appeared to have been around longer than my grandma. And there were two windows. One was over the sink with a view of an alley and the building next door, but the other, across from my bed, had a view of the city around me.

It was that other view, the one of the city, that gave me butterflies. It wasn't a particularly beautiful or notorious view, but it was still of Manhattan. The part of it that became mine. I would sit and watch night fall over the upper east side, soaking in a reality that years ago I had begun to believe might never happen for me.

I kept an ongoing note in my phone of ideas—things for the magazine that I was planning to get up the guts to pitch and things to write just for me, not for any publishers beyond my Word document.

One morning I woke up, and I started a note in my phone titled *Things to Say to Gabe*. I added to this note daily. It was long, sometimes serious, sometimes ridiculous. It was full of things I should've admitted to him years ago. Things I should've admitted to *myself* years ago. But there I was, alone in NYC, and finally being honest with myself about who I was and what I wanted. I was someone who wanted things that scared me and a man who scared me.

And I was someone finally ready for all of it—my notes said that. They told him, *I'm finally ready.* That note still reminds me of walking under a sky of towering concrete, passing stranger after stranger, missing him.

. . .

I didn't just write in that little apartment. I also had lengthy phone calls helping plan Katie and Canada Man's wedding. There was even an infamous four-hour-long call about the guest list. Since the wedding was happening on the Hernandezes' expansive property, Katie felt anyone and everyone should be invited, but her parents were far more hesitant. Terrence and I got called in for perspective. It got heated. But Katie won.

There were also short, frantic, decisive phone calls helping plan Katie and Canada Man's wedding that sounded like, "Hurry, tell me sunflowers or lilies?" These mostly happened while I was wandering around the city.

I would be walking down the street and shout, "Lilies!!"

Within my first days there, I had a coffee shop I visited every morning that quickly felt like *my* place. There was also a Thai restaurant that I had so many times, I felt sad to leave when the time came. I stopped into a gorgeous, brick Episcopalian Church down the street that was so welcoming that I came back the Sundays and Wednesdays I was there. They had future events scheduled that, in another life, I could imagine myself attending.

I figured out how many shopping bags I could handle. My main mode of transportation became my sneakered feet. These were things that I knew I would miss when I left. And I also knew, as I was heading to the Thai place for dinner, these were things that could be the beginnings of a life.

I could build a life here, I realized. I could build a new life outside of everything comfortable and cozy. A new life was not as scary as it felt when you were driving down the same roads you'd always known. Because there were roads everywhere—some more traffic jammed than others.

I could adapt. I could dig up roots and replant them, especially because a new life didn't mean shaking loose everything you loved from the old one. I didn't have to fight so hard to protect what I loved because the things that truly love you back fought to stay in your life.

Katie and I were adjusting to her big life changes naturally, because our roots were strong and healthy. We loved each other, trusted each other. We could adapt to whatever big life changes I made next. *It was my turn, wasn't it?*

I pulled up my note of *Things to Say to Gabe* and wrote that I could build a new life with Gabriel. His family, and Katie, would adapt and adjust. And more importantly, I wrote that *I could adapt and adjust*. Wait, no, I deleted that last line and wrote I could do more than adapt and adjust, *I could thrive*.

Forty-Five

One afternoon, I was sitting in a coffee shop working, but my mind didn't want to think about work—it wanted to think about Gabriel Hernandez.

I, on a whim, pulled out my phone and sent him a message.

ME

Just wanted to check in.

As if I were his coworker and knew he was home sick or something. I awaited his reply for an hour, full of anticipation. I fell asleep that night, unable to get the bubble of hope out of my chest that at any moment my phone could light up with a message from Gabe.

But days passed, and nothing.

I thought I'd regret sending it more, but I didn't. I'd been painstakingly spending the entire time wondering if I should send another message or not. Now I knew the answer.

Maybe it was selfish to reach out. He obviously didn't want to hear from me. But I wanted him to know I was available. That this time, I wasn't going to hide or run. That, if he was ready, I was ready now to talk. I was going to send messages now. No more ignoring them.

Now I would just be hoping for a reply.

When I was in college studying journalism, I used to imagine a future where I lived in big cities and wrote in busy parks, watching the world around me. But I had found myself often writing in my little apartment or the café down the street where there was air conditioning.

But finally, one day, I decided to brave the heat and go write in Washington Square Park. I needed to get out of my head, and my deadline was quickly approaching, as in a couple of days away. I was doing some of my final work before sending it over for feedback and edits. Plus, why not make that dream come true? It was just a subway ride away.

I found a spot on the grass under a shady tree and worked on revisions for a few hours until my phone started ringing, startling me out of my fog of focus. It was my mom. I answered on the second ring.

"Hey, Mom," I said.

"Hey honey, what are you up to?" Her voice sounded far away like I was on her car speaker phone.

"I'm sitting at a park working. What are you up to?" I had on my earphones, so I rested my head against a tree for a moment.

"I'm driving home from an appointment and was thinking about you. I miss you."

"I miss you, too, Mom," I said and meant it. Hearing her voice felt like a hug through the phone.

"I was wondering how you're doing up there. We had that long talk about Gabriel. Then the next thing I know, you're boarding a flight to New York City. Have you guys spoken about everything?" I heard her blinker clicking.

I sighed deeply. "We haven't spoken at all. I mean, I've tried. But he's not answering me at all. Which feels like karma for when I didn't reply to his message for, you know, ever."

"Well, that's stupid. He should reply to you. Why would he

ignore you like that? Especially if he knows how bad that feels. Plus, come on, you know he wants to talk."

"I'm just giving him his space. I think he's clearing his mind or whatever. I know—"

"*Clearing his mind*? Of what? You two need to finally talk. It's been years of mind clearing. Your last talk ended abruptly—"

"I'm the reason it ended abruptly, Mom." I brushed a bead of sweat from my forehead.

"Who cares? You said you didn't want to talk right then. If he took that to mean you didn't want to talk ever, then he did that defensively. I mean, you have both been fumbling the ball."

"You mean fumbling the bag?"

"You're both fumbling it up." My mom muttered.

"Well, I don't disagree." I closed my laptop. I was sweating and being lectured by my mother. "I obviously want to talk to him, but I'm not mad or anything. He can be defensive. I mishandled our last talk, and then I blew him off again on the plane. After years of pretending we'd never kissed. I mean, I had some defensiveness coming my way."

"Do you think he'll *ever* answer you?" My mom said gravely.

"I assume he will. I've been thinking he just needs some time. Do you think he's *never* going to talk to me again?"

"I don't know, hon." Mom yawned into the phone. "He was pretty cold at the engagement party."

"What, you think I blew it for good with Gabe?" I gathered my purse, put my laptop into it, and started toward the subway. I needed to get out of the sun. The subway was hot and humid, but it would at least take me home.

"You two have been playing this back-and-forth game for years. For all I know, this is just another break in the game."

"I'm done playing the game, Mom," I said, making my way through the busy sidewalk.

"That may be true, but I do think it's time you talk to Katie about all of this."

· · ·

I was in my head the entire subway ride back home, so much so that I almost missed my stop. Once I arrived in my doorway, I dropped my purse to the ground and let out a weighty exhale. I poured my thirsty self a giant cup of water and then collapsed onto the couch.

My clothes were sticking to me from sweat. My feet always ached after a journey back to the apartment. My brain was fried from writing, and after talking to my mom, my thoughts kept circling around what she'd said.

What if he never answers me?

I had been living with the assumption that eventually Gabe would talk to me. He would, at some point, send me a text or give me a call. Or in some dramatic fantasies, show up at my doorstep here in NYC. But either way, be it the dramatic drop in or a casual message, I had been expecting he would talk to me. Probably sooner rather than later. Leave it to my mother to get my mind stuck on The Worst-Case Scenario. Could Gabe be officially and fully blowing me off?

Had I gotten a handful of chances with Gabriel Hernandez and wasted every one of them?

His eyes when I rejected his olive branch of conversation on the plane kept appearing in my mind. The disappointment, the hurt, all of it left a lump in my throat. I burrowed deeper into the couch.

I closed my eyes, willing a nap to overtake me, when my phone buzzed in my pocket. I needed to send an update on my project. I rolled onto the ground and went to the kitchen to find my laptop bag by the door—but the only thing there was my purse.

I halted in my tracks. Hadn't I dropped it to the floor with my purse when I walked in the door? I replayed the memory in my mind, but I didn't remember feeling my laptop bag on my shoulder—just my purse.

"No," I said, panic vibrating in my veins. I had my laptop bag with me when I got onto the Subway. I remembered keeping it close. But I was deep in my thoughts, distracted, and frazzled when I almost missed my exit.

I must've left my laptop bag on the Subway. That bag had my laptop *and* my external hard drive. It had everything I'd written. Past and present.

Including every word I'd written since arriving in New York.

Forty-Six

Sweetie, I think you could still find it. Don't lose hope!

I found the Subway schedule online. I called any person I could call tied to the Subway. I asked about Lost and Founds, but my laptop bag was gone. I'd lost it.

I lost my work. I lost my articles, my essays, my random musings, my journal entries, past work I was proud of, works in progress, silly memories, and all the work I had put into my New York project. Every page...lost somewhere in Manhattan.

I cried. I called my mom. I called Katie. My mom told me not to lose hope that maybe it would somehow find its way back to me. Katie told me it sucked but that I would write so much more. She encouraged me that there was all the work still living on in the internet. But I still cried. It still hurt.

I spent the whole night stressing. I didn't eat. I didn't really sleep until the wee hours. The reminder on my phone that my project was due tomorrow afternoon woke me the next morning.

I kept looking around my apartment, just in case. I walked back to Washington Square Park and looked everywhere in the morning light—just in case. But it wasn't anywhere. I was a sniffling mess.

I started to walk back home, each footstep like a tick on a clock as I marched closer and closer to my deadline. What would I do about my project? The question was louder than the city around me. I had to finally admit to myself that I couldn't get it to them tomorrow afternoon. There was no way that could happen.

It was embarrassing. I had to call and tell them that my work wouldn't be in on time, couldn't be in on time, due to my own carelessness. Small town girl goes to NYC and doesn't even know how to travel on the Subway safely. And this from the writer who was working on a project about visiting New York. I groaned in shame.

When I called and asked for an extended deadline, I explained the loss of my laptop, and they told me I could have a few more days but that the deadline was based on the editorial calendar, so they couldn't offer any more time than that. The calendar was locked in.

Then I was asked, "Can you still write it?"

It was a valid question. I'd been working on this lengthy piece for weeks, and now I was starting over with only a few days to go. Could I write it all in a few days? It was an exit ramp I could zoom down. An easy out.

"I wrote that piece and got to know it really well. I can rewrite it. I'll get it to you in a few days. I won't set us back," I said over the phone, curled up in a little ball on the couch.

After we hung up, I grabbed my purse, headed out, and got myself a cheap laptop, a triple espresso latte, and a giant breakfast burrito. I took all of it home and holed up in my apartment to write nonstop for days.

. . .

I sat on my floor with my notebooks, lying open around me, trying to rebuild my essay page by page from memory. I was sketching out the progression, trying to remember different lines and sequences, noting different quotes and references. It was hours just remembering and outlining like that.

It reminded me of the night I stayed up helping Gabriel rewrite his project in high school. It felt like muscle memory piecing something lost back together from memory.

I was up late drinking coffee and typing away on my computer, rewriting lines in a new way, feeling relief and victory when I hit on something I remembered from last time. And honestly? Joy when I felt like maybe I rewrote it in a better way than before.

I decided to close my laptop around 3 a.m. to get a little sleep, thinking how funny it was to feel like I was back in high school rewriting a project, back where I started. It was full circle, I thought as my eyes started to close. Except this time, I was all alone.

Gabe had me, but there I was all alone, sitting on the floor. And I could do it alone, I knew. I didn't *need* anyone. I didn't need Gabriel. But I wanted him there in these moments. I knew what it felt like to be laughing through the pain, turning obstacles into memory with him. And that's what I wanted.

On the day it was due, I hit "submit" and actually felt really good about the work I was submitting. Rewriting it gave me a new perspective on the piece, and remembering certain sentences led me to write even better ones. A certain kind of magic that almost made it better than it was before. I could feel it in my bones.

I had my laptop on my lap in bed, and I fell backward with relief when the project was done, submitted, and all I had to do was wait for feedback. I pushed my laptop away and took a few breaths before it really hit me. I could piece this project back together from fresh memories, but I couldn't rewrite all I had lost.

I had gotten so wrapped up in the rewrite that I had forgotten how expansive the loss truly was. Journal entries, past work, personal projects—every word lost in New York City. And there was nothing for me to do but accept it.

Katie called to check on me, and I was still in bed. "How are you doing? I know today was the due date."

"The due date." I pulled the fluffy white covers over my head. "It really did feel like I was laboring the last couple of days. But I got it all submitted and feel so relieved."

"So relieved," she said. "I'm proud of you for rewriting it and not giving up."

"Giving up felt impossible. I mean, I'm out here in New York for this. I needed to finish what I started."

"You know what? It reminded me of that big rewrite you did with Gabriel in high school. Do you remember that night? I left you two worker bees and went to sleep." I heard running water on Katie's end of the call. It was early morning in Texas, too, and she was getting ready for work.

"You had track early the next morning. You needed sleep." I didn't mind one bit when she left the two of us.

"Well, you two always had your little bubble. I couldn't get into the bubble. It was like a forcefield I couldn't penetrate. I would've just been sitting there, awake for no reason." Her voice was muffled like she was speaking through a hand towel as she dried her face.

I admitted, "Gabe and I have our little writer bubble. It is true."

"Writer bubble, sure. You guys get all bubbly about more than writing, though. You're supposed to be *my* best friend, but you guys have this like... I want to say electricity or chemistry, but that'd be weird to say. But I guess that's the best word for it. Do you know what I mean?"

I was quiet. Still hidden beneath my sheets. My heart started to race.

"You have to admit, I'm right?" She started talking over my anxious silence. "I noticed it that night. He called *my* best friend in his time of crisis. I was like, 'Am I sharing Emma?' Is she also his best friend or something? You two have always been each other's...*other best friend*? I don't know. Like he hurts his leg this year, and he needs *you* like medicine. I've been sharing you all this time."

"Well, he ran off without his medicine pretty easily, huh," I mumbled. I pulled at a loose thread on my pajamas. "But...I get what you're saying... It's true."

"Speaking of, since he's your other best friend, do you know what's up with him?" She said, her voice edged with concern.

"What do you mean?"

"He's off figuring out his book, but he's acting like, exactly how you said it—like he ran off. He seems like he's running away from something, hiding away." It was quiet now on her end of the call. I could imagine her standing by the phone, worried about her brother.

"He hasn't been talking much to me. He hasn't answered a single call." I spoke around a lump in my throat.

"That's weird. See, that's what I mean. He's being weird. I'm worried about him. He seems down. He was already kind of down when he got injured, but things had seemed to be coming together." She let out a breath. "I guess healing isn't always linear."

"He's seemed down?"

"Yes. I thought he would be giddy about his book coming together. His meetings are going great, but he just sounds kind of sad."

"I wish he would talk to me, too," I said. She had no idea how badly I wished he would talk to me. "He didn't even tell me he was leaving."

"I cannot believe that. You two were inseparable the past few months. You were literally just running all over Cambria. Then he ghosts you? See, *something happened*."

Something did happen, I thought. *I hurt him*. He should be celebrating right now, but he's sad. I squeezed my eyes closed. I was such a fool. I left us both alone on opposite coasts.

"Are you there?" she said, interrupting my thoughts.

Tell her, I thought. "Well, you know, actually in Ca—"

"Hold on, babe, speak of the devil. Gabe is calling me." She clicked over to the other line. A minute later, she switched over to me and told me she would call me back.

I sat in my bed as rumpled as the sheets wondering how much of my life was wasted on missed moments. Things were full circle, even Katie noticed, from one late-night rewriting session to another years later, yet nothing had changed.

I still wanted Gabriel. Not in a perfect, tidy, easy package that would easily fit like a puzzle piece into my life. I wanted him with the messy, challenging strings attached. Things hadn't changed much, but *I finally had*.

I only had a few days left in New York City. I was trying to decide how best to spend the rest of my time when I received a call informing me that my laptop bag had been found by someone. They wanted to get it back to me.

This was a big, harsh city, and my assumption had been that someone had stolen my precious, irreplaceable body of work. I was wrong. It hadn't been stolen; it had been found by a kind woman who made sure to get it back to me.

In a matter of hours after that call, I had every word back under my care and everything saved in online storage. I cried again for the millionth time this year. Grateful tears. I thanked God. I immediately called Katie.

"Wow, I thought it would be stripped and sold for parts by now," Katie said in awe.

"Me too," I said, shaking my head as I clicked around on the laptop, back on the same floor where I'd rewritten my project. "Look at the world taking us by surprise."

"Are you going to submit your original draft? It's barely been a day since you submitted the other one. I bet they would still take it."

Quickly I said, "No, I honestly love the one I submitted. It's way better."

"Ah, yes, it's your baby."

"You know, the first thing I did was open up my original piece and read it, just to see if it was the better version. But it didn't even compare." I beamed with pride.

"Do you think it's because when you wrote the new version, you had something to prove?"

"I think sometimes things turn out better when you have to start over, and that's exactly what I did."

Forty-Seven

Terrence called me near the end of my work trip to tell me he'd be in town for a day for a couple of meetings to wrap a few things up before the wedding and honeymoon. I requested a meeting with him, too. It felt very official and maybe even presumptuous, but I did it anyway. It felt like the perfect way to end this page-turning little season of my life.

We met at my new favorite coffee shop, me always gravitating to the familiar, even on an adventure. I wore a serious black dress with my hair slicked back in a low bun. He brought a couple of other staff from his team.

We sat a table by the window, a nonstop flow of people buzzing by. We had chitchat. One of the women on his team, Molly, was nearly nine months pregnant. Terrence had a lot of questions about the work I was doing here in Manhattan. We talked about my past work.

Then, Molly mused, "Emma, what do you hope to do with your career?"

My mind flashed to how many times I'd responded to this question with, "I don't know," stuttering over my words as I stumbled over my desires and my fears like a rocky path I didn't know how to walk. But, this time, I'd been hoping for this question. I was armed with answers.

I told Molly and everyone at the table that I wanted to write full-time for a magazine, theirs or one like theirs, or a paper—somewhere that sent me off in the world. I said I'd keep freelancing until someone hired me, but I intended to keep hunting until I found this job.

They were nodding and opening their mouths to respond, but I could hear Katie in my mind when she said, *"I'm going to give it a future,"* and how those words had stayed lodged in my heart since she said them.

So, I quickly, added, "I can see a future for this magazine with me. I have a ton of ideas for different verticals and directions we could go. My work has gained traction for you already. I fit with this team. I get the vision."

I felt breathless after I said it. As if when I spoke, I had let out a breath I had long been holding. A big grin spread across Terrence's face. He said they wanted me on permanently.

Molly said they wanted me to have my own section as an editor. I'd still write my own pieces, but I would also edit and assign pieces. I had my serious, professional questions. We discussed and strategized, and really, we dreamed together at that table about the future of the magazine. I couldn't stop smiling the rest of the meeting.

Maybe I should've ruminated for a while or said I'd get back to them, but I took the job right then and there.

As I walked back to my little spot in the city, I decided that if something was on your map, there might be misdirection, U-turns, ridiculous detours, and a lot of questioning your destination, but no matter how long it took, you'd get there. I wanted Gabe to be a destination on my map. If it wasn't "meant to be," I would write him in. In big, bold letters *GABRIEL HERNANDEZ.*

Because after that meeting, there was no one in the world I wanted to share the news with more than him. To show him that I had claimed this version of me he'd seen for so long. That I gave her a future. So, right there, on the busy street, people all around me, heat coming off the concrete, I called him.

He didn't answer, of course.

But I left a long, happy, rambling, laughing message as if I knew all along he was going to call me back someday. That I knew, no matter how mad he was or how unclear his mind, he would be happy to hear my news. I knew it in my bones.

At the end I said, "You don't have to call me back." Then, like an exhale, I added, "I just wish you would."

I flew home the next day, a jumble of excitement and giddiness. The wedding was only two days away.

I landed early. I went to sit at baggage claim, waiting for my bags to arrive. I opened my phone to see that my dad, who was picking me up, had an appointment run late and so he too was now running late. I also saw a message from Katie. She had sent me an address and told me to come see the house she and Terrence were making an offer on. She was panicking.

I told my dad not to come, and after my bags arrived, I had an Uber drive me straight to Katie's prospective house. It was one of the oldest houses in town. It was downtown but right on the edge of downtown in one of the original neighborhoods. I had ridden my bike by this house thousands of times while growing up.

It was white with a big wraparound front porch, but the yard was thick with overgrown grass. The paint faded and chipped. I walked inside and my first thought was, *Well, this would be a project.*

"Hey, you," I said when I found Katie walking through the kitchen, fingering the sink and the cabinets.

"Hi. Oh my gosh, you're back! How was New York? How was

the flight? Terrence and you both called me last night about the job." She ran over to me and wrapped me up in a big hug.

"Katie, the trip was amazing, and I am thrilled about my job. But, oh my gosh, you're getting married the day after tomorrow, and we're standing in what might become your new home." I pulled back from her hug so I could look at her face.

She looked pale. Nauseous, even. I knew this look. Katie was overwhelmed.

"Come on. Why are you panicking about this house? It's beautiful." I looked around the vintage kitchen.

"We were going to wait to take this step. We just got engaged. We're doing it all so fast, you know? We decided to just move into his apartment for a while and wait on a house until way into the future. We're literally buying the coffee shop right now. There are a lot of balls in the air. But then this house popped on my radar... and it is the fixer upper of my dreams." She said everything fast and flowing, like a shaken-up bottle after the top has blown off.

"Do you think you'll regret not getting it, just because, you know, it's another ball in the air?"

It was quiet while Katie sorted through her thoughts. She turned her back to me and looked out the window over the sink.

"I think..." she said slowly. "I think I could end up regretting getting it, pushing us before we're ready. Jumping the gun. I feel off about it."

I peeked into the falling apart living room. "It would be a project," I said. "Did you bring me here to talk you out of it?"

"I think so."

"Miss Bold Moves is going to pass on this one?" I raised an eyebrow.

"I make bold moves when they're the right moves, my dear," she countered effortlessly.

We started laughing. Then her phone vibrated from her purse resting on the kitchen counter. She dug it out.

"This is the caterer; I'll be a minute," she said, looking at the caller ID. Then she disappeared into another room to take the call.

I stepped out onto the big porch. I sat down on the front steps and closed my eyes for a moment. That's when I heard a familiar rumble.

I opened my eyes to see a beat up old truck pull up in front of the house. Gabriel. I was so happily surprised I laughed out loud at the sight of him. When did he get back to Texas? Then I tried to bite back my smile. This man had been ignoring me. Was I supposed to be mad? Should I play it cool? Wait, or was he mad? Should I be ready for a confrontation? A thousand thoughts at once, like buzzing bees. And, really, I was just glad to see that truck again.

"You're hard to track down," he said, slamming his driver door shut. His voice quieted every buzzing thought.

"Me?" I stood up. "Where have you even been?"

"Here and there." He shrugged all mystery and cockiness.

I rolled my eyes. I wanted to wrap my arms around him. I wanted to kiss him. But I rolled my eyes instead.

"I got your voicemail," he said, walking toward me. "And man, I missed your voice. I had all these responses, but it was a voicemail. I kept thinking how we really need to talk...but then I realized I've been the idiot not answering your calls."

"Or text messages," I narrowed my eyes.

"Or text messages." He winced. He was standing in front of me now. We were eye to eye.

"Why? And don't give me that whole needing-to-clear-your-head spiel. I want the real answer, exactly how you think it in your head," I said. I resisted the urge to pull him closer.

"You know, Emma, I hadn't realized how bad the end of our trip was going to hurt. But it really hurt to go from kissing you to getting rejected, all in a matter of hours. It felt like this whirlwind that left me hopelessly confused." He swallowed. "It felt eerily similar to those months after your twenty-first birthday."

"Gabe, I'm so sorry," I said, my voice raw, quiet. "I hate that I hurt you like that again."

"I was really, really messed up when we got back. And there you were, in that dress at Katie's engagement party, sitting at the table, looking me down with those big eyes. And I know you were looking me down," he said pointedly. I blushed at his words.

"I was just aching at the sight of you. You were there in front of me. You know how bad I want you. I agonizingly wanted to go talk to you, it was hard not to, but I kept thinking about your message 'It's best we don't,'" he said. The air was humid, thick around us. Cars rumbling in the distance.

"But I just meant—" I started to interrupt him. He held up his hand.

"I don't need to go over exactly what you meant. I'm sure you didn't mean to never talk again. I just felt like I was one of those variables you were unsure about—like what job do you want, where do you want to live, and do you really like Gabe?" He said counting off each option on his fingers.

I nodded apologetically. Because maybe for a while, even though it wasn't true, I had stashed my big, scary feeling for Gabriel in the Variables file in my heart.

"When, for me, there is no question. No variables. No choice. I want to be with you, plain and simple. It's you, no matter what, no matter how, no matter the wreckage—it's you. It *has* to be you, Emma," he said, his voice gravelly, a rasp.

I stepped closer to him, feeling the heat between us. My skin was acutely aware of his every move.

"You're not just a variable for me," I said. "I'm not unsure of how I feel about you. Maybe I didn't want to admit it to myself for a while. But your place in my heart is one of the surest things in my life. It's been you since I was a little girl." I started laughing at the agonizing undeniable truth of it all. Like I was really realizing it as I spoke it. "It's been you every single day, year after year. It's been you on the best days, the worst days. It's been you even when I hadn't seen you in years—even when I was seeing you hold someone else's hands. It's been you even when I was trying to convince myself to be okay without you."

His eyes were on mine in a way I could feel to my core.

I took a deep, steadying breath. "You're not one of the options I'm choosing between. You're a destination on my map that I was desperately trying to find the right path to."

There we stood, just us two, the sun on our shoulders.

"Then why..." his voice cracked.

"I hadn't meant to end it between us. I was trying to press pause on the conversation, but I didn't want us to stop talking. I definitely didn't want to hurt you the way I did. I should've spoken up and explained it, but I was so... I was scared." I swallowed. My mouth was dry, and my heart was pounding. "You were right when you said I was scared to admit what I want. I was scared to admit I didn't want Jordan. I was scared to admit I wanted to move on from my job. And I wanted you most of all, so I was scared of you most of all."

"I saw you talking to Jordan at the party—" He looked down at his feet as he said this. A curl fell over his eyes.

I shook my head as if to immediately brush away the thought of Jordan. "He was telling me he was back with his ex."

"The girl from the auto shop?" He looked back up at me.

I nodded.

"Wait, why are you scared of me most of all? Is it the family thing?"

"Mostly."

"I get that. But you also said something that night in Cambria about me running off to California?" *Of course, he had held onto something from the last conversation that plucked one of my most sensitive nerves.*

"I do get scared that you will just leave me behind. I think when I didn't get the job in California and you did, and I had to stay behind and watch your life blossom there without me, I felt like I couldn't keep up with you. Like I'd be left behind like your old small town."

"I will never leave you behind. I never did. You were here." He patted his chest. Then pointed to his head. "And you're on repeat up here twenty-four seven."

I swooned a little, but the realistic part of me replied, "But logistically."

"Logistically, we'll figure it out together. No one gets left behind. I would much prefer to be around you as much as possible, so that can be considered as we plan *together*." He grabbed my wrists and pulled me a couple of steps closer.

"The feeling is obviously mutual," I said. "I am so sick of missing you."

"And with the family—" He started, but this time I held up my hand when he tried to interrupt me.

"That's just growing up, isn't it? Family dynamics and friendship dynamics evolve and change. I'm going to be with you because I want to be, and whatever happens, happens."

"Whatever happens, happens?" he repeated, skeptical but hopeful.

"The whole lot of 'em will get over it. And you know what? If we crash and burn, they'll get over that, too, won't they?" I took another step closer.

He entangled his fingers in mine. "So you want to give this thing a shot?"

He'd asked me this a couple of times before, and I always regretted my answer. I never had the guts to answer him honestly. This time I wanted to get my response right. I wanted to say exactly what I wanted.

"I want us to start kissing on a regular basis," I said, bringing my face closer to his, harkening back to something he had said back in Cambria. And because I really did want to kiss him as often as I could.

He grabbed my arms and pulled me in, his eyes dropping to my mouth. "Then let's start."

And we kissed. I don't know for how long.

"What?" Katie said, standing on the front porch, mouth agape at the two of us kissing in the driveway.

I pulled away from Gabriel, my hand to my mouth. I should've expected her to walk out at any moment. "We were just..." I started.

"Kissing?" Katie's squeaked.

"Yes," I said. Gabriel was half laughing, half grinning at the situation.

"When did this happen? The kissing? Is this new?" She walked down to us.

"Newish?" Gabriel offered. Her ran a finger through his hair. "Well, it first happened a few years ago. Then it happened a lot on the trip."

Katie's eyes were huge. My eyes were huge, too. I put my hand to Gabe's mouth to quiet him.

"Okay, let me explain," I said. Gabe kissed my hand. Katie gasped. "You're not helping," I whispered to him.

"Why are you hiding stuff from me? What is happening?" Katie's voice kept getting higher. "Why are you here?" she asked Gabe. "You're supposed to be flying in tomorrow morning for the rehearsal dinner."

"I hopped on an earlier flight," Gabe said far too casually in my opinion. "I wanted to come see Emma."

"You wanted to come *kiss* Emma. Are you guys... I shouldn't even have to be asking this question. How am I, the sister and best friend of you both, having to ask this question?" She put her fingers to her temples.

"We are not dating," I said. "Or actually, now we... are? We're... There's you know...feelings. Of course, we didn't just kiss for no reason. We're in the talks."

"In the talks?" Both Katie and Gabriel repeated.

"We're like right in the middle of talking about everything. Literally," I gestured between us.

"It's true," Gabe added.

"Well then, sorry for interrupting your secret relationship chat!" Katie stormed off toward the house. I chased after her.

"Katie, wait." I raced into the house. Katie stood in the empty kitchen with tears down her cheeks.

"I'm sorry, Katie. I wasn't hiding..." But I realized that wasn't true as I said it.

"I feel so stupid," she said, her voice thick with hurt. "You two have always had your stupid secret little world. How could I not have guessed it? Maybe I did guess it. I just always assumed if anything happened, even an inkling of anything, I would be the first to know. You know, I would've thought I'd know even before Gabe since you'd tell me if you felt anything for him. But instead, I have zero idea what's going on."

"Honestly, Katie, I felt like I had no idea what was going on half the time."

She blinked at me.

"Okay, the thing is...I've.." I stuttered. Hadn't I been rehearsing what to say to Katie? My mind was blank. "I've been in love with Gabriel since I was like twelve years old. Do you remember his first girlfriend?"

"No," she almost laughed. She leaned against the kitchen counter.

"Well, I do. I was insanely jealous of her. I couldn't figure out why I was so jealous of her. I wanted *to be* her. Those feelings went on for years, confusing me. I was in denial. I was also too young to really understand." I walked further into the kitchen so we were standing side by side. "When I slowly I started to realize what those feelings were, they felt hopeless, like a kink in the perfect machine of our little world. I didn't say anything because I was too busy trying to pretend they weren't real."

"Why didn't you tell *me*? Me, of all people. I told you every single thing, even when I dreamed of someone." She wiped her eyes.

"Come on, Katie. This was Gabe. He was your *brother*. You can't understand a little?"

She was quiet. She leaned against the kitchen counter, looking at her hands.

"Everyone called me the Other Hernandez girl. I didn't want to jeopardize my standing. I also didn't want to make the vibe weird between all of us. What if you started teasing me or giggling around him? What if you started to question me? What if you wanted us together, and then we broke up? I mean...it felt big." I spread my hands wide to emphasize just how big it felt.

"I get it. It is big," she finally said. "Tell me what I've missed."

"It's just that. We've liked each other for a long time." I shrugged a shoulder.

"Even when you were with—"

"Even while we were with other people. I mean, I still liked the people I was with. My feelings for Gabe were just sitting there on the back burner."

"You know, this actually explains a ton," Katie raised her eyebrows.

"When I turned twenty-one—" I started.

"Gabe flew out to see you—" Katie said, glad it was finally something she knew.

"Yeah, and you all left us there at the restaurant? Do you remember that? Gabe drove me home. We kissed for the first time that night." I felt terrified and giddy to finally be sharing this monumental moment with her.

"You didn't tell me!"

"I barely told myself. I tried to ignore it. I tried to force him to ignore it. We honestly never kissed again until he went to Cambria with me." I turned toward her.

"Another kiss! I can't believe you didn't tell me." She shook her head in disbelief.

"I tried the whole 'let's just ignore it' thing again. You see how that's gone."

"Wait, wait. I'm so confused. Are you two dating now?" She turned to face me, too.

"Katie, we literally just now decided we want to be together and give it a try right before you walked up. That's why we were kissing when you walked outside."

Katie ran to the doorway and looked outside. "He's gone," she said wistfully, looking out at the front yard and driveway.

Nothing was left of Gabriel except his tire marks on the driveway.

"He left," she said to me. As if he were some broody romantic male lead and not the punk older brother she used to say smelled like farts.

"He probably realized you and I needed to talk this out a bit," I said. "And he's right. I mean, how do you even feel about your brother and me?"

"I don't know. I barely know what you feel about him and you." She walked out onto the front porch. "What do you feel?"

We sat down on the steps, the sky with its pink streaks hanging overhead, the sounds of downtown coming to life.

"Your brother has been the one for a long time, Katie. It's terrified me, annoyed me, confounded me, and thrilled me, but at the end of the day, I think it's so strong because what we have is so good. That's kind of the gist of how I feel."

Katie giggled in surprise. "Gah, who knew how dramatic you

could be about a guy. You've always been Miss Sensible. I feel like I should steal some of that for my vows."

I gave her a shove.

"And he feels the same?"

"You could probably ask him all about it. But from what he's told me, yes. It's equally undeniable." I thought of the things he had said less than an hour ago. My stomach so full of butterflies I felt like I might float up into the sky.

"What's he said to you? Like, do you have any quotes?"

I started laughing. "Katie, oh my gosh."

"What? I'm curious now." She shrugged.

"What do you feel about it? I have to know. I've been worried about your reaction for years," I said, my gaze intent on her.

"It upsets me that you never said a word about it to me. I get that you were scared and confused, but really, after Cambria, with us being grown adults now, I'd have thought you would open up to me about it. That upsets me," she said honestly. She looked at me and then cocked her head to the side. "But the two of you being in love? Being together? I think that actually makes a lot of sense. Some things are finally clicking."

I nodded. "I wish I'd told you." It felt like I'd just taken a breath after holding it in for so long, the relief radiated all the way to my toes.

"You two *just now* decided to give it a try. *You turtles.*" Her voice was soft, accepting.

"I was hesitant, surprise, surprise. Hesitant since we kissed on my twenty-first birthday."

"What's been going on in that head of yours?"

"Way too many things. It probably would've really helped to talk to you about it all this time." I said. A warm breeze rippled through the trees, our hair. "You know how your brother is just so brave and go-go-go? I think that intimidated me. I know that with him, he wouldn't let me sit it out. He wouldn't let me cling to the past—"

"He's always seen right through to the real you. Since you were in school. He's always been reminding you what you want."

"Always calling me on all my crap."

"And vice versa," she noted, tossing me a sideways grin.

"It felt like I was not only facing my feelings for him, but I was also facing the version of me that wanted to be with him. That version of me wanted a lot of things that scared me. That version of me called up Terrence. That version of me is the woman who went to New York."

"That version of you is you." She said so sincerely it made my heart tug.

"I know. It's me with the training wheels off."

Katie grabbed my hand. "I love you no matter the wheels."

"I know that. I think I know it too well. Our friendship has always been one of my favorite hiding spots from the rest of the world." The sun was hanging low in the sky now. I wondered how long we were allowed to hang out at this house Katie had decided not to buy.

"You think?"

"Back when we were about to head off for college, Gabe had to confront me about copying your major just because following you around college felt like such a safe choice." I shook my head at my younger self.

"Oh yeah." She crinkled her nose. "I forgot about that."

"I followed you back home after college instead of following Gabe as badly as he wanted me to."

"I've liked our time together here." She grabbed my hand.

"I've used us as an excuse not to go after Gabe when I think I knew deep down that this," I squeezed her hand, "would be your reaction."

"Should I call you on your crap more?" She joked.

I shook my head. "I got your brother for that."

"Our friendship has always been a touchstone for me, too.

Not so much for hiding but for reminding myself who I am. Growing up, working, getting married, and moving out, it gets easy to get so caught up in the grind and moving so fast that my self-reflection becomes a blur. I've gotten used to our friendship being one of my touchstones that reflects me back to me."

"But all that growing up grind reflects you, too. You're the heart and soul of your job. Your love story with Terrence—how you listened to your gut and fell in love with arms wide open. The way he moved here for you. And I'm sure wherever you end up living will be a further reflection of you."

"I know, I know," she said breezily. "I guess I'm talking about the way you remind me of the young, carefree Katie."

"Well, dido. I love young Katie and young Emma." I said tenderly, nostalgically.

"Can you believe this year, though?" Katie asked.

"No, not at all. If you'd told us a year ago, heck, even in January, that you'd be getting married the day after tomorrow—"

"Or that you'd be kissing Gabe?" Katie let her jaw drop. "Well, maybe *you* wouldn't have been so shocked."

"Oh, I'd be shocked," I said. "Or imagine telling yourself in January that you'd be owner of Coffee & Commas."

Katie fell back on the front porch. I fell back, too.

We lay there with the wooden beams behind our back with our shoes kicked off, laughing. We could hear the murmurs of bustling downtown, but we could also hear the crickets singing in the grass.

"I feel like I've always known you and Gabe were meant to be. Like I always knew you were two lovesick puppies panting after each other. Like I'd just forgotten I knew," Katie whispered.

"Maybe you did," I mused. "My mom did."

"My mom probably did, too." She snorted. "Maybe you and Gabe were always meant to be together, but maybe it's also that you and I were always meant to be sisters."

"We've always been sisters, Katie. That's one of the top

reasons I didn't want to admit my feelings to anyone. I didn't want to ruin what we have in any way. I wanted to preserve us."

"We don't need preserving, Em. We are made of the strong stuff, the withstanding stuff. We are bound to change, to shift, to share—but we'll always last."

"Always." I reached my hand over to hers. We latched on to one another, and I felt her diamond ring against my pinky.

It was different than when we were little girls grabbing each other's hands to drag one another on to the next adventure. But it still felt easy, comforting like kin.

"You didn't want to tell me because you wanted to preserve our friendship but also because you didn't want to tick me off," she said in a knowing voice.

"Duh," I admitted readily.

She then flipped onto her stomach, resting on her elbows. "Okay, now I need the quotes from Gabe. I need all the details. Starting with what was said during the Cambria trip, but then also work backward to when you guys were teenagers. Wait, you two danced together on New Year's Eve. Was that like a romantic time for you guys, and I was totally oblivious?"

Forty-Nine

Texas was moody and temperamental. One day it was blue skies, bright sun, and then you could wake up the next morning to clouds gray as smoke and torrential downpour. The hardest part to deal with was the lack of warning.

We'd been told it could possibly rain a couple of days ago, but no warning it would be such an angry storm that flights would be delayed and venues panicking about their outdoor ceremonies.

Texas was moody and decided she didn't want any visitors today. Check back tomorrow though tomorrow was the wedding.

Today was the rehearsal dinner, and now Terrence's Canadian family and friends would not be able to attend. They had departed from Canada and stopped for their connecting flight in Denver to find their flight to Austin was canceled due to the harsh storms.

"They're hanging around the airports to see if they can get aboard another flight, but it appears any flights landing in Texas are canceled or delayed until further notice," Katie told me over the phone late that morning. Her voice was heavy with stress and exhaustion.

"Oh no, I'm sorry, Katie. How are you doing?" I was sitting at my bathroom counter, putting on my moisturizer.

"I'm trying to enjoy the day before my wedding, but it's hard to do with all these unknowns. I can't imagine Terrence and I getting married without his family there. I'm not sure what to do."

"Do you think they will be delayed tomorrow, too? The storm is supposed to let up, right?" I wondered aloud.

"It's all unknown. Terrence is glued to the weather channel like an old man," Katie said, trying to find humor in the situation.

"If they can't..."

"If they can't, I think we should delay our wedding. But Terrence is adamant against the idea."

"Why is he? I mean, you're having it in your own backyard, so the venue if flexible," I asked.

"It's the abundance of guests we'd have to notify, plus rescheduling the flowers, food, and music. We also have our honeymoon flight and hotel booked. It'd be costly and a headache!" Terrence chimed in from the background.

"We don't even need to be talking about this because I'm sure they will get here in time!" Linda added. Her voice echoed in the way it did when she stood in the kitchen.

"I agree with Mama Hernandez," I said, deciding my role as best friend was to remain optimistic. "My weather app says the storm stops tonight."

"I'm betting on Linda and Emma," Terrence said, his voice louder now, getting closer to the phone.

"A safe bet," Gabe said.

"You bet on the bride!" Katie said, exasperated. "Come on, guys."

"You bet on the bride's mama," Terrence joked.

"Emma, are you going to come help us set up for the rehearsal dinner downtown?" Gabe's voice was loud, as if he was speaking straight into the phone's microphone. "I think we need extra hands."

"No, no, no, you can get your Emma fix later. We have too many hands helping set up a place that sets up for us anyway. Emma has a list of errands she's running for me that is very important—more important than y'all's little shenanigans," Katie said in a commanding tone.

"Wait, what are these little shenanigans?" Linda asked, all bubbly and curious.

"Fun shenanigans," Gabe said. I could imagine him there in his baggy sweatpants, white tee shirt, and a twinkle in his eye. I sighed quietly to myself.

"She didn't tell you about the shenanigan last night?" Terrence said, presumably to Linda. I should've known Terrence would know now.

"Linda, let's talk about it all after the wedding," I said, blushing even though it was a phone call.

"Is there something to talk about? What happened last night?" Linda ignored me.

"Em's right. The next two days, we need to focus up!" Katie said loudly over murmuring in the background. A few more voices were questioning the shenanigans, and I could hear Gabe saying something about how they could probably guess.

"Guys, focus!" Katie was saying.

"Should I let y'all go? I should start my errand list," I said.

"You haven't started? I thought you were calling from the car," Katie said, her voice booming through the phone.

I hurried off the call.

. . .

The rehearsal dinner was at the fanciest restaurant downtown. The one we went to before senior prom and where my dad always reserved a table on Mother's Day. You wore your best when you walked in the doors of The Vintage Table.

I could hear my high heels click against the wet pavement as I hurried toward the tall French doors with my big umbrella open overhead. I told the well-dressed hostess waiting by the door that I was there for the rehearsal dinner. She promptly led me through the chandelier-lit rooms winding to the backroom.

I had on a dark blue satin sleeveless dress with a sweetheart neckline. My hair was curled in a way that made me feel like a 60s movie starlet, and my lips were red. When I thought of my lips, I thought of him.

This night was about Katie and Terrence, I reminded myself, as I walked into the party. *Not Gabriel and me.*

Immediately, Gabriel's eyes were on me from where he stood in a far corner of the room. He grinned devilishly when he saw me. I had been thinking about him all day long, but I swallowed down the feelings and looked for the bride.

The backroom was all lavish with rich reds, sparkling golds, and vintage French chandeliers hanging overhead, just the place for Champagne toasts.

Katie, in her white silk slip dress, was encircled by people, her friends and family. I joined the circle. She saw me and grabbed my arm, pulling me to her.

"I put the bags in the back of your car before I came inside," I whispered.

"Perfect. Thank you," she said to me. Then, she turned to the whole crew. "I was just telling everyone how our Canadian guests are staying the night in Denver. They're staying at a hotel by the airport and keeping an eye out to hop on the earliest flight to Texas that they can."

I could hear the thunder through the rain-soaked windows.

"I'll be praying it lets up soon," I said.

"Hey," Gabriel whispered against the back of my neck. I quickly turned to him, leaving the group.

"I like this." He touched my dress, also touching my waist.

"No shenanigans tonight, remember?" I said quietly, trying to remember how to breathe a single breath. "Katie's special orders."

"I would never shenanigan on Wedding Eve," he promised in earnest. I raised an eyebrow. He winked.

Then, Mr. Hernandez tapped a glass, so we all turned to listen. It was time to find our seats, he told us. I wasn't seated by Gabriel. I was seated with a couple of other bridesmaids and close friends who weren't related to Katie. Gabriel was at a table behind mine, but I was seated at an angle where I could see him out of the corner of my eye. He noticed.

He kept leaning back in his chair and glancing at me. To me it felt like we were making a scene, though no one else would think anything of it. Except maybe those in the room who knew what we were up to yesterday. When someone said something funny during a toast, we would look at each other and laugh together, as if sharing each joke, like passing a note.

Terrence was belly laughing at Katie's brothers' shared stories, tearing up at her parent's prayers, and squeezing Katie's hand. I watched all of it. He was enjoying the evening even though it wasn't going to plan, wasn't his vision of perfect, and was lacking essential people. The person who seemed the most distracted by the family missing was his soon-to-be-wife. I sipped my Champagne and said another prayer for the rain to stop, even as I heard it hammering on the roof.

The dinner ended. People were taking photos and exchanging hugs before running out the door armed with umbrellas. I was talking to Tanya, letting her newest son chew on my finger, when Gabriel appeared beside us.

"Gabe," she said to him. "I might head out early. I'm worried about London. He was really scared when the storm started up, and now he's at our house all alone."

"He would appreciate the company, I'm sure. He's not a fan of thunder," Gabe said, then to me, "Jack London was kicked out of Mom and Dad's due to wedding festivities and his love of chewing."

"No one wants a chewed-up wedding veil," I said.

"Okay, can you tell Mom and Dad for us? I haven't been able to get either of them alone to talk to them. I'll stop off at home to deposit my husband and the kids before I join up for the bachelorette festivities. I still need to pack my overnight bag, anyway."

"Sure," he said. She disappeared into the party, leaving Gabe and me alone.

It was like the moment our eyes locked, all the air left the room, along with all the chitchat and music. It was just us two.

He stepped closer to me. "So, about yesterday."

"Before we were interrupted," I said.

"You said, and I quote, 'I'm going to be with you.'" His voice was a notch above a whisper.

"I did." I bit my lip.

"Was that an invitation or an order?" He asked.

"More of an announcement."

"Thanks for letting me know." He touched his fingers to mine.

"You're welcome," I said, interlacing my hands with his.

"Do you want to walk outside for a minute?"

"It's pouring rain," I said, though everything in me was thinking *yes*.

"There's a covered patio, remember?"

I nodded. He took my hand and started to lead me through the dwindling party. My whole body was humming with reckless excitement. He looked back at me right before we were going to turn down out of the back room and into the hallway. He grinned that sideways grin of his.

"No shenanigans!" Katie shouted across the room, breaking the moment like glass. "It is my bachelorette night. No sneaking off! The smooching can wait until tomorrow night!"

"No, it really cannot," Gabe said roughly.

I just blushed, ignoring any people looking over. I turned my back to the room in mortification but gave a measly thumbs up to Katie, who was laughing at us. Terrence, playing Gabe's brotherly wingman, was pleading our case with her.

Gabriel nodded toward the hallway as if suggesting we duck out anyway, but I shook my head.

Katie marched over to us and declared, "Bachelorette time!" and away we went.

The Bachelorette party splashed through the rain to get spicy margaritas and sing karaoke. Then, sleepy and tipsy, we were chauffeured back home to don face and hair masks until we all decided to turn in early-ish with the big day in the morning.

Tanya and Katie were sharing Katie's bed, and I had a sleeping bag on her bedroom floor. I was nestled in with my eyes closed while Tanya and Katie whispered.

They were wondering if the rain didn't stop, could the barn be cleaned up quickly enough? Maybe if they started cleaning it out at six a.m.? Or could they just arrange furniture in the living and dining area of their house? Or maybe they just slosh out in the rain and offer everyone umbrellas? Then it was quiet. I assumed they had drifted to sleep.

I snuggled deeper into my sleeping bag to open my phone so I could check the weather forecast. I repeated my prayer from earlier.

Then, I got a message from Katie.

KATIE

I can see the light from your phone, so I know I can bug you.

KATIE

I just want Terrence's family here and to get married standing under my big Texas sunshine.

ME

this message found me already praying. I've
been praying all night.

KATIE

that's my bestie

Then, another message popped up.

GABRIEL

Shenanigan meeting outside?

ME

it's pouring rain outside

GABRIEL

we have a covered patio

ME

you've become such a recent purveyor of
covered patios

GABRIEL

you know you're going to be meet me out
there

ME

fine

I found Gabe sitting on the steps, just missing the rainfall,
looking out at the inky night sky. I sat down beside him. The
steps were damp under me, but there was nowhere else I wanted
to be. He pulled me in closer to him, tucking me under his arm.

"Finally," he said, release a breath.

I felt like my whole body sighed. Maybe I could fall asleep
here for the night, in his arms, to the sound of rain.

"I missed you so bad," he whispered against the top of my head.

I wasn't sure if he meant for the past few years or for the past few weeks, or the past twenty-four hours, but either way, I said, "I missed you, too."

I reached up and pulled his chin until he was looking at me. "But we're here now."

He leaned his lips down to my hand and kissed my fingers.

"This changes everything, huh?" I said, because since when did Gabe and I have sneaky rainy meet-ups to kiss?

"But does it?" he asked, cupping his hand around my face, running his thumb against my jawline and then down my neck, almost leaving a trail of smoke at how hot it was.

Until the sliding glass doors opened, and there stood Mama Linda. "Oh, it's you two. I thought I heard voices out here and was a little spooked."

Gabriel said, "No intruders, Mom. We were just talking."

She raised an eyebrow. "Shenanigans?"

I stood up abruptly. "No shenanigans."

Gabe moaned. "We cannot even have five minutes together?"

I grabbed his hand and pulled him up. "We have a big day tomorrow, bud."

"After everything the past twenty-four hours, and I'm getting *bud*?" He continued his moaning.

"Go to bed, bud," Linda said, as we trailed back inside the house.

Fifty

The next morning, we woke up and the rain was completely gone. The earth was soft, but the air felt crisp and cool. As if God had decided to spend all night cleaning for the wedding today, everything was a bright, shining green.

"It'll be perfect. Everyone will just need to wear a pair of boots. I'll send out a mass message," Tanya said that morning as we stood drinking coffee standing on the back porch, dripping in relief like dew.

Terrence's crew hopped on an early morning flight. Katie and Terrence woke up to celebratory messages telling them they were boarding along with their arrival details. Katie had run out in her pajamas to announce the news, dancing around the kitchen. Mr. and Mrs. Hernandez were enlisted to pick them up in a few hours at the airport.

Katie was having a semi-spa-like morning in her room with a massage therapist first thing in the morning. She'd booked herself a long bath before her stylist and makeup artist arrived. I felt like some sort of floater being whisked from job to job without making much of an impact and with no real direction.

I started out helping set up in the backyard with Victor, Ricky, and Luis. Then I was back and forth, prepping and chatting with Katie. Then I helped the florist. Then I was answering catering questions I wasn't even sure about. Then I was answering calls asking where the actual people in charge were.

I was standing in the kitchen when I realized we had a couple hours left until the wedding began, and I didn't have my hair or makeup done. I tiptoed into Katie's room, and the makeup artist offered to help me a little. Music was playing, and Katie already looked like a wedding goddess from your dreams.

She was giggling with Tanya, Sarah, and her mom while her hair was primped. So, I relaxed and tended to my own appearance. I had been chatting with the stylist about my new job when Katie gasped, "Mom!"

The stylist and I both turned to Katie as she exclaimed, "Dad just texted. He got a big stain on his suit!"

There was scrambling, murmuring, and a speaker phone call where they learned a cup of coffee was the culprit. Linda griped that she had told him to wait to put on the suit until the very last minute.

Sarah shook her head and said, "Men."

It was decided that Mr. and Mrs. Hernandez would rush off to the dry cleaners for an emergency appointment.

"But..." Katie buried her head in her hands. "What about our Canadian crew landing in like an hour?"

"I'll go," I offered. "I can race to the airport and meet them at baggage claim, then rush back here, throw on my dress, and go."

"We're already running late with this whole fiasco. Are you sure you can go right now? If not, maybe I can have one of the boys go?" I watched Katie reach to chew on her nails but then resist the urge.

"You know they're busy—they were doing all the setup. I'm already primped, and I have no real duties. I'm the best person to go."

"Are you sure?"

"Of course."

"Okay. Okay! Can you leave, like, right now?"

I was starting my car when someone pounded on the passenger side door. I glanced to my right and watched Gabriel open the door and climb inside.

"I'm happy to see you, but I'm in a major hurry." I gave a weak smile.

"Katie told me to assist you. She thinks you need help hauling luggage."

"What? I don't know if the wedding can spare you!" I was starting to catch the pre-wedding panic.

"I think me not going, or discussing it further with Katie, will stress her out more."

I pressed on the gas and backed out of the driveway. "You're right. It's crunch time."

I sped out of there.

"I forgot what a speed demon you can be," Gabriel said, dramatically clinging to his seat.

"I am barely going over the speed limit," I said as he eyed the speedometer.

"Careful with the turns." He winced as I rushed through a turn. Then he laughed. "Do you remember how we were late to my highschool graduation?"

I broke into a grin. "Yeah, Katie and I had thought it would be cute to surprise you by blindfolding you and taking you to a big breakfast at Bread & Butter. But we had not planned for traffic on the way back."

"You terrified me that day. You had me pull over and took over the wheel so you could get us there on time. I feel like you worried more than I did about me missing my graduation."

"Do you remember the time you made me late to the Beyoncé concert? Because you drive so slowly..."

"We all move slow in our own ways," he said suggestively.

"What's that mean?" I shot him a glance.

"I make us what, fifteen minutes late to a concert. You take a few years to answer me when I ask if you want to give us a shot." He smirked.

"This isn't going to be a thing we joke about. This was an actual serious thing." I tried to fight a smile.

"You also said the Beyoncé concert was a very serious thing."

I realized I'd let my foot off the gas a little and tried to focus on the road again. Suddenly his hand was resting palm-up between our seats. I dropped my hand in his. We drove like that together.

The sun was shining, my best friend was getting married today, her in-laws would be there, and I was holding Gabriel's hand like it was an absolutely normal and right thing to be doing. Then we drove up onto a literal stand-still, bumper-to-bumper traffic on the exit ramp to the airport.

"I think you could probably map another way to get to the entrance, maybe bypass this?" Gabe said, peering out the window.

"This is the only way to the entrance. That's why there's a traffic jam." I said.

"We just need to get to the parking lot. We don't have to get in front of the airport. You don't think there's another way to get to a parking lot?"

We started to squabble about alternate routes, even after cars lined up behind me and there was no backing out. Terrence called to tell us his family had landed and that they would be waiting for us at baggage claim. He asked for an estimate, and we explained we really had no way of knowing. My chest felt tight. The clock felt like it was ticking each minute to taunt me. Gabe and I were both staring out the windows anxiously.

We crept along until we eventually eased our way into the entrance and made it to the parking garage for arrivals.

We raced out of the car and ran through the parking lot all the way toward the airport.

I briskly led us down the sidewalk, weaving through the people until we made it to the second set of doors. They opened before us. I walked in and started to look around the sets of baggage carousels.

I felt Gabriel's hand tug on mine. Before I could respond, he was twirling me around until I was in his arms.

There were people all around us. People rushing. People embracing. There was a time crunch. A wedding we needed to rush back to.

But there was Gabe, and his warm body pressing into mine and his lips against mine. Everything else melted away, just for a minute. My arms around his neck, his fingers gripping my waist. I pulled away, out of breath, laughing.

"No one else I'd rather argue about directions with," he whispered in my ear.

Fifty-One

Terrence's family was full of excited, relieved energy. They didn't care we were late; they were just grateful they were able to be here. We hugged like we'd known each other for years.

When we walked into the house, Terrence was waiting for his family, and his mom burst into tears upon seeing him. They embraced.

His dad was holding back tears, only saying, "Son."

Terrence buried his face in his dad's shoulder and took in a jagged breath. "You're here," he kept saying.

His sister and best friend were sniffling. I couldn't help but think of Katie's persistence, demanding we needed to reschedule if Terrence's family could not be there. Her late-night request to pray the rain away.

Terrence spun his sister around in the air, beaming.

The wedding happened in the sweet, balmy Texas summer air that only comes after a storm. It smelled like lilacs. Katie walked down the aisle in a strapless ivory dress with a lacy train as the pecan trees swayed overhead. Her hair was in loose waves down her back.

I wore a spaghetti strap sienna dress and old worn cowboy boots. My hair was in a long, loose braid. Gabe had on a suit jacket and his curls as tamed as they could be. He stood across from me during the ceremony. The guests sat in old church pews laced with lilies and ivy.

During her vows, Katie told Terrence we called him Canada Man when she first met him and that it felt like magic then—and it felt like magic now. Terrence said that one of the first things he said to Katie was, "I'm sold," seemingly in reference to her baked goods, but really, he had meant her.

The breeze blew my hair across my face as they exchanged rings. Gabriel's eyes lingered on me like we were magnetic.

Twinkle lights hung overhead during the reception, weaving through the branches of trees. A DJ was playing some sappy old love song as I got myself another cocktail. I'd had a plate full of food and swayed around the dance floor with the flower girl. My parents were at our table, clinking glasses.

We'd taken what felt like a million photos. I'd hugged Katie and Terrence and took credit for bringing them together.

"I'm happy to share you with him for life," I'd whispered in Katie's ear.

I had known Gabriel would be preoccupied with the kind of obligations the brother of the bride was bound to have with photos, visiting relatives, and crisis management. I was sipping my drink as the post-storm breeze rippled through my hair when Gabe snuck up and wrapped his arms around me from behind.

"You are out to torture me when you put on dresses," he groaned into my neck.

"That is actually my one goal every time I don an outfit—torture Gabriel Hernandez."

"You excel." He spun me around to face him. His arms around my waist, my arms resting on his. He looked at my lips.

"The only kissing that we should be discussing at this

wedding is that of the Texan and the Canadian," I said, against my own instincts. "Our kissing would definitely be discussed."

He looked down at our embracing selves. "This won't be discussed, though?" He raised a brow.

"Potentially," I admitted.

He sighed deeply and released his grip on me. Then, he grabbed my arm and said with a gleam in his eyes, "I have an idea."

He led me away from the reception party until we were at the front of the house where he always parked his janky old truck.

"You sure are bossy," I teased, leaning my back against the truck, his hands holding mine.

"You sure are stubborn," he countered, leaning into me.

"I ran off with you, didn't I?"

"Yes, you did," he said, in that knowing way, only stupid, annoying, get-my-heart-beating Gabriel could. Like I was sixteen again, accidentally confessing I was a willing accomplice. But I wasn't hiding anything anymore.

So, I leaned into the distance between us and kissed him. There we were, after all this time, on a hot summer evening. The guy still thrilled me.

Like nothing had changed.

Like everything had changed.

Epilogue

I slid open the window and let the crisp, lilac scented breeze sweep through the hotel room. I had just checked in, but Gabriel had arrived hours earlier than me. We'd been following each other across the globe like a game of cat and mouse the past year—me meeting him on his work trip, him meeting me on mine. Sweet River for holidays, and my new apartment in Austin when we needed to catch our breath. As a woman hopping from place to place, my favorite place was in Gabriel's arms.

This reunion in Cambria was a little birthday trip he planned for me. I had been back in New York weeks ago for a friend's book signing, when he sent me a photo of the flights, and the hotel from our trip over a year and a half ago, with a one word question.

Birthday?

I had promptly replied,

yes, please

It's funny to remember where we were just a year ago, our relationship so new, so fresh. Staying up all night to rehash the past through laughter and kisses. Long phone calls across distance talking excitedly about our future. *Our future.* I'd fall asleep thinking: *am I already dreaming?* Gabriel was mine, all mine.

I was his first call. His home base. He bought me hiking boots and a backpacking bag, so I could accompany him and London on the trails. (Which terrified me, but nothing, not even the dog being a superior hiker to me, would keep me from this man again).

He was impulse to my hesitation. I would get lost up in my thoughts like the sun fading away on a cloudy day, but he would reach over and run a finger along my bottom lip and say, "I love your thinking face."

I quickly slipped into a pink bikini top and a pair of linen pants. I pulled my hair into a thick French braid that fell down my shoulder. Our hotel had a walking path that led from the back-door to a rocky beach. I basically ran down the path to him.

I arrived on the pebble laden sand, breathless and beaming. He was sitting on the beach only inches from the crashing waves, wearing a black tee shirt and linen shorts. His tan skin glowed in the sunlight. My smile widened when I noticed the pizza box beside him.

I bent my body over his planting an upside down kiss on his lips. He weaved his arms around my waist and pulled me into his lap.

We kissed, tangled up like that, as the sun set around us, all pinks and violets.

"I missed you," I whispered into the side of his neck. We'd been together just a week ago, but I didn't care. I would've loved a daily dose of Gabriel; an hourly dose of *this*.

He let out a gravelly breath that sent goosebumps everywhere. "I could do this all the time," he muttered against my collarbone.

My gaze fell onto a little gift bag sitting beside the pizza box. "Is that my birthday present?" I wiggled my eyebrows. My bikini strap had fallen down my shoulder.

He traced his thumb over my exposed skin. "I had a whole

thing planned, actually," he said almost shyly. A new look on Gabe.

I cocked my head. "I was going to wait until after the pizza, and when the stars came out." He gestured to the red wine sky overhead.

I looked at the box and felt all the pieces settle into place. *He had something planned.* I knew what it was without a doubt.

"Don't wait," I whispered, my heart racing.

He swallowed, then gave my waist a little squeeze as he lifted me from his lap and then crawled over to the bag.

He pulled a little ring box from the bag. My jaw began to tremble, my eyes stung in the sweetest way. I put my shaking hand to my lips. *I knew what this was.*

"Emma Brown," Gabriel's voice broke as he dropped to his knee. "You have no idea what you do to me...I had this whole speech..." He blinked away a tear. "I just love you so much and—" He popped open the ring box to reveal a silvery, shiny diamond ring. Simple, perfect. *Gabe was asking me to marry him.*

I tackled him before he could finish. "Yes, yes, yes, yes, yes!" I covered him in kisses.

We laid there on the sand, teary and giggly. He kissed me forcefully, emotionally, then rolled us onto our sides, till we were looking at each other.

He'd managed to keep a grip on the ring box. "So, yes?" He asked with a trembling voice, holding it up.

"*For me, there is no question.* It's yes. Yes. Yes." Warm tears flooded my cheeks. I sniffled. "I want this..." I placed my hand on his warm chest, I could feel his heart pounding beneath his black tee shirt. "...forever."

He yanked my body against his, the two of us on our sides, two magnets pulled together. "Forever," he said possessively, before placing a kiss on my forehead.

I twisted my hand up to his and grabbed the tiny box. I looked at the sparkly ring, but all I could see was airplane rides with snack bags for our kids. Katie standing beside me as a maid of honor at our wedding. Gabriel every morning and every night. His arms around my waist as we set the table for dinner. Riding beside him in his truck talking about the rest of our life. *All I could see was our future.*

Cheering in the distance interrupted my thoughts. I glanced at Gabe who was fighting a grin. I sat up and peered across the beach to spot Mama Linda with her arm slung around my mom, my dad, Victor, and a few more people. My eyes widened as I realized it was the whole Hernandez crew. My whole family all together on the edge of the beach. Someone popped a bottle of champagne.

"She said yes!" Gabe shouted, sitting up beside me. Katie ran toward us sand flying under her feet and Terrence trailing behind her. The happiest little tear dropped down my cheek, Gabe reached up and brushed it away. "Once Katie and our moms found out, they were already buying the champagne and figuring out the carpool details," he whispered.

I smiled at him gratefully. What had begun over homework on Linda's kitchen table had turned into *for as long as we both shall live.*

Bonus Chapter

GABE AND EMMA'S BACHELOR & BACHELORETTE PARTIES

GABE

Victor and Luis are taking this poker game
way too seriously

where are you, beautiful?

EMMA

I'm two margaritas in and watching Katie sing
Party in the USA.

It's karaoke night at Chauncey's, the place to
be if you're a Bachelorette ;)

*sends a photo of herself wearing a headband
with a bridal veil attached and a white tank
top that says BRIDE in hot pink letters*

GABE

I didn't realize how hot I'd find all this bride
stuff.

maybe we can meet up?

EMMA

That's against the bachelorette party rules!
Katie said no boys—especially no fiancés!

GABE

did she actually say that?

EMMA

You know Katie. She definitely said that.

GABE

eh, I'm not too worried about those rules.
we're pretty good at making out behind
Katie's back, if history is any indication

Katie slid onto the barstool beside me at the bar. Eyeing the phone in my hands immediately, she asked, "Gabe?"

I nodded, smiling giddily. "He's just checking in."

"You know, I found it annoying when Gabe was always stealing my best friend's attention *before* you were a couple. Now it's just off the charts." Katie shook her head.

I shrugged. "I'm sorry, that's what you get for having such a *dreamy* brother. How do you expect to bring him around and not have me fall for him?"

"I've already accepted that fact. Now, all I want is for you to put your phone down," Katie said as she grabbed my phone. "And get on stage," she pointed toward the stage where the two redheaded Rhodes sisters were singing "I Wanna Dance With Somebody."

"You're up next," Katie narrowed her eyes.

A couple of our old friends, and bachelorette party attendees, were standing at the front of the stage waving their phones in the air like lighters. "Should we go join them?" I asked.

"I need a drink first," Katie said before ordering something pink and icy.

Katie might tease Gabriel and I the most, but she was also our biggest supporter. Always giving the best advice, making room for our relationship and going out of her way to affirm and embrace our love story. She'd laugh the hardest at all the signs she missed and told me she wanted me to write a novel about all of it. Gabriel even showed me the text thread where she helped him slyly plan his proposal.

My phone vibrated. Katie flipped it over to reveal a message from Gabriel. We both leaned in to read it.

Gabriel: I've had a few and I wanna see you

Gabriel: I brought up Chauncey's to Vic

Katie flipped the phone back over. "Victor will shut it down. He knows we're at Chauncey's. It's bachelorette party territory."

I raised a brow. "What if I text Victor and tell him Olivia Rhodes is here singing Whitney Houston?"

"How do you think you'll do that?" Katie folded her arms across her chest, the words MAID OF HONOR stitched over the front. "I have your phone."

The two of us broke into giggles. Katie was all bark and no bite. "Do you really think Victor would break our agreement that easily if he knew Olivia was here?" she asked.

"A thousand percent," I snorted. Something had been simmering between Victor and Olivia for a while now and it had reached a boiling point this fall.

"I kind of want to test it," she whispered, the alcohol making her sloppy in the cutest way.

"We have to test it," I encouraged her, because selfishly, I knew it'd definitely bring Gabriel's party to mine. I'd been booked up with bridal showers and wedding dress try ons, and as fun as they were, they kept us apart. Since Gabe had become mine, I hated wasting anymore time apart.

Katie said into her voice to text, her voice lilting, "Oh Victor, *Olivia Rhodes* is dancing around on stage at Chauncey's. Should I tell her you say hiiii?"

We clinked our glasses together and went to dance with our friends to Olivia and Lucy Rhode's now singing Sabrina Carpenter.

I was warm and flushed on the dance floor, hips swaying, and eyes closed, when I heard the beginning of Fall Out Boy's "Alone Together" echo through the speakers in a warm voice I knew all too well. My eyes shot to the stage.

Gabriel Hernandez was grinning down at me rakishly. He held the microphone to his lips, dark hair falling over his eyes. My heart hammering in response. *How can he still make me nervous?*

He winked, singing about being alone together, and all I could think was *I want nothing more than to get him alone*. He fell to his knees, dramatically singing out the words, his voice rough, passionate and offkey. A loud carefree, laugh shook my body.

Katie bumped her shoulder into mine. "Get up there!"

"What?" I squealed. I'd skated by without getting on stage so far.

"Go sing with your groom!" Katie said.

The crowd was squealing and dancing, and I thought of young Emma, and how often she regretted saying *no* out of fear and hesitation...when her heart was screaming *yes*. Since I'd finally said yes to Gabriel, I'd made it a resolution to keep bravely saying yes over and over again, to make up for those moments younger Emma lost.

I had to keep up the resolution. Even if it involved crashing my fiancé's serenade on stage.

Gabe's eyes lit up when I climbed up the stairs, like I was still his favorite surprise. He grabbed my wrist, pulling my body against his, sharing the mic between us with his other hand. The spotlight bright over us, the crowd shouting the song in unison. Gabriel's body heat warm against me.

We were offkey, messy and tipsy, but we were in love and having so much fun.

The song ended, and Gabriel dropped the mic so he could lift me up to spin me around. My body sliding down his as he slowly brought me back to the ground, his eyes ravenous as they met mine.

Our lips collided and the crowd went wild—as the girl in the bridal veil got herself a dramatic kiss. I dug my fingers through his hair, kissing him right back.

"No one can ever keep you two apart," Terrence said with a smirk as we joined him and Katie at the bar. "Why do we even try?"

"So, how was the bachelor party?" I asked.

"Fun," Gabriel said, wrapping his arms around me. "Not as fun as what happened up on stage, but really fun. My brothers were cracking me up with how seriously the poker game got." Gabriel and I had been traveling around so much over the past few years, that we both revelled in family and friend time when we were here in Sweet River. I knew Gabe missed his brothers when we were away.

"Oh man, the game was getting intense," Terrence said, his eyes wide.

"I know how competitive a Hernandez game night can get," I said. "Honestly, just a one-on-one game of scrabble can get intense with Gabe."

Gabe and I chuckled, exchanging a laugh—I was pretty sure he was remembering the same night of Scrabble as I was. Gabe and I had created this little life together full of inside jokes and glances where it felt like we could read each other's minds.

"This one is the same way," Terrence shot a glance towards Katie.

"Don't sign up for a game night if you didn't really come to play," Katie said. Someone wailed an Adele cover across the room.

"Say what you want about the Hernandez brothers, but no one is as cutthroat as Katie at...well, anything you can win," Gabe raised his brows.

"All right, Gabe, you came, you got your kiss, but we have an itinerary to stick to," Katie tapped her phone, where the itinerary was laid out and bullet pointed in her Notes app.

"We can't leave yet. What about my kiss?" Terrence asked her, voice smooth. Katie melted into his arms. While the two were distracted, Gabriel slid his arm around my waist pulling me through the crowd, until we were alone in the dark hallway at the back of the bar.

"Finally," he whispered against my ear, as I stumbled backwards into the hallway. "I've got you to myself."

He spun me around to face him. Nose to nose. Lips to lips. He pushed my back against a closet door. Our chests rising and falling, nearly breathless.

I ran my fingers through his hair, yanking him closer, until his mouth met mine. My whole body buzzing at the contact. Kissing Gabe on stage while the crowd cheered was going to be a fun memory but getting him all to myself still felt like finding fortune I didn't know could be mine.

Gabriel dragged his lips down my jawline, to my neck. I twisted my hands in his dark grey shirt.

"Three," he growled against my neck.

"Three?" I asked.

"Three days until you're all mine."

I press my forehead into his. "Gabe, are you kidding me? I've *always* been all yours."

REBECCA JO JACKSON Q&A: A DISCUSSION WITH AUTHOR, SARA NORTH

Sara North: Hi Rebecca! I'm so grateful to get to ask you questions about your gorgeous books and your life as an author! You're one of the kindest, most thoughtful people I've met in this space and it's so lovely to have connected over our mutual love of reading and writing books. Ok, so, let's start with Sweet River...

Did you always know that Sweet River would be a series?

Rebecca Jo Jackson: I didn't! *It Couldn't Be You*, which is the first in the series, started as a stand-alone book and honestly went through a few different versions as I worked on it! But while writing ICBY, I fell in love with Sweet River and realized I didn't want to be done with it – or the characters. I love that through the other books we get to check in with characters and their stories, in a small way, continue to be told. I'm currently working on the latest book in the series...and we get to visit Emma and Gabriel's wedding!

SN: Ahh! I can't wait to read more about Emma and Gabriel! And, it's fun that the idea of it being a series was more of a surprise. Readers often tell me that they wish

they could visit the world in my books and I wish I could do the same with yours!

If you could have one day in Sweet River, how would you spend it?

RJJ: I would definitely schedule a visit during the Sweet River Summer Festival (wink, wink to Lucy Loves Him Not) and my first stop that day would be Coffees and Commas! I'd HAVE to bump into each couple (and their families!).

SN: Always stop at the coffee shop first, I love it! When I think about the books we write, I think of themes or emotions that summarize what I was trying to say or a central focus.

If you could use one word to summarize each of your books, what would they be?

RJJ: Oooh, good question...

It Couldn't Be You: Growth

Lucy Loves Him Not: Sunshine

One Little Chance: Hope

Sweet River Book 4: Vulnerability

SN: That's so beautiful! It brings such clarity when we can think of our books in such a succinct way. I can absolutely see those themes in your books (while I wait for Book 4!). Now, about your writing process...

RJJ: Every writer I've met has a different process for how characters or stories unfold - how do your characters reveal their stories to you?

It's been a little different with each book so far! For instance, It Couldn't Be You began with daydreaming to music (angsty Olivia Rodrigo songs) while Lucy Loves Him Not began with the idea of Sweet River getting a new City Manager, so I started with an outline for Lucy Loves Him Not.

It's been different with the subsequent books, as well! Music is a huge part for each story, though, and I'm someone who loves outlining (even though the outline is always evolving).

SN: I'm the same way! And I must have music while I'm

writing, always. It's such a fascinating thing when characters become who they are. Even though we're the writers, I find that they surprise me and take on elements that endear me even more to them. When you think about the books you've written so far:

What do you love most about your characters?

RJJ: I love how they grow. Often they begin the story with a hesitancy, or a fear, some old bruise that might make them hold back in romance (and often other areas of their lives), but by the end they take a chance. They push themselves. I find it inspirational, and therapeutic, to write.

SN: Yes! There's always a deep source of pain which turns into a way they sabotage themselves somehow and an obstacle to overcome. To me, it feels like a gift to be able to write and know the characters I do...

Do you still think of your characters, even when their stories have ended?

RJJ: ALL THE TIME. It's why I love that I get to revisit Sweet River in other stories.

SN: SAME.

What movies do you think your characters would watch?

RJJ: I have a tendency to bring this up in each book! My FMCs love '90s Romcoms.

SN: Oh my word I literally say this about my books, so I love this so much. My characters and yours could have a movie night! When it comes to the whole process of writing (because it's really hard work!)...

What encourages you to keep writing?

RJJ: For me it's as good for my mental and emotional health as exercise is for my body. I feel the difference when I've been putting it off.

SN: Yes, I resonate with this so much. It can feel like a part of me isn't present when I'm not writing. We

mentioned music a bit ago and, for me, I mentioned I have to have music playing while I write.

What's an essential part of your writing process?

RJJ: Pen to paper. I have a journal for each book where I workout problems, jot out characters, scene sketches or bits of dialogue, before I bring them to my laptop. Something about pen to paper flows for me.

SN: Ahh! Why are we the SAME. I did not know this about you! There's just something so satisfying about a pencil (for me) and paper that feels like I'm finally getting to the story I need to write. It's essential. Let's talk about when you have your characters, you know your story, and you've got your books into the world...

What's been the most surprising thing about your author journey so far?

RJJ: That people will actually read my books, haha! The other thing would be how it's brought such beautiful connections with women I wouldn't have connected with otherwise – I love when readers, or fellow authors, message me and we connect over stories and characters.

SN: It's true! And it still surprises me when people read mine, as well! But, you're right, the comments, the kind words, the relationships that are created are beautiful. I know I'm so grateful to have met you!

We're both indie authors and I know we work incredibly hard to get our books into the world - what's your "why" for publishing books? When did it move from "I might publish" to "I must?"

RJJ: It felt like a nudge from God. I was querying and researching and PRAYING. God brought various indie authors into my world through incredible books and it felt like him showing me another way.

I also had this urge that...*I'd waited long enough*. I wanted to put my stories out there, however I could. I have a lot of books I want to write and I wanted to get started.

SN: Well, I'm so glad that you did and I really admire that - you took action on what was in your heart to do and that took courage. Creating always does, but now you get to see it unfold and create something really lovely in the world. Romance is the most popular genre, but it's also what we've both decided to write.

Why do you think romance books are so valuable?

RJJ: I have so much I could say about this. There are so many things valuable about romance books. One big thing for me is how healthy love and relationships help us to grow and challenge us to be brave, to hope, to put pride aside, etc. Throw love into someone's life and a really interesting story immediately unfolds and such rich character growth. We learn about ourselves through love and romance.

SN: Sweet - that's so true. We learn more about ourselves through the relationships we're in, throughout every area of our life. I think it's also an opportunity, like you've mentioned, to bring hope and also healing to the world. It's a universal need and dream - to be loved.

Sometimes I get asked if my characters are based on me or my life - if I feel like they represent me - and, of course, while they're fictional, there are emotional parts to them that I resonate with deeply. Do you think that your characters reflect who you are as a person in any way?

RJJ: Each character carries different pieces of me, for sure. Whether it be personality traits or struggles, or pieces of who I've been or reflections of my own history or family. They each carry glimmers.

SN: "They each carry glimmers" - I love that! Such a perfect way to put it.

What do you hope readers feel when they read your books?

RJJ: I hope my books feel like a warm hug or a really cozy, sweet escape.

SN: Your books are so cozy and sweet. I definitely feel

that when I read your books. Thinking back on your experiences with books...

What's a childhood memory that now, as an author, you look back on as confirmation that writing books was always going to be a part of your story?

RJJ: I was always writing little stories and poems in journals growing up. And, as a little girl, I would follow my mom around telling her made-up stories while she did laundry or ran errands! She would always listen and ask questions. Now she's one of the first people who reads my books and still listens to me discuss my books and asks the best questions.

SN: That's so wonderful that you had a parent be so supportive (and still so involved!) to encourage you in the creative process. It's so valuable to have people close to us believe in a gift that sometimes we don't even know we have or haven't fully developed yet. I love that for you. And, to also find support from people we maybe haven't met yet!

What does the Bookstagram community mean to you?

RJJ: Just that – community. It's full of supporters, cheerleaders and inspiration. I love the Bookstagram community so much...I can't imagine sharing my books without them!

SN: They really are so lovely. I've laughed, cried, and have felt immensely grateful over and over again for the people who have held onto my books and have told me that they've resonated in any way.

What's the most surprising thing a reader has said about your books?

RJJ: I was surprised at how many readers saw themselves reflected in my characters (like Emma, for example!). It's always the messages from people that see themselves in my characters or stories (or even specific quotes) that bring me to tears. That anyone could find catharsis or a balm in my books is the best surprise ever.

SN: It feels like such a gift, doesn't it? I love this, Rebecca! You are so encouraging and supportive and have

become such a sweet friend. I love hearing more about your series and the process of becoming a writer and now being an author. Ok, let's end this chat with a way that we can all get to know more about you through more things that you love!

Now...the One Answer Only round:
Favorite Rom-com: You've Got Mail
Go-to coffee or tea order: London Fog
Favorite season: SUMMER
Age you knew you wanted to be a writer: 8
Number of new book ideas you have in mind: 5ish?
Place you want to travel to next: Mountains

A name for a character that you'll never use: [Ok, breaking the rules for you to also answer "why!"] That would probably be an ex-boyfriend's name haha

If you weren't writing romance you'd be writing: General fiction

A trope that seems scary to write: Love Triangle
Favorite trope to read: Second Chance
Favorite snack: Chips and salsa!!
Favorite dessert: Chocolate covered strawberries
Current song "on repeat:" Risk by Gracie Abrams

Thank you to all the readers who joined us for this bookish discussion with my sweet and creative friend, Sara North! And a big thank you to Sara for coming up with such thoughtful and fun questions!

Sara North is a closed-door romance author whose first series, full of humor and heart, is set in the fictional New England small town of Birch Borough. With a book celebrating each season, Sara's books are standalone but are best read together. It all starts with I Love You in French (fall) and I Love a Good Challenge (spring), with the rest of the seasons coming soon!

The Sweet River Series

Lucy Loves Him Not
One Little Chance
Olivia's Only Pretending **coming Fall 2025**

Sign up for Rebecca Jo Jackson's newsletter at rebeccajojackson.com or follow along on Instagram @AuthorRebeccaJoJackson to stay up to date on the latest book news.

Acknowledgments

Thank you, Joseph. This book wouldn't be here without your support, encouragement and time. You read each book with such enthusiasm and love each character *almost* as much as I do. My gratitude for ALL you do is endless. *And you still thrill me.*

Thank you to my whole family. You guys have always taken my writing seriously and it gave me the courage to do the same.

And a special thank you to my mom, Jenna and Hannah Marie, for reading messy drafts and giving invaluable feedback and support.

Mom, you're my first call and biggest cheerleader. I thank God he gave me a mom who loves to read— and will read my book over and over, and discuss the characters like we're discussing small-town gossip. Dad, you interrupted your regular historical fiction and westerns to read my sappy romcom (without me even having to ask you to)— your support and love is something I can always rely on.

Jen, truly, I am so grateful for the lengthy conversations in mom's kitchen about fictional characters, about how quickly you respond to my panicked story related texts. I would take you for coffee at Coffee & Commas if I could.

Many writing sessions happened because of Grammy's babysitting efforts. My in-laws give so much support, excitement and love for this book. You even loved my silly formatting mistake of a first print. You all make my heart swell.

Thank you to the early readers who encouraged me and loved

these characters at their messiest. Every email and text was read over and over.

A big thank you to my editor, Jen. You were kind, encouraging and skilled. I learned so much working with you.

My illustrator was my talented niece Emma Grace Haskell. She's one to watch and captured the heart of this story with such skill and love.

Sutton, Ivy — the sound of your giggles and pitter pattering feet will always sound like Sweet River to me. I can't wait for you to grow up and read this. Mommy will always be here to dry you off after you dive in.

Thank you to God for giving me so much to be thankful for.

And to all my bookstagram friends...it's the most beautiful surprise to find out how kind, generous and supportive strangers can be.

Thank YOU for giving this indie book your time.

About the Author

Rebecca Jo Jackson writes sweet, but angsty love stories. She hopes her books feel like a warm cup of coffee from Coffee & Commas. She grew up in a small town in Texas, but now has a home in California with her husband, two daughters and pup.

- www.rebeccajojackson.com
- instagram.com/authorrebeccajojackson

Also by Rebecca Jo Jackson

Sweet River Interconnected Standalone Series

Lucy Loves Him Not

One Little Chance

31 Days for the New Mama

www.ingramcontent.com/pod-product-compliance
Lightning Source LLC
Chambersburg PA
CBHW020343010826
48973CB00005B/1250